£5

88

First published by
David James Publishing in 2013
Copyright © 2013 by A.L.McAuley

Cover Design Copyright © 2013: Jacqueline Stokes
Author Photograph by Chris Neely

A CIP catalogue record for this book is available from the British Library
ISBN: 978-0-9575610-6-9

Dedication

For Helen
without whom this would never
have come to page

Acknowledgements

There are so many people to thank for their support & encouragement during the writing of this novel, not least my close family (they know who they are), Emma Jensen, Kate Gibbs (my moral compass), Diane Corrigan, Mags Flynn – and the Angel whose hand I held and continue to hold each night before I go to sleep.

88

by

A.L. McAuley

DAVID JAMES PUBLISHING

Prologue

ANDRUS TAMM SAT PATIENTLY STARING OUT through the corner of his window on the second floor of the 3 star hotel. Three star by Somali standards was a liberal use of the hotel grading system. The gaudy paper was peeling away from the walls, with only a bare light bulb to illuminate the dingy room. A single chair sat against a well-used table, worn at the edges, and covered with old graffiti, making claims of faceless names being gay or offers of cheap sex being just a phone call away. Business cards from local prostitutes were delivered and placed on it daily, offering favours from the mundane to the depraved.

Andrus was Estonian and born only months before the fall of Russian communism. His father was a Soviet and detested the new western thinking by their former communist leaders. He enrolled his only son in the Gagarin Air Force Academy at Monino outside of Moscow, using some of his old Cold War contacts to have the boy accepted. He was fifteen years of age when he first walked through the doors of the academy. Thirteen years, two wars and several covert operations later, he had been posted to Mogadishu. He spoke perfect Russian, Finnish and English without trace of an accent, as well as his native Estonian.

The FSB had recruited him two months before his twenty-fourth birthday and were instrumental in his intense weapons,

11

explosive, counter intelligence and covert training expertise. After numerous missions, his reputation grew. He was impossibly handsome and had a personality, not usually associated with such fine looks.

He was currently deployed in Somalia as an adviser to one of the local warlords opposed to American interference and influence to encourage oil, mineral and media based contracts.

And now he sat in his shabby room waiting, as commanded, staring uninterestedly through the dusty cracked window, for contact from the FSB regional superior. He was unaware that his orders had been cancelled. He would not be contacted, at least not from regional command.

Andrus weighed up his options. He was of course prepared for any unforeseen eventualities. That was basic training. He now understood that his services were obviously no longer needed as the time allotted for contact from his controller had passed.

He decided to break with protocol and attempt direct contact with central headquarters in Moscow. The emergency contact number no longer responded and so now he fully understood that he was on his own.

He watched as two heavily armed pick-up trucks sprayed clouds of dust as they skidded to a sideways stop in front of the hotel. He counted five men exit from each truck and run towards the entrance carrying assault weapons and light machine guns. He figured that his superiors had lost control of the fragile hold they had on the *Al-Shabaab* militia.

He would likely be used as a bartering tool in some future exchange, part of a deal drawn up to secure the continued loyalty of the warlord; a token gift to sweeten negotiations. He would be tortured for information and eventually traded, in a mutually beneficial exchange, or killed and left for the local wildlife to dispose of him. He didn't like the idea and was ready to make a quick exit.

From this moment on he was self-employed and would later enjoy settling the score with his former employers. Not one of them or their family would ever be safe from his reach regardless of where they hid themselves!

He picked up his cellphone, cracked open the back and removed the SIM card. He then tossed it down the dirty, brown stained toilet, rechecked his weapon and exited the door of his room.

He could hear the sound of the heavily armed men take the stairs two at a time, whispering orders to each other, ready and eager for violence. It was ten against one, so easy odds for them.

His room was second from the end of the corridor. He favoured this position, as it was anonymous and provided easy access to windows and fire escapes. He had previously unlocked the window and now exited and descended the ladder to make his way to the rented Hyundai. He got in the car and lowered the seat back half of full recline. This enabled him to have a full view of the scene. He inserted the ear protectors, adjusted the focus on his camera to where he knew would be the epicentre of the blast, then with his free hand, withdrew the remote detonator and waited for the show to begin.

A huge invisible magnet pulled plaster, fittings, furniture, militia men and hotel staff into a maelstrom of chaos and destruction. Glass and debris all became one lethal dirty ball of utter obliteration. The first of the men to reach the top of stairs saw his vision blur as the shock wave increased in intensity, expanding outwards from its epicentre.

A nanosecond later, what was left of his torso and limbs was embedded with rubbish and shrapnel. His body was consumed, initially from the blast wave, then by the intense orange fireball that followed. Anything that wasn't shredded by the shrapnel was incinerated a split second later. The interior of the hotel's first floor appeared to swell outwards like a gigantic balloon constructed from bricks and mortar, anything that impeded the blast wave was demolished instantly. The explosion was pure and indiscriminate. It didn't care who the enemy was. It was being generous and including everyone.

Andrus wound down the window of his rental car and savoured the familiar smell of his work. He wasn't completely dissatisfied with the result. He felt the old familiar sensation between his legs, stifled for so long less he show his true nature to his military superiors. That phase of his life was over now and this would be the last time he suppressed his sexual fantasies. Next time he swore to himself that he would enjoy his work to the fullest.

He reached into his jacket pocket for the electric cigarette, finding it, he put it to his lips and took a long drag, blowing out the fake smoke before slowly driving away from the demolished hotel. He would burn the car later before making his way to the Kenyan border and crossing over, posing as a Finnish tourist.

Part One

Chapter *1*

JOHN GREER FLICKED THE SWITCH ON IN THE LAB and watched as the fluorescent tubes reluctantly hummed then blinked into life. He usually disliked their cold sterile light, but, since the beginning of the heat wave, they had a psychological cooling effect from the blistering temperatures outside. But still it didn't deter him from scowling at them as they reminded him of raw grey winter mornings and driving cold icy rain.

The current heat wave had lasted for five weeks with no sign of ending anytime soon. The Irish were not used to the constant high temperatures and few of the houses, other than those belonging to the very rich or very optimistic, had air conditioning. 29-36 degrees was positively Mediterranean; perfect Sangria weather, but in the sweltering streets of Belfast it was torture. Tar-macadam on the roads turned to sticky black slush, spattering car windscreens with gooey tar.

The news channels reported daily of farmers complaining of the threat to livestock, or gorse fires that raged across the province started by teenage arsonists. The city had developed its own style of cafe culture with neighbours chatting and gossiping at their front doors long past their normal bedtimes. It was too hot to sleep regardless of how many windows they left open to encourage a breeze through their tiny rooms.

An hour and a half earlier the six thirty alarm had sounded on his digital radio. The chirpy and overpaid English disc jockey prattled on about London's parking problems and congestion charges.

"And why exactly would I give a shit?" Greer ranted at the radio. His eyes were stinging and his bladder was bursting. Soaked with sweat, he rose then shuffled his way to the toilet. "Surely to God Almighty - how in the name of all that's Holy do I have any fluid left in me to pass?"

He relieved himself of his full bladder using audio, as most men do when they try to deny the fact that they're awake and attempt to pee with their eyes closed. He swayed back and forth in front of the narrow toilet bowl. Not bothering to raise the seat before relieving himself would be a decision that he would later regret after taking his shower; when he would sit on the plastic seat now coated with fresh tepid urine. He listened for the reassuring sound of water on water, refusing to let the morning sunlight bring him to the harsh reality that sleep was over for yet another night.

Greer finished without bothering to wash his hands - that was for restaurants and company. He had remarked, when once asked by an ex-girlfriend if he'd washed his hands after using the toilet, "I don't need to as I don't piss on my hands."

He gave a chuckle, remembering her reaction and the look of disgust on her face. Unsurprisingly that relationship, along with a list of others hadn't lasted very long. He knew it was a foolish idea, but still he considered going back to bed for just another quick ten minutes. It was already too bright to sleep and the feckin' DJ would only torture him when the snooze alarm went off again. Admitting defeat, Greer flushed the toilet, reversed, turned and walked straight into the half open sharp edge of the toilet door. Luckily his chest, primarily his left nipple, took most of the force of the impact instead of his face.

"Jesus Christ, I'm ruined!"

Greer staggered out of the bathroom, massaging his stinging nipple, then turned back to check in the bathroom mirror to see if he had torn away any of the soft flesh. Reassured that although now bright red from the impact but still fully intact, he continued to rub his stinging breast as he tossed aside magazines and yesterday's newspaper from the coffee table to search for the

TV remote control. As usual, it evaded him, so instead he surrendered, flopped on the settee and lit a cigarette.

Greer glanced at the five foot IKEA print of the zebra's head and wondered again what the hell he was thinking of when he bought it. Blaming one of the daytime home makeover programmes for his poor interior design choices, he stubbed out his cigarette in the remains of last night's full ashtray and was about to head for the shower when he spotted the TV remote in the last place he would have thought to look; happily perched on top of the set.

"Oh come on! Why? Why would I leave it on the bloody TV?" ranted Greer.

He walked across the room, picked up the remote, tossed it onto the settee as he passed, then made his way back to the shower.

Chapter 2

T HE LABORATORY WINDOWS OVERLOOKING THE campus quadrangle of Belfast's Queens University were covered with a neutral film, the purpose of which was to prevent bright sunlight affecting the natural growth cycles of the test samples. The adverse effect was that the observer looking out had little idea of the time of day, or whether it was sunny or overcast outside. Also, the internal lighting was turned off during the daylight hours to simulate the perfect conditions for growth of samples. This meant that Greer and his colleagues spent most of their working life in perpetual twilight.

John Greer had been a lab assistant at the University's marine laboratory, situated on the outskirts of Belfast City for the past eleven years. His days consisted of rechecking the research notes he received by email or delivered from the University's main Marine Research Centre for further analysis. The Victorian building where he worked was of magnificent brown brick construction, erected in the mid eighteen hundreds; the design based loosely on Magdalene College Cambridge. It had a sizeable entrance hall, adorned by beautiful memorial stained glass windows, which led to an ornate staircase that meandered up to the Great Hall. There was a wide expanse of driveway covering the short distance from the road to the front of the huge nineteenth century structure bordered by an area of perfectly manicured lawns. The paths surrounding the main building were designed to lead students to the adjoining outbuildings. Inevitably, these paths, put in place in the nineteen sixties, had detracted from the original Victorian splendour of the campus.

Over the years the University had grown and spread over various streets of south Belfast. It now occupied many of the surrounding town houses and office buildings that had been acquired by the growing academic departments.

Greer was on the wrong side of forty and was getting ever more resentful of the fact that promotion was becoming increasingly beyond his grasp. The years of sedentary lifestyle and passion for red wine, fast food and cigarettes had left him soft and pudgy. The clothes he wore were standard casual bordering on bland and uninteresting. There was nothing remarkable about him and his five foot eight inch frame other than his ability to pick up virtually any musical instrument and produce a tune from it. This meant he had a guaranteed invite to every party thrown by his friends and co-workers. Most of these he declined, preferring to practise alone on his first passion and continuing love affair with the acoustic guitar.

As the day began to get into its swing, teaching and research staff steadily filtered into work, all with a collective desire to be somewhere else; probably, imagined Greer, somewhere out in the sun with a few cold beers.

The cleaners and domestic staff had finished their night shift and left, talking noisily amongst themselves, oblivious to him or his dark mood.

Greer's current project was assisting Doctor Eva Ballantine. They had been jointly working on several projects over the past number of years. Eva was in her early thirties, although it was difficult to tell her age precisely as she spent most of her free time outdoors and the weather had added some premature lines to her face, though not too unkindly. She generally lifted his mood when they met at work yet Greer still hadn't figured out if he fancied her or not, even after all this time together.

Their current project was a study of algae exclusive to Strangford Lough where Eva was mostly based. The Lough's name was derived from Old Norse: *Strangr-fjord* meaning 'strong fjord.' A beautiful village sat at its harbour, located thirty miles south east of Belfast on the opposite side of the Newtownards peninsula and connected to its neighbouring Portaferry by a short ferry ride.

Greer occasionally accompanied Eva to collect samples but his work was primarily here in the lab in Belfast. Sometimes, if they got a dry or sunny day, she would wangle them both a trip down to the Lough. He liked her. She was clever, independent, attractive, had a love of life and little time for silly, girlie nonsense.

Chapter 3

S HIT, SHIT AND SHITE! EVA STARED AT THE RED digital numerals of her bedside radio alarm in disbelief. The display read 08.40. It had obviously gone off but it was equally obvious that she had slept right through it.

"What? That can't be the time!" She knew that the drive down to the university would be slow and frustrating as the traffic would be thick with morning commuters.

She threw off the light sheet under which she'd slept and was about to leap out of bed when she remembered her injured foot. Despite her oversleeping she took the time to lie back on the mattress and pull her foot up to her chest to inspect the dressing. Thankfully, it was clean and still firmly in place, but she reckoned that she should change it when she got into work or at lunch.

She partially hopped over to the wardrobe, as she didn't want to risk putting her full weight on the injury in case she reopened the fresh wound. She needed to protect it so, ignoring how strange it may appear, a suit and white trainers would be her wardrobe choice for work today.

The next twenty minutes would be lost forever as she grabbed sterile dressings from the medical drawer, a banana from the fruit bowl and slammed her front door behind her as she left. Forty-five minutes later, a Styrofoam cup of scalding cappuccino in each hand, she entered the lab in a worse than usual, Monday morning fluster!

John greeted her with his own unique brand of humour.

"Afternoon. Who was the lucky guy?"

Eva ignored the comment as she attempted to set her handbag down on her desk while simultaneously talking on her mobile phone and trying to scan today's case notes.

John would, as usual, attempt to predict where she might eventually set the cups of hot coffee without causing harm to either of them or the delicate equipment that surrounded them both. He knew from experience that if he simply backed away she would eventually glare at him for not helping and place the coffee down in a safe place when she realised he had no intention of assisting her. It was worth the dirty confused look for not helping.

Eva was used to Greer's odd sense of humour, as always exaggerated because it was Monday. She hit back with, "Is your period a particularly heavy one this month?"

"Oh you're just too witty," he replied.

"Heaven help us when you reach puberty love, your moods will be even worse, if that's possible!"

She made it into her part time office after giving Greer his coffee. She took a seat at her desk, which she only ever used on Mondays and Fridays to write the beginning and end of her weekly reports, without interference or disturbance.

The bulk of her research took place at QML Portaferry. Her current project was finding new strains of micro-algae, which had much greater growth rates than those of terrestrial crops. The research would eventually assist in the large-scale production of bio fuel. The figures so far had been more than encouraging.

The theory was that using algae would eventually be the only viable method of producing enough bio-diesel to replace the current dependency on traditional fossil fuel. The area of land that was needed to produce enough fuel was finite so the use of marine crops was the obvious answer. On average the yield of oil from algae production could be anything from 7 to 31 times greater than the next best crop of oil or palm.

Chapter 4

E VA SLID INTO THE CHAIR AT HER DESK AND
slipped off her shoes. She put her feet up on the cross bar
under the desk and pushed back on the chair leaving her
balanced on two legs. She rocked herself backwards and forwards
flicking through the itinerary of supplies they would need for next
month's order of stationery and chemicals. Her auburn hair was tied
up into its usual ponytail, which emphasised her sharp jaw line and
piercing brown eyes. She wore a pale grey skirt and matching
jacket. She had been the same size in clothing since her late teens.
Her figure was slight but not rakish and she possessed the rare gift
of 'presence' that she inherited from her father without appearing
either unapproachable or aloof. Her body was toned without being
muscular and was a result of her training; not an excessively careful
diet.

She gave a yelp as she remembered the cut on the sole of
her foot as it rested on the desk foot bar.

She sat bolt upright and pushed the chair away with the
back of her leg, almost falling over as she made a grab for the edge
of the desk to stop herself toppling backwards. She regained her
balance and hopped on one leg, waiting for the inevitable wave of
pain to come followed by the stream of fresh blood. When it didn't
arrive she hesitated, not wanting to look at her injury for fear that
she had reopened the wound.

Feeling sorry for herself, she sat down, then raised her foot
up to inspect for any new damage. She gave no thought or

consideration to the fact she was wearing a short skirt. She poked at the dressing hoping it wouldn't be necessary to redress the wound. She gingerly peeled back the sterile pad so as not to disturb the tape that secured it but could thus far see no sign of fresh bleeding or the wound itself. She continued to pull at the material until the tape gave way exposing the entire sole of her foot.

Chapter 5

T HE COLOUR DRAINED FROM HER FACE. THEN panic turned to confusion as she dangled the blood stained dressing from her hand. "Holy crap! Where's the…?"

She checked and rechecked repeatedly, her brain refusing to register what it was currently witnessing. There was no sign or mark of any damage to her now healthy foot. She just stared down at the sole, totally bewildered as she tried to figure out what was happening? Her heart was racing as her adrenalin was fired into the ends of her fingertips!

"Now, you take a minute and think about this," she said out loud, but her mind was still reeling. She couldn't think straight! She needed a second party to help make sense of what she was seeing. She called through the closed office door for Greer.

"Johnny, come in here and take a look at this for me, will you!"

She couldn't take her eyes away from the place on her foot where she knew that the glass had penetrated. She ran her thumb back and forward over the area where the now vanished wound had been.

"Take a look at what?" he shouted from the adjoining lab.

There was a pause that went on for, in his opinion, just a little too long. He lent back on his chair and shouted through the closed door in an attempt to have his voice thrown further. He could just about see the top of her head outlined through the frosted glass that separated the partition wall from the ceiling. "Oh God, I'll have to get up and see what she wants eventually," but thought he would shout one more time just to test her patience. "Again, take a look at what?"

"Come in here, will you, please!"

Chapter 6

EVA STILL REFUSED TO TAKE HER EYES AWAY from where the injury should have been, instead staring blankly down, almost wishing that it would reappear. She even wondered if there was any history of mental illness in the family, or at least something to explain what was happening to her?

"Okay, just a second!" Greer sighed, put down what he was doing and just about made it through the door when his eyes met the un-ignorable vision of inadvertently displayed ladies underwear.

Generally in his recent permanently single circumstances, the only time that he caught sight of women's undergarments was either on mannequins in shop windows or on TV pay per view channels. Not for some time had he seen them in real life. He did his best to avert his eyes and maintain his focus above her waistline.

She was nursing her right foot in her lap. He tried to ignore the fact that she had reclined almost fully back to get a better view of her foot and was thus displaying too much thigh, full on flesh coloured panties and part of a luxurious, cellulite-free buttock.

Incredible what a man can see in the time it takes a high velocity bullet to hit a target from fifty yards given the right, albeit inappropriate, motivation.

Eva continued sitting, oblivious, with her foot held in her hands staring transfixed down at its sole and ignoring him.

Trying his best not to take any more advantage of the obvious wardrobe oversight, slightly ashamed and a little embarrassed, Greer scolded himself and felt his face redden.

"What's wrong, Eva?"

She pointed the sole of her foot at him, hovering her leg over the top of the desk.

"Are you going to take a look at this for me or not?

Greer stayed in the doorway. "Eva!" he pleaded.

She looked up at him again.

"For God's sake. What? What are you doing over there anyway? You're not going to see anything from the other side of the room!"

"Eva. I'll help as best I can, but can you please adjust your clothing?"

Embarrassed, she folded the skirt between her legs as best she could while at the same time muttering about men and their stupid crap. He made his way round to her side of the desk and reluctantly pulled up a chair.

"Okay, let's have a look."

She moved her leg across onto his knee.

"So, what am I supposed to be looking for?" he asked.

"You're looking for a laceration. About an inch long."

"Where?"

"On my fucking foot, you idiot!"

Last night's excess of wine had left John in more than his usual Monday morning fragile state. He attempted to stand but the weight of her leg made it difficult.

"Listen, I'm not having that. Whatever it is that you want me to see isn't there. I have no idea what you're talking about and as far as I can see, there is absolutely no injury present - oh and one other thing, Doctor, don't ever use that tone with me again!"

Eva revised her attitude. It wasn't his fault that he couldn't see any damage or injury. How could he, when even she couldn't see it?

"John, I'm sorry. Please. Look again. I cut it on glass in the Lough yesterday. It bled like buggery and hurt like hell but now there's no sign of the wound or even any trace that I ever had any injury."

He could see by her face that she was genuinely distressed, but as he listened to the story, he decided the reasons for her behaviour were either down to excessive alcohol usage or hysteria. He attempted to settle her further and come up with a reasonable or plausible explanation.

"Look, maybe you dreamt it or something," he suggested.

"I didn't dream it!" she protested, her voice rising again. "It happened. It was real and now it's gone. Do you understand?"

In his opinion the atmosphere was becoming much too heated for a Monday morning.

"Okay then, how do you explain it, Doctor?"

Greer was now getting annoyed for the second time and he decided that he wasn't putting his feelings on hold for this crazy person. He lifted her leg off his lap, stood and left her office, half slamming the door as he exited.

Chapter *7*

E VA HASTILY SLIPPED HER SHOES BACK ON, snatched up her bag and bustled her way out of the building, dodging the students on their way to and from lectures. Doubting her own sanity and reason, her thoughts returned to the episode with Greer and she felt sorry for the way she had spoken to him. Was it any wonder that he had reacted the way he did? Even she was finding it impossible to comprehend.

Her heart was thumping hard in her chest and in an attempt to gain some measure of self-control she forced herself to walk rather than run. It turned out to be a little of both as she hurried her way through the campus to her car.

"Okay, this is crazy," she said to herself. "Stay calm. If you're not calm, you won't be able to make rational decisions."

She tried her best to regain composure and recount the events leading up to incident when she had cut herself on the broken glass. She was now, for no logical reason, limping. Possibly it was a psychosomatic reaction?

She at last made it to her car and went straight to the rear door of the hatchback, raising it with the keys still in the lock. She dropped her handbag down onto the ground beside her, spilling some of its contents out onto the gravel. She ignored the Chanel lipstick as it happily rolled away under the car. So far out of reach that she would either have to lie on the ground in an undignified way to reach it or run the risk of moving the car and possibly crushing it. Forgetting it for now, she continued to toss aside wet suits and pieces of her mobile wardrobe. She leant as far into the car as she could without getting fully inside and rummaged around for the towel she'd used as a makeshift bandage to wrap her foot in that day at the Lough.

Eventually finding the corner of the towel she pulled it from under the pile of wetsuits and running gear. She raised it up to inspect it. The fresh blood was still there! She scolded herself for being so untidy. Then thanked God for not putting it in the wash and removing the evidence of the wound. She was so relieved on finding it that she draped it over the passenger seat headrest in case the evidence should disappear before she could show it to someone.

She hurriedly tossed the contents of the car back into in an untidy pile and got into the driver seat. She turned the key in the ignition, giving one last look at the towel as she selected reverse gear. The blood stained towel hung over the headrest like a trophy smeared in the loser's blood.

"I knew I wasn't going crazy."

Chapter *8*

E VA TURNED THE STEERING WHEEL CLOCKWISE
and the rear of the car moved out and away from the metal
bollards that prevented drivers from making deep ruts on
the grass as they turned their vehicles. She felt the rear of the car
lifting slightly on one side and wondered what the problem was?

"Oh crap!"

She let the car roll forward, slipping it into neutral and ran
to the back of the car to see her handbag squashed down heavily on
one side. She picked it up and checked to see if her mobile phone
was damaged along with anything else that was fragile. She had
been lucky; there were a few casualties but no major drama.

She got into the car, tossed her handbag onto the seat and
took one more look at the towel, reassured that the blood was still
clearly visible.

She re-engaged the car into drive and as she moved
forward, heard the crunch of the most expensive lipstick she had
ever bought being pulverised under the wheels!

Her head slumped forward at the realisation of what had
happened and she momentarily brought the car to a second stop.

She crossed her arms across the steering wheel and rested
her head on her wrists in mourning for the lipstick.

OK the lipstick's gone, stay focused Eva.

She refused to allow herself to continue with the journey
and instead took a few minutes to calm down and think about the
events of the previous day that had caused this incredible situation.

Eva spent her free time running and cycling in training for triathlons. In summer she added open water swimming down at the Lough to her regime. It was her best part of the three elements of the sport. She was an above average swimmer, but not elite by any means and had never come close to winning a race.

Yesterday, she had been out in the Lough, enjoying the solitude and weightless feel of the water. Her swimming time provided her with the perfect opportunity to think without any distractions. Midway into this session she had felt a change in water pressure and became aware of an unusual hum that was resonating around her. It felt as if she was being gently pushed sideways through the salty water and towards the shore. She swam on towards the slipway that was off in the distance.

As she finally made towards the shallows she could just make out the murky bed of the Lough and the weeds, swaying from side to side in the ever changing current. It was a comfort today for whatever reason. Not seeing the seabed when she swam didn't bother her normally but sometimes when alone in the water with little noise but the sound of your own breathing and the splashing of your hands hitting the surface, your mind could begin to play odd tricks on you. With plenty of time to think and few distractions the brain pricks at a swimmer's fears and phobias.

She at last saw the concrete of the slipway rise up through the water and reached down for it. Her hand felt the first slippery weed covered piece of rippled man made traction. She clawed at it a little too hard removing some of the surface skin from her fingertips that were now softened because of the time she'd spent in the Lough.

Her feet made contact with the ferry's slipway and gravity began to take hold of her again. She felt her own body weight after spending an hour supported by the water. She teetered and zigzagged as she made her way up the concrete slipway and out of the Lough. It took her some moments to fully regain her focus and balance, breathing hard and trying to remove her earplugs and nose clip. She was just preparing to clear her mucus filled nostrils, without anyone seeing her, when the pain hit!

She automatically shot up on to the ball of her foot. The adrenalin sent her body into self-protection mode as the foreign object pierced through her skin and penetrated into the soft tissue of her foot. Her body reacted automatically in a bid to both protect itself and register that harm had been done without allowing her to feel the pain fully yet. That would come soon. For now it needed her to get away from the present danger!

Eva hopped up the greasy slipway to reach drier level ground, losing her footing on the weed covered incline causing her to ground the damaged sole. She could almost hear the crunch as the glass penetrated deeper through the harder tissue.

She wept at the agonising pain and the thought of the possible damage that may have been done. She eventually made it to flatter ground and leant against a wall balancing on one leg and holding her injured foot in her hands. She pulled the thin glass shard from her flesh and threw it into a gorse bush in disgust. The blood flowed freely now and the cut was in such a position that it was difficult to apply pressure to stem the bleeding. She gingerly ran her fingers across the wound, flicking blood aside, trying to see if there was any more of the glass still remaining. She could find none, but still doubted her own judgment.

The harsh sound of the horn from a passing truck distracted her from the injury and the wolf whistles coming from the driver and directed at her were silently responded to with a scowl of disgust as they passed by, laughing and unaware of her distress.

Chapter *9*

HER CAR WAS NOW ONLY FEET AWAY AND SHE reached it easily by hopping across and landing heavily against the side window. As usual she had hidden the keys in the tyre well making them difficult to reach as she tried to keep her foot off the ground, away from the dirty road.

She hunkered down on one leg, fumbling and struggling to reach her hidden keys. There was now a small pool of congealing blood on the concrete as she balanced tentatively on the ball of her foot. Finally she grasped hold of the keys, stood up and opened the car door. She then hobbled to the back of the hatchback and raised the tailgate. She pulled a towel and a water bottle from under the usual junk in the rear. The cut was long and fairly deep. She poured water over the wound, washing away the diluted blood and hopefully anything nasty that may have been in the water. Fresh blood continued flowing as she bandaged the foot up as best she could in the towel, tying it in a clumsy makeshift knot around her calf.

She rechecked the wound again. The bleeding had appeared to be easing a little. She rewrapped it back up in the towel and again secured it. She started the engine and mentally thanked her ex-boyfriend for talking her into buying an automatic car instead of a manual shift.

The pharmacy at the top of the hill was open. She was just preparing to get out of the car when she noted the time on the plastic dashboard. It was 12.31pm.

"That couldn't be right!" she said out loud. By her estimation the swim session should have lasted forty minutes or forty-five on a poor day. She remembered clearly checking her divers watch, as she always did, before starting out. It read 11.20am, she was certain. She glanced at it again and it verified the time as now 12.31pm. Even with the time it took her to check and clean the wound it shouldn't have taken much more than an hour; give or take, but according to the time on the cars clock, she had somehow lost twenty minutes.

She could figure it out later, for now she needed to buy dressings, iodine and antiseptic cream and apply a makeshift field dressing that should suffice until she got home. She doubted that she would need stitches. The glass hadn't gone as deep as she'd feared, but she bought some paper ones just in case. Easing her foot back into her sandal was agony but necessary for what was to be a painful drive home.

A niggle buried in the very back of her mind was telling her that something else had happened other than the injury, but it was hiding from her now, somewhere in her subconscious. She drove the short distance home and limped across the pavement to her front door.

Sitting down on her favourite chair, she removed the dressing covering the wound and tossed it aside. The bleeding had stopped but she applied the paper stitches just in case and protected them with a fresh dressing.

Content now that no other fragments still remained, she poured a huge glass of medicinal red wine, slipped into a warm bath, dangling her foot out over the edge, then went to bed. She raised her head off her hands not content with her recall of yesterday's events, something was escaping her.

On the drive home from the university Eva tried to convince herself that the wound was only a graze; but it was a graze none the less and it had hurt and just as importantly, it bled. So where the hell had it gone?

She didn't notice the older woman sitting in the rear seat of the black Mercedes that was parked with the engine running, fifty feet away from the scene of the lipstick's unfortunate demise. The woman who watched Eva as she fumbled in the rear of her car, instructed her driver to leave as she had now seen enough.

As the Mercedes pulled away from the gates, the woman reclined back into the padded seating and pressed the button to raise the black privacy glass of the rear passenger window.

She opened her purse to check her make-up and noticed the new wrinkles on her neck, not that she cared, but the circles she moved in socially would notice such a disappointing neglect of one's appearance.

She directed the mirror further down towards her chest to see what other cosmetic procedures were needed next. Liver spots were noticeable even through her deep tan, the platinum diamond encrusted pendant shone all the brighter against the dark skin of her throat highlighting the brilliant diamond 'JS' hanging perfectly on its platinum chain.

The limousine slipped away into the morning traffic on its way to her next destination.

Chapter *10*

Stockholm

VALENTINE SERE SAT AT HIS DESK IN THE Stockholm office, staring out over the harbour of Skeppsbron at the eastern waterfront of Gamla Stan, Stockholm's *Old Town.*

The setting sun bathed the medieval buildings in golden light as the town's reflection shimmered on the waters of Lake Mälaren.

He had just returned from yet another wild goose chase; this time to Kiruna, Northern Sweden, approximately 150 miles inside the Arctic Circle. Sere had visited Sweden several times over the years and its northern wilderness appealed to his sense of isolation.

Kiruna had become an industrial and functional town with a large permanent mining community. It was bleak and inhospitable but it was also very accessible. Direct flights from Stockholm and London were regular even in the depths of arctic winter and the worst of weather.

For hundreds of miles in every direction, there were only small hamlets and lakes. The frozen wilderness intrigued Sere. He loved the howling of the huskies, eager to get started hauling incoming, insufficiently dressed, passengers from their flights to their destinations by traditional dog sleigh. They would enjoy the first ten minutes of the ride until the minus thirty degree temperatures, which translated to minus forty when you factored in the wind chill, took effect. Even with the protective clothing supplied, frostbite was a constant worry especially at night as the temperatures could drop even further.

Most of the motor vehicles had cracked or broken windscreens due to the extreme variations in temperatures, from the warm 20 degrees inside the cabins, to the -30 to -50 degrees outdoors. The glass cracked under the numbing temperature differences.

The contradiction in modes of transport amused him. *From first class to frozen ass, what a way to travel!*

Despite the extreme temperatures, he had his people acquire a fifteen thousand square foot site for a winter lodge. The planned facility would be equipped with everything from underground secure bunkers with safe rooms to hot tubs and helipads on the terraces. He flicked through the papers on his desk to see where the stars would guide him next. The information gathered by his local research team regarding a previously undiscovered type of bacteria found in the biggest underground mine in the world had turned out to be incorrect and another waste of his own time and money. This meant that Valentine Sere was, again, on the move. The lodge, however, he would keep, such was the fortune of his position.

Valentine's father, Wilson Sere, was the CEO of a multinational pharmaceutical company, which, as he was told many times during his childhood, his great grandfather Isaiah Sere had started. The family still retained the majority 52% share in the company, so his research and travels were funded by petty cash to keep him amused and out of his, mostly absent, father's way.

His father, Wilson, was a ruthless man who showed little respect for anything but power and position. He rarely called anywhere home and interacted with his only child very occasionally, or when he was forced to by his also generally absent spouse. So Sere was raised in a sterile environment where he called his father 'Sir', his mother by the only name that she would allow herself to be addressed by him, which was 'Mother,' and his long standing bodyguard, who he called 'Papa.'

Even with his travels and experiences, he could never have foreseen or predicted the events in which he would be entangled and which, unknown to him, were already beginning to unfold.

Chapter *11*

E VA HAD SPENT ALL OF THE LAST THREE YEARS focused on a specific project to find a new species of micro algae which would further advance the research in bio-fuels. So far she had little result and with only a year left of her four-year grant she was running out of time.

She was concentrating her attention entirely on Strangford Lough. The Lough was unusual because of its currents and strong tidal flows. It was a dangerous place to swim as many unfortunate sailors and bathers discovered to their peril, due to the speed of the Irish sea entering through its narrow inlet. The Lough could fill and empty again in less than a day. It recently had the first prototype submarine turbine electricity generator installed beneath its waters, which supplied a significant chunk of energy to Strangford and neighbouring Portaferry.

Eva was a local girl. She grew up in neighbouring Downpatrick, Co. Down, said to be the home of Saint Patrick and where, according to folklore, you can still visit his grave. She had a lifelong love affair with the sea and had studied marine biology at Newcastle University's School of Marine Science and Technology; her speciality being marine bio-geochemistry and applied marine science.

Four years later, with a fully qualified diver's licence and after two brief, but passionate romances, she graduated with first class honours and a PhD in research into the microbiology of sea surface micro layer (SML). She found work straight away at

Queens University's Marine laboratory as a research assistant to Professor Barthold Fischer OBE. The world may have been her oyster, but she decided to stay and work in her native Ireland.

Eva's area of expertise was in particular algae and domestic marine fauna. She loved to tell her friends that way too much emphasis was put on the depleting South American rain forests while so few took any notice of the most abundant oxygen giving organism on the planet – to be precise, algae farts.

It would be these 'little green bum burps' that would keep all of us living and breathing; not the bloody Amazon rainforest.

Chapter *12*

THE SUMMER OF 2014 WAS, BY NORTHERN IRISH standards, unusual. July through to September saw above average temperatures that remained constantly in the mid to high twenties with the occasional 30+ spike. It hadn't dropped below 19 degrees at night for the past three weeks. People moaned as they always do about global warming and climate change.

Eva's research studies had shown that the normal domestic algae thrived in hot weather but the heat didn't appear to have any effects on that of her newly discovered samples. They looked a little more fluorescent than normal and would grow marginally faster, but that seemed to be about it. No spectacular bursts of colour or smells, unlike that of the dangerous toxic blue fresh water variety that emitted a heavy unmistakable aroma and could be lethal if swallowed or cause permanent liver damage.

She also noted that any fluctuations in temperature appeared to have had no or little affect, even extreme cold caused no notable damage or change. This is what intrigued her about this species in particular. It was impervious to pretty much everything but drought, and even that had yet to be tested thoroughly.

Most marine plants, like terrestrial plants, died off or decreased in growth in colder conditions. Her experiments and results could prove that she may have discovered the first non-deciduous localised algae, impervious to climatic or seasonal variations. Variations which, according to the experiments she had carried out so far ranged between -2°C and 33°C.

I should name it after my mother. She would have loved pond slime named after her, Eva had thought on more than one occasion during her research.

Chapter *13*

TERRY BEST WAS THE CHIEF ENGINEER ON THE underwater turbine project in Strangford Lough. Up to now his talent and training were wasted. The *Sea-Gen* turbine produced 300 kilowatts of electricity and powered approximately one thousand homes. It ran like a Swiss watch.

As far as Best was concerned, it was easy money for easy work. He rarely needed to go near the machine apart from the occasions when it was raised to de-scale or safety-check the bearings of the massive tungsten carbide blades that measured 43 meters from tip to tip.

Best heard the shrill of the initial alarm, but put it down to a routine safety drill that was part of the automated fail systems installed within the turbine's self-protection protocols. The turbine had bespoke factory set default software installed that self-diagnosed and tested all of its systems as part of a daily cycle. The turbine was fitted with sensors designed to pick up any abnormal pressure or resistance on the rotational speed of the blades. When the phones and bells started ringing, he feared for an underwater snag, or worse, that a diver or seal had gotten too close and had been entangled and drowned!

He threw his life preserver over the high visibility jacket then untied the RIB. It took minutes to reach the turbine site. The bulky hand-held remote he carried still refused to respond. The batteries were charged daily and sometimes hourly in winter, as their charge depleted quickly in the cold.

The secondary shutdown switch on his remote, which was the last option, was still not responding regardless of how many times he pushed it. Best was worried. The water around the turbine for one hundred yards in all directions was vibrating and droplets were bouncing on the otherwise millpond surface. *"BOLLOCKS!"* was his first response.

The data he was receiving on his handheld remote was telling him the blades were rotating at 37rpm and increasing. They were now at 3rpm above the critical working limit. The normal limit for optimum power harvest was 14rpm.

He tried to figure out the reason for the malfunction. He checked his readouts and ran his hand under the safety helmet to scratch his now sweating scalp hoping to maybe find an answer under there.

He tied the RIB to the mooring point on the turbine and watched as the water appeared to boil at the surface violently churned by the increasing speed of the massive blades. He climbed the ladder up to the control cockpit, then entered the narrow turret of the turbine and hit the manual kill switch to cut the power.

The blades responded by slowly rotating upwards, using the resistance of the water as a brake.

The whole incident began and ended in nineteen minutes and 47 seconds. A diagnostic system check was carried out and four hours later the turbine was back in business.

Whatever had caused the malfunction had somehow been corrected, so he just put it down to water gremlins and thanked his lucky stars that no one had been killed or injured.

Chapter *14*

WHEN EVA GOT HOME SHE SLUMPED ON HER sofa. Confusion gave way to educated, logical thinking. She gathered her thoughts. She began to write down the course of events on the day of the injury as she remembered them.

- She was swimming.
- Nothing before or after entering the water was unusual.
- She cut her foot on broken glass.
- That was less than twenty-four hours ago.
- No wound or sign of any tissue trauma.

What the fuck is going on!

Chapter *15*

THE SHELL COMPANIES THAT VALENTINE SERE had begun in his teens had gathered momentum. He had little idea how to run a business, but he had the funds and resources to employ the people who did. Despite his success, he was not a man to boast about his achievements and that endeared him to those he encountered. It disarmed them and they poured information into his receptive ears.

He was now one of the wealthiest people in the United States and he treasured his anonymity above all else. He wore better than average jeans, expensive shoes and a stainless steel *Rolex Submariner* wristwatch. Apart from that there was nothing special or noticeable about him.

He was handsome but not overly so. He wore his wavy hair in a heavy continental style. Long at the top with a floppy fringe held erect by a strong kink at the front. His time in the sun had highlighted the ends to a caramel blonde and his skin still retained the memory of time spent in the Miami sun. He could walk through any hotel lobby without a concierge pestering him with invites to celebrity parties. No one knew except him, his true wealth. The bank managers and accountants he employed could only guess, but even they didn't know for sure the extent of his wealth and power. His father's company still paid for his business class tickets and he loved the idea of it.

He scouted for IT experts through gaming competitions on the internet. He couldn't care less for the age, colour or the gender of his *techies*. If you could reach a certain gaming level, which his senior technicians had constructed, you were offered a lump sum to be deposited into a bank of your choice, which was of course untraceable. They didn't even need to leave home if they chose. Their account was monitored and the prospective new employee was kept under surveillance and tracked for a year, unless they had adverse government or competitive security connections.

He supplied the latest computers and software and some that were still only in development. He bugged the data processing units. If successful they were employed in one of his fake companies and registered as IT consultants. They were then assigned to hack into every university computer system on the planet, every publicly and privately owned research lab and every museum. He had Trojans planted in US, Chinese, Russian, Middle Eastern and British Scientific facilities.

If there was something new out there, Valentine Sere would know about it almost immediately.

Chapter *16*

EVA WANDERED AROUND HER OFFICE, STILL numb regarding the healing event. She audibly exhaled and contemplated phoning the smartest person she knew. It had been quite some time since they had last spoken and it hadn't ended well. The conversation was terminated sharply, with cross words and accusations.

This was commonplace since their confrontation over their parents. *Time to take charge for once*, she thought and tapped in the numbers on the keypad of her mobile. The phone rang five times. She almost hoped it would go to the answer service.

"Hello?" There was a short pause before she steeled herself to answer.

"Hi, sis."

"Is that you, Eva?"

"Yes, it's me. How's things?"

"Um, yeah good, I suppose. What's up?"

The tone was a mixture of coldness, confusion and surprise.

Her sister was the last person Estelle Ballantine had expected to hear from.

"I know it's been a while, but I need some advice," said Eva.

"*You* need advice from *me*?" Estelle retorted.

She was completely taken aback by her sister's request, as advice had been both abundant and ignored in their recent turbulent past. So much hurt had been both given and received and Estelle had found it difficult to hide her anger at the lack of support from her little sister following their father's death. The old wounds were still very raw.

"I'm sorry, Elle, I shouldn't have troubled you."

Eva recognised the recent normal, hostility in her sister's voice, that of late had become commonplace in the rare times they had spoken since their loss.

"Please, wait. I'm sorry," said Estelle. Something about Eva's tone made Estelle regret her hostility and her natural protective instincts kicked in. She gathered herself and began again. *Too much water under that particular bridge, your sister needs your help, so grow up for God's sake!*

"What can I do for you, Eva?"

"It's a bit hard over the phone. Can we meet up?"

"If it's going to end in another row, then no, I don't think so!"

The hardness in Estelle's voice had momentarily returned.

"It won't. I promise," said Eva quietly.

Chapter *17*

ELLE WAS THE FAMILY NICKNAME FOR EVA'S older sister. They hadn't spoken for two years after the untimely death of their father, but Eva was her only sister and now her only family. Their mother had died in a senseless explosion attributed to a forgettable terrorist splinter group in a shopping centre in Belfast. Her father had been waiting for her, sat watching golf in the bar, killing time, drinking his Guinness, eating the stale bar nuts and reading his newspaper.

Their parents met at a twenty-first birthday party held by the parents of one of Patricia's friends. Joseph had been nineteen and Patricia eighteen. She was the most beautiful person he had ever seen and he fell in love instantly. She took a while longer to be swept off her feet, but eventually would come to love him in her own way.

She gave no indication to him as a young woman that she would be so entranced by material wealth and possessions. She had been determined to finish her law degree, and continue to practice until her husband's company became so large that she and he found it no longer necessary for her to work.

As the years passed and the fortune grew, she craved the attention that the family's financial standing and reputation would bring them. It would get her seats in all the best places and heads would turn as she entered any room. She loved to shop and was easily entertained by the lure of the sales. Ironic really, as the family now owned most of the prime property tenanted by the fashion retailers she frequented and bought from.

As a result of her new wealth and status, she sat on several committees and gave her free time to charitable organisations, both pastimes a long way from the backstreets of Belfast where she grew up with her four younger brothers and three elder sisters. In her mind she was a good spouse and mother, but she had been easily swept away with the trappings of wealth and the liberties it brought. She sat across the table at a respectable distance from the man on the other side. They met when they could and always in public. She wasn't prepared to commit to the physical side of the relationship, as that, in her eyes, would have been a betrayal to her husband and family. She adored the attention and compliments he gave her, but policed her emotions heavily.

His number was on her mobile phone as her hairstylist. He was ten years younger than she was and he genuinely cared for her, hoping that she may someday leave her husband and that they may have a life together.

The receipt for the men's Cartier watch she had just put around his wrist was found later in what remained of her Louis Vuitton handbag. The police investigation would put two and two together and the news would be leaked to the press.

The massive explosion blew them both side-wards at an impossible survivable velocity. Their necks snapped instantly. The flying debris and intense heat did little to assist their speedy demise.

Dust settled, screams started, and sirens blew as they drew closer to the scene of the blast.

Chapter *18*

JOE FELT THE WINDOWS RATTLE AND HEARD THE massive explosion. He knew his wife was in serious trouble!

He saw the plumes of smoke rising from the shopping centre as he ran towards the scene of the bomb. The police were doing their best in trying to hold people back from getting close to the blast site. Witnesses and casualties with minor injuries, covered in dust, did their best to evacuate the area, desperately trying to get the seriously injured to safety; coughing, crying and wiping their eyes to remove the dirt and dust left from the explosion.

Joe tried to explain to the young panicked police officer who he was and his concerns for his wife, but the police officer shouted into his face, splattering him in saliva, that, there may be other devices in the building!

This wasn't uncommon during the thirty years of civil conflict. The first bomb would kill and maim. The second would be detonated when police and military had arrived at the scene. Killing and injuring as many more as possible.

The young police officer had been less than fifty meters from the centre of the explosion when it detonated. His youthful reactions had saved him as he dove for cover finding shelter from the flying pieces of people and buildings, but not the sound or the shockwave. Joe saw that he had blood trickling down from his dust caked ears. He realised the young man was now probably deaf and despite the hell going on around him was doing his best to be a professional, regardless of his now tattered uniform and the uncontrollable shaking of his hands.

Joe stood in horror as dead and mutilated were carried away from the scene. Too few ambulances had arrived at the still smoking building to deal with the injured, so the dead and dying were laid out on the pavements covered in coats and table cloths, or anything that could be used as makeshift shrouds to leave the dead with at least some dignity. The force of the blast had stripped them of most of their clothing leaving them bloody and naked on the cold pavements.

Eleven dead and many more injured, with Patricia Ballantine and her friend among the fatalities. No warning was given before the explosion and the terrorists got all the publicity that they were looking for!

Chapter *19*

THE DEATH OF THEIR MOTHER WAS SPLATTERED across the TV news channels worldwide. It wasn't headline news for long, but it filled a vacant space until some other more interesting breaking story nudged it into the annals of history. No great surprise. Yet more innocent human beings ripped to shreds in another pointless bomb blast in Northern Ireland.

Soon the reporters would put the pressure on Estelle. She was the elder daughter and when the press got tipped off about their mother's affair from a greedy, corrupt police officer on the media's payroll, they were relentless.

Joseph Ballantine was a mechanical engineer. Ballantine was not his given birth name. That was Kelly. However in the late sixties and early seventies some Catholics found it hard to get jobs in engineering in Belfast, so he changed it to Ballantine, a name that could be used without having him pigeon holed as either Catholic or Protestant. He kept himself to himself as he learned, then honed his trade. He double jobbed to put himself through college and got his degree in mechanical engineering. Four years of hard work paid off when he graduated with first class honours.

He worked in East Belfast Tool & Die. The company was a precision engineering firm and he became their chief design technician. He saved hard to earn enough money for a deposit on an old building in the Markets area of the city. He finally got his break and made his fortune patenting a radical new design for the die casting of egg boxes.

Eggs were fragile everyday items that needed to be transported cheaply and safely. Soon every supermarket and egg producer in Europe and eventually America wanted his die cast specifications. He sold the patent and received royalties for his design from a multinational packaging company and enjoyed a semi anonymous life between Belfast, Boston, Massachusetts and Mallorca. He offered no bells and whistles and most business people knew him as *Yolky Joe*. He rarely moved in the expected circles and kept his old friends close. He protected his daughters from becoming famous because of their father. He was a gentleman and cherished his privacy, never allowing himself to be swept away with the trappings of wealth or the notoriety it brought. Unlike his beloved late spouse Patricia.

He was struggling to accept the fact that the love of his life wasn't the love of hers. The affair was milked to death by the local press ghouls and Estelle, in a bid to protect her father and sister, took the flak. Her younger sister Eva shrank into the undergrowth and privately mourned her mother's passing while trying to understand the reason for her infidelity. She felt as betrayed as her father and knew that Estelle felt the same way. The mixture of loss and anger at their late mother's actions would drive a wedge between the members of the family. None of them knew that at the time. Their mother had not appeared to be unhappy but had put her own selfish need to be adored above the family's welfare.

Elle took a year to come to terms with their mother's double life. She adored her father and watched him steadily become more introvert as the months and years passed. He stopped answering his telephone and became a recluse in his own home. His health was failing as he spent his days watching the blank screen of his television and drinking himself to sleep in his armchair. He dismissed the domestic staff that had cared for the family for the last twenty years and continued his decline into full-blown depression.

Estelle had been left with no other option and eventually was forced to take the decision to have her father sectioned when he stopped eating. He had been seventeen stone and had taken good care of himself in his prime. He was a handsome man and turned heads when he entered any room. He shunned the looks of admiring female company but secretly dreaded the idea of becoming old and invisible.

The doctors and psychiatrists tried numerous treatments but to no avail. It wasn't a body dysmorphic condition or self-loathing. The truth was that his heart was broken and he just didn't want to be here anymore. The daughters watched him wither away in front of their eyes. Eva came home from university at Estelle's request when he stopped responding to her in the hospital. At the end he even refused to drink water. So his lips cracked and his tongue ulcerated resulting in him being so dehydrated, he couldn't even say goodbye or tell them that he loved them. Every attempt by the medical staff to administer a saline drip, he pulled from his own arm. He was nine stone when they put him in the clay. No cancer and no disease. You can't put *self-destruction* on a death certificate. So they put *myocardial infarction* (heart failure), which seemed apt under the circumstances.

Eva refused to accept the fact that her sister had been left with the lonely decision to put her father into a mental institution. Estelle was the elder child and knew that Eva couldn't or wouldn't do the only thing left to try to save their father's life. The man was no longer in control of his own health or decisions and as a last ditch attempt to save him, her only choice became psychiatric intervention. When that didn't work, the end was inevitable.

Chapter *20*

JOSEPH BALLANTINE, PREVIOUSLY KELLY, WAITED until the girls were absent. He died on his own, tended to by strangers in a secure private ward. When the nurse telephoned Estelle to come as quickly as she could, she knew it was already too late. She phoned Eva on the way to the clinic. As they both arrived he was lying on the hospital bed with his eyes still open. They could both see that he was already dead.

They stood over him hugging his lifeless body and sobbing as endless tears streamed down their cheeks and flooded into his dead eyes. For all appearances, it seemed that he was joining them in their grief as his daughters' tears rolled down his face.

Eva was in mourning and confused. She had just turned twenty-two and graduated from University. She hadn't been there through most of her father's illness and blamed Estelle for his subsequent death. She needed someone to focus her anger on, so Estelle was the only available target.

"I suppose you were just too busy to be bothered, Elle! You had more important things to do. Cases to win and a reputation to make. The family always played second fiddle to you and your career!"

Estelle tried as she could to understand, but she was hurting too.

"Where the hell were you, Eva? I was left here to deal with the press, the doctors and the bastards that I stupidly thought were friends. I had to sort it because you couldn't or wouldn't! You were too busy tie-dying your fucking cheesecloth skirts and burning incense sticks with your bohemian classmates. I needed help and support, but you only managed to come home for a bloody fortnight!"

"You know what? Fuck you!"

Eva turned, slamming the door of their family home and left. She would never enter it again. It would eventually be sold and the money sent to a charity that their late father regularly donated to.

That was the last time they had spoken and it hadn't been with any civility.

Estelle had tried making contact several times over the following weeks and months. She was the elder sibling and saw it as her duty. They both met at a friend of the family's funeral a year past and had a polite exchange in front of the mourners, but time moves on and she eventually gave up trying to heal old wounds. She missed her parents and she missed her sister. It sometimes felt like they had all died in the bomb blast.

Eva continued to be disappointed in herself for not being there to help when Estelle needed her. It was her responsibility as much as her sister's and she failed in it.

A cocktail of embarrassment, shame and pride prevented her from reconciliation with her sister. She knew in her heart that Estelle had been left to deal with the mess and she was too much of a coward to admit it to her. That was hard to admit. She had lost them all and hated herself for it.

Absence just seemed the easier option.

Chapter *21*

New York

THE SUN BLAZED ACROSS THE EXPANSIVE DECK of the two hundred foot yacht, which was kept permanently moored at the Newport yacht club, New York. The views of the Manhattan skyline were breathtaking.

Magnificent as the vessel was, Wilson Sere rarely spent time on it, as work, wealth and the acquisition of power were his preferred ways to live his life. Once a year he would have it sailed out into international waters as yet another means of tax evasion. He was as usual joined by a host of his cronies, most of whom were every bit as ruthless and greedy as he was. Fresh supplies were brought out for the prolonged stays at sea. The provisions could range from fresh milk and fruit to $1,000.00 a day prostitutes, or whatever else his guests needed or requested.

This was one reason he retained the yacht, the other being that he got little pleasure from the company of his wife or son and could easily escape them when at sea. He saw his son Valentine only occasionally, but today was special as it was his seventieth birthday.

His wife Julia had organised a party on board and she refused to take no for an answer, publicly protesting that they rarely saw their only son and heir. Wilson reluctantly agreed and so the invitations were sent. The yacht was bedecked with bunting and coloured lights for the occasion and Julia had scheduled the $70,000 firework display to be started as her husband blew out the candles on his cake. She couldn't care less if Wilson approved or appreciated the gesture but appearances had to be kept one social step ahead of her wealthy bridge-playing partners.

Valentine's takeover of his father's company would be completed the next day. BION Pharmaceuticals would soon at last be in his hands. He had stealthily set up thirty-one companies spread all over the globe, then slowly over a period of six years had bought shares in BION, which now totalled forty-eight percent of the entire organisation, plus suppliers and sub-contractors hidden under various names of his choosing. Wilson Sere and his board members would never suspect a thing. Valentine's father still retained forty-two percent of the shares, his wife five percent and his son an equal five percent. The markets would open in the morning and Wilson Sere would be surprised to find out who his company's new, now senior, controlling partner was. Valentine would simply use the five percent he already owned to take over BION as the majority shareholder.

He greeted his father on the yacht with the usual formal handshake.

"Congratulations, sir. Happy birthday."

"Thank you, Valentine."

Wilson barely made eye contact with his son, instead picking at some canapés from the tray that the waitress was passing around the guests and sipping his $275,000 a bottle, 1907 *Heidsieck* champagne. The rare liquid had been rescued from the bottom of the ocean off the coast of Finland where it had sat for the past eighty years until his thoughtful wife Julia had procured ten of the bottles for his birthday party.

"I trust you're keeping well, sir?"

"Better than you would hope, I should imagine, Valentine."

There was no humour in his father's statement. Valentine believed that his father thought him incapable of doing anything other than whittling his time away and spending the company's money. He reddened with embarrassment and looked around from guest to guest for a kind face or sympathetic word to indicate that they found his father's remarks towards him to be hurtful and unkind. He of course found none. Everyone on the yacht was on Wilson's pay roll one way or another, so would nod their heads and

61

smile whatever their employer said or did regardless of anyone's hurt feelings, especially Valentines, as most regarded him as a time waster or playboy.

Valentine took a small but noticeable step backwards. This, as he predicted had ended the way it usually did, no matter how much Valentine wished things to be different, it had been the same behaviour since his childhood. His parents were strangers for the most part and not particularly good ones at that. He inwardly scolded himself again for appearing weak and needy, holding aspirations to something that was unattainable. Embarrassed and angry, the only course of action was a dignified departure.

"Enjoy the rest of your birthday, father."

Wilson Sere didn't respond, but instead carried on the conversation he was having before his son's interruption.

Chapter **22**

VALENTINE MADE HIS WAY THROUGH THE sniggering guests and well-wishers. He found his mother and kissed her on each cheek. He told her that he loved her, and then said his farewells. He walked the fifty feet to the gate and gangway, where armed security guarded the entrance to the yacht. His mother half-heartedly tried to stop him leaving and went through the usual process until one of the waiting staff spilled a tray full of glasses containing the champagne.

She called the girl who spilled the tray over to her. She spoke quietly and calmly as the poor girl went pale with fright.

"That Fizz you were so clumsily juggling until you dropped it was worth ten years of your pathetic salary my dear, so this is what you're going to do. You will go immediately to the servants supply store and retrieve the black and yellow striped tape."

Valentine tried to intervene but was silenced by a sinister stare from his mother.

Julia readdressed the waitress without apology.

"As I was saying, get the tape and section off the area where you dropped the tray. Get a magnifying glass from the Captains deck and pick every shard, no matter how tiny from between the grooves of the wooden planking. I will have it inspected when you're finished and if one bit has been over-looked, I'll have you deported back to whatever third world toilet of a country you're so desperately trying not to be repatriated to and that includes any dependents or children you may have shat out of that ridiculous ass of yours! Do we have an understanding my darling?"

The girl was now in tears and scampered off to perform her task in full view of the smirking guests. Julia returned her attention to Valentine and politely protested that his visit was so short and that he should settle down soon and give her some grandchildren.

It wasn't the first time he'd heard her say it and it still sounded like she had rehearsed the line after hearing it from a cheesy television show without any real meaning in her words. She didn't persist long, being easily distracted by some of her bridge club friends, who insisted that she must come immediately and see the new million dollar trinket they had just bought at on line auction on their personal aide's laptop.

He stopped to look back at her in disgust as she left without saying goodbye. He paused briefly to look at the stars that twinkled over the New York skyline. He rechecked his watch. The markets opened in nine hours. The takeover of BION was almost complete. He made a mental note to have the yacht moved or sold. *I'll discount it for a Chinese buyer, or even better, I'll let the Russians have it.*

He held his champagne glass at chest level and wondered again why his parents had even bothered to go through the process of having a child. It must have been the fashionable thing to do at the time because he felt like more of an inconvenience than a cherished son.

Oh well. Time to stop trying at last, he thought and angrily dribbled a long string of saliva down into the expensive wine.

He looked at the froth of the saliva floating on the surface then mixing with the rarest of champagne bubbles. He dropped it over the side of the yacht and watched it hit the water with a light plop, before walking down the gangway to shore, vowing never to willingly board her again.

Chapter **23**

EVA SWIPED HER SECURITY CARD AND ENTERED the lab. No time for small talk. She was in a hurry and singularly focused on her task. She bagged specimen jars, assorted chemicals and her laptop, then loaded them into her rucksack and left without speaking to anyone. The only connection she had to the miraculous healing of her foot was the swim at the Lough. She had racked her brain for any other explanation and could find none.

That's where she got injured, so it was a logical place to start her investigations. The drive down to the Lough passed without her noticing. She arrived in Strangford and parked the hatchback close to the ferry terminal. She tried to remember exactly where she had thrown the glass shard as she sat on the wall nodding to the odd passer-by. She even seriously considered getting down on her hands and knees and rummaging through the litter beneath the gorse bush to find the offending object, but knew that was pointless among the rubbish.

She mentally retraced the events between entering the water and the accident occurring. The only thing she could recall that was any way out of the ordinary was the unusual hum and vibration in the water during her swim. As a scientist, her mind was trained to be measured and methodical.

Start from the seemingly unremarkable tiniest detail and work your way up until you find what you're looking for.

A nagging thought remained no matter how hard she tried

to dispel it. *There has to be a connection here somewhere. No sign of visible trauma twenty-four hours after the injury, no scabbing, no pain or even mild discomfort!*

Eva began to retrace her steps from where she left the water until the point where she reached her car. She had to make sure that nothing was missed. If something had been overlooked or temporarily forgotten, something that had occurred between the panic of the injury and reaching the car, then she had to systematically rule out all possible factors in the quest to find the answer to the bizarre rapid healing. She leaped down off the wall and walked along the road looking out to the main body of water in the Lough, then made her way down to the water's edge, staring out onto the beauty of the scenery. She was momentarily distracted by the view, just simply gazing out at nothing in particular, lost in her thoughts. The horn from a passing truck woke her from her daydream. She continued on, walking down along the shoreline taking fresh samples of the algae, water, sand and seaweed; of anything in the area that could provide a clue to her own, very personal, miracle.

John had already started the initial testing of the original algae samples back at the university.

Chapter 24

TERRY BEST ORDERED A COMPLETE DIAGNOSTIC check of the turbine's systems. His team turned every screw and tightened every metaphorical bolt from top to bottom, but no faults were found. The event hadn't even registered on the historical readout. According to the machine, it just simply hadn't happened! He had the blades raised and cleaned, as a precaution just in case he was missing something. He knew he wasn't, but had to be sure.

No big deal. Nobody died, he thought. *Lucky this time!*

Eva watched the operation in progress and waited for one of the maintenance crew to come ashore. She approached one of the workers busy tying up a small rowing boat and excused herself to the man for appearing nosey.

"What's going on with the turbine?" she asked.

"Don't know, love. Some sort of breakdown."

"Who's the boss?"

"The guy over there talking on the mobile," came the reply.

"That's John Starkie, isn't it?"

She was bluffing. She had no idea who the chief engineer was. She was just probing, fishing for a name.

"No, love. That's Terry Best."

She thanked him and made her way over to where Terry was standing and waited until he finished his call. He watched her out of the corner of his eye as he continued the phone conversation. When he ended the call, Eva introduced herself.

"Mr. Best?"

"Yes, that's me."

"Pleased to meet you Mr. Best. I'm Doctor Eva Ballantine."

"It's a pleasure, Doctor. What can I do for you?"

"I've recently been doing some research, down here on the Lough."

Eva produced her Queens University ID and showed it to him.

Terry's initial thought was, *Here we go again, another bloody 'seal hugger' looking for a reason to shut this thing down and put me out of work!*

"I don't want to be rude, Doctor, but I'm a little busy here."

"Of course you are, I'm sorry, Mr. Best, I won't take but a minute of your time. I'm just trying to find out if there has been anything unusual or out of the ordinary happening recently?"

"Like what, Doctor?"

"It's Eva, please!"

"Okay. Like what, Eva?"

Terry's tone was neither hostile nor friendly but if you had to choose, you'd say it was tinged with a hint of exasperation.

Eva audibly exhaled and reluctantly gave Terry an edited account of the events of the experience she had, trying as best she could not to appear a lunatic.

"Look, Terry," she said, not caring now if she was being unduly informal, "I've had a bit of an event take place here. Nothing to do with your turbine I'm sure. I'm just trying to pick up the pieces of the jigsaw and quite frankly, I've no idea what I'm looking for. I'm a local girl and when it's safe, I swim here every other day in summer. I was kind of maybe hoping you could help me out?"

Terry could sense the tinge of panic and the desperation in her voice and that she seemed to be genuine enough. He decided to let his guard down a little.

"There was a minor problem with the turbine. No big deal. The whole thing began and ended in fifteen minutes."

"What happened?"

"You see that's the strange thing. The turbine accelerated

for no reason. Then after a few minutes it just righted itself again."

"What time was this?"

"Again that's a tricky question. There's no record on any of the systems that it happened at all. Possibly some minor computer glitch, but whatever it was, it's fine now. We've taken this thing apart from the top down and still have no answers yet. It's purring like a kitten now."

"What time would you roughly estimate this happened, give or take?" she asked.

"I can only make an educated guess. The alarm went off at 11.45 am which meant it was reaching its working safety limit. It took me about five minutes to get out and manually shut it down, which is the part of this that concerned me the most. The *hand held* should have shut it down from shore. That's what it's designed to do in case of heavy seas or rough conditions but it wouldn't respond. I've personally rechecked the batteries twice and it works perfectly now. Weird right! So to finally answer your question, the event probably started and ended between roughly 11.40 and noon."

"Okay, thanks, Terry."

"No problem. Hope it helps. By the way, Doctor. You didn't hear any of this from me."

"No worries your secret's safe with me!" called Eva as she turned and made her way back towards her car.

Well that's something anyway. I went in the water at 11.20am. That would have put me 20 minutes or so into the session. What else? I know something happened out there that I have yet to remember!

Her mind was still drawing a blank. She shook her head. *Listen, it will come back to you. Now stop talking to yourself. You're acting like a crazy person. You'll be shouting at the pigeons next for crapping on your car!*

Chapter **25**

E STELLE BALLANTINE SAT QUIETLY SIPPING HER barely drinkable coffee, waiting for her sister Eva to eventually show up. *Late as usual; some things never change*, she thought.

She slumped back in her seat and took out her diary, checking tomorrow's appointments. She took a third refill and again endured the waitress giving her the *'are you ever going to order anything'* look.

"Okay, that's it. Five more minutes and I'm out of here!" she grumbled to herself. *You know what? Balls to this, I've been waiting long enough!*

She pushed the chair back, pulled a £5 note from her purse, tossed it on the table and made her way to the door. As she pressed the remote for her car from outside the cafe, she heard her name being called by her sister.

"Elle!"

She ignored the shout pretending not to hear, now angry and with the unwanted old familiar wall going up. She carried on with the business of getting into her car. She was pissed with her sister and didn't want an explanation or a confrontation.

"Estelle!"

That one stopped her. She turned towards the caller; she, of course, knew who it was.

"I'm sorry, Elle. I got tied up," she half panted. "If you ever carried your phone, I would have called you."

"This is crap, Eva, and you know it. This is the first time we've purposely met in I don't know how long and you're so lacking in manners to be late! By the way, I do carry my phone, I'm seriously pissed off, and I don't like it one little bit. What continues to make your time more precious than mine?"

"Please, Elle, I'm really so sorry, but I think I'm in terrible trouble!"

Elle's tone softened.

Here we go again. How many frigging times does she get yet another second chance?

"What kind of trouble?"

"Let's go back in."

"Not here," said Elle, "down the street. The waitress in there is a total *bitch*."

During the next hour, Eva tried her best to explain the course of events at the Lough and the strange rapid healing of her foot.

"Are you sure that this really happened, Eva?" questioned Elle.

"No, no I'm not sure. I'm not sure of anything at the moment. All I know is that I sliced my foot on glass and the next day there's no sign of any injury, it's like it never happened. I even have the bloodied towel lying in the back of the car if you want to see it? I haven't washed it yet, as it's the only tangible evidence that anything happened at all."

"That's impossible, Eva, and you know it every bit as well as I do. If this is some long tale of yours in a bid to heal our wounds, forgive the irony, then you had better think again."

"I know it's impossible but it still happened and it's not some, as you now appear to think, plot of mine. I'm sorry now that I ever called you."

They both sat in silence for a while and wondered if they should just get up, leave and go back to the all now familiar distance that had come between them, or try to calm their tempers and share some mutual trust for a change. The connection had been lost between them for too long. They both sat stubbornly staring out at the passing traffic and pedestrians from the window of the cafe.

Elle was struggling to comprehend what her sister was telling her and still for the most part angry. She hadn't figured out if she was angry over this meeting or just angry with her sister for the events of the past or the time they had wasted apart.

How can you make sense out of something that makes no sense? Maybe this really is some concocted story on Eva's part to somehow initiate contact? She had never been that subtle in the past. If she had something to say, she would always have said it.

Estelle's brain still continued to refuse to accept the information Eva had fed it. In an attempt to bring normality and sanity back to the situation, it scrambled for a solution in logic.

"What about the samples you took?"

"They're back at the lab."

"Anything odd or unusual?" asked Elle

"I haven't started my tests yet."

"Well, shouldn't you start there then?"

"You're right, of course, you're right."

Eva's mind needed a jumpstart and Elle could always get her focused when she lapsed into a state of confusion. She stood up from the table and gathered her belongings, fingering through her purse for the money to pay the bill.

Estelle stopped her from trying to find enough loose coins to pay.

"I've got this. You go on and get started with your research."

"I'll get right on it and call you when I know more."

"You do that. Listen, Eva, I'm sure you'll figure this out. I'll bet it's something simple, something logical and easily explained. Get to work and call me when you find something."

They walked out of the cafe together into the bright sunlight and afternoon heat both standing at the edge of the curbside to avoid the passing pedestrians.

Elle didn't know what to think of the story. She reckoned her sister may have had some sort of episode, but she was still her only family, so she understood that it was her duty to humour her sister no matter how odd or strange the circumstances. It was the first real contact they had had in so long, so what if it was some phoney made up story. At least they were speaking face to face again.

Eva put her arms out to give a parting pensive hug. She needed the long lost physical contact and reassurance from her big sister. Elle almost reluctantly responded as this could mean all was forgiven in the past and she wasn't sure if she was ready for that just yet.

It was for the first time in almost two years and it took Elle some seconds to fully embrace her sister.

Chapter **26**

SO MUCH HAD HAPPENED IN THE TIME SINCE their parents' death. Estelle felt Eva had thrown her to the wolves. Anger and disappointment in her sister and herself, partly for making the only decision with regards to her father, but also the lingering doubt that Eva may have been right about her being too busy to see the signs of their father's mental deterioration early enough to save him.

She had watched him wither away in front of her eyes. Angry at her sister for the lack of support, angry at her mother for the double life she had led and frustrated and angry at her father, for starving himself to his own destruction while she had to watch, helpless as he committed his lengthy suicide. But most of all angry at the world for making her do it on her own. She was only a girl herself and it sat like a lump in her throat. She was the elder of the two and she hadn't asked to be born first, but it was in her nature to protect and take control.

She had been doing it her whole adult life, now, finally understanding that it was unfair to blame Eva for not being more supportive. Why would she? It was learnt behaviour. This could be uncomfortable, but it was in the past and neither of them had anyone else.

Seconds after they made complete contact a surge of energy passed from sister to sister. Elle convulsed and backed away from Eva suddenly breaking the embrace. It felt as if every atom in her body had decided to shift position and rearrange themselves. She felt her hair was standing on end and her fingernails had become too large to be accommodated by the beds they sat in. She shuddered and stifled the urge to vomit as her head spun and her coffee rose up from her stomach. She teetered then steadied herself against a parked car, visibly shaken and pale. She continued to lean against the car until the nausea passed and she could muster the words to speak again.

"What the hell happened there?"

"I don't know. What's wrong with you?"

Eva stared at her, bewildered and wondering what was going on?

"What. You didn't feel anything?"

"No, nothing why what's the matter?"

"What's the matter? You nearly blew me off my feet is the matter!"

Eva apologised, not entirely sure why.

"I'm really sorry, Elle. You look okay now. I've no idea what you're talking about. Honestly!"

"Shit. Okay, maybe static electricity or something."

She knew that it wasn't.

"If you're sure you're alright. I have to go back to work."

"Yeah sure, I'm fine, honestly, I'm fine. Go."

Eva turned to go when Ella finally gathered herself and asked, "By the way, Eva. When did you start wearing contact lenses?"

"Contact lenses? I'm not wearing any contact lenses."

"Then why are your eyes cornflower blue?"

"*Blue?* My eyes aren't blue!"

She didn't say goodbye again, but rushed inside and through the cafe to its restroom, to check her eyes in the mirror. What was Elle talking about? Her eyes were as normal, still brown!

Chapter **27**

VALENTINE STROLLED INTO HIS FATHER'S former Chicago office, the very nerve centre of BION pharmaceutical. Every major company decision was made here. The Board was due to meet in thirty minutes to greet their new CEO. The door burst open and Wilson Sere stood before his son, apparently furious at having to fly in from New York at such short notice. He had received the takeover information from his personal aide that his seemingly idiot son had been successful with a hostile takeover of the company.

"What the hell do you think you're doing boy?"

"Ah father, I see I have your attention at last. Nice of you to make a personal appearance."

Valentine knew his father would be furious. After all, he would have been the same in similar circumstances. His father, unusually for him, decided to hold himself in check until he heard what his son had to say. This was business now and self-control was never his strong point. Wilson Sere stood wearing his bespoke handmade Italian suit. It seemed that no matter how much money he spent, his clothes always appeared just a little too snug. They strained at the seams across his massive back and his shirt collar dug into the fatty folds at the back of his permanently tanned neck. He stood five foot eight inches in height and had a fifty-eight inch chest making him a bear of a man. His massive fists were clenched in a bid to control his anger. Even at seventy years of age he remained a threatening figure. His face was purple with rage contrasting with his pure white hair which was oiled flat to his scalp.

"Don't be clever with me, Valentine!"

"Surely, father, that's the one criticism I thought that I'd never hear from those lips?"

"You may think you have the upper hand now, son."

In Valentine's memory, he never called him son. Something had apparently changed now. Was this finally recognition that they could at last be related or a simple slip of the tongue?

"But beware: long runs the fox."

"You must excuse me, father, but as we are using canine metaphors, you will understand that I have heads to pat and noses to smack. Now, let's go see who wags their tails shall we?"

Wilson declined to join his son in whatever he had planned next. Instead he would concentrate his time and effort on how, either legally or illegally, he could regain control of his company. Valentine left his father standing, halfway out in the hallway. Wilson stood mumbling to himself as he left.

"He'll be a sorry boy."

He half smiled to himself as he left the building, descended the forty floors in the elevator and made his way towards his chauffeur polishing one of his many cars. Perhaps the boy had learned some useful tricks, may not be a complete disappointment, and achieve his potential after all. His driver opened the rear door of the Rolls Royce and Wilson climbed in. As he reclined back into the deeply cushioned leather seat, he picked up the cars telephone and dialled his wife's number. The call was answered before the first ring had ended.

"Yes, Dear?'

"We have a beginning."

The line went dead without a response. Wilson instructed his driver to proceed onto the airport. This would require some careful planning. His next call would be to the latest in a long line of protégés.

Chapter *28*

VALENTINE CLOSED THE DOOR OF THE OFFICE and locked it to make a further point. He walked down the long corridor to the boardroom, taking little notice of the works of classic and modern art that lined the walls of the forty-fourth floor of the BION building.

It was said that his late grandfather had laid the foundation stone of the building himself and had designed the structure to be the most state of the art and grandest in Chicago. He only stopped short of making it the tallest in the western seaboard less it caused annoyance to some of his New York and Washington contacts for usurping their own claims to have the world's tallest buildings. He had never met the man himself or knew anything about him other than his business successes. He strode down the intricately laid polished wooden floors that led him to the double fifteen feet high Art Deco designed boardroom doors. He stopped short of entering the boardroom and took out his phone and hit a button. Joanne, his aide, answered in one ring,

"Mr. Sere?"

"Jo, please, for the hundredth time, it's Val."

"Sorry, yes, Mr... Sorry, Val."

Joanne pushed the heel of her hand against her forehead in frustration at not remembering to, as instructed, be less formal with her boss.

"My father has been put on indefinite garden leave. He's tired and needs a rest. He's not a young man anymore."

"Of course, sir. Sorry Val."

He didn't say goodbye. Just ended the call and returned the device to his pocket of his jeans.

He entered the boardroom without ceremony or introduction, taking the time to ready himself as he walked across the room, ignoring the board members sitting around the twenty-foot long mirror polished Tiger Maple table. He opted instead to admire the sprawl of Chicago's buildings and dark waters below. He had to hand it to his grandfather for choosing this location to erect the BION building. To the left he had the John Hancock Centre with its crossed bracing steel girder construction that would surely be one of the last man made buildings left standing if man ever became extinct, then the magnificent triangular Lake Point Tower in the distance. The view down took his eye to Navy Pier, which was doing its best to make an incursion into the vast Lake Michigan.

No one in the room made a sound as he turned away from the panorama and made his way to the head of the table, he quietly pulled back his seat and sat down.

All the board members invited to the meeting sat gathered around the table, still surprised at the news that as of today they had a new CEO. The smarter ones knew that it was Valentine. The not so clever didn't even know what he looked like.

He recognised several of the smirking faces from his father's birthday party on the company yacht. None of these people had given him the time of day over the years, except one, Kay Kane. She had been protective of him since she joined BION four years ago. She sat midway down the table in a position that made her important but apparently not irreplaceable. Her honey blonde hair and contrasting cherry red lipstick were worn, in the main, as a protest against her pinstriped suit wearing Ivy League superiors. As with everything Kay did, it was for a reason, known only to her rather than some pointless feminine protest.

His father had his aides headhunt her while she was the deputy chief adviser for a major domestic arms manufacturer. The lucrative package that BION had offered was appealing to her, but she didn't need it or the money.

79

She rarely went on corporate trips, unless she personally needed to show her face. Many of the customers she sold weapons to also needed drugs for their casualties. Naturally she provided them to the defeated side as well, at a hugely inflated rate.

Put simply, she could name her price! She was as cold blooded and ruthless as they come. She couldn't care less for human tragedy or suffering and saw conflict as a major marketing opportunity.

She smiled at Valentine as he got comfortable on his new throne. Valentine bowed slightly to her in acknowledgement and began his address.

"Ladies and gentlemen. Good morning. For those of you who are unaware, I am your new employer."

Mumbles rose from around the table, some feigning shock and surprise while others inwardly hoping for more control of the company under their new CEO.

"May I ask each of you to switch off your telephones so I may, for a brief time have your full attention."

Continuing mumbles of outrage and protest resonated through the room, made louder at being momentarily cut off from their precious links to the outside world. Each of the board members had just received a simultaneous text message from a withheld number. Everyone ignored the message on the screen containing the strange arrangements of jumbled letters.

Everyone, except one. The symbol on that phone was an all too familiar one!

Several of the clever ones rose to their feet to congratulate him in their sycophantic manner. He knew through his research who could be trusted and who would continue to be loyal to his father. As usual Valentine had a detailed plan of action.

Chapter **29**

VALENTINE OUTLINED THE SIMPLE STRATEGY for his designs for the future running of the company, one that would increase its market value and lead to securing its already firm grip on the national pharmaceutical market and future dominance globally. He revealed plans to branch out into renewable energy technologies and in particular bio fuels. He ended his address and relaxed back into the chair to unanimous applause from the board members.

"I trust the new order of things will be smooth and lead us all to even more prosperous times ahead at BION."

Again the heads surrounding him nodded to each other across the table in joint agreement in the knowledge that the injection of fresh blood and the boy's new dynamic thinking would now take them forward with the promise of even more obscene amounts of wealth.

He waited for them to settle down and began his second statement.

"I would like to take this opportunity to introduce our new vice president. She has, since her appointment been an invaluable asset to BION and a major new force in its growth."

His audience looked around for someone to enter the room.

"Miss Kane, would you mind?"

Kay Kane looked up in shock as she realised she was being offered the promotion. She slumped back in her chair for a second. She had no idea that she would be promoted ahead of some of the more senior board members. She simply stared at Valentine as he nodded his head gently for her to accept her new promotion.

She steadied herself, stood and graciously accepted what would be her new role in the company, avoiding making eye contact with anyone other than Valentine.

"Thank you, Valentine. I'll do my best to reward your decision."

She sat down, still without looking around to seek approval from any of the others.

The mumbles of differing views on Kay's surprise promotion over some of the more senior members, rose again regardless if she heard them or not.

Valentine spoke through the chatter, silencing the gathered.

"Ladies and gentlemen, I would like to speak to Miss Kane in private for a few moments so I would ask you to adjourn to the restaurant where food has already been prepared by one of Chicago's finest chefs."

Chapter *30*

THE BOARD MEMBERS LEFT WITH RENEWED rumbles of protest, leaving Kay and Valentine alone in the vast boardroom. Valentine waited until the last one was gone and Joanne his aide closed the door behind her as she escorted them out.

"Are you on board with the choices I'm about to make Kay?"

"I like the one you've made so far."

"Okay. Let's get on then."

He picked up his phone and asked Jo to bring back the members of the board he'd chosen along with the sealed envelopes he'd given her before he'd made his address.

"Jo. Have Miss Cohen, Mr. Goldstein, Mr. Houston, Senator Hamill and Harvey Wright sent into the boardroom please. The rest of the members may leave on vacation to the company's villas if they wish. I will contact them, I'm sorry, Miss Kane, will call them in due course."

Kay nodded again in approval.

Five minutes later the five board members took their seats spaced out around the table with Valentine at the head and Kay to his right. Each had two manila folders placed in front of them by Joanne who left again closing the doors behind her. Each envelope had their name hand written on the front.

Valentine knew that he had them exactly where he wanted them. It had taken time, resources and money to gather all the information he had acquired on each of the individual members. So, unusually for him, he dispensed with the pleasantries and spoke generally to the members seated.

"You have in front of you two options. The envelope with the *Smiley* face has 16 million dollars in ongoing indexed linked shares in BION pharmaceuticals and any of its subsidiary companies, plus $860,000 per annum as pension. This is to be regarded as severance pay, effective immediately. You may not return to your offices once leaving this room and will be asked to hand over any laptops, tablets, and cellular telephones or any other item pertaining to BION pharmaceuticals should you accept. The company lawyers have drawn up the conditions of the agreement and they are contained in the smiley envelopes. You simply sign and the agreement is complete."

The protests and outrage from the indignant board members resonated around the room. Valentine refused to respond and waited for relative silence before continuing.

"If I may be allowed to continue. The second envelope with a *Sad Smiley* contains, shall we say…you know what? Let's not say. Let's play show and tell! Mr. Goldstein, would you open your envelope, please, and give your colleagues your decision?"

The rest of the group stared in fascination as he tore at the top of his envelope with *Smiley's* down-turned smile drawn on it. Ira Goldstein shook the contents onto the table. Photographs and receipts dating back five years were revealed and he knew he was helpless.

His forearms tensed and a bead of sweat rolled down the inside of his glasses. He took them off and wiped them on his silk tie.

"Well, Ira. What's the option?"

"You bastard, this is blackmail! How did you get these?"

"That was easy Ira. You and that little club of deviants and swindlers that you belong to make you very predictable."

Valentine knew he was of course in control of the situation and was enjoying watching Ira's reaction. His was the first of the sniggers he'd heard as his father had so rudely treated him at his birthday party on the yacht the day before.

He wasn't enjoying it half as much as Kay! She never liked the arrogant fool and was fascinated by the contents of the envelope.

"Well, Ira what's your decision?"

Ira slumped his head and mumbled that he accepted the *Smiley* package.

"You can leave now Ira and take both envelopes with you. There is only one copy of the contents of your *Smiley Crying* pack so take it with you and good luck!"

Ira Goldstein rose from his seat and left without saying goodbye: not bothering to close the door behind him.

"Rachel, would you go close the door for us please?"

It was more of an order than a request, and Rachel Cohen knew it. She was not a person used to carrying out menial tasks but reckoned she may receive some leniency for her seeming lack of pride and compliance. She rose, walked over and closed the open door, returned and took her seat without protest.

"Do I need to go through this drama with the rest of you? Let me assure you all that the contents of Mr. Goldstein's envelope pales beside some of yours! So if business is concluded?"

Valentine rose from his seat and began to take a second admiring glance at the Chicago cityscape and give them a chance to make their decisions. It only took a moment to hear what he had been hoping for.

Senator Hamill spoke. The man just simply couldn't help himself.

"You'll fucking pay for this, Sere. You have no idea who you're dealing with!"

It was the very thing that Valentine was waiting for and he knew without any shadow of doubt than when the contents of the Senator's envelope were revealed that he would have immediate agreement without further negotiation or protest.

"I know, regrettably for you, exactly whom I'm dealing with Senator and in response to your threat, it's not me who will pay but you, and you will pay dearly." Valentine returned to his seat beside Kay. "I think I'll retain your services and your vote in the Senate. Your sins are of a particular interest to me."

"What fucking sins, you upstart?"

Valentine addressed his statement generally to the gathered.

"Heavens, isn't this just better than Christmas and Thanksgiving all rolled into one! Kay, would you open the Senator's *Sad Smiley* envelope for us please?"

She moved down the table and picked up the envelope that lay innocently in front of the Senator. He leant back in his chair with his arms folded in front of him, smugly smiling at her as she lifted the package.

"You have nothing on me, Sere. I'm as pure as the driven snow and everyone knows it. It's my campaign motto for Christ's sake."

Valentine ignored him but could sense he was panicked and nervous through his bravado. He looked to Kay to reinforce that she continued with her task. He didn't need to, as she was more than eager to see the contents of the package.

The remaining members stared at the manila envelope in morbid fascination.

The Senator then watched in horror as photographs and a memory stick were strewn across the boardroom table. Kay picked up the stick, as the Senator hastily gathered up the photographs before his colleagues could get a closer look at the images. Kay ignored the Senators desperate efforts and walked casually up the length of the boardroom watched by her audience and inserted the memory stick into the fifty inch wall mounted TV monitor. The remaining board members stared at the screen, enthralled as to what they may be about to witness.

There were scenes of the Senator taken on a high-resolution video camera of a packed smoky bar room in Mexico. He was standing in the midst of several other men, cheering and whooping, swinging his shirt around his head whilst holding a bottle of half empty tequila as a young girl was being sexually assaulted by a long and growing succession of drunken, drug fuelled men. The girl was barely 18 and not a willing participant, as she was being restrained by a further two semi naked sweating thugs. The assembled crowd were in various states of sexual drunken arousal and cheered as the line of perverts was guided in their depravity.

"I will be holding on to these images for sentimental reasons," Valentine smiled.

Senator Hamill sat finally silent. It was one of the rare occasions in his life that he knew he had been discovered in one of numerous depravities; unveiled for what he had always known he was since his earliest memories, a pervert, a sadist and a paedophile.

Valentine readdressed the Senator as Rachel Cohen was throwing up under the table.

"Senator, as you well know this little piece of video gold is one of the lesser that I could have chosen, but I think it's sufficient to end your glittering career and produce the required outcome to my more than generous offer."

The Senator walked across to the television and yanked the memory stick from its side. He then walked back across the room and gathered the rest of the scattered contents from his package, dropping the data stick inside. The door of the boardroom refused to be slammed as he stormed out.

Valentine knew that he wouldn't need to close the door and thought it even more intimidating to any one of the members to have the contents of their envelopes fall on public ears.

Valentine now addressed Rachel Cohen.

"Ms Cohen. Shall we open your envelope?"

Her reply was short. She wiped her mouth clean of saliva and sick, then had to swallow back some of the vomit that was still determined to exit her body.

"No thank you, that will not be necessary, your offer is more than generous, Mr. Sere."

She stood up from the table, tearing up the *Bad Smiley* envelope including its contents without looking at them, then threw the mixture of torn photographs and envelope in the trash can as she left.

Each had their own sins and shame at being discovered and couldn't care less for the others humiliations, instead desperately trying to protect what was left of their remaining dignity.

"Mr. Houston. Are we agreed on the terms?"

"We are," he said, lifting both envelopes and leaving

without protest.

While Valentine watched the last one leave the room, he turned to Kay. She hung up her mobile abruptly ending a call and turned to him, unfazed by the film footage.

"Clever. Do I need to expect one of those paper goodie bags someday?"

"Let's hope not. What did you think of the deal?"

"Generous."

"Any thoughts?"

"If I had your say so."

"You do."

"Leave it with me."

Chapter *31*

ELLE BALLANTINE SAT AT HER GLASS KITCHEN table and thought about the meeting with her sister and the odd event outside the coffee shop. Considering it had been their first contact in months, it hadn't been ideal. She returned to her notes to try as best she could to put the incident out of her head. There was a big case tomorrow with plenty of last minute preparation to do, so it needed her full attention.

Elle had made the choice early to follow in her mother's footsteps and become a lawyer. She had been extremely successful in her profession and after years of being the prosecutor, now only took the side of the defence. She was also very particular when it came to choosing those cases.

The latest involved a former priest named Father Hugh Doggett. He had been accused of child abuse and the police believed that any accusation of that gravity warranted investigation. They questioned Father Doggett on several occasions, even taking him into custody for a formal interview. They took statements from the family of the boy who made the sexual abuse claim but could find no physical evidence to support the accusations; either from the boy or his parents. Despite the lack of evidence, the parents decided to proceed with the action.

Father Doggett had been arrested for the second time and questioned for six hours before being released; again without charge. The accusation had been made out of spite.

The boy had made the claim when he had been overlooked

for a place on the team for an amateur boxing competition. Father Hugh, as he was known, realised his fate when the allegations were made and immediately left the priesthood. With the recent and very public scandals involving sex abuse claims by the catholic clergy, it wouldn't be too difficult for his parishioners to believe what they read in the local newspapers or heard in whispers at the corner shops. Even in the understanding that his name and reputation were now cleared, the mention of child abuse was enough to have you branded regardless of the verdict!

Elle opened the door of her chambers to find Father Doggett sitting quietly with his eyes closed at the leather embossed desk. She liked him the minute she saw him and with years of practice, could spot a liar or criminal at a glance. He was lightly built and in his early fifties with strands of white flecks through his ebony hair which was cut short on top and razored close at the sides and back. He still had tiny pieces of hair cuttings in the wells of his ears from his visit to the barber this morning and spots of fresh blood on his collar from giving himself one of the closest shaves she had ever seen.

He stood immediately as if to attention as she entered the room.

"Father Doggett, I'm Estelle Ballantine. Please take a seat. As you may be aware, my colleague, who was to represent you, has decided to pass your case over to me at the last moment for reasons known only to himself. I'm sure you can appreciate that a case of this nature may not be to everyone's taste."

Hugh answered her with a short and precise reply.

"Of course, Miss Ballantine. Thank you for your candour."

"So Father; let's get you prepared for this hearing by going over the course of events and accusations that have led you to the unfortunate position in which you now find yourself. If I'm to properly represent you in court, I'm afraid I will have to ask some uncomfortable and difficult personal questions. I understand how painful this may be but regrettably it is a necessary evil to have your name cleared of these allegations."

"It's no longer Father, Miss Ballantine. However, I'll answer what questions I can."

Chapter 32

ELLE BEGAN TO SCAN THE NOTES IN HER HAND, secretly sneaking a glance at Hugh over her papers to judge his body language. He sat quietly with the palms of his hands laid flat on the desk.

The boy who had made these claims had obviously done so out of malice. None of his times and dates matched up on either of the statements taken by the police or social care representatives. There was no indication of prior history of anything untoward on the defendant's record.

"So, Mr. Doggett," she paused and exhaled as she began. "Did you on this instance or in the past, in any way interfere in a sexual way with the plaintiff?"

"No, Miss Ballantine, I did not."

Hugh kept his answers simple and honest.

"Have you ever had any relationships with any of the people entrusted into your care either past or present?"

"No, I have not."

He was calm and measured and she knew within a heartbeat that he was without question telling her the truth.

"Okay then, Mr. Doggett. The opposition council are going to attempt to lead you with various questions that may place doubt in the Judge's mind that you may be morally impaired, or suggest that you may be a sexual deviant or predator of minors. Do not and I emphasise do not under any circumstances permit yourself to become angry; that's exactly what they want you to do. Stay calm and let me have my turn to question this boy and his parents. Now if you're ready, they're calling us so let's go in."

Hugh thanked her again and made his only request.

"May I have a moment before we go in, Miss Ballantine?"

"Of course, Father; we have some minutes to spare."

Estelle had been raised Roman Catholic as was her sister. So calling an ordained priest anything but Father regardless of the charges against him was near to impossible.

Hugh let the reference go and made his way over to the window that overlooked the buildings leading to a view of the river and mountains. He stood quietly absorbing the scenery.

"This may be the last time I get a view like that for a long while Miss Ballantine. Thank you again for your representation. I'm ready to go through."

They both made their way through the door of her chambers. Hugh listened to the clicking of Estelle's stilettos as they made their way along the marble tiled corridor and into the ornate courtroom surroundings. Elle greeted the opposition council, then arranged her legal papers on the table.

They both wore the formal attire of wig and black gown that covered their suits. They exchanged a few pleasantries as they waited for the judge to enter.

The plaintiff and his parents sat at the prosecution side of the court while Hugh sat on his own by the defence staring up into the packed gallery of onlookers. The parents of the child stared across at the lonely figure of Hugh as he sat, waiting for his fate to be decided.

The doors behind the Judge's bench opened and the court official ordered all to rise. Judge Geoffrey Coyle took his place behind the oak panelled bench and instructed the proceedings to begin.

The prosecution was the first to speak laying out the charges and Estelle settled back into her chair to hear the accusations made against her client.

Hugh 'Dogs' had been brought up a Romany gypsy. His adopted mother found him as a week old baby; left at the steps up to her caravan one winter morning in early February 1961. It was freezing cold and the baby woke her with his crying. She took him into her family and gave him, against the protests of her husband, the name Hugh. Her husband was a difficult man that objected to her taking the infant into their care; he neither wanted nor needed another mouth to feed, especially one from outside the community.

She eventually got her way as she knew she would and Hugh was raised by them, under one condition, "If that bastard child is to be raised by me, he's not taking my fucking name. He's a stray Teresa and that's what we'll name him after! You gave him his Christian name so I'll give him his surname. Dogs, Hugh Dogs. That'll do him well," his father slurred through the whiskey.

Chapter *33*

TERESA OBJECTED BUT HAD TO CONCEDE THE point if she wanted to keep the baby and so Hugh Dogs was raised a Gypsy and was just about as tough as they came. He grew up fighting and dealing his way to earn respect and position within the gypsy community. At 17 he stole a police car to go joyriding with some of his gypsy friends. They crashed the car over turning it and killing one of the passengers. The family rapidly fractured, fell apart and fought amongst themselves, promising revenge on Hugh as the driver of the ill-fated stolen car.

Hugh changed his surname to Doggett. By using that surname he could cover himself in new company, should anyone from his past call him Dogs. He fled to England with the money he'd made by dealing and trading horses. He held both a British and Irish passport, which he kept secret from both his adopted parents. Having two passports was one of the perks of coming from the divided North of Ireland with its estranged 26 counties to the South and its 6 in the North.

He enlisted in the British army, using his British passport and served for five years. He later served a further two years in the Royal Engineers and was then transferred after re-enlisting in the Royal Marines. The army gave him an education and he got his commission at 26.

He shone as a marine junior officer and was selected for the Special Boat Service (SBS), the naval equivalent to the SAS. He co-led various missions, most of which were successful with limited losses. The military life suited him perfectly.

He excelled in marksmanship and hand to hand combat, a result of his history of fighting from a young age to protect his adopted family's name. However it was the conflict in the former Balkan states that would change him forever.

In the midst of the worst possible human conflict, he'd seen enough of the terrible things people could do to each other. He hit the bars and the whiskey bottle and was eventually, after several minor misdemeanours, albeit reluctantly, demoted, losing his commission.

The army either failed or ignored to understand what toll the conflict had taken on him or his comrades, but discipline had to be maintained regardless of the person or the circumstances.

His career in the service was ending when he met an Anglican Army Chaplin in a field hospital outside Sarajevo. A man who gave his all to care for casualties that he treated regardless of their religion or political persuasion. He inspired Hugh to save souls rather than take them.

Hugh soon gave up drinking altogether and resigned from the military; much to the relief of his commanding officer, and began his studies for the priesthood.

He was later ordained and became a parish priest in a small village on the outskirts of Belfast. It was here at the boxing club he ran with some of the volunteers that his time as a priest ended and his future friendship with Estelle Ballantine began.

Chapter 34

T HE PROSECUTION BEGAN THEIR QUESTIONING, first with the plaintiff then Hugh. The boy who made the claims produced fake tears as his parents had instructed. If they won this case, it would become high profile and present the possibility of receiving compensation from the Catholic Church regardless of the fact that they regularly attended mass given by Hugh each Sunday morning. They could not care less if Hugh was sent to prison or not or if his reputation was left in tatters.

The prosecution began the cross-examination. On one line of questioning they presented a long drawn out suggestion that was designed to lead Hugh into the trap of their next more direct supposition. Hugh took more time than he needed to digest the question and then, as if to further throw the opposition lawyer off, he asked him to repeat it as he hadn't quite fully understood the line of questioning.

Exactly as he had hoped, his ploy worked; much to the frustration of the prosecution lawyer who was now off track and had to reword the question more simply and directly.

Elle smiled inwardly as she watched the opposition lawyer fumble his words as he attempted to regain control and again manoeuvre Hugh into possibly incriminating himself.

Hugh continued to keep his answers short and was returned to his seat again leaving the prosecution lawyer frustrated and without further direction. Justice Coyle put added pressure on him when he instructed the prosecution to either direct their line of questioning more simply or desist in their vague cross examination of the defendant.

The court appearance was brief. Estelle was instructed to proceed with her defence and as instructed produced numerous character references from senior army officers, senior clergy and statements of support from parents of children involved in the boxing club as well as a petition signed by members of the parish. She cross-examined the social worker assigned to the case as well as the investigating police officer. All of their testimonies pointed to non-physical or otherwise improper contact made by Hugh.

When Elle finally, but gently, cross-examined the plaintive, he simply crumbled and admitted to the lie. The judge apologised to Hugh for the trouble he had been caused and scolded the boy and his parents for wasting Court time and instructed them to pay all costs. Hugh was free to leave to a life now without the priesthood or military; both of which had formed the greater part of his working life. He was lost. No friends to speak of and now homeless.

Hugh followed Elle out of the court to face the waiting press. She had prepared a statement regarding the unjust and inflammatory testimony that had been directed against her client at the hands of an over indulged and spoiled child and how easy it was to end an innocent man's ecumenical career and moreover how easy it was to destroy someone's reputation by an unjust smear, then abruptly left, leaving the boy and his parents to face the microphones and cameras.

When out of sight of the gathered media circus, Hugh put out his hand to thank Elle and instead she gave him a surprise hug. She wasn't generally known for her displays of public emotion or affection, but she felt satisfied that justice had been seen done and that Hugh could now, after his sacrifices to the army and to his parishioners, get on and lead a normal life.

"Good for you! I know how difficult that must have been, but it's over now."

Chapter **35**

HUGH DOGGETT WAS NOT A MAN USED TO physical contact from a female but nervously accepted it. He didn't quite know what to do with his hands, so he just let them droop at his sides. Elle released him, sensing his discomfort.

"Thank you, Miss Ballantine."

"It's Estelle, Hugh, or Elle to my friends! What will you do now?"

"I don't know. I hadn't made any plans with this ordeal looming."

"I may know someone who might be able to help, if you're interested?"

"Sure! What kind of thing?"

"I'll make a call and get back to you."

"That would be more than kind of you, thank you again."

They parted with both knowing they had a new friendship in the making.

Chapter *36*

KAY KANE WAS THE UNDIAGNOSED TEXTBOOK definition of a borderline sociopath. She held an almost total lack of feeling or remorse for the pain that she caused to others. She could no more empathise with the lives she had destroyed than a predator could relate to the distressed mews from the helpless pray held between its teeth.

She arrived in the underground car park that led to her apartment. There was no front door key or any visible means to enter or leave the building.

She drove her silver Mercedes through the lower level and arrived at the grey iron gates that only she could access, taking her the further one hundred and fifty yards of the reinforced concrete wall lined entrance to the private elevator. The passage way and elevator had been designed 'off plan' by Kay to accommodate a large car. She pressed the remote button that she had had rewired to the cruise control switch. The doors of the elevator slid open and she drove the car in.

The CCTV together with an in-car wide-angle camera meant that she could easily see if anyone tried to enter the gates or the elevator from behind or to the sides without her knowledge. She was careful and over the years had made many enemies. Therefore, spending money on domestic security was not only essential, but also tax deductible.

The doors of the elevator slid open at her apartment level at the opposite side to which they had closed, allowing her to drive the car directly into the interior of her apartment. She got out of the car and hit the lock button twice on her key fob. The circular metal diamond plate covered carousel turned the Mercedes around one hundred and eighty degrees so pointing the nose of the car back towards the entrance of the elevator.

It had been custom installed as part of her design requests when paying the $5.5 million for the three thousand square foot apartment. She had been offered a larger space for similar money by the developer but opted for the smaller dimensions as she thought them 'bijou' and more fitting to her solitary life style. No one else could use the same elevator so the Mercedes became part of the interior decor.

Her living space was for the most part open plan and sterile with no indication as to the gender of the person who lived there. It featured high ceilings and under-floor heating. Most of her furniture was rented from a theatrical props company excluding the Louis XIV bureau and chair that she had been presented as a gift by a former client from Angola.

She had broken the international arms treaty to supply him with neurotoxins in his successful attempts to quell a rival takeover by domestic rebels.

It was believed that this was the same chair and bureau that Marie Antoinette had used to write her farewell note to her family before being taken to guillotine for execution.

Kay owned nothing else that could bind her to any one place for long. She would regularly have her domestic staff create displays of exotic flowers in an attempt to make the living space seem homely; should anyone have the privilege to ever be invited. All the work surfaces of the unused kitchen were burnished stainless steel with low voltage lighting reflecting on the various unemployed appliances that were placed there.

Chapter *37*

KAY WALKED TO THE SAFE IN THE KITCHEN that she had installed in the false freezer compartment and pushed the ice tray aside revealing a frosted over menu pad. She scraped away ice that covered the pad and typed in 'Cold'. The panel popped open a millimetre allowing her to hook her nail behind the plastic flap and fully open the panel before removing the mobile phone that was hidden inside.

The wine cooler sat at the side of the freezer and was well stacked. She tore at the Velcro thermo lined case that protected the telephone from the cold of the freezer while taking out the remains of last night's bottle of Chablis.

She spat the telephones protective cover onto the work surface, holding the bottle and telephone in one hand and removing the tall wine glass from the kitchen cabinet with the other. She splashed the wine into her glass then emptied the contents of her purse out onto the kitchen's steel surface. Lipstick, gum and loose change spilled in all directions over the counter top, leaving the packet of Marlboro Gold that she was searching for exposed.

Kay depressed the power button of the telephone while turning on the gas from the hob on her cooker. The blue gas flame ignited as she pulled her hair safely to one side, protecting it from the flame as she bent down to light her cigarette.

She leant back against the steel counter top; the hand holding the wine glass dropped by her side as the smoke hit her lungs and the nicotine entered her system. The wine glass tilted precariously almost spilling its contents as the cigarette worked its potentially lethal magic. Kay stared up into the low voltage light inhaling then exhaling the cigarette smoke and prepared to make her call. There was only one number on the cell phone's memory and she dialled it as she refilled her glass with wine then lit her second cigarette.

Her decision to make the call was an easy one. Why should BION spend millions on pointless redundant assets when in this town $1,800 could get you someone killed and for two grand you got to keep the gun! However this plan would require a little more finesse and money. If you wanted the best then you had to pay for the best. The telephone rang four times before it was answered.

"Darling, how are you, it's been an age?"

The voice was layered with drama and the 'R's' where heavily rolled in what she supposed was a camp middle class English accent.

"Oscar, I trust you're well and keeping up with all the latest trends?"

"Always sweetie always, you know old me!"

"I'm looking for a new act, Oscar, Something fresh, never before seen. I have a performance that may take a particular type of talent and was wondering if you had any new fresh and creative faces?"

Kay rested her wine glass on the counter top and chewed on the corner of her bottom lip as she awaited the answer.

"As if by coincidence I do. A gorgeous young talent from the Balkans I'm informed. By his resume he's been classically trained and just released from his last contractual obligations. Perfect for your needs I should think. If he doesn't fit the part, just you give me a call darling. I'll have him replaced immediately. Free of charge, of course. He's divine to gaze upon I'm told and so young."

"Can you send me some of his reviews?"

"Already on their way, darling!"

"I take it your rates haven't changed?"

"Dear Lord, no sweetie. Not for my regulars."

"I knew I could rely on you, Oscar."

Chapter **38**

THE DIRECTOR OF THE OSCAR WILDE THEATRE Company was both merciless and ruthless, only the wealthy or people with the right connections knew of his existence. He was one hundred percent discreet and kept no records of any operations performed by his *list of talents,* as he referred to them.

If you needed an assassination or the services of professional mercenaries, or someone framed 'air tight' with absolutely no paper trail that could lead the event back to the client, then he was the man for the job. Oscar Wilde was of course not his real name. No one but him knew that, but he appeared to like the dramatic and literary connection to his profession.

Kay had no idea as to his sexuality; if she sat next to him in a cafe or restaurant she would still have no inkling that it could be him. One thing that was made clear to you by those that introduced you to him, was that if you in any way alerted the police, FBI, INTERPOL or any national or international law enforcement agency to his existence or whereabouts; without any doubt, you, your family and anyone you held dear or were connected with, would be, in his terms of contract, *sanitised.*

Those were the rules. As long as they were understood and you agreed to the terms, you could be included on his *mailing list.* The line went dead. Kay dismantled the mobile, removed the sim card and held it over the blue gas flame until it melted the circuit board. She walked over to the waste disposal unit in the basin and dropped it in, then hit the grind button.

The email came through on her laptop almost immediately and she scanned the contents. Very impressive, quite accomplished for a young artist, as Oscar would refer to him.

She clicked on the hotmail account and typed, "I need a performance."

The email was answered within minutes.

"I love to perform."

"It's a complicated play that needs the part filled without delay!"

"Can you send me the script?"

"It will be with you in a moment. I'm sending you the cast of characters as we speak. There may be one further member you could work with in the future. I haven't decided if I want him in the production yet."

"It's just come through. Is this a drama or set piece?"

"Set piece or drama, the choice is yours. I'll let your creative talent decide the scenes layout."

Set piece was code for an accident. *Drama* was when a message was to be sent, very public and usually noisy and always messy.

"Okay, it seems an interesting play. I'll get back to you when I get time to digest the part and get into character. Within the week I should think."

Kay terminated the connection and raised the glass to her lips, sipping the wine and tapping the delicate glass against the front of her teeth. She walked over to her main computer terminal and hacked into the accounts that Valentine had set up for his *Sad Smileys* as he childishly referred to them. There had been no activity yet, as apart from the odd minor transfer.

She wondered what to do with the money Valentine had offered as severance, when her plans for the now redundant board members came to fruition. It would be simple to falsify sub clauses in the contract should the event of suicide or terrorist attack claim the lives of any of the relevant parties. One thing she was determined to do was to ensure the money went on positive PR for BION and make sure that none of the funds went to the greedy, undeserving members of the already over indulged relatives. A substantial charity donation or maybe a new school or hospital wing would be preferable.

Her decision was made purely on a financial basis. The lives she was preparing to end would only benefit the company. It was simply time to get rid of some of the 'old guard' and start afresh. Paying millions to placate unnecessary redundant staff made no sense to her.

She made a mental note to take young Valentine in hand once she had dealt with this matter and steer him in the direction that she thought most appropriate to her and her benefactors.

Chapter **39**

E VA LAY STILL, SOAKING IN THE HOT WATER, watching the steam rising, barely keeping grip of the glass of red wine that she let sag over the side of the tub. Gradually she felt her shoulder muscles relax and begin to soften after the stress of the day. Her eyelids drooped as she soaked in the hot water, slowly drifting into a doze. Her brain was trying unconsciously to recall all the craziness of the last two days.

The memory of standing on the glass shard snapped her out of her daze and she returned to reality with a shiver, spilling some of the wine with a splash on the tiled floor.

She reached out and placed the glass on the pine cabinet, drew her foot up and again looked in vain for the wound. She returned her foot to its resting place on the edge of the tub and again gradually relaxed.

Her swim and time in the Lough went quietly through her mind. She was getting settled with her new stroke since taking the private lesson. Then a memory began to slowly materialise. The combination of wine and warm water was gently coaxing them from her.

Twenty or thirty minutes into a swim, the mind begins to switch on to an alternate frequency. Its active unconscious meditation is brought on by the repetition of stroke after stroke and breath after breath, combined with the muted noise of the passing water over the earplugs. The normal everyday worries slip away along with the passing scenery.

She was breathing on the fifth stroke instead of the third. This meant she had to slow her pace to allow her lungs and muscles to adapt to the lack of oxygen thus giving her the advantage of being able to keep her face in the water longer to reduce drag if she needed a sprint finish in a race.

When she did inhale, she almost rolled half way onto her back, resulting in an uninterrupted view of the sky above and enabling her to breathe more safely on a choppy surface, mitigating the risk of inhaling salty water. Her eye caught the silhouette standing by the water's edge. It was a female, but she took little notice as spectators were a regular occurrence. They would point you out to their children like you were some odd spectacle or a bonus part to their day out.

The figure was standing on an outcrop at the Lough's edge and remained, as far as she could see perfectly still and staring out into the water. She was closing the distance some fifty feet away and on her current course would pass within thirty feet of the figure that remained standing by the shore.

Her natural reaction was to alter course and put more distance between them. It seemed strange to her that you could pass within inches of someone on the high street, but somehow feel more vulnerable out of your element, plus it wasn't uncommon to have teenage hooligans lob missiles at you from the shore.

Eva became increasingly uneasy, even though she was positive that no one could reach her without her easily getting away. She continued on, ignoring her concerns and concentrating on her stroke. Suddenly she stopped and began treading water, focusing more clearly on the figure by the shore. She fixed her gaze upon the person, she was now for whatever reason almost hypnotised and had to remind herself to keep her legs moving to stay afloat.

The figure was that of a woman probably in her mid to late thirties, taller than average height and lightly built. She was utterly stunning, transfixing even and accompanied by an equally beautiful young boy, aged between twelve and fourteen years. The woman was dressed in a simple summer white ankle length dress and leather sandals. Her hair was copper gold and cascaded over her shoulders disappearing down her back.

Eva watched as she bent down, putting one knee almost to the ground. She placed her right hand into the water and gently moved it back and forth, making small ripples in the surface. She made no attempt at verbal contact, but Eva felt an instant connection with her. It seemed as if she was somehow being caressed by the rippling waters, which was, of course, ridiculous. The boy sat down behind the woman, bringing his knees up to touch his chest, wrapping his arms around them and securing them with his joined hands. He sat quietly watching what Eva now took to be his mother.

The figure made eye contact with Eva and simply, slowly nodded her head approvingly and smiled towards her.

Eva reluctantly smiled and nodded back appearing to agree to a yet unasked question. A feeling of love washed over her in waves; all she desired at that moment was to be close to this stranger and her child.

She remained hovering in the Lough's salty waters, almost floating, while staring at the female and the boy.

The blast from the horn shook her from her trance and she spun around out of fright. She had drifted farther out into the Lough, almost getting into the path of the ferry. She altered her position in the water; safe now and returned her gaze to shore, the woman smiled again, now seeming to understand that the spell had been broken. She reluctantly continued with the rest of her swim, looking back between five counts to see if the figures were still there.

They were, and remained standing watching Eva swim away, smiling after her as she left. The boy had most likely lost interest or had gotten bored with the event and was jumping over invisible streams and hurdles as he gradually vanished from sight. Eva watched her as she walked away, then saw her fade into the scenery as she followed the child over his make-believe obstacles. Five more strokes, she turned again to check one last time, but the young woman had vanished.

Why hadn't she remembered this before now and how was it that she must have allowed the current of the water to carry her almost into the ferry's path without noticing?

Again why, when recalling the encounter, did she now yearn so much to be back again in the woman's presence?

And why was a memory, which had escaped her till now, so incredibly vivid?

Chapter *40*

ANDRUS STUDIED WHAT WAS REFERRED TO AS *the play and the cast of characters* on the list that Kay had sent him. All were involved in the manufacture of drugs and medication in the pharmaceutical industry. All were senior board members of BION, which meant they had made plenty of enemies in the past.

Ira Goldstein

Rachel Cohen

Harvey Wright

Graham Houston

All the *cast members* on the list so far were high visibility, public figures. Carrying out the contract on them individually would raise too much suspicion.

The simplest way to complete the operation was to have them all gathered in one place. That meant a wedding, a party or a funeral!

The choice was an easy one: a funeral.

He minimised the email screen, sending it down to the bottom of the computer's icons and brought up the internet search engine.

Radical groups were easy pickings for his profession if you required hot-tempered, easily manipulated tools of the trade. He would generally opt for right wing religious zealots but this required a connection with chemicals, vivisection or animal testing as it was more generally known.

He googled *animal rights activists in Illinois* and found what he was looking for, Steve Dearie.

Steve Dearie had joined POAW, *Protection of Animal Welfare*, when he attended college in the mid-1990s. Over time he had apparently become increasingly right wing and as the years went by, an added bonus was that he was well known to the police as he had previously been cautioned and processed through the police register.

Scenes of the remains of wasted dogs left in piles outside research laboratories, forgotten to be disposed of properly by the auxiliary staff, neglected emaciated horses with grotesquely overgrown hooves and bears made to dance on hot iron plates for the entertainment of eastern European audiences; dug deeper and deeper into his soul. The images of rhesus monkeys having detergent dropped into their eyes by researchers dressed in white coats as they screamed in pain, restrained and terrified as their test subjects.

It was torture for Dearie to have to endure the adverts on television and billboards, of beautiful girls strolling down sandy tropical beaches, combing their perfect fingers through their glorious tresses of wonderfully shiny hair. It incensed him to anger and eventually would lead him to militancy and violence.

Dearie's on-line blog claimed that in his opinion, the worst offenders were the cosmetic companies that used the 'we don't test on animals' slogans. They bought test results from the companies who did, produced their filth, then marketed it to the stupid and naive. Steve Dearie fitted the profile that Andrus needed perfectly. He was like a gift and would almost criminally easily be exploited. Andrus made a point of introducing himself at one of the POWR internet chat room sites and spun Dearie a story of extreme animal cruelty right here in their own town.

He had the address but couldn't approach the place where the wretched creatures were kept alone for most of the time and starved of food and water. They agreed to meet the next night to gather some evidence.

They arrived separately and on foot at the rendezvous point and shook hands as they made their way to a diner roughly two miles away from a seemingly abandoned gated compound. Andrus wore an army fatigues jacket with the lapels covered in an array of buttons ranging from 'Ban the Bomb' to being a member of the global socialist party. They left the diner after exchanging email and phone numbers and vowed that if this mission was successful it could be the beginning of their revolution.

Andrus had set up false untraceable email accounts so in the unlikely event that tonight's plan was thwarted, it would be easier to contact Dearie directly rather than use the internet chat room again. He knew that the site would be monitored by homeland security, so it was safer to construct a false identity and keep their plans to themselves. He introduced himself to Dearie as Ernest Serna, telling him that he had changed his name on his twenty-first birthday and had abbreviated the name of his socialist hero *Ernesto Guevara de la Serna* or *Che Guevara*.

The two men made their way towards the compound and became aware of dogs barking in the distance and what appeared to be the sound of primates screeching.

They skirted the perimeter wire separately and Steve found a gap in the fence that Andrus had made earlier that day. Steve led the way as Andrus had lied, telling him that he'd never broken into a building.

"Follow me, man. It's a piece of cake."

He didn't answer but followed closely behind, keeping a look out for guards that he knew were non-existent.

Of course there was no security. Andrus had paid cash to rent the building for a month on a short-term lease, again using a false name.

The faded paint of a yellow and red sign showing a cartoon character of a friendly farmer driving his old reliable tractor above the shutters that advertised pet and farm feed supplies, only angered Steve even more because of the blatant connection with the crimes that were committed behind these rusty steel doors. He expected to find plastic partitioned rooms used for experimentation at the end of the filthy corridors when they got inside and Andrus didn't disappoint with his preparation of the scene. They entered the building through a service door at the rear, snapping the corroded padlock with the short iron prize bar that Steve carried in his backpack. Steve handed him a pair of night vision goggles that he had bought from the internet *spy store.*

Andrus pretended to struggle to put them on; so Steve instructed him how to focus the vision and began to help him with the tensioning straps around his head. As he raised his arms to adjust the fittings, Andrus quickly withdrew the drug filled syringe from his pocket and inserted the steel needle into Steve's armpit. He pushed Andrus away in fright and was about to protest when the drug took effect. He raised his hands to his heart then bent over double sagging to his knees.

Andrus supported him under his shoulder and guided him down the empty corridor that was littered with old discarded newspapers and empty cardboard coffee cups, then he manoeuvred him into the sound proof room he had prepared earlier. He sat him gently on the cot beside the chemical toilet and watched him as he passed out into a drug-induced sleep.

He ejected the CD of animal sounds and inserted a new one from the pile on the table counter. He switched on the projector and synced the images projected onto the wall to the sounds coming from the CD player.

There was a montage of flashing images of cattle being slaughtered and the sounds of blood spilling on the floor as their throats were cut; donkeys being made to carry heavy loads until they collapsed and died of starvation; whales being harpooned and their calves left to starve.

All grotesque and heartbreaking.

Andrus inserted his own ear protectors and took out one of the packets of assorted premixed drug cocktails. The noise was deafening, as it would be for the next three days, torturing and utterly relentless.

Steve would be subjected twenty-four hours a day to the continual bombardment of images, drugs and music as well as the constant sound of guns firing, police sirens and heavy metal music.

Andrus would ply him with *Provigil* to keep him awake so there would be no sleep or rest until Steve's mind was utterly broken.

113

The second injection that he received was a mixture of LSD, Heroin and methadone. By this stage of his brain washing he was barely conscious. Andrus had stripped him of all his clothes and he now sat, tied to the padded seat of the commode, naked, except for the foil blanket that Andrus secured around his shoulders.

He then inserted the saline and antibiotic drip into Dearie's left arm to keep him hydrated. The heart monitor band he had fitted around the man's chest would alert him if his captive suffered heart failure. He had set the alarm to go off if it fluctuated dangerously and a message would be sent immediately through to his hand held phone alerting him to the danger. He knew it probably wouldn't as he had hacked into Steve's dental records, which gave him the history of his captive's general medical condition or relevant allergies. It was safer than using his doctor's records as they would be more closely scrutinised if anything went wrong with the operation.

He switched on the small blow heater to keep him warm, took the syringe, a vial of saline and a bottle containing a white powder from the top of the trolley that he used to medicate his prisoner, then put them in his jacket pocket. He rechecked Steve's condition. Content that he was stable; he opened and quickly closed the door behind him as he left. There was no sound whatsoever coming from the room as he made his way to the exit. He took a new shiny padlock from his other jacket pocket and secured the door of the building before leaving Dearie to his narcotics and brain conditioning.

Chapter *41*

EVA'S MIND STILL SEARCHED FOR HIDDEN memories as she fumbled through her bag to find her phone on her way into work the next morning. She flicked through the list of contacts and pressed the dial out button to connect with John Greer. The call was answered with the familiar reply.

"Eva! What's up?"

"Johnny. Can you start sorting the latest test samples from the Lough? I'm on my way back to the lab and I'll see you in five minutes. I need to send the rest of the samples down to the main labs in Portaferry for further analysis."

"Sure. I'll have everything ready for you. See you in five."

Greer replaced the telephone in its cradle and walked over to the cool cabinet, opening it and removing several of the samples for their travels. All the samples were dated, weighed and labelled. He prepared the counter top, setting out alcohol solutions, distilled sterile water and anything else he thought Eva would need to carry out her preliminary tests. He shook several of the test tubes containing the algae and observed that they appeared duller today; less luminescent. *That's a little concerning,* he thought. *I don't know if you kiddies are feeling very well today.*

Eva entered the lab, tossed aside her handbag and put on her lab coat.

"Well, how are our babies?"

"You may want to check them, boss. I'm not sure, but I think some of them are deteriorating."

"Really? Let's have a look."

They walked into the next room together. John stopped in his tracks as Eva approached the test tubes.

It was as if someone had put a light under them as she drew near. They instantly regained their colour and even appeared to swell as she got closer.

"What are you talking about, John? They look fine to me. Actually, they look better than they did when I took them from the Lough."

"Eva, they look better than fine! Ten minutes ago I would have considered putting them in the trash bin. Now when you come into the room they're almost glowing!"

"Sorry? Are you certain that you have a degree in biology? That's just the stupidest thing I've ever heard you or anyone else say!"

"Eva, I took these samples from the cool cabinet when you called me and they were grey in colour and definitely dying. Now when you arrive, it appears that they have made a complete and total recovery. Not just recovered, but blooming."

"Maybe they've simply returned to room temperature?"

"Let's see, shall we?" He opened the cool cabinet and noticed that the rest of the samples were also now back to their full colour. "How do you explain that?"

"I can't; at least not yet. Let's stop speculating and do some work."

For whatever reason, Eva was rattled and she wasn't entirely sure why.

They carried out some basic tests. Subjecting the samples to heat, cold, diluting them in distilled water then alcohol, and a mild solution of acetic acid. No apparent changes occurred. This went on for the rest of the afternoon. Test after test, separated and stored and the results recorded, all at room temperature.

John left the lab and returned twenty minutes later with a syringe full of clear liquid. He applied it to the last sample and they decided to call it a day.

"Let's see what Monday brings. I have a courier collecting the remaining samples for Portaferry, but if you agree, I think we

116

should leave these ones here," he remarked to Eva.

"Yes, that seems like a good idea, see you Monday!"

Greer's head was spinning! He knew what he had seen. Those samples were for the best part dead until she entered that room, but why? Why would a simple organism respond to a single individual? It was ridiculous to even contemplate such a thing, but there it was. Right here in front of his eyes. He knew there had to be a logical scientific explanation. He also knew he would be back into that lab before Monday morning and he wouldn't be claiming overtime.

Chapter *42*

ELLE STARED THROUGH THE GLASS DOORS OF her seventh story apartment overlooking the mouth of the River Lagan at the entrance to Belfast Lough. She watched as the last cross channel hydrofoil ferry slowly made its way towards the dock and wondered at the marvels of man's ingenuity.

The sun was beginning to set behind the Black mountains and the lights and sounds of Belfast's nightlife began seeping into the room.

She loved the city and she loved her new home. It suited her perfectly. Belfast was recovering from years of unrest and turmoil. It was the proverbial phoenix rising from the ashes and this apartment in its new regenerated Titanic quarter of the city was the jewel in its crown.

We even have tourists now, for God's sake! Who would ever have thought that? Tourists in Belfast! she was thinking.

Friday night and no plans. Perfect. Pamper night.

Face pack, wine, music, Chinese takeaway, and not necessarily in that order.

She started to turn away from the view when something down below on the river's paved walkway caught her eye. A boy, possibly aged between twelve and sixteen, was looking directly up at her.

The last rays of the setting sun reflecting on the surface of the water were blurring her vision. It appeared that the child was smiling and was attempting to have a long distance conversation with her. He seemed to be cradling what looked like a young baby in his arms and his words passed between her and the infant that he was holding. A younger brother or sister perhaps? That child shouldn't be on his own at this time of the evening with a tiny infant.

She leant over the balcony and put her hand to her ear, trying to amplify the sound of his voice, but it, of course, didn't help and the child carried on talking as if she understood what he was saying. Elle stopped herself from carrying on any further attempts at communication with the child. It seemed obvious now that the boy must be using a hands free connection on his phone and that not only could he be playing a prank on her but she was helping him make a fool of her.

As Elle began to turn away, the child became increasingly agitated and gestured to her again - pointing at something in the water. Her eyes followed the direction in which he was pointing but could see nothing due to the reflection of the setting sun on the wake of a passing cargo vessel. Try as she might she could see nothing from this distance. She held up her hands in submission to indicate that she was giving up trying to understand what the child wanted to show her. The child continued to address her as if she did. He then, in an act of utter stupidity or threat, dangled the infant in his arms over the cold water of the river holding onto it only by its ankle as it screamed in protest!

"Jesus Christ! What are you doing? What are you *doing!*"

Elle threw open the door of her apartment not waiting for the elevator she ran down the stairs of the interior fire escape two steps at a time to reach the exit. The doors security bar smashed against the wall as she hastened towards the child and the infant in peril. She ran around the apartment complex as fast as she could only to see the child standing alone and no sign of the infant he had been holding.

"Oh, Mother of God, no! Where's the baby? Where's the baby you were holding?"

The boy smiled as she approached, raising his index finger over his lip to silence her.

Her concerns for the infant and child were now at odds with

each other. Was this some sort of elaborate trap? There had been some muggings of late so she calmed herself and became understandably cautious despite her concerns for the missing infant. As she approached the child put up its hand in a gesture for her to stop!

"What happened to the baby?"

The child was both serene and beautiful at the same time; his manner more that of an adult. Again he pointed down into the water and her eyes followed the direction of his pointing finger.

"Oh my God. He's thrown the baby into the water!"

She ran towards the water and stared down into the depths, but could see nothing of the missing infant, just the waving reflections of the buildings on the opposite bank of the river.

"There's nothing there, you little shit! Where is the baby you were holding over the edge of the rail?"

The young boy remained silent, continuing to point down into the empty black waters. Then she saw it. Next, she smelt it! What was left of her lunch spilled from her stomach down over the handrail then splashed over the concrete and into the water!

Her eyes awash with tears from the shock and the effort from vomiting so violently, she rested her head against the cold metal railing that ran the length of that section of the river, ignoring the child to her right. It felt cool against her brow and the contact helped her to realise that this vision wasn't simply some kind a nightmare that she couldn't wake from. Elle wiped the remains of sick away from her mouth and swallowed hard forcing any bits of bile and partially digested food back down into her stomach. She slowly gathered herself and turned to the boy, begging a simple question.

"Can we do anything to prevent this?"

"Your sister doesn't know it yet but she has the answer and she will need you. She has given you a gift."

"I'm not strong enough!"

"You have to be. She won't do it without you. You now have a gift of your own to give. Choose your friends well as you may need them."

The child smiled a sympathetic smile and looked down at

the baby that he was again miraculously now cradling in his arms, soothing it until it became quiet. He turned and walked away without any farewells or goodbyes. She contemplated calling after him but the tears were still rolling down her face as she re-entered the building and stood in a trancelike state as the elevator doors opened on her floor. She exited the lift and walked the short distance to her apartment. She sat at the kitchen table and stared blankly at the wall in front of her still stifling the urge to vomit as the scenes from the water were recalled. *Sweet mother of God! What am I meant to do? Do I tell Eva? Does she already know and hasn't told me?*

The images she saw in the water again came flooding back to her and her stomach convulsed for the second time. She steadied herself and made her way to the kitchen sink and bending down, splashed water over her face and dried it on the hand towel, then reached down into the wine rack. She poured herself a glass of wine, filling it to the brim then took a gulp. The alcohol scorched the back of her throat on the way down. She winced and took another full swig ignoring the discomfort; emptying the glass.

She next took the brandy from the cabinet and poured a full triple measure then downed it in one. Her legs weakened and her vision blurred. She sat with her head in her hands for a moment then felt around for her mobile phone, retrieved a number from her list of contacts and dialled. The call was quickly answered.

"Hugh, it's Elle!"

"I know who it is. What's wrong, Estelle?"

He could sense the level of distress in her voice.

"I need some help from a priest, Hugh. Even an ex one like yourself. I've had a bit of a fright tonight!"

"Anything I can do! Where are you?"

"I'm at home."

"Give me your address. If it's in town I can be there in twenty minutes."

She gave him the address details, hung up the phone, refilled her wine glass then fell out of love with the view over the River Lagan.

Hugh immediately ended the call, hailed a taxi and within minutes was on his way to help his new friend.

Chapter 43

ANDRUS TAMM PRESSED THE DOORBELL OF Rachel Cohen's downtown apartment. She answered, first checking the caller through the security peephole in the door. Satisfied that the caller was genuine she scanned the false identification that Andrus had forged earlier.

Suspicions allayed, she undid the security latch and, prepared to welcome him into the apartment behind the half opened door.

Andrus had been monitoring the escort agency that Kay Kane had detailed in the information pack she had sent concerning the movements of her fellow board members.

Andrus picked the softest target and zeroed Rachel Cohen as the easiest prey.

He arrived thirty minutes early for the appointment she had previously arranged with her usual escort agency. He had taken the precaution of pretending to be Rachel's aide and contacted the agency to rearrange her genuine date to arrive one hour later than the original time, as 'Miss Smith' was unusually running late this evening.

He stood at the entrance waiting to be invited in. She opened the door fully now wearing too much make up and too few clothes.

Rachel had been shy as a child, however her family and in particular her father's family wealth and power had purged the shyness from her. He sent her to an all-girl French boarding school for seven years of her adolescent life with rare visits home to her original hometown of Chicago. She was their only daughter and the youngest, with four male siblings. She found life at the boarding school traumatic, being horribly bullied by the other girls and on several occasions over her time spent there, abused sexually by one of her female teachers.

She eventually learned to suppress her shyness in public, appearing to be outward and confident to the extent of presenting herself to be arrogant and self-important. It was, of course, all an act. Few people including her family had been aware of the abuse and bullying she had undergone at the school. If anyone had bothered to speak to her in French, which was now her second language, they would have discovered that she spoke her native English perfectly but whilst using French, Rachel spoke with a severe stammer as a direct result of her ordeals during her dreadful time at the private school. As a further result of the secret abuse she developed a preference for solitude in her private life and a fundamental hatred of herself and females generally.

She had reached her fifty-third birthday and still coloured her hair as black as jet, stretching it tightly back in a ponytail to assist in hiding some of her facial wrinkles. This had the unfortunate side effect of making her appear stern and severe. The constant traction of her hair being tightly scraped back had receded her hairline, leaving her almost bald at the front and exposing the scalp two inches more than was natural.

"My, my. Wherever have they been hiding you?" Rachel enquired of her visitor.

Andrus bowed his head slightly in submission half answering the question to the floor.

"I'm your escort for the evening, Miss Smith. Shall we be dining out or in?"

"Oh, in I should think!"

She turned away allowing her purple silk gown to drop to the floor as she led the way into the luxurious apartment. She wore latex underwear, stockings and stilettos. She had maintained the figure of a trim twenty year old if not a little on the scrawny side in his opinion.

Too much time in the gym, he thought. *Still, I've seen worse.*

"Drink?"

"Whatever you're having, Mistress."

"Oh you can lose those jeans now, darling. They look much too uncomfortable."

He did as she asked along with the rest of his clothes and piled them neatly on a chair.

Andrus was in superb shape, a lifetime of training and regular distance running had given him the physique of a professional athlete. All lean muscle and sinew, he had no issue with standing naked in front of a woman or a man for that matter.

Rachel Cohen, or 'Miss Smith' as she was to be called this evening watched him undress and smiled.

"Oh my dear boy! You're just too gorgeous to harm!"

"That's disappointing, mistress. I was told I would enjoy my visit!"

Rachel rose from her seat on the expansive leather corner settee.

"Let me fetch some of my toys for us to play with."

She left him alone in the room, while she went to the section of her wardrobe containing her box of tricks. This gave Andrus just enough time to put the five milligrams of *propofol milk* into her drink. Two mills would be enough to fully sedate a grown man, but urgency was required as to a possible but pending timing issue.

Rachel returned carrying an array of devices, ranging from leather horse riding crops to strap on penises.

"A toast to a mostly violent evening, my darling boy."

They clinked glasses, looked into each other's eyes, and then, without any warning, Rachel kneed Andrus in the crotch! He doubled over in a cocktail of shock and pain.

I'm going to enjoy watching the light drain from this one, he thought as he crumpled on the rug.

"Thank you, mistress," he moaned through the white pain that steadily rose from his groin to his stomach. "More please," he managed to say as the pain continued to rise further.

She sipped at her wine staring down at him; then set the glass down on the black granite table. She drew back the riding crop and began her night of fun. Andrus was still kneeling on the rug and could feel the trickles of blood from the wounds she was inflicting. It lasted for three minutes until the drug took full effect.

Rachel dropped the riding crop that only seconds earlier she had been vigorously wielding, and fell like a stone against the settee.

He stood up still stooping slightly to avoid any of his blood dripping on the wooden floor and walked into the bathroom. He stepped into the cold shower allowing any trace of his blood to drain away completely then dried himself with toilet tissue and flushed it down the bowl. He then returned to the living area to see Rachel Cohen with her upper body lying half on, half off the leather settee; her legs limp and apart, leaving her undignified and vulnerable. The pointed heels of her stiletto-clad feet took the weight of her legs as they had found some purchase between the grooves in the planks of the wooden floor, stopping her from completely sliding onto the ground. She was catatonic. Her eyes had rolled fully back leaving only the whites staring at her killer as he prepared to complete his work.

Andrus put on his rubber gloves. He was still naked except for his wristwatch, which he checked to see how much time he had left to get this element of the contract completed. *Nineteen minutes, plenty of time.*

He removed Rachel's *Fun Gear,* replacing her latex outfit with a simple dressing gown that he took from her bedroom. He tossed the latex garments, together with the riding crop in the refuse sack he had taken from under the kitchen cupboard. He bundled up the rest of the toys she had brought out and returned them to the wardrobe with exception of the crop that was now contaminated with his blood and skin tissue.

Andrus checked the syringe that he had removed from its plastic wrapping and filled with adrenalin before knocking on her door.

He heaved Rachel's body back onto the leather settee, resting her head on a cushion; then raised her limp foot up placing it

125

onto his knee to get a better view of where he would insert the needle without leaving any trace or mark.

He gently injected the needle into the cuticle of her little toe, slowly depressed the plunger and watched as the contents of the syringe emptied into Rachel's system.

Despite being completely unconscious, it was as if Rachel's body became aware that it was dying.

As the convulsions started she began to foam at the mouth, her arms and legs thrashing violently. Andrus picked up two of the blue velvet cushions that adorned the settee and used them along with his body weight to restrain her. The cushions would prevent bruising of her arms where he held her down as he knelt on her chest. He knew he wouldn't have to hold her long as the adrenalin was sending her rapidly into shock and causing her internal systems to crash.

He was right. The thrashing soon ended and Rachel Cohen had only seconds left on the planet. He raised her up further on the cushion to get a better view of her final moments. The protests were finished now as she had become more settled with her breathing more shallow. Her chest barely rose as she inhaled.

Andrus sat on the edge of the settee, naked, and watching her die, now holding himself in his hands. Tissues were at the ready for the inevitable spume of semen.

Her convulsions restarted and became violent which only spurred him on to quicken his own strokes. As Rachel Cohen took her final breath, Andrus reached orgasm and ejaculated into his tissues. He then rolled the now-dead Rachel onto the floor and lay back, taking the time to fully enjoy the rest of his orgasm as he watched the last vestige of life pass from her.

He set about cleaning himself, walking naked into her bathroom, flushing the semen-filled paper down the toilet. He then ran the faucet, draped his genitals over the edge of the sink and washed himself with the soap from the dispenser, then thoroughly cleaned the basin. He dried himself with more tissue and re-flushed the toilet. He dressed and began removing any further trace of his visit; for Andrus this was a standard enough procedure. He found everything he needed; again under her kitchen sink.

Rachel had died within fifteen minutes and Andrus, satisfied with his work in every way was ready to leave. He rechecked his watch. Seven minutes over schedule. He was beginning to enjoy his work too much and was becoming tardy. Thankfully so was Rachel's bone-fide date. He must also have been a poor timekeeper.

He scanned the room one final time, content that the area was clear of any trace of his ever having been there, then quickly left the apartment and the now dead Rachel, leaving the door ajar as he made his exit. He waited in the maintenance room at the end of the corridor for Rachel's genuine escort to arrive at her front door. He was of similar size and build with an identical haircut; Andrus had had his cut to match the photograph from the escort's online brochure. He had obviously been to the address before and called through the open door when his several rings on the bell and knocks on the doorframe went unanswered.

The young man entered the apartment cautiously, then ran out screaming for help some minutes later after finding Rachel Cohen lying dead on her settee.

Andrus casually walked to the elevator and pushed the button for the lobby avoiding the CCTV cameras. He exited the building through the service door and strolled out into the rainy Chicago evening.

Chapter *44*

IT HAD BEEN SIX HOURS SINCE HE AND EVA HAD left the lab together and Greer could wait no longer. He gave a customary scowl to the dreadful zebra print on the wall, grabbed his car keys and headed to Queen's and the algae samples.

It was now late and the night shift security guards gave him a suspicious look as he fumbled with his keys. He entered, flicked on the lights and didn't bother to wait for them to stop flickering to full illumination. He knew where he was going and only needed partial light to get there.

He understood that if he needed to carry out further tests he would require the resources of the main research laboratory in Portaferry, but it was too late at night to make the journey down and anyway the courier had yet to take receipt of the parcelled samples for delivery.

Out of habit, he routinely began to put on his lab coat, then checked himself for being idiotic and instead went straight to the cupboard where they kept the algae test subjects.

As he knew would happen, the first three samples were shrivelled, almost beyond recognition. However the last one with his mystery substance had virtually disappeared.

"Let's see you come back from that kiddo! Hydrochloric acid will do the job every time!" he said out loud.

He took pictures of the samples and downloaded the resulting photographs on to the lab's computer, then emailed the results to his computer at home.

He returned the test tubes to the shelf and locked up the lab for the night, happy that his mind wasn't playing tricks. He knew that no plant or animal could withstand being immersed in acid for that long and still manage to survive.

Chapter *45*

HUGH DOGGETT ARRIVED AT ESTELLE'S apartment and pressed the buzzer on her intercom. He took no interest in the view over the marina or in any of the female revellers that were out on their hen night.

The intercom was answered as he watched the party goers disappear around the edge of the apartment complex.

"Hello?"

"Estelle, it's Hugh."

"Hugh, hi! I'll buzz you in. Just come up. It's the seventh floor, apartment 12."

Her speech was slurred and he hoped he hadn't been called over because she'd been dumped by her boyfriend or some other equally benign reason.

He entered the elevator and pushed seven on the control panel. The automated elevators voice reaffirmed that he had made the correct floor choice and the automatic doors slid quietly closed. As the doors opened on the chosen floor, Elle was waiting outside the lift; she clearly appeared to be upset and seemed to have been drinking heavily.

"Hugh, I can't thank you enough for coming over so quickly!"

"No problem." They both stood for what to Hugh seemed like awkward minutes. "Can we go inside?"

"Yes, sorry, of course. How stupid and rude of me, please come in."

Hugh entered the apartment and neither commented on the decor or the view across the river. He did, however, see what was obviously an orderly organised apartment now in semi-disarray. Her coat was lying on the floor where she had dropped it, used cigarette ends spilling from the makeshift ashtray with one still burning away in its corner and a wine bottle lying on its side behind the seat, slowly dripping its contents onto the white carpet. Hugh worked out quickly that children were not a factor in Estelle's life due simply to her choice of snow-white carpet and sharp edged modern furnishings.

Elle made her way to the kitchen area, trying her best to appear sober and gathered, shouting in from the other room.

"Can I get you anything?"

He saw that she needed some purpose and distraction. He now took time to admire the view from the glass doors looking out over the river.

"What have you got?"

"Beer, wine, coffee, tea…"

"I'll take a beer thanks."

She went to the fridge and took out a bottle of German pilsner beer. She searched around in the cutlery drawer for a bottle opener then remembered she had used it to open her wine earlier. She returned to the living area and picked up the opener from the coffee table.

Her hands were shaking as she fumbled with the bottle. After the third attempt she managed it and handed him his beer. She then refilled her wine glass from a new bottle in the fridge, not remembering the half empty one lying on its side on the floor.

Elle sat on the seat opposite and asked how he was doing, in a veiled attempt to appear casual and unruffled.

"How are you since I saw you last?"

"I'm fine, thanks. What's new with you?"

"Oh you know how it is, work, work, work."

"Elle, I'm not a man generally known for my tact but I can feel there's something serious going on, or you wouldn't have called me. Now what's up?"

She steadied herself and tried to relax back in the chair. It

131

didn't work, as within seconds she was perched back on the edge of the seat again.

"If you have little tact, Hugh, I hope you make up for it in patience."

Her voice became unsteady as she wound herself up to tell a relative stranger the stupidest thing he would ever hear from any lawyer; drunk or sober. Hugh's directness seemed to snap her out of her current distraction, but how could she even try to explain what happened?

"I'm a professional woman, Hugh. I don't scare or freak out easily, but I saw something tonight which scared the living crap out of me!"

She described the events with the child and the rest of the time leading up to her calling him.

"I know I'm not dreaming any of this, Hugh. It was all as real as you and I sitting here."

"What did you see in the water, Elle? Tell me everything."

She hesitated not wanting the images returning to her, while at the same time needing to give an accurate description of what had happened. Hugh watched her as she nervously pushed the cuticles of her fingernails back until they bled.

"When the child pointed to the water, it took a while for me to see that my sister Eva was there. She was screaming from just under the surface, fighting for breath and inhaling the black water! She was surrounded by countless thousands of small children, some alive, some dead and some in various stages of decay. Most of them were only weeks conceived and had been aborted at various stages of development. All had died badly in agony with grotesquely distorted heads and faces. Their skulls were massive, covered in bleeding sores and ulcers. There was barely enough water to even get between the bodies because they were so tightly packed! It wasn't a vision, Hugh, it was like playing back an event that had really happened. It was as if someone had pressed a rewind button on time itself and showed me a glimpse of hell."

She went across the room and poured two large brandies.

"Bring that bottle with you, Elle."

Hugh hadn't drunk hard liquor since the bar fight in Belize.

He had never allowed himself since to be, in any way, not in full control of his temper or his senses, but this was different. This was scary even by his standards and he knew that Estelle needed a drinking partner. The girl was no liar and he knew by the countless confessions that he had heard as a priest that this wasn't some made up fantasy of a hysterical manic depressive. He was conflicted so why lie to himself? He didn't know what he was getting into with this girl, but she needed a friend and for the time being at least, that was him.

"Okay, Elle, first things first. Right now, we don't know what any of this means so let's begin by eliminating the obvious. Are you under any undue stress at work or taking medication?"

Elle put her temper on hold at such a ludicrous question, but in light of the story she'd just told him she let it slide.

"Listen, Hugh. I didn't call you over here if there was any doubt in my mind that this happened. I'm not some hysterical, desperate drug addicted female with her finger on an emotional trigger. I know it sounds ridiculous. If I was sitting where you are, I'd be thinking the same thing, but this happened and it was right at my front door. I still can't get the smell of death and shit out of my nose!"

"Have you contacted your sister to ask if she's safe?"

"Christ. No."

"Let's give her a call and see how she's doing."

Chapter *46*

HUGH WAS AWARE THAT HE WAS SIPPING HIS brandy much too quickly. He watched Estelle as she fumbled drunkenly for her phone. She called her sister, relieved when she answered. Not wanting to panic or scare her she adopted her usual tone.

"Hi, Eva. How are you?"

"All good, Elle. You?"

Eva was surprised at receiving the late call from Elle but knew that all was not good with her no matter how much her sister tried to hide the strain in her voice.

"Yeah, good. Listen, Eva, this is going to sound strange, but has anything else unusual been happening lately?"

"Unusual, what way unusual? You mean apart from the super human foot healing thing?"

Eva could hear that Elle was slurring her words a little and tried to make light of the situation. Eva doubted her sister would remember because of the alcohol she had obviously taken, but carried on listening patiently.

"I don't know. Bizarre, bad dreams, you know strange, unusual weird, anything else out of the ordinary?"

"No, not really; just working away at finding some answers to my condition. Why do you ask?"

She continued to hide the reason for calling and asking ludicrous questions by being matter-of-fact.

"Well, that's good. I've been thinking about you and I

134

thought I'd just give you a call. Maybe try to meet up? I have a few more questions for you."

It was all Elle could think of. She knew her sister would take the bait quickly, due to her curious nature and did her best to give nothing away to avoid further alarming her.

"Questions? What kind of questions? I still haven't any answers yet regarding the wound."

"I've been thinking of mum and dad a lot lately and just wanted a catch up. Nothing earth shattering. What are you up to tomorrow?"

Elle was stamping her foot on the floor as Hugh looked on. She was digging an even deeper hole for herself and both she, Hugh and probably now Eva knew it. Hugh gestured with his hand, using his thumb and finger to simulate the motion of hanging up the telephone. At the other end of the line, Eva decided that her patience had now run out and she had had quite enough of her sister's obvious drunken ramblings and changed the direction of the pointless conversation without appearing rude.

"I've got a race coming up soon so I was planning a practice swim down at the Lough, but I can miss it!"

"No, I'd love to go down home. I haven't touched base for ages," said Elle. "I have a guy here with me who can swim like a fish. Maybe give you a pacesetter."

"A guy, really. That's interesting. Who is he?"

Hugh was shaking his head, making gestures and waving his hands to indicate that he was not prepared to go.

"It's not like that. He's just a friend, Eva."

"Okay, whatever you say. I'll be down there at 9.30am before the place gets too busy."

She thought it would be unkind to tease her sister further given the strange circumstances and questions she had been asking.

"See you down at the Lough side at nine thirty then. I have some research notes in the car that I need to pop through the lab's door, so don't give me the usual hard time if I'm a few minutes late, OK?"

Elle hung up the phone, leaving her sister wondering what was going on and who the new man in her life was. It wasn't like the Estelle of old. A lot of troubled water had passed under the bridge, but not enough for all of the issues of the past to be swept away so quickly. Eva still wasn't entirely comfortable with the rekindling of the relationship that in her eyes was still fragile and she would have expected her sister to feel the same.

"Sorry about that, but I will seriously owe you if you come," Elle said to Hugh.

"I haven't been swimming in years, Estelle, I'm not even entirely sure if I have a pair of swimming trunks!"

"It will be like riding a bike to you. We can get you some on the way down if you can't find yours."

Elle wasn't taking no for an answer. She wanted Hugh there at the swim with Eva. He was the only one that she had told the story of the vision to and that gave them a connection. He was involved now whether he liked it or not.

Hugh drained the last of the brandy and began to leave.

"I'm sorry for dumping you in this, Hugh; I truly am. You're a good man."

"I'm a pushover, Miss Ballantine."

The brandy had relaxed them both and distracted them a little from the day's events. Hugh stood up and lifted his house keys from the table.

"I'd better go, Estelle. It's been an interesting evening. Will you be okay here on your own?"

"Yeah, I'll be fine, and thanks again for coming over and listening to me rant on about what was probably an allergic reaction or something."

She didn't believe that for a second and by the look on Hugh's face, neither did he. Elle put her arms around him in a *thank you* hug.

The shock of the embrace sobered him instantly. Hugh put his hands behind him to steady himself against the wall.

"Sheesh! That brandy's brutal. No more of that! Good night, Estelle. See you in the morning. You have to pick me up by the way, as I don't possess a car yet. I'll be ready at eight and no more booze. I think we've both had enough OK?"

"Yeah, fine and again thank you."

He had to continue to steady himself as he left the building. He took a minute to take in some fresh night air while holding onto the metal railing at the waters' edge. He wandered over to the spot at the river where Estelle had experienced her vision. He stared down into the dark waters, but could see nothing of the horror that Estelle had witnessed earlier below the surface.

He felt a chill run down his spine and turned the collar up against the night's cooling air.

"I think I'll walk a bit," he said to the river.

He made his way into the first church he came to and knelt down and prayed at the altar.

Chapter *47*

THE STATE CORONER'S REPORT PUT RACHEL Cohen's death down to misadventure, caused by a drug and alcohol induced overdose. Andrus had left traces of *propofol* in her bedside drawer and in her bathroom cabinet.

The police assumed that Rachel had used *prop* as it was known, to induce amnesia. This lady most likely had bad memories to suppress or numb. That particular drug was known as *milk of amnesi*a.

They also found cocaine and heroin in small quantities, but still more than enough to kill her. The case was closed and the family informed that it was death by misadventure.

She would be buried in the family plot at Chicago's Memorial Park Cemetery. There was no further enquiry at the family's bequest and the burial would take place six days after her passing; two days after her body was released from the coroner.

Chapter *48*

S TEVE DEARIE WAS READY! HIS MIND WAS broken and he was angry. "Fuckers! Fuckers! Dirty fucking Fuckers!" he repeated over and over. He was taking control. No more protest marches. No more placards and demonstrations outside office buildings.

His new friend had showed him the way. Proactive statements. Positive action. Show them the same mercy and compassion they show to the poor creatures they torture and experiment on for money and greed.

He stood as if in a trance, mentally thanking Andrus repeatedly as the vest packed with high explosives was attached to his chest. It took thirty minutes to set and fix the detonators and the *dead man* switch that Andrus would carry just in case Steve's drugs wore off early and he maybe had second thoughts.

"Ready? Are you ready soldier? It's time to finally bring an end to these atrocities, Steve. Your name will start a revolution! This is only the beginning. Many more will follow where you lead! People have children to leave their legacy to, but forgotten in a generation or two. You will live in history forever as the man to make a stand and fight back for the defenceless! Do it for the children who won't have to see what you've seen, but most of all, do it for yourself! Now one last time: ARE YOU READY?"

"I'm ready," he said calmly and resolutely. His gaze was fixed and his life willingly forfeit.

Kay Kane received the instructions from Andrus on the

mobile *pay per go* phone that he had supplied. She was to stand at the funeral service with whomever she wanted to keep from harm, directly opposite the Rabbi who would be giving the eulogy.

Her instructions were to 'wear heavy undergarments and use ear and eye protection. The performance will be directed away from you, but I can't guarantee debris deflection. The event will happen during the service.'

Steve Dearie's vest was a work of art. It was loaded to the front with Semtex with nothing at the back but a thick steel plate to direct all the blast forward. The nails and ball bearings had been soaked in rat's urine for days, so anyone injured by the flying shrapnel would die from Weir's Disease or septicaemia if not treated. It all had to appear genuine.

The mourners gathered round the coffin as the Rabbi gave his eulogy and Rachel's coffin was slowly lowered down to its final resting place. No one paid any attention to the van pulling up fifty yards away. All of Rachel's friends, family and fellow board members stood at the graveside. Ira Goldstein, Harvey Wright and Graham Houston stood to the left and right. Senator Hamill was in Washington on a charity fundraiser for injured veterans.

Kay came well prepared. She wore *Phoenix skin* body armour under her trouser suit and blouse. The technology was still in its infancy, but it was the latest the military had to offer. It could repel subsonic ballistic debris from twenty feet and had a smart suit reaction cushion, which protected the vital organs from a pressure wave at a comparable distance.

The sunglasses she wore were also cutting-edge, made to look like expensive designer shades, which they of course were. Just not the kind you walk into your local department store and buy over the counter. She had received the explosive stats via email from Andrus and with luck the gear would work.

She reached out to hold Valentine's hand as the coffin rested at the bottom of the grave. He felt the moisture on her palm as they made contact.

"Are you okay, Kay?"

"Yeah I'm fine. Why do you ask?"

"Your hand is sweating a little."

"Really, I had it in my pocket. Sorry."

"I'm sad to see that Rachel is dead. She wasn't the worst of them. I read some of her historical notes that I dug up from her files. The family are financially rich but emotionally poverty stricken. She had it tough as a kid in France."

"Unfortunate. She wasn't the best either, Val. She pulled plenty of dirty tricks in her time. You should know. You had them documented and included in that envelope you gave her."

"Anyway she's gone now. May God rest her soul."

Kay continued to hold his hand. She was less than comfortable with the physical contact.

A few heads began to turn when they saw the man running at an inappropriate speed towards the closely gathered mourners. The limited security started talking into the microphones hidden in their jacket cuffs, but no one seemed to be too concerned at the mad man heading in their direction. It was probably just some drunk or crack-head needing to rant at the privileged.

The closest security guard heard the first screams from the assailant and started to react, but by then it was too late. Steve Dearie made a dive into the grave and righted himself as his body hit the solid wood of the coffin's lid. The mourners gathered round in fascination at the *mental case* who was shouting at them about animal rights and justice for the tortured! As instructed he put his back to the corner of the clay wall of the open grave and pointed his chest towards them. Mourners peered around and down at the crazy man in fascination.

"This is for the ones who are helpless at your hands you murdering bastards; this is for the ones who can't fight!"

It was almost amusing to watch until he opened his jacket, exposing the suicide vest packed with the high explosive. The mourners with the better view now understood what was about to happen and began forcing their way backwards through the rest of the crowd of people who were still pushing forward to see what was going on in the grave.

Unlike the rest however, Kay took a step back, taking Valentine with her.

The blast debris and shrapnel flowed out in a supersonic

wave. Gravity was defied and chemistry was left to its destructive beauty. Light first, then followed by the blast wave, wet mud and metal. Most of the blast felled the mourners like a sharpened scythe sweeping through wheat.

As the first three rows fell immediately, some of the blast was deflected backwards and down blowing the lid partially off Rachel's coffin and leaving Rachel's body and part of the interior of the casket exposed. Just enough of the debris had been thrown backwards to cause minor cuts and grazes. Valentine fell to the ground holding his hands up to his eyes. Kay feigned shock and confusion forcing tears while all the time trying to comfort her boss.

"I'm blind! I'm blind!"

Kay forced his hands away from his damaged eyes and stared at his scorched face.

"Look at me! You're not blind now LOOK AT ME!"

Valentine tried to open his eyes. Grit and dust filled his sight. He held his head downward and waited for the tears, hoping they would clear his vision.

"You're not blind. It's dust and debris. Pull yourself together until I get us out of here!"

There was no statement issued to the press of anyone or any group claiming responsibility for the bombing. There would be no promised revolution.

The late Stephen Theodor Dearie would soon be forgotten and immortalised as just one more ill-informed delusional domestic terrorist with a personal grudge.

Andrus watched the explosion from his car. The mission was as predicted a complete success. The wheels of his car slowly turned as he drove away from the carnage. The broadest of smiles washed across his face as he drove through the panicked mourners and out the cemetery gates with his arm resting out of the cars open window and that familiar electric cigarette resting between his fingers.

Chapter *49*

W ITH THE BRANDY AND WINE STILL IN HER system Elle arrived at Hugh's front door at 8.30am. If stopped by the police and breath tested she could lose her driving license and even damage her career. She had little choice as arrangements had been made.

She was about to give a short blast of the horn when the door opened and Hugh appeared. He locked up, got into the car and passed her a cheery 'good morning.'

"Morning, Hugh. How's the head?"

"Ah, no bother! Yourself?"

"I'll live! Why do we do it to ourselves? I'm getting too fond of the bottle."

"We've all been there. Do you drink every night, Elle?" Hugh enquired.

"Oh God, yeah! I need help to wind down. You're not going to give me a moral lesson now, are you, Father?"

Hugh didn't bother to respond, instead checking himself for the stupid and inappropriate question. He couldn't preach to anyone regarding excessive alcohol consumption.

Elle put the car into drive and began their short trip down to the Lough.

"That sounds like a touch of dependency, but not addiction. Right?"

"Listen, Hugh. I enjoy wine and the thought of never having another glass of it keeps me from becoming an alcoholic."

143

Hugh chuckled out loud at the clarity of her statement.

"There's a logic in that, I suppose."

They both smiled at each other and some of last night's drama disappeared.

"Got your Speedos on?"

"I do."

"You haven't?"

"Yup! Went for the 'budgie smugglers.' It was a toss-up between that or the 'Mankini.'"

"Oh my God! You're either very gifted anatomically, or have no style or shame."

"All three, woman. Keep your eyes on the road; you'll see them soon enough."

Estelle laughed out loud as Hugh made himself comfortable in the BMW's black leather passenger seat, smiling as the car filled with the sound of Elle's laughter and feasting his eyes on the passing beauty of the familiar countryside.

It was going to be another hot day in the province and the swim would be a welcome change of pace for Hugh, as well as helping to dispel the remains of the hangover he lied about not having.

He hadn't been in the water for a while and didn't until now realise how much he missed it.

The rest of the journey down passed in relative silence. The scenery of the Peninsula was spectacular on a bad day, but on a good one like today it was beyond stunning.

"You know I've been all over the world and I would still put this drive and the one up to the North Antrim coast up against any of them."

"I agree. We do take it for granted. I've driven down this road so many times I think I'm oblivious to it."

They arrived in Portaferry village and parked the car in the queue for the short ferry ride across the Lough to Strangford on the opposite side. The ferry was small and could accommodate around fifteen cars and foot passengers.

As the ferry's engines rumbled to life and the captain raised the metal ramp and prepared for the journey across the Lough, they both got out of the car and stood on the deck watching as the water around the stern began to bubble and froth white as the propellers chopped their way through the sea. They stood in silence, taking in the view of the Lough and the village of Strangford approaching in the distance on the other side. Elle stared down into the waters depths as the ferry ploughed on to its destination.

Approaching the shore, Elle caught site of a figure in the distance who she assumed to be Eva, removing her gear from a car. She had parked along the wall next to the water and was getting prepared for her meeting with her sister and the training session. She reckoned it wouldn't be so much training as socialising and hopefully further reconciliation. They drove down the exit ramp and off the ferry, pulling up alongside Eva and blocking the traffic. Elle hit the button to wind down her window.

"Morning you!"

"Oh, Hi. Good morning."

"Eva, this is Hugh. Hugh, this is my sister, Eva."

Hugh lent over low enough to say hello.

"Hi, Hugh. It's good to meet you. I think you're holding people up. If you pull in on up the road a bit I'll meet you there."

Elle checked her mirror and realised she was stopping the traffic.

"Oh God, you're right. Okay. See you in a minute."

She waved at the frustrated driver behind, drove off and parked the car some fifty feet away. They both got out and Hugh reached for his rucksack while Elle went to the back of the car and popped the boot open. Like many female's cars, there was almost an entire wardrobe of shoes, coats and last minute impulse buys still in their bags.

"My God. What haven't you got in there?"

"Shut it, Slim. I need all this stuff."

She took out the bag containing her swimming gear and towels then closed the trunk of the car and locked it.

"Let's go."

They began walking towards her sister, who still appeared to be moving piles of assorted belongings around in the back of her own car. Estelle had no idea or plan of what to say to her. *Let's just wing it Elle and see how things go*, she thought.

Eva was still fiddling with stuff in the rear of the car when they approached.

"Morning again."

"Oh, hi again. Good morning. I'll be with you in a second."

"No hurry."

Eva was busy hauling bundles of clothing into her arms and struggled to close the hatch on her car.

"Okay, that's me ready to go."

Hugh put out his hand to shake Eva's. She was struggling to keep hold of wet suits, swimming caps and goggles. He turned to Estelle and asked if keeping a mobile wardrobe was a family or gender trait? Eva looked at her sister confused at the statement.

"Ignore him. He's been incarcerated in a religious sect for years!"

"I wasn't in a religious sect. I think the Roman Catholic Church spans the crank, faith-loving loony brigades."

"He's indoctrinated and irreversibly brainwashed," continued Elle. "Just ignore him. He told me he's wearing Speedos, so my case is well and truly rested."

Hugh was about to retort but thought the sisters could have their bit of fun at his expense. It was becoming playful banter, most of which was lost on Eva.

"Am I missing something here? I've brought enough wet suits for everyone. If you don't mind Hugh, I'll shake your hand when we get down there."

Eva felt like she was on the periphery of some odd private joke. Not knowing if her sister and her friend were teasing her. Hugh sensed her confusion and decided to change the subject.

"Can I help you with anything?"

"No, I've got everything thanks Hugh, oh! If you could close the car up that would be good."

He did as requested and dropped the car keys into Eva's bag.

Chapter 50

THE TRIO WALKED OFF TOWARDS THE WATER to begin their swim, with Estelle remarking on her sister's apparently newly found organisational skills. "You brought wetsuits for all of us. Do we need them in this weather?"

Hugh answered the question for Estelle.

"Jellyfish. Right?"

"Correct!" came Eva's reply.

"I hadn't thought of that," said Elle. "Good call."

"I had to borrow one for you, Hugh. It should fit okay I think."

"Thanks again. I'm not a fan of jelly stings. Though it's more what you have to do to ease the stings that I'm not a fan of."

Eva laughed. She knew what Hugh was hinting at. It was apparent that Elle did not.

"I'm not too sure if that even works."

Their exchange was totally lost on Elle. "What do you have to do? What does who have to do? What works?"

Eva and Hugh just smiled as they walked ahead leaving Estelle to continue her interrogation.

"What do you have to do? I bet its horrible right?"

Hugh wasn't about to tell her, so he gestured to Eva to educate her sister.

"She's your sister. You'll have to do it, if or when the time comes."

"Listen, you shits! No one is doing anything until I find out

147

what the hell you're talking about. Now would one of you two please enlighten me?"

Hugh still refused to answer leaving Eva to explain.

"The theory is that you have to urinate on the sting to neutralise it."

"Really! Well, just to let you know, no one, but no one is peeing on me! I don't care if I go into anaphylactic shock. You can let me die first!"

Both Hugh and Eva were in fits of laughter.

"I'm serious, don't even think about it or you'll be walking home Doggett!"

They continued to make their way down towards the water's edge; still listening to Estelle's threats of retribution while Eva and Hugh continued to laugh and discuss who would have the honours of applying first aid to Elle if she got stung.

Hugh took the conversation further, as the image of having to administer body fluid first aid to a woman refused to be purged from his imagination.

Laughing out loud he said to Eva, "You would have to pick the place right? To be honest; you couldn't just do it on a public beach. I mean what would happen if you froze and couldn't produce the goods when needed? Dear God, this is going to haunt me forever. You know, some people would pay good money for that sort of thing."

"Yeah, well not me, so balls off both of you. No-one is going to empty their bladder on me!"

They eventually came to a sandy, rock free outcrop at the water's edge.

"This will do; not too many rocks here and no nasty jelly fish."

"Up yours, Jacques frigging Cousteau!" came Elle's reply.

Hugh was still laughing as he took off his trousers and shirt. Both Eva and Elle had put on their bathing suits before the journey to the Lough, as did Hugh. As Hugh undressed both sisters said it at the same time, "Jesus! Hugh what the hell happened to you?"

"Pay no attention, old wounds and a colourful, if painful, past."

He hadn't figured on the effect of removing his clothing in public without warning. Hugh Doggett was covered in old scar tissue. Burns mostly with a few raised welts where stray bullets and shrapnel had done their damage.

Eva couldn't help but ask. She noticed the distinct tattooed insignia on his upper right arm.

"Is that an SBS tattoo? You were in the special forces?"

"Yeah, among others, that was back in the day," replied Hugh.

"What happened to you? How did you get all those scars?" asked Elle.

"Buy me a drink someday and I'll talk you through them all."

"I bloody will do!"

"Me too," said Eva.

All three entered the Lough at the same time. As they waded out into deeper water Hugh asked, "What do you prefer Eva. Speed or distance?"

"Your choice, Hugh. I'm just glad to be in the water again."

"Elle, how's your swimming?"

"It's okay. I'll try to keep up for a while anyway."

"Stick to shore side, then, if that suits you?"

"Fine by me," came Elle's reply.

"Everybody ready? Eva, I'll follow your lead."

"Okay. Let's get going."

Chapter *51*

ELLE SWAM THREE TIMES A WEEK AT HER LOCAL pool. She wasn't fast, but could swim fifty, twenty-five metre lengths in twenty-five minutes, which was a good pace by most swimmers' standards.

Hugh held the regiment record for the mile and to this day, to the best of his knowledge, it had yet to be broken.

Eva had rated herself as average at best. She tinkered with the mp3 player attached to her goggles and inserted the earplugs.

The music she had downloaded had a constant beat that she could match her strokes to. The sound of Fat Boy Slim's *Weapon of Choice* filled her ears.

She usually swam at three strokes, then a breath, but the new five-stroke method was becoming more comfortable now. She could feel the others beside her in the water, keeping pace with similar strokes.

Ten minutes in she began to find her rhythm and relaxed into the swim. Twenty after that she stopped to turn for home.

Neither Hugh nor her sister were anywhere in sight. *Shit! Something's happened to Elle. We shouldn't have tempted fate. I bet she got stung on the hand, foot, or worse the face!*

Eva headed back as fast as she could and as she neared the shoreline she saw Elle and Hugh sitting at the water's edge with their feet dipped in the Lough. She made her way towards them and shouted over the music still playing in her ears if they were okay and why had they stopped?

"What happened? Where did you guys go?"

She left the water as fast as her legs could carry her, at the same time removing her goggles and earplugs.

"You guys okay? Where were you?"

Elle looked at Hugh as he made the hand gesture for her to speak first.

"Where did *we* go? You were gone after the first few minutes. I couldn't stay with you and I know Hugh did his damnedest."

Eva tried to compute the information.

"I wasn't going *that* hard!"

Hugh was matter-of-fact when he spoke, waiting for Elle to finish.

"Eva. You left me for dead. Do you have any kind of buoyancy aid in your wet suit?"

"No, of course not. Why?"

"Your body was halfway out of the water!"

"I'm sorry, Hugh. I have no idea what you're talking about! *Halfway out of the water*? How could that be even possible?"

Eva had no clue what they were possibly accusing her of. She stood, feeling herself becoming defensive. Hugh could understand her confusion and eased the tension of the conversation.

"Okay Eva. Take off your skins."

Skin was a military term, now widely used to describe wet or dry suits for swimming or scuba diving.

"Why?"

"Please Eva. Just take your skin off!"

Eva reluctantly began to take the wet suit off. She pulled her legs out and threw the suit to the ground.

"Now what?"

"Feel the back of the suit Eva."

"Why?"

"Please. Just feel it."

Hugh remained calm and silent as Eva reluctantly picked the discarded wet suit up from the sand. Estelle just stared at her sister in disbelief.

"What am I meant to find, Hugh?"

"Check the back of the skin."

Eva turned the wet suit round to see what Hugh was talking about.

"It feels okay! I'm still lost here."

"Feel it again, Eva. I think you'll find it's dry."

"*Dry*! How could it be dry?"

"You tell us."

Eva ran her hands over the suit again and again. Hugh was right. The back was dry. Estelle needed some answers.

"Eva. When I asked you on the telephone had anything else unusual happen to you, did you forget to tell me you could beat the Olympic 100 metre free style record and then some?"

"You folks will have to give me a minute here," said Eva quietly. "I'm trying to get my head around this."

"Look, we're just trying to understand what's going on here as well. Can you tell us anything that might shine some light on it, or give us something to go on?"

Eva told the story again of the day she was swimming in the Lough, the turbine malfunction and the figure by the water, cutting her foot and the miraculous healing.

Elle waited for Hugh to digest the story. He stared at Eva then at Estelle in utter shock and disbelief. He turned his gaze to Estelle and asked her as directly as his manners and military training would allow.

"Estelle, why didn't you tell me any of this?"

The tone of his voice stunned her. She knew and understood that he was upset, but masking it as best he could. She could sense the thin veil of control in Hugh's question and for the first time could get a feel for what it may have been like to come face to face with a professional killer. The expression on his face could be translated as benign or waiting for termination orders.

"Estelle, I repeat again, why haven't you told me about this?"

She didn't answer.

Hugh Doggett couldn't remember if he had ever threatened a woman, but he would remember this one.

"Listen and listen well, both of you. If any of you girls have anything else to tell me, you'd better do it now. I am not sure what you've got me involved in here, but I'm not one bit happy about it."

"Hugh, we're as baffled and as lost as you are, honestly!"

"Estelle, have you told your sister of the vision you experienced outside your apartment?"

Hugh decided that the time for tact and diplomacy had ended.

"*Vision*? What vision, Elle?" asked Eva.

Estelle tried to figure out a way of describing the vision and still protect her sister from the scene of her with the children that she had been witness to. She told her of the things she saw but omitted to tell her that the girl in the water was Eva.

Hugh was about to force her when he noticed that her eyes were filling with tears. These two girls were all each other had in the world and from what he could gather their relationship appeared to be on a tenuous mending process. Telling your only sister that she would drown in a sea of dead children could send her into meltdown. He decided that for the time being he would leave well enough alone. Elle jumped in.

"What about the tests you're doing? Anything odd there?"

"My lab assistant seems to think so. He reckons the algae test samples appear to react to me in some way."

"React to you. How?"

"I'm not sure really. According to him, they just seem to react positively to me somehow. They grow brighter in colour when I'm near them."

Hugh stepped in again.

"You got the test subjects here at the Lough I take it, Eva?"

"Yes, well no, not here. Just further round by the point."

"Is it faster to walk or swim?"

"Walk I should think," came the reply.

"You want to take a look, Elle?"

"Of course, I do. Let's go."

Chapter **52**

ALL THREE REMOVED THEIR SUITS AND BEGAN the ten-minute walk to the point that overlooked the mouth of the intersection with the channel. Eva stopped them when they came to the spot where she had collected the samples. She pointed to a small stretch of sand at the waters' edge that became visible through the thicket.

"This is where I took the samples."

They each made their way down to the shoreline to look for anything unusual. Nothing seemed out of place or extraordinary. They scanned the shore for anything that may give them some clue to the events of that day but everything seemed normal. All of them were equally baffled.

"Look folks," said Hugh, "I don't know about you two, but I'm getting hungry and we still have the wet suit issue back there to sort out. It must be almost lunchtime, also I reckon that it's faster to swim back than walk. I'd like to do a little experiment of my own. How about we go thirty feet from shore to check if there was anything odd about Eva's wet suit that she was unaware of, then at least we can eliminate that for starters?"

He checked his divers watch. It was 11.41am.

Estelle concurred.

"I agree. Eva, how about you?"

"Yeah let's get going, I don't think we need to go back for our suits, no one will find them here until we drive round after lunch and pick them up, and as Hugh said, it's only an experiment."

"Estelle, can you watch at eye level, as Eva and I swim out the first fifty yards?" said Hugh.

"Okay. That's fine. I'm happy right here thank you."

Hugh and Eva waded out into the Lough until they were out of their depth, then called for Elle to join them.

"Well, Elle, did you notice anything unusual as Eva and I swam out?"

"Nothing, Hugh, it all appeared normal to me."

Eva almost sighed with relief at her sister's answer.

None of them, especially Eva, could touch the bed of the Lough. They were still talking when Hugh noticed that he was having to work harder to remain in one place.

"Are either of you two finding it harder to move in here?"

"I hadn't noticed but now you mention it!"

"Me, too."

They all looked around to find the cause.

The water was noticeably denser with the green algae. It was quickly becoming the consistency of syrup and rapidly getting thicker!

Hugh could see the panic rising on the girls' faces as they all now struggled to move their limbs. They no longer had to tread water to stay afloat as the algae was already supporting their collective weight. The green mass was now as thick as sticky porridge and getting thicker by the second, pushing them closer together. Their struggling appeared to make the plants task easier. Hugh knew he had to do something to ease the situation.

"Okay! Let's stop. This isn't helping. Let's just all try to relax for a minute and take a breath. We don't appear to be in any particular danger. We're not drowning and this will pass in a moment. I'm sure of it. Let's all count to three and then we stop kicking and just see what happens! Ready? 1-2-3!"

They all looked at each other and unnaturally, for being out of their depth in water, simply softened and relaxed. The algae instantly drove them together, each reached out to grab hands in the unexpected surge of green stew. The three faced each other until they had no option but to embrace. The algae now began to creep up from the water and encase them from the backs of their heads to their feet in an organic suit of living Lycra, spreading down over their eyes and faces leaving their mouths and nostrils clear. Estelle began screaming and Hugh now blinded like the rest, did his best to calm her.

Everything went quiet. No sounds of gulls, waves, or white noise from the town or passing boats, just an eerie stillness. Estelle was the first to break the silence. She was beginning to understand that she wasn't in any immediate danger apart from the lack of vision, which was now clearing like the others. She managed to open her eyes fully to see the other two staring at her.

"You two okay?"

Both answered 'Yes' at the same time.

"I don't know what you are seeing, but I'm watching dolphins doing hooplas."

A pod of at least thirty to forty dolphins was leaping ten to fifteen feet out of the water. They got so close to the three swimmers that Hugh and Estelle could make eye contact with them. If any of the two had ever doubted there was real intelligence in these creatures, they wouldn't from today on. The dolphins knew exactly why they were celebrating even if they didn't.

Eva started to take notice now and craned her neck around to see the display. The dolphins and porpoises were having one hell of a party.

"You ever seen anything like this, Hugh?" she asked.

Hugh didn't answer as he seemed to be distracted and was trying to wiggle out of his bonds.

"You okay, Hugh?"

"I don't know. I don't think so!"

The panic returned as Hugh was now obviously getting increasingly distressed.

"Hugh. What's wrong?"

He ignored the question and began to writhe around desperately trying to struggle free of his algae suit.

"*Hugh! Hugh!* What's happening?"

He almost screamed as the relentless pain that wracked his body increased. His face was contorted in agony and his body writhed around in the water. The algae held him tight; there was nothing Eva and Estelle could do but watch.

"I'm burning. I'm burning in water!" cried the ex-Priest.

The sweat poured from his forehead running down each side of his face. His head sagged then drooped forward as he passed out.

Eva was now screaming, partly out of concern for Hugh, but also the fact that she had no control over what was happening to them.

"*Hugh! Hugh!* Wake up!"

Elle was next to feel the pain. It began with what felt like an itch deep inside her knee. The sensation was like some invisible force moving the atomic structure of her right knee around without an anaesthetic and the pain was unbearable! The same sensation began in some of the knuckles on her left hand. She was in too much pain to even cry. As suddenly as the pain started it then stopped.

At the same time, Hugh began to regain consciousness. He mumbled as a drool of saliva trickled from the corner of his mouth. He tried to speak, but it came out as a whisper first then a slur.

"Get me to shore."

"Hugh, are you okay?"

Hugh repeated his plea. Still dazed and exhausted.

"Please. Get me to shore."

"We can't yet, Hugh. The algae still has a grip on us."

He remembered that he had been fully buoyant in the water, so lolled his head back to ease the tension in his neck. He stared up at the gin clear sky and thanked God he was still alive and almost out of pain.

"What happened?"

"We don't know. You passed out. How are you?"

"I'm not sure. Tired I think and my skin still itches."

The algae began quickly to release its hold on them and the movement was returning to their arms and legs. Within a few moments they were free.

It was as if it had never happened. The water around them was again totally clear with no sign of any floating plant life. Even the dolphins had gone and their party appeared to be over. Eva

157

knew they could still be in danger and that Hugh was in a very weakened state.

"Let's get him to shore, Elle."

Estelle nodded her head and they both rolled Hugh onto his back, to make it easier to float him in to land. The two sisters held Hugh on each side keeping his head out of the water until they reached the water's edge. Hugh, although of light build, was deceptively heavy. The girls gently lowered him to the ground, both exhausted from the effort. Eva took a step back when what she was seeing registered in her brain.

Estelle was too preoccupied with Hugh's welfare to notice anything, supporting his head and talking to him. Eva softly spoke to her sister.

"Elle, leave Hugh. Leave him alone and come over here."

Elle didn't hear her sister due to her concern for Hugh. Eva raised the tone of her voice an octave and repeated her request for Elle to come to her side.

"*Estelle!* Leave Hugh alone and come over here now, please!"

Elle spun her head around to protest, then she saw the expression on her sister's face.

"What's wrong, Eva? I'm trying to help Hugh."

"Please, Elle. Leave him and come and over here to see what I'm seeing!"

Elle got to her feet and moved the few yards to her sister's side.

"What's wrong?"

With the drama in the water and her concerns for her friend, she was losing patience and her nerves were understandably shredded.

"I want you to slowly turn around and take a look at Hugh."

"That's what I was doing until you called me away!"

"Please just look."

Elle turned round to see what her sister was talking about. She took a little time to notice anything different in their fellow swimmer.

Today was the first time she had seen the man without

clothes on, so with all that had just happened, she didn't understand what her sister had begged her to see.

Estelle registered and now stood open-mouthed staring down at the man still lying at their feet.

Hugh Doggett was in fighting shape. He carried little if any body fat. He had obviously kept himself very fit, a relic of his days in the armed services. He was beginning to regain his strength and became aware of the two girls staring down at him.

"What? What are you two looking at?"

There was a pause before any of the girls spoke.

"Take a look at yourself, Hugh."

"What do you mean: take a look at myself? What's wrong with me?"

"Your scars, Hugh."

"What about them?"

"They're gone. Your scars are gone!"

"What?"

"Your scars and burns, Hugh. They're gone. All of them!"

Hugh Doggett looked down at his arms and torso in utter disbelief. There was no sign of any scar tissue whatsoever, or any sign that they had ever been any there at all. Even the hairs had grown back where the scar tissue had once been.

"Feck me! What's happening?"

That was the first time Hugh Doggett had sworn out loud or in company since entering the priesthood.

Chapter **53**

DIABETIC RETINOPATHY IS THE MOST COMMON of diabetic eye diseases. Damage is caused to the blood vessels in the retina leaving the patient with partial or no sight. Her condition was advanced and progressing to the most severe Proliferative Retinopathy, now rendering her almost totally blind. There was no cure.

If she'd caught it earlier Audrey Walsh may have retained at least some of her sight with treatment, but it was too late for that now. She had tried every homeopathic remedy, every snake oil selling quack she could find with the help of her husband Cyril, but all to no avail. She was still losing her remaining sight at a rapid rate.

She spent her days with Cyril driving her to some new hope of cure for her condition.

They'd sold their house and most of their belongings to finance trips to both domestic and foreign destinations. They had even taken a trip to Lourdes in France regardless of the fact that neither was a Roman Catholic. They were desperate and would both try anything to help in the restoration of what remained of her sight. They had met at a dance in a community hall in Belfast at the height of the *Troubles*. Few people in those days, ventured far from home at night and certainly not to the city centre. Thirty years of killings and bombings had left a generation still battling over sectarian division.

Random killings and kidnappings were commonplace and

many areas, including towns and city centres were out of bounds to both sides of the religious divide. Each side of the community stuck to where they felt safest and that was generally their own areas. The entire working class sections of Northern Ireland became insular and paranoid of strange cars or people they didn't recognise coming onto their streets. Unfamiliar faces had the potential to be enemies.

Cyril Walsh worked as a painter and decorator. His first wife died from cancer in 1987. He had married young aged nineteen and lost her twenty-one years later. They had no children of their own, leaving Cyril a widower until he met Audrey.

He rarely went any further than his local pub, bookmaker or the recreational centre. Audrey had worked in the Lyric Theatre as a wardrobe mistress. Her first husband was in the Royal Ulster Constabulary and was killed in an IRA bomb blast in a bus station in the centre of Belfast in 1978. He was twenty-nine and made a widow of Audrey and an orphan of Angela, their only child and daughter of seven months.

She raised the child with the help of her mother and sister Joan. She was diagnosed late with diabetes and hadn't been on a proper date since her husband's death until she met 'her Cyril.'

It didn't take long for them to fall in love. Cyril was forty - two and Audrey was thirty-nine. Eight years later they married in the registry office at Belfast City Hall. That had been 1997: seventeen years ago this coming October. They loved each other every bit as much now as they did back then.

Today Cyril had had an idea.

He walked through the open front door of their mid terraced house to find Audrey hanging the washing on the line in the small yard. He shouted out to her through the open window as normal to alert her that he was home. He filled the kettle and put it on the gas hob to make tea for them both.

"Audrey, I met an old pal of mine at the bookmakers and he was asking after you."

"Oh really. Who was that?"

She didn't bother turning round to address him as it took her full concentration to feel for the line and pegs to hang the wet washing on.

161

"Do you remember Tommy Spears who used to be a neighbour of your mothers?"

Audrey now turned, looking at him. Her feet hurt today and Cyril could see by the look on her face that she was both impatient and in discomfort. She didn't answer so he thought it best to carry on the one sided conversation.

"Anyway, I was telling him you were well, but your eyes were giving you bother."

"What the hell did you tell him that for?" asked Audrey, her voice rising in frustration.

"I don't know he just asked. Do you want to hear what he said or not?"

"I don't mind."

In reality, she did mind. She wasn't happy with Cyril discussing her condition with strangers he'd met in a betting shop.

"He says there's a well in Downpatrick, supposed to have some sort of cure in it. He also said that it was claimed to be a cure specific to the eyes and I thought as it's a lovely day we could drive down and have a look around and maybe have our lunch on the way home?"

Audrey pretended not to be that interested. The fact was she was almost bursting with excitement. Why hadn't they heard of a possible cure so close to home?

"Where in Downpatrick? Haven't we been there already?"

"I don't know love, I can't remember. We'll have to ask somebody when we get there. I think you go through the town and head towards Ardglass. He said it was signposted. It's ten-thirty now, you finish hanging the washing and I'll make the tea. If we leave here at eleven we could be down there for noon. What do you think?"

Audrey's tone softened. She knew his intentions were good and her welfare was paramount to him. A smile caressed its way across her face.

"Oh I don't know, love. Can you be bothered driving all the way down there?"

Audrey knew he was tired and fed up with running her round the country looking for miracles that didn't exist.

162

"Of course, I could be bothered," replied the love of her life. "What else do we have to do?"

Audrey broke her personal best for hanging the washing and threw half of her tea down the sink when Cyril wasn't looking.

"Okay, handsome. That's me ready."

Struell Wells are located on the Struell Well Road outside the town of Downpatrick. Said to have been blessed by Saint Patrick himself, it had been popular with pilgrims from the sixteenth century. It was once a pagan place of worship and was particularly associated with a cure for the eyes. Hundreds if not thousands visit the place every year, hoping for a cure.

Cyril and Audrey parked their car and walked the short distance to the site of the well. They passed a man walking his yappy mongrel dog. He paused and asked Cyril if he had the correct time?

"Sure, no problem. It's just after 11.30."

"Thanks. By the way, it's your lucky day folks. You'll have the waters to yourselves down there. It's usually busy here at this time. Good luck to you both."

Cyril gave the man a smile and a 'thank you' while trying to stay clear of his dog.

"Good luck to yourself, young fella."

He led Audrey along the path and down to the well site. The wells had been there for thousands of years. The area was well maintained with an area of neatly cut grass surrounding the small, stone-gated entrance to the water inside.

"It's lovely here, Audrey. It's a shame you can't see it that well, love."

Audrey linked Cyril's arm as he led her down towards the narrow stone building containing the clear pool of the well. Water boatmen skimmed across its surface chasing their microscopic prey.

"Here, let's give it a go, sure you never know, we might be lucky this time."

Audrey trusted her husband completely and let him guide her down to the water.

"Where are we, Cyril, what do I have to do?"

"The water's down here, love. Don't panic, I'll help you."

163

Cyril led Audrey to the spring in the ground and helped her bend down to reach the water.

He checked his watch. It was 11.43am. If he timed this right he could be home to watch the three thirty race at Kempton. He had got a hot tip on a horse running and put a fiver on it. If Audrey found out, she would kill him.

"I think the best thing is for you to hold your head back and I'll trickle some of the water into your eyes."

"Have you washed your hands?" asked Audrey, ever mindful of cleanliness.

"Look, do you want me to do this or not?"

She didn't reply, but held her head back to receive the water.

Cyril made a cup of his hand and immersed it in the well and quickly withdrew it thinking he'd been stung or bitten!

"What's wrong? My neck's getting sore."

"I don't know. I think something just stung me."

"Stung you; where?"

"It's no bother. Hold your head back woman."

"Don't you woman me, Cyril Walsh!"

"Okay, Audrey. Would you please hold your head back so I can get this water into your eyes."

She gave him a withering look and tilted her head again. He hadn't remembered breaking his little finger when he was a young child, playing games with his pals on the streets of Belfast. He stared down at the wrinkled skin of his finger where he'd felt the sharpest pain of what he presumed had been a wasp or bee sting. There was no reddening or indication of a puncture mark and the pain was dissipating now anyway.

Cyril looked for bugs swimming in the water then gingerly submerged his cupped hand into the liquid for the second time. He held his water filled hand above her damaged eyes and carefully trickled liquid first into her left then right eye. She reached for a tissue to wipe away the excess water.

"Give me your handkerchief, Cyril."

Cyril began to rummage in his pocket, searching for a clean tissue when his wife began scratching at her eyes.

"What's wrong, love?"

"I don't know; stinging!"

She almost whimpered with a sense of increasing panic.

"Okay. Give it a minute or so and it will settle down."

"It's hurting, Cyril! It's ..."

Audrey Walsh crumpled on the ground holding her head in the palms of her hands. She would have prayed for it to stop, but the searing pain prevented her from having any thoughts other than the needles that seemed to be driving into the back of her eyes. She lost her grip on the world and fainted.

Cyril made a feeble call for help, but his concern for his wife had taken his full attention.

"Audrey! Audrey, love, please!" He shook his wife as her arms fell limply by her sides. "Oh God no. No, please don't take her. It's my fault. Take me instead!"

Cyril knelt at her side and put his hand on her chest to feel for a heartbeat and nearly fell over backwards. Her heart was thumping like a racehorse; it seemed as if it was trying to beat its way out through her chest! He sat for a moment shocked. Then he saw life gradually returning to her rigid body. He took her by the shoulders and shook her again.

"Audrey are you okay, Audrey. Audrey?"

"Of course, I'm okay, you old fool. Give me some air."

It took a second for Audrey Walsh's brain to take in the colour of the trees and grass on which she was lying. The sun was blinding as it dappled through the foliage of the overhanging branches that Cyril had somehow managed to guide her to.

The past years without full sight had left her with only the memories of colour and entire outlines of everyday objects. Now here it was; all summer's glorious beauty and splendour right before her.

Cyril remained holding her head in his lap with his arm around her shoulders for support. Staring into her eyes and wishing to God he hadn't had the bloody stupid idea of coming all the way down here, only to cause her further harm.

"Cyril. We have to tell people."

"Tell people what, love? I know it was a stupid idea."

"I can see sweetheart! I can see. I can see again and I love you."

Cyril slumped back on the grass and stared at his wife. It was the first time in almost ten years that she looked directly at him when she spoke. The idea that his wife had been cured of her loss of sight was beginning to slowly seep its way into his brain. It's a fact that the Irish have a skill of turning fright into humour as a coping mechanism and so the first words that Cyril blurted out were, "Thank Christ, love. I need a pint and you're driving home for a change!"

He flung his arms around her and they rolled on the grass like teenagers. He kissed her eyes over and over. Then kissed her wet cheeks and hugged her.

"Home?" he whispered to his wife. "Yes Cyril, home. I want to see my home again."

Chapter **54**

Chicago

THE INSIDE OF THE COMPANY LIMO WAS KEPT AT a constant 21 degrees, summer and winter. Marcus, one of the company's most trusted senior drivers, almost spat his neat vodka into his lap when the explosion went off. He dropped the open bottle on the floor and tried to retrieve it without the entire contents emptying onto the carpet in the footwell of the car!

"What the fuck?"

He leapt from the car to see the cloud of dust and smoke rise into the afternoon air. Mourners from the funeral were scattering in every direction away from the explosion in panic.

He quickly threw the half empty bottle behind a nearby headstone.

"Oh holy crap. Some wacko's set off a bomb!"

He had worked for BION, for the last eleven years and had made a tidy fortune from conversations that he had overheard from the passengers he carried during his time chauffeuring them to and from their hotels or business appointments.

He could facilitate any desires that they were willing to pay for, drugs, women, men, girls or boys. He didn't care, tax free gratuities and favours potentially returned in the hopeful near future.

He leant back into the car and withdrew his sidearm from the glove compartment and started to break into a run, no mean task for a six foot four, three hundred and fifty pound man wearing a suit and new tight shoes. He searched through the oncoming mourners for Mr. Sere and Miss Kane. He suddenly caught sight of them staggering towards him and the waiting car.

Kay Kane was doing her best to get them both beyond the reach of danger; Valentine Sere was obviously hurt and stumbling, desperately trying to flee from the melee. He directed his sidearm towards what he could see as the epicentre of the chaos. Kay spotted him and shouted over the screams and distant sirens.

"Start the car, Marcus!"

"Are you okay, Miss Kane?"

"I said start the fucking car, Marcus!"

He holstered his weapon and helped Mr. Sere into the back of the limousine, ignoring protocol by not closing the door behind them, but instead running round to the driver's side to quickly get the car started. He floored the gas pedal almost causing more casualties by nearly running down some of the mourners in a bid to get his passengers out and away from any present danger.

His two passengers flopped into the back seat. Kay was holding Valentine's chin in her hand staring into his dust filled eyes while trying to clear the dirt and caked mud from around them with a tissue. They were streaming with tears and badly bloodshot.

Blood was seeping from his tear ducts and she started to think that the situation should have been handled with a bit less drama and a bit more finesse. *I mean, he was her boss, for God's sake!*

"What happened, Kay? Who the fuck was that?"

"I don't know, Val, some crazy with a bomb!" she replied.

"How is everyone?"

"I don't know. Let's get you to a doctor fast. Marcus, call Harmony Rodgers at the clinic and tell her we're on our way. I need her to check Mr. Sere's eyesight."

"Yes, Miss Kane."

Kay removed a bottle of still water from the car's refrigerator and tried to dribble its contents into Valentines eyes. Marcus searched for the doctor's number; not an easy task while driving at almost twice the legal speed limit and dodging pedestrians and casualties through the narrow roads of a cemetery packed with fleeing mourners.

The number rang a few times until one of the duty receptionists answered the call. Marcus asked to be put through to Harmony Rogers, stressing that it was a matter of an extreme urgency!

"One moment, please, and I'll put you through to Doctor Rodgers aide."

The car was filled with the sound of the surgery's call waiting *elevator musak*. If Richard Clayderman had been so unlucky to be inside with them in person, Marcus reckoned, Kay Kane would have relieved him of his side arm and shot the man herself. Kay's face was growing redder by the second as she continued to scowl at the speakerphone.

After what seemed to Marcus to be an eternity, Harmony Rodgers' overly cheerful aide picked up her extension.

"Hi. This is Miss Rodgers' aide. How can I help you today?"

Marcus spoke as calmly as the crisis would permit.

"I need to speak to Doctor Rodgers. I have an inbound VIP emergency with facial trauma that needs her immediate attention!"

"I'm sorry, sir, but Doctor Rodgers is in surgery at the moment and can't be disturbed under any circumstances."

Marcus was about to plead when Kay leant over his shoulder, putting her hand on his neck to silence him. Kay leant further forward and spoke into the hands free system in the car through the open aperture.

"What's your name sweetie?"

"I'm sorry ma'am. I don't have to give you that information."

Marcus could feel the pressure beginning to steadily build and self protectively moved himself a little more towards the driver side window. He despised this awful woman. The sooner he got them to the clinic, the happier he would be.

"Okay then whatever your name is? My name is Kay Kane and we fund that slaughterhouse you draw your monthly wage from. We will be arriving at your front door with a very important casualty in approx...."

She redirected her attention to Marcus.

169

Marcus replied quietly, "Three to four minutes."

"That would be five minutes maximum, Miss Thingy! So you do whatever you have to do and have the lovely Doctor Rodgers standing at the front door when we pull up or you, she and whoever I take as much a disliking to as your good self, will be flipping burgers or filling shelves in some warehouse tomorrow morning. Is that understood?"

At the other end of the line, the colour drained from Miss Thingy's face.

"I'll just go alert Doctor Rodgers to your arrival, Miss Kane!"

"You do that, and be quick about it!"

The connection was severed and Kay was about to return to her seat when she took hold of the partition that separated the driver from his passengers. Her tone became matter-of-fact. She stretched over to Marcus and spoke to him in whispers, not letting Valentine overhear her conversation. Oblivious, he continued to rest back on the seat with his eyes still tightly closed.

"Marcus. Have you been drinking today, son?"

Marcus could feel his face go red then pale an instant later. He knew his future may just about to be flushed down a very deep and most likely very dirty toilet.

"We had a few people over last night ma'am. Family gathering, you know the kind of thing?"

"No, no. I don't fucking know Marcus." She was being thrown around the inside of the car as Marcus took the corners at speed. When the car finally straightened she continued her address. "However what I do know is that I won't have privileged company staff abusing their positions. So when we arrive at the hospital, you will wait outside until I and your soon to be former employer have been seen by the tramp of a doctor who's going to attend to him." Kay Kane continued to whisper into Marcus's ear. "Now, there's a chance that I might let you keep the money that you made from the loose tongued idiots you've been driving around and listening to their conversations by using the cars intercom. But, when this day is over, you can seek employment elsewhere and if I ever see your face or hear your name mentioned again I'll have you crippled at best. Is that clear?"

Marcus stared through the windscreen, trying to come to terms with the fact that he had not only lost his job but had absolutely been scared out of his wits. He could only guess what this *Harpy* was capable of, but he had no desire to find out.

"Crystal clear, Miss Kane."

"Good. Now, chop-chop. There's a good boy."

Kay reclined back into her seat and smiled as Marcus cast a glance at her in the rear-view mirror.

"Two minutes, Val, and we'll have you good as new."

Chapter **55**

Louisiana

THE VILLAGE OF MADRON LIES ON THE MOST western edge of Cornwall, situated two miles northwest of Penzance. The town boasted of having the worst soccer team in Britain as well as having its own *holy wells*. Most of the buildings were constructed using old local stone or granite and still stood solid after hundreds of years. The American tourist and his wife hadn't seen anything like the twisty country lanes before and wondered at the British traffic roundabouts. There appeared to be a rule regarding joining the traffic flow but it remained a mystery to them. They carefully descended the steep twisting stairs of the coach for a walk and some sightseeing to stretch their stiff legs.

Lyndon and Dordi Butterfield had spent less than a week of their vacation in England with one more week still to go on the first leg of their trip. Next they would take in the sights of Ireland, but first a flying visit to Wales then on to Scotland to see Edinburgh Castle and finally on to Norway, their last stop before flying home; Dordi still had distant relatives living in Oslo.

She had never met or even heard of some of them, but she had done some detective work on their computer back home when the couple had made the decision to travel.

After that they would see how their finances held out and how Lyndon's condition was faring.

This was their first time out of the United States and their second trip together out of Louisiana - once to visit Lyndon's cousin in Saint Louis, Missouri and the second time to see the oncology doctor in Mississippi. Until a month ago neither of them had owned nor needed a passport.

The day before they left for Europe, Lyndon had given one of his rare sermons to his wife of nearly forty-five years. They had been standing in the kitchen, which adjoined the small bait shop they ran together. He had taken his wife's hands in his and looked into her eyes, kissed her on the forehead, then on her nose.

"If I have one regret in this life, it's that I didn't tell you often enough how much I love you. Pride I'd imagine. Men's stupid crap, I guess."

Dordi tried to pull her hands away.

"Oh Lyn quit it now, you old fool."

He had held her tighter, ignoring her protests.

"Okay then, enough of the soppy stuff. I've been working on that little speech for days. I had it rehearsed and everything. I even practised it in front of the mirror. Now listen please. I know things have been tough for both of us, but I want to leave this world with nothing but the good memories. So, when we get to going, I don't want to hear any talk of me dying or what will you do without me, blah-de-blah-de-blah. Agreed?"

"I guess."

Dordi had agreed. She looked at the clock on the wall as a distraction. The thought of losing him was too unbearable to even contemplate.

"Well, okay then. I'm as excited as a school kid."

Dordi smiled at her husband and replied, "You should be. You got about the same mental age as one."

He slapped her on the backside as she turned away.

"HEY!"

"You still have the wiggle, gorgeous."

"Don't push it Dopey. The sympathy card's fading fast!"

She had turned away from him with a smile beginning to spread on her face and left him to his whistling in the kitchen as he finished up with the dishes; still grumbling to himself through the whistling about his unheard speech.

Lyndon received the news that his cancer had returned from his best friend and Doctor Tom Derrick. They'd known each other for fifty something years, spending countless fishing trips and family gatherings together. Tom had been best man at his and Dordi's wedding and Lyndon had given the eulogy at the untimely funeral of Tom's wife, Margie. They were as close as family considering they weren't related.

Lyndon made his way across the street in the stifling humidity of the Louisiana mid-afternoon sun.

Rehearsing the second speech that he had prepared, going over it in his head had been a mostly uncomfortable new discipline for him. He supposed when you knew that you had a limited number of words left to say in this life, that they better be well thought out before expressing them.

Lyn opened the door and stepped into the air-conditioned reception of the surgery, wiping the sweat from his brow with his handkerchief.

He checked himself in with the receptionist Magnolia and took a seat on one of the plastic chairs, going over and over what he would say to Tom. Just sitting looking up at the ceiling fan spin and tapping the back of his head against the wall as Magnolia went about her work in her own distinct way. No matter what your troubles may be, you just couldn't fail to follow her every movement. Magnolia Breaux was seventy-nine years old, or at least that's what age she would admit to.

Her white uniform was pulled in tight around at the waist of her 112 pound frame and secured with a wide black patent belt and silver buckle. She had Tom sign the forms confirming that her latest breast augmentation surgery would cure her of feelings of inadequacy and severe depression. It was more than his happiness was worth to refuse and they both knew it.

The buttons on her uniform strained hard to retain her new double 'F' sized store bought breasts. She wore the reddest lipstick that Lyn had ever seen, further emphasised by the multi-layers of pale pan stick makeup and bright blue eyeliner. Magnolia was one of the sweetest, most eccentric people that a person could ever wish to meet. It also helped that she was as close to Cajun royalty as was possible to be; her family had settled in Louisiana at the time of the first settlers in the South and just happened to own one of the biggest natural gas fields in the Southern states of America. She didn't need the money; she just liked being social and useful.

She called Lyn's name and walked him down the corridor, knocked, then opened the door of Tom's treatment room without waiting for him to call her in.

"Hey Tom; I got your girlfriend here for you to snuggle up to, looks to me that she's raring to get at yah!"

"Thank you, Magnolia; now off you go now and frighten the school kids."

She closed the door behind her as she left but not before making the sign that Lyn should call her.

Lyn smiled, "She's a treasure Tom."

"Oh, she's priceless all right," came the reply.

They passed a few more pleasantries before Lyndon finally sat down on the opposite side of the desk. He was nervous and still sweating from the afternoon heat and needed to get to the point of his visit without appearing rude. They both spoke with a heavy Cajun drawl.

"So, Lyn, what's on your mind today?"

Doctor Thomas Derrick scanned through Lyn's notes down through his half-moon spectacles that sat permanently perched on the end of his bulbous nose, a nose which had reddened over the years due solely to his love of Californian red wine. He placed the sheets of the medical reports down on his desk and reclined back on his swivel chair and waited for his friend and patient to speak.

"Now listen, Tom. Both you and I know things ain't looking too good for me. If I'm to hear the bad news I'd soon as it is from you. I want Dordi knowing very little of the details about this until we're sure of the time that I have left. Deal?"

"Sure Lyn I'll get the final test results on Monday and I'll speak to your specialist when I look at the stats. I'll come see you when they arrive."

"I think I'll come see you, if that's okay," replied Lyn. "We can go grab a beer over at Ned's."

"Whatever you like, Lyn, it's your call."

The weekend passed and it was soon Monday morning. Doctor Tom Derrick rechecked the results on the report in front of him for the fourth time; hoping that he had missed something that may offer a glimmer of hope for his friend's survival.

He tossed the papers down, removed his glasses and massaged the end of his nose. He then finally plucked up enough courage to make one of the toughest phone calls of his life. He was about to tell his best friend what he already knew. That he was dying and dying fast. The cancer was spreading and no further treatment was available. He threw the results across the table scattering them around the surgery as he glared at the anatomy diagram poster on the wall. He blew the air hard out of his cheeks, picked up the telephone and dialled Lyndon's number.

"Hey buddy, it's me."

They met later at Ned's bar for their beer as prearranged and sat in one of the booths as Tom reluctantly gave Lyn the prognosis.

"How long Tom?"

"No one can really tell for sure, Lyn. With all the new drugs and breakthroughs, it would be impossible to say."

"How about an educated guess? I need to get my affairs in order."

Tom sat staring into his beer glass, hoping for an easy way to pass on the results of the tests. He knew that this was part of his job; he had given plenty of his patients similar bad news over the years, but this time it was different and very personal.

For the first time in his life, he felt what it must be like for a judge to pass a death sentence. There was also a reminder here of his own mortality as they were both close to the same age.

"Tom!"

"Yah?"

He sighed and looked up at his old friend.

"How long, Tom?"

"Maybe a year, possibly a few months more, with further more aggressive treatment."

"A year?"

There was another pause and Tom looked up to the heavens, through the roof of Ned's bar.

"Okay Lyn, you've got six months, at best. It's gone into your ribs."

"Six months! Okay, okay, ummm, okay. I guess that's that then."

He shrugged his shoulders as if he'd just let an unimpressive bass get off the line. He was doing his best not to make this any more difficult for Tom. Truth was he was scared out of his wits but trying to be as strong and philosophical about it as he could manage.

"Listen, Tom. I know that had to be tough on you, but thanks anyway."

"I'm sorry, Lyn. Truly I am. I'm sorry for both you and Dordi. I know how much you kids mean to each other."

"I know you are Tom and I appreciate that. I better get home. Dordi will be worrying."

Lyn sat in the car park and watched his friend come out of the bar.

How do I tell Dordi? How can I break my baby's heart?

He sat his wife down in her chair in the kitchen and handed her the coffee he'd made for her. The view out the window seemed all the more beautiful as the thoughts of not seeing it for too much longer made it more cherished and finite.

Dordi's coffee cup slipped from her hand and bounced on the stone tiles, spilling its contents and smashing on the rebound, sending fragments of shattered crockery scattering across the floor. The tears welled up in her eyes. She knew the news was coming. She just didn't know how long they'd have left together.

"What are we going to do, Lyn?"

"I'm not sure yet, but I've been thinking of us taking a trip."

Dordi's grandparents had moved to America at the end of the nineteenth century with their two children. The eldest, a girl called Kari, Dordi's mother and Albert her uncle. Her mother had married an English miner and had three children together. Two of which later died from smallpox leaving her as their only child and daughter.

She met Lyndon in a veteran's hospital in Biloxi Mississippi, where she had been nursing. He had been discharged from the army on medical grounds after serving in the infantry in Korea for seven months. He'd contracted malaria in the army and the disease had left him needing treatment for three months in care. He had mustered enough courage to ask Dordi out on a date and they married two years later. They had one son, Brady, who was now married with three children and living in Vancouver, Canada.

She had always dreamed of seeing Norway, and Lyndon could think of no better time to go. The childhood fairy-tales of Trolls and Huldras, the forest witches that could suck the life from a man, had both frightened and fascinated her since her mother told the stories on freezing winter nights.

For some strange and unexplained reason Dordi needed to get Lyndon to the old world. She couldn't explain it to herself but now that he'd suggested it she knew one way or another they needed to go.

"Where will we get the money, Lyn?"

"I've been putting some money by for a few years. I knew it would come in handy someday. Now, how about that vacation?"

Dordi fixed her white hair back into its usual braid, scraping the loose straggly ends into their proper place with the hairpin she held between her teeth. It was her usual way of showing determination in dealing with situations and focusing her mind. She straightened her apron and tied it tight at the back, showing her still slender waist. Her tiny four foot nine frame was dwarfed by Lyndon's six foot two stature as he held her head against his lower chest.

"Let's get to us fixing that vacation."

Chapter 56

Cornwall

THEY PLANNED THEIR TRIP, BOUGHT TICKETS and applied for their passports. The date was set and the two of them left American soil for the first time as they began the initial leg of their trip of a lifetime to Europe and Scandinavia.

The coach made its way through the twisting country lanes of west Cornwall. Dordi sat at the window seat and frequently jumped away in fright as the large coach skimmed the hedgerows and low hanging branches. Eventually they came to a stop at one of the picturesque villages for which Cornwall is famous. Their mildly annoying tour guide had given them a photocopied homemade laminated map of the village with some of the *must see* sights. It was twenty-two degrees outside, but they still wore their coats as they had yet to get acclimatised to the English weather.

Most of the passengers made their way to the nearest toilets and tearooms, but Lyn and Dordi decided to stretch their legs and take a walk to have a look around the village and the church.

They strolled arm in arm up a lane that meandered out of the village then stumbled upon the view looking out over Mounts Bay. From their high vantage point they could see the English Channel as it merged with the wild North Atlantic. The smell of the sea and the rolling of the waves in the distance held them fast for what seemed like an eternity.

Dordi checked her wristwatch. It was 11.22 and the bus was leaving at 11.30, 'on the dot,' as the tour guide had repeatedly stressed.

"Oh my God, Lyn, the bus - we're going to miss the bus!"

Lyn checked his own watch as they both realised their mistake.

"*Craparolla!* Let's go!"

They hurried back towards what they thought was the pickup point of the coach, but got disoriented and took a wrong turn that led them further away from the rendezvous point.

"Which way, Lyn?"

"Let's back up. I think we took a left instead of a right back aways!"

"I hope they don't leave without us?"

The anxiety in Dordi's voice was clearly apparent. Real panic set in on both of them until Lyn had a thought and stopped dead in his tracks.

"You know what, baby? Let's leave it. We're on vacation here. If we have to we can get a cab to the station and grab a train or even stay here for the night. We're in no rush to be anywhere."

The panic immediately left his wife's face as she took a second to remember that they were on what was very likely to be their last vacation together.

"You know what honey, you're right. We can do whatever we like as long as we do it together."

Dordi took her husband by the hand and they ambled down the lane, leaving the coach and the irritating tour guide to their fates. She watched as Lyn kicked pebbles down the narrow road as she admired the rolling green fields and hedgerows. They were walking down what appeared to be a farmer's lane with fresh wheel ruts in the mud leading straight down the trail, when Lyndon caught sight of the rags and ribbons hanging from a tree all roughly at the same level or slightly lower to the ground.

It appeared that a major flood had happened right here in this one spot and deposited all kinds of flotsam around some but not all of the few trees and gorse bushes that grew there.

"Hey, what's over there?" asked Lyndon.

Dordi's gaze followed the direction in which he was pointing.

They made their way through scrub and followed a path

through thicket until they came to the trees with the scraps of cloth and paper tied to the branches. It was there that Dordi noticed a small hand written sign stuck in the ground. *Please leave the Clouties be – they are not souvenirs.*

"What are *Clouties*, Dordi?"

"I'm sure I don't know. I've never heard of such a thing," his wife replied.

It is believed that the *Clouties* or strips of cloth were torn from the part of the body which was affected by illness and were thought to be gifts to the *Naiads* or water nymphs as offerings to cure their ails. As the cloth rots on the branches, so it was said that the illness would disappear with it.

"Maybe it's the rags and pieces of material that's hanging on the branches. I don't see anything else around."

People had left photographs and prayers tied or pinned to some of the lower branches of several of the bushes and nearby trees. Lyndon put on his glasses and crouched down for a closer look. He leant over the stone surrounds that protected the ground from damage as pilgrims visited the site where the well water gently flowed. His gaze was focused on the now faded snapshot of a child, most likely placed there by a parent or relative. It was of a little girl of maybe six of seven years. She had died or been lost he reckoned. There was faded handwriting at the bottom and he crouched down to get a better view of some more of the hand written notes.

Suddenly, Lyn lost his footing and slipped sideways on the muddy ground, ending up thigh high in the waters of the well.

He struggled and grappled for a handhold when the searing pain in his stomach hit! It was as if someone was twisting his intestines around with an invisible fist squeezing at them until they were ready to burst. He gasped for breath holding his stomach and struggling to keep any sort of hold on firmer ground to stop him sliding deeper into the well.

"Dordi! Dordi, help!"

Dordi spun away from the photos she was looking at to see her husband flailing and at the same time trying to protect his stomach. He was growing weaker and more distressed by the second and she thought she would lose him right there and then.

She mustered all her strength and grabbed the shoulders of his jacket. Bracing her foot against the largest stone she could reach she hauled with all her might, and managed to pull him from the water and roll him out onto the grass. Lyndon was now fading into unconsciousness and his breathing had become shallow. She knelt beside him with her hands resting on her knees trying to recover from the effort of hauling a two hundred pound man from the slippery edge of a narrow pool.

"Help! Somebody, help!" she yelled through her gasps.

Dordi was faced with a dilemma. Should she run for help or stay here with Lyn? She reckoned she wouldn't get far, so given her options she sat down and cradled her husband's head in her lap and began to pray. His breathing was laboured and his very life force appeared to be draining away from him before her very eyes. Someone had told her once in conversation that alcoholics can have a moment of clarity when everything just makes simple sense. She now understood what they had meant.

The probability was that her husband was going to die right here in this field. She could feel his dead weight in her arms as his breathing had almost stopped. She knew that sooner rather than later, he was going to die. Which would he prefer? Passing away here in her arms with the English sun on his face, or eaten to the bone with tubes and wires coming out of him at the County Hospital?

Dordi lifted her eyes away from the face of her dying Lyndon and spoke to God as if he was standing right behind her watching them both. Not daring to turn around in case he should leave them, she spoke over her shoulder as if in a plea.

"Lord if you're going take him from me, then take him now, here with me holding him in my arms! If it's your will, just you take him home to you. I'll be just fine here on my own."

She closed her eyes and tried to remember the words of the prayers she had been taught as a child. Most of them evaded her now. She could remember the first few lines of one or two. So she just joined them all into one long prayer and managed as best she could. She took off her jacket and wrapped it around him. She'd read something in the first aid manual they kept in the drawer at the

182

bait shop that another person's body heat was the best thing to raise and maintain someone's temperature. So she curled up beside him on the grass, put her arms around him and tried to stay calm as she stifled back the tears. Maybe someone would come and they could get some help.

It was torture! The thought of just lying here was driving her insane. She began to move away and decided to go with option 'B' and make that run for help. Lyn had lost consciousness and his breathing was becoming even shallower. Now was as good a time as any to make her move. She prepared to manoeuvre his head onto the makeshift pillow of her jacket when Lyndon spoke.

"Ah baby, don't go. It's nice just us two just lying here in the sunshine."

She sat bolt upright and strained her neck in the fast movement! Lyndon was still lying on the grass and resting his head on the pillow she'd placed under him although his eyes remained shut.

"Have you been fakin?"

Her Louisiana accent was more pronounced now that she was seething with anger. Her concern had quickly given way to fury. She scrambled to her feet and she now stood over him with her hands on her hips.

"Oh just shush. I'm still recovering."

"You old bastard! I thought you were dying on me!"

Lyndon sat up and felt at his stomach. The look on his face was a mixture of confusion and surprise at the change in sensation he was feeling. Dordi was stomping around, probably looking for something blunt or heavy to hit him with, he reckoned. He rose to his feet and dusted some of the wet mud off his trousers. His wife was still pacing round in circles and ranting at him and the innocent bushes.

"Dordi, stop!" She continued swearing under her breath and trying her best to ignore him. She thought she might never forgive him! "Dordi, please stop and listen to me. Something's different here, something's happened."

His wife snapped out of her tantrum and concern returned to her face.

"Different? Different, how?"

"I don't know. I feel kinda strange!"

"Can you walk?" she asked.

"Yeah, I think so," came the reply.

"Dordi. This is going to sound really odd, but the pain has gone!"

"The pain's gone! What all of it?"

"Yes, all of it. Give me a minute here to see what happens when I move around some more." Lyn gingerly raised his arms up in the air, hoping that the constant pain in his abdomen would still be absent. He let his arms drop by his sides as a child would. "No. Don't feel a thing. In fact, I feel great!"

"Let's get you back to the town and have you checked over by a doctor."

Chapter **57**

T HE THREE SWIMMERS MADE THEIR WAY BACK towards their respective cars. Elle had yet to mention that for the first time in almost nineteen years, she was pain free from the old injury to her arm and knee. At the time it hadn't been a serious injury but was enough to keep her in plaster of Paris for a couple of months. She hadn't even thought about it for so long that she had to remind herself that it even happened at all.

An old boyfriend had taken years to fully restore a classic motorcycle and was dying to show it off to her when he had finally finished it. He had spent two years and God only knows how much money, sourcing parts and having some custom made in her father's factory. It was his pride and joy and to be fair, even though she had no interest in it, she could appreciate the dedication it took to complete it. Her father loved it; it appealed to his engineering mind as well as the love of anything mechanical and getting his hands dirty again.

He let Ricky use one of the tool rooms in the factory on a regular basis to store and tinker at it at nights and weekends. It was, as she recalled, one of the main things they talked about or more accurately, he talked about for most of their pleasant relationship. Odd how the pain ebbs, but the stupid stuff you still remember. Elle couldn't remember Ricky wearing any other clothes but a maroon Led Zeppelin tee shirt and black jeans.

He never wore the same jeans again. On the first time she had ridden pillion, the engine seized flinging them both on to the road, resulting in her breaking her arm and chipping a bone in her knee and Ricky shredding his beloved jeans and shattering his ankle.

For the whole time that she'd spent in the cast, she hadn't been able to wash the right hand side of her body properly. She would come up with ideas for specially adapted tools to get to the parts of herself she needed to clean. The waste refuge bag tied round her leg taped at the top was a stroke of genius to keep the water out.

Most of her ideas were never that successful, so she spent much of that time sniffing as discreetly as possible under her right armpit to make sure it wasn't smelly. That habit stuck with her for a long time after the break had healed.

Why at a time like this would I remember that? she thought to herself. *Maybe it is the brain's way of handling difficult situations and making something seem normal out of totally abnormal scenarios?*

She had fallen behind the other two and called for them to wait.

"Hey hold up a second you two!"

They carried on either ignoring her or lost in their own thoughts.

"Can you two please slow down and wait for me?"

Eva and Hugh stopped and turned around to see what she wanted.

They hadn't been speaking, just walking silently back to the cars. Eva now looked at her sister.

"What's wrong?"

"Nothing wrong. Just about to add something weird into an otherwise totally normal day!"

"Quit kidding around, Elle. I've had enough strange goings on for one day thanks."

Hugh interjected, "What's wrong Elle?"

All three of them should, by this stage have been considering psychiatric evaluation. An event like this had never happened to anyone before, at least not in recorded history. Maybe whatever the algae had done to heal their bodies had a similar coping mechanism on their minds. It helped them all to deal with what should have been to anyone else, impossible!

"Eva. Do you remember the motorcycle accident I had when I was going out with Ricky Shaw?"

"Of course I do. You tried to talk me into washing your armpits and God only knows what else."

"Yeah, thanks for not being much help there. Anyway, I haven't woken up a day since, without hearing my knee crack or be able to make a fist properly. Until now that is. Look."

She opened and closed her hand, making and remaking a fist.

"It's perfect. It's as though it had never been injured!"

All three stood looking at each other, waiting for someone to speak first. Eva directed her gaze at Hugh.

"What's your take on this, Hugh? What do you think's happening here?"

Hugh took a minute to try to make some logical sense of the day's events. He came to a stop and rested against the dry stone wall.

"Girls, I've given this some thought in the short time since the event, mulling it over and over in my head. There are many words and terms we use today, awesome, magical, epic, etc. I don't have any more of an explanation than you do. However, what I would say is, without being excessively dramatic, the events that have taken place here would be a textbook case of a bona fide, honest-to-God miracle.

"There is simply no other explanation for it. If you take my advice, Elle, I wouldn't go telling too many people about your newly healed arm and knee. Not if you still want to practice law and not end up in secured care. I think we should all go home and get unpleasantly drunk.

"Except for you, Eva. You are the scientist among us and therefore you're the one that needs to get back and try to figure out why we have had our injuries healed. And more to the point how? You were the first to have this healing experience and you think it could be something to do with the algae that grow here. It's our only lead at the minute and you're the only one who can provide us with any real answers. I would ask a question of both of you, if I'm permitted?"

Both girls nodded.

"When I was in the water the pain was unbearable when the algae coated me. Did you two suffer any pain?"

Estelle was the first to answer.

"I thought my arm and knee were on fire from the inside, but I was so focused on you I didn't mention it!"

Hugh then directed his question to Eva.

"How about you, Eva? Any pain from the healing of old injuries?"

Eva had no clue where Hugh was going with his line of questioning but Estelle was beginning to understand. Eva hadn't appeared to be in any distress apart from the initial panic of not being able to move in the water with the rest of them and she was as interested as Hugh to hear what Eva had to say.

Eva could sense that they both needed some answers. She hadn't suffered pain like Hugh or Estelle. She had broken her wrist while roller-skating when she was eleven years old and had to have surgery to realign the damaged bones. So why no pain in the water like the other two? She didn't have a clue.

"I didn't suffer any pain, Hugh, and I don't know why. Estelle knows I broke my wrist once. She had to write the answers to my homework for me."

"How about the time you cut your foot?"

"Yes, lots of pain, but it was still bleeding when I got home that day. I didn't have a conscious dramatic healing experience like you two. Mine took overnight to heal. At least I think it did. I checked then changed the dressing before I had a bath."

"Eva, you hurt your foot on the slipway, you weren't in the water at the time of the injury. You still had it before you had your bath later that night. It appears to me that it was only after you had your bath that your foot healed, which by that rational means that it was contact with the bath water that the healing took place. Sound reasonable to you both?"

No one else had any better answers so Hugh continued.

"If I'm correct, Eva, if you have contact with any water that is contaminated with the same algae that we all had contact with today, it will result in healing of one kind or another. When you got into the bath you would have had the same algae on your skin from the swim earlier. I believe that today was no accidental occurrence. Unknown to you, you made that happen. I am also convinced that there was no intent involved. Your assistant John is right. You are connected to this plant life, no matter how strange that may sound and I firmly believe that for whatever reason you have been blessed with the power to heal. We should all go home and give ourselves some time to digest this. What about we meet up in a couple of days and take it from there? If any of us has any further revelations we want to share, then we are all just a phone call away. Sound good?"

Both Eva and Estelle nodded in agreement.

Estelle hugged her sister and whispered in her ear, "Get some answers for us kiddo."

"I'll do my best."

"I know you will. Call me when you find something."

All the old injuries, even the emotional ones appeared now to be gradually healing.

"I will, I'll give you a call tomorrow or the next day, soon as I find anything out."

They parted and both cars drove along the same road towards home.

Chapter **58**

ELLE CHECKED HER REAR VIEW MIRROR TO SEE if her sister was still following behind. She was now, for obvious reasons, being protective and concerned for her sister's welfare and safety. If these 'events' that had done nothing more than bring her and her sister closer again, then it could only be a good thing.

She understood that Eva was still a little distant and unsure how to handle their relationship. To be honest, she felt the same way herself but any progress was at least progress of sorts.

The past had been tough on both of them. Watching their father fade to a skeleton and the betrayal and the selfish acts of their mother would be enough to drive anyone apart. Elle still stung about it.

Maybe she was just a stronger personality than her late mother, or maybe times had changed. Women more empowered these days and didn't have to depend on the men in their lives handing over their wage packets on Friday nights to feed their family.

"I know I can be a pain in the ass but my heart's good. Unfortunately I wear it on my sleeve a little too often," she mumbled to herself.

"Give her some time. If I'm correct about her healing abilities then this is monumental. It doesn't always have to be on your clock, Elle. Oh and stop talking to yourself, Hugh will think you have Tourette's."

The red traffic light caught her sister on the town bound entrance into Downpatrick and she vanished from her sight. She thought about stopping and waiting for her but dismissed the idea as being over protective and drove slowly and reluctantly on towards home, in the hope that Eva would catch up with her when they both reached the open road.

Chapter **59**

Chicago

CRYSTAL CHANDELIERS HUNG FROM THE HIGH ceilings, projecting twinkling spectrums of light down onto the marble floor of the private hospital. All of it was lost on Kay Kane who was impatiently sitting in the waiting area checking the texts and emails coming through on her Tablet.

The names of her chosen targets were amongst the dead and injured lists she was receiving using intercepted police radio messages fed into her ears by headphone.

She would have to give an interview to the press and news stations as she was now BION's most senior surviving board member under Valentine, so she began making notes on how sorry she was at the pointless loss of life and how her heart went out to the bereaved families.

Yeah, frigging yeah, what a waste of life and talent, blah, blah, blah. Fucking over paid drones that they were, and good riddance to the waste of skin.

Of course, she could not publicly express her true feelings, and the fact that she had orchestrated the whole event.

Valentine was still being treated, so she needed somewhere quiet to prepare a full statement once she had gathered all the relevant information. She would be careful not to say anything other than that she condemned it as a senseless act of terrorism and would pass on her regards to the families and friends of the deceased and injured.

Kay walked over to the reception area where both the

receptionists were busy taking calls and waited for one of them to make eye contact with her. Being ignored was not something she was used to so she stood with her arms folded, tapping her foot on the tiled floor until she ran out of what little patience she possessed.

She leant across the desk and took the telephone out of the girls hand and calmly told the caller to call back later, then slammed the handset down on its mounting.

"Excuse me, ma'am. You can't do that. That was a patient on the line!"

"I need a room. Somewhere quiet where I can make a call."

"Ma'am, if you don't take a seat I'll call security and have you removed immediately!"

"Listen to me," she said, looking down at the girl's name badge, "listen to me now, Becky. I don't want to waste time repeating myself. So you go talk to Miss Thingy, Doctor Rodgers' aide and she can give you the low-down on who you're dealing with. Do it and do it now!" She addressed the second receptionist who now had her full attention. "You, go get me some coffee and an ashtray."

"I'm sorry ma'am but you can't smoke in here, it's a hospital."

"You morons are really beginning to test my resolve. Now contact Doctor Rodgers' aide."

Most people would speed up their words in agitation or redden in the face at having to deal with the 'jobs worth' attitude she was receiving.

Not Kay. She had spent her career dispatching much harder nuts than these two idiots. The first receptionist glared at her as she dialled the extension number.

"Hi Trish, it's Becky from reception here. We have a Miss..." She paused and looked across to Kay who dramatically mouthed the word *Kane*. "We have a Miss Kane demanding a private room to make a call and she told us to.... I'm sorry, say again."

Becky's eyes were now directed up intensely towards Kay. The information she was receiving was leaving her in no doubt the need to supply this individual with anything she desired.

"I see. Yes... I understand, yes, thank you." Becky addressed her colleague, trying to avert her eyes away from the 'I see you've got the message' look from Kay.

"Joan, can you go get that coffee and ashtray now please and have it brought to treatment room three?"

"What? No...you can't smoke in here. It's a hospital!"

Joan had not been privy to the information that Becky had just received; if she had, she wouldn't have questioned her request. There was no time for niceties. All could be explained later.

"Joan! Bring the coffee and the goddamned ashtray!"

Her colleague almost jumped from her seat at the tone of the order and speeded to find what could be used as a makeshift ashtray.

Chapter **60**

VALENTINE LAY BACK ON THE HOSPITAL BED as the attending nurse cleaned the dust from around his face and applied sterile gauze over his eyes, then allowed him to settle down while Doctor Rodgers made several internal calls for a specialist to be contacted if needed.

Harmony wasn't taking any chances with this patient. She entered the treatment room and approached his side. She gave instructions to the nurse attending on what she may need for the preliminary examination.

He seemed like an okay sort of guy; unlike the Witch that he chose to keep at his side. She placed her hand on his shoulder after introducing herself to make him aware that she was about to examine him.

"Now, Mr. Sere, I'm just going to remove the gauze and have a look at your eyes. You hold on to my arm and if you find it too uncomfortable just squeeze it and tell me to stop, OK?"

Valentine took hold of her arm waiting for the pain to intensify once the dressings were gone. She removed the dressing, first over his right eye looking for any remaining foreign objects or superficial damage to the areas around the ocular orbits.

The skin around the right eye was scalded and his eyelashes had been burned away but apart from minor scratches and lacerations, there was no significant damage. Then she turned her attention to his left eye.

He kept his eyes closed tight, afraid to open them to the

painful white light. The remains of soot and dust covered his face. His hair had been singed and the smell of the blast and burnt fabric from his clothing lingered in the air.

"Can you open your eyes as wide as you can for me please Mister Sere?"

Valentine attempted to open his dominant right eye, but the pain from the overhead theatre light was akin to looking directly into the sun. Harmony knew instantly that this was much more serious than a simple trauma to the surface of the eye. There was some sort of coating that gave the appearance of a cataract but appeared much denser and harder than normal tissue. She was able to touch the sensitive outer layer of his eyeball with the end of her light pen without him noticing.

"Okay that's fine, Mr. Sere. Could you try to open the other eye for me now, please?"

Valentine forced himself to open his left eye but again the pain was still too intense.

"Let me dim the lights a little and we can take another look for you sir."

She gave a signal to the nurse who adjusted the lights to half of normal illumination.

"I'm going to shine a light pen into your eyes, Mr. Sere. It shouldn't be too uncomfortable for you this time."

Valentine squirmed as Harmony now directed the light of the pen into his right eye.

"Okay that's fine, Mr. Sere, now the left again."

Valentines eyes streamed with tears as the light from the pens beam burned into his eye. The same basic retinal test was repeated on the left eye. She could see by the now dull reflections coming from both of his eyes, it was clear that they appeared to have somehow been riddled with thousands of tiny microscopic shards of metal.

What initially seemed to be a burned layer of the eye's surface, now gave the appearance of them having been dipped in molten lead, with tiny patches of bloodshot ocular tissue interspersed between the metal coating. She had never seen anything like it before. She was no expert, but if this patient retained any of his sight, it would be a miracle. It chilled her to the bone to even look into them. *Pity*, she thought. *Good looking guy.*

"One more test, Mr. Sere." Harmony held her finger up in front of Valentine. "If you can, follow my finger for me please?" She moved her finger back and forward in front of his eyes. If they were moving, she couldn't see it. All she could see was a dull reflection of the examination light reflecting back from where his pupils and iris should be!

"Okay, that's fine, Mr. Sere. If you'd like to lie back and relax I'll give you a little something for the pain. Jaclyn here will be your nurse and look after you until I make a phone call. I'm not an eye specialist so I would like an expert to give a second opinion. Jaclyn, please rinse out Mr. Sere's eyes with some saline solution and put some drops in for the pain. Okay? I'm going to speak to a colleague of mine over at St Joseph's General. He's the best man to have a look at your eyes for you. Let me call him and have him come over."

"What's wrong? What going on with my sight doctor?"

"You have some debris in your eyes sir and I need a specialist to check you over. Now I know it's difficult, but try to relax. As I said, Jaclyn here will take good care of you."

She gestured for the nurse to carry out the saline rinse and administer the sedative. Jaclyn Gates had been a nurse in General Medicine for thirty years. She'd worked the weekend and graveyard shifts in A&E for the last five years in the Jacobi Medical Centre in the Bronx, New York City; it was listed as one of the most dangerous environments in the world, to nurse or treat patients. She now held the senior sisters position at the private clinic. She knew Harmony had taken a risk when she had employed her. Not many would as she had officially only ten and a bit years to retirement but her triage skills and experience were the best. The pay and the hours were infinitely better, she got a pension, dental and every other weekend off and, up to this point, no one had pointed a gun in her face.

She approached the patient with the trolley containing the saline solution, cotton pads and the morphine syringe. They were all laid out neatly on the sterile green paper that covered its surface.

197

Harmony Rodgers stood aside as her best nurse prepared the saline wash.

She knew she was her most experienced nurse on the staff and had just about seen it all over the years. Jaclyn got busy with the business at hand. She spoke gently to Valentine and put her hand on his shoulder to let him know she was about to begin the procedure.

"Now, Mr. Sere, I've kept the lights down and I want to get some wash into your eyes if that's okay with you?"

Valentine nodded his head to show that he understood, tears still streaming from the corners of his eyes and rolling down his cheeks. He lay still keeping his eyes closed and away from pain and discomfort for as long as he could.

She rested the kidney dish by his chest and brought the dropper full of saline water up above his damaged eyes. As she carefully prised open his eye to apply the rinse she unconsciously took a step backward, dropping the saline rinse down his shirt and then watched as the dropper rolled under the bed.

She turned to look at Doctor Rodgers in confusion. She was totally bewildered and seeking some reassurance that her own eyes weren't deceiving her. Harmony Rodgers stared back and shook her head; nodding in joint amazement. She gestured for her to continue and pointed to outside, holding five fingers up and mouthed five minutes.

Jaclyn accepted the fact that this was a real situation and not some bizarre prank and tried as best she could to carry on with the procedure. Trying to stop her hands from shaking as she dripped what was left of saline solution into Valentines damaged eyes.

The metal shards that had partially covered the patient's corneas were now becoming ever more disturbing. The foreign objects were beginning to completely cover the entire surface of his right and left eye as she watched in morbid fascination.

There was no visible sign of the pupil or iris now present in either eye. They appeared to be independent from the patient, seeming, as if it were even possible, to have a will of their own, responding independently of the demands of the casualty.

They tracked her movements as she moved and she felt as if

they were penetrating deep into her soul. She could make out her own reflection in their surface. She knew he was almost unconscious with the morphine she had quickly administered and he lay on the bed sleeping.

His heart monitor told her he was out cold but the metal coverings on the eyes were fully alert and aware of her still standing over him. The colour had changed to a metallic dark green that she could only translate as being in no present danger.

The surfaces rippled like emerald mercury. It was beyond impossible!

She finished up and left the treatment room as fast as she could without alarming the patient, then raced down the corridor and flung open the release bar on the fire door to exit the building. The fresh hot air and sunlight gave her welcome relief from the vision she had been witness to and reminded her that she wasn't in some frightening daydream.

Harmony was waiting for her outside.

"What the hell's going on?"

She was frightened out of her wits and dispensed with formalities.

"Have you ever seen anything like that?"

"Give me a minute, I need a smoke. Let's get some air."

They both walked out into the rear service area of the clinic. Jaclyn took the pack of cigarettes from her trouser pocket and was about to light up.

"Could I have one of those?"

"I didn't know you smoked!"

"I didn't, until now."

The last cigarette Harmony smoked was dipped in 'poppers' at high school. She threw up for hours and hadn't even thought of trying one again until now. The smoke filled her lungs and she coughed at the first drag.

"You okay?" asked Jaclyn.

"Yeah, just need some practice."

The nicotine hit her system and ran down her arms and into her fingers. Her head spun as she steadied herself against the Italian scooter that was parked illegally in one the loading bays.

"Who owns this thing? They ought to know they can't leave it here?"

"It's mine. And to answer your earlier question, no Harmony. No one has ever seen anything like that. The metal shards in his eyes seem...don't tell me I'm crazy...but his eyes now look like mirrored surfaces. That guy looks like his aviator sunglasses have melted onto his eyes. When I did the initial exam I thought I was going nuts! Sorry for dragging you in, but I needed someone measured and with your experience to verify what I was seeing."

"Any idea how to treat him?"

"No. I've contacted Ted Duval over at Saint Josephs. He's the best ocular surgeon in the county. He's just out of theatre and will come over soon as he finishes up."

As he lay immobile, Valentine had unwillingly been witness to all the sins and past failings of his medical attendants. He saw in his mind the letter that Harmony had written and secretly delivered to the offices of the Eastern medical board alleging that her former business partner had been guilty of negligence and behaviour unbecoming of a doctor, resulting in him being struck off the medical register. And all as revenge for him ending their brief affair and his decision to stay, instead, with his wife and family rather than make a new life with her.

He saw Jaclyn's stepdaughter plead with her not to tell her father that she was pregnant to a coloured boy of thirteen. The threat was enough for her to agree to an abortion that had been performed by a back street butcher paid for by her. The child subsequently contracted an infection in her uterus; rendering her sterile and incapable of having children in the future. Valentine struggled with the litany of sins and mistakes that were being drilled into his conscious mind by his new ability thanks to whatever substance that unknown to him, Kay Kane had infected him with through the simple act of holding his hand at the funeral.

The one image that kept trying to fight its way back into the forefront of his mind was tantalisingly close but he couldn't quite grasp it. There was something...something else about the nurse Jaclyn that had been treating him, something that he somehow knew was important. It was like trying to remember the name of something familiar but no matter how he tried, he frustratingly just couldn't quite grasp it. He was sure he'd never met her before, but still…

The bombardment of images took over again and any chance he had of remembering was gone. He lay on the trolley, now fully awake mouthing silent pleas to any God who would listen. Praying for the orchestra of nightmare images to end and never return. This was the most horrendous and lucid nightmare he had ever had.

Chapter *61*

Belfast

OR THE FIRST TIME IN MORE YEARS THAN SHE could remember, Audrey drove herself to the Medical Centre. She had a 9.30am appointment with Doctor Payne. Her usual doctor was on annual leave. Audrey Walsh couldn't care less.

Feeling fit and well, she parked the car in a space as far away from those reserved for disabled drivers that she could find. The sun was shining and the birds were happily chirping in the trees. She walked with a long-lost spring in her step as she entered the surgery and approached the reception desk. There was already a queue in the waiting room and it had only turned 8.40am. The receptionist greeted her as if she were a family member.

"Morning Audrey! How are you feeling this morning?"

"Couldn't be better, Laura. How are those grandkids of yours?"

Laura McCartney took a second to figure out that all wasn't quite right.

She couldn't just yet put her finger on it, so continued to make small talk while she tried to work out the changes in Audrey.

"I was looking after them all weekend while our Tina was on a Hen do with her pals. I think she's still in a blind mess after it.

"Oh my God, Audrey. Sorry about the blind remark."

"Never think a thing about it, Laura."

"Who's this new Doctor I'm seeing this morning?"

The poignant use of that term had never before held any

gravity with her. Seeing anyone or anything was a recent and welcome blessing.

"You're with the dazzlingly bright 'Doctor James E. Payne', as he likes to be continually referred to. He's just three years out of medical school and thinks he can cure cancer, a pain in the arse, with all the personality of a dry roasted peanut. The most interesting thing about him is that he's fat and bald. Call him Doctor at every opportunity and he will write you a prescription for anything. You can see me again when he's treated you. Christ Almighty, there I go again with sight references."

Audrey began to laugh when she saw the expression on Laura's face.

"You're all right Laura, don't worry at all. I'm not offended. Now take me to your healer."

Laura came around the desk as usual to lead Audrey to the examination room. She linked her arm to steer her safely away from any obstacles or danger, then began to pick intensely at her nose then scrutinising the results of the damp nasal matter that she had successfully retrieved from it. It wasn't as if anyone was going to notice.

She threw the ball of snot on the corridor carpet then knocked on the surgery door before opening it.

"Doctor this is Mrs. Walsh to see you."

"Good morning, Mrs. Walsh. Please come in and take a seat. What can I do for you?"

"Good morning, Doctor."

Laura was just about to close the door when Audrey turned back to her and remarked, "For a second there Laura I thought your head was going to cave in, you were picking that hard at your nose. Some of these days you'll pick your brains out altogether."

Laura McCartney stood speechless. There was no reply to the statement that she could think of. She simply stared at Audrey in bewilderment then continued to close the door behind her. She guiltily checked her finger on the way back to her post, then took the precaution of wiping it on the front of her apron and tried her best to carry on as normal with the rest of the patients still waiting in reception.

Doctor James E. Payne gave a quizzical look at the odd exchange between the two women then checked over Audrey's notes. As he did so, Audrey scanned the medical room, staring at the array of instruments that lay on top of the Doctor's desk. She had never seen a smart phone before and wondered what it could be? Maybe some new medical device?

"Well, Mrs. Walsh. You appear to have been managing your condition well, so what brings you to see me this morning?"

"I'd like a check –up, if you have the time please, Doctor?"

"Of course. Anything in particular on your mind?"

"If you could have a look at my eyes I would be more than grateful," replied Audrey, who was about to become one of the most sought after human beings on the planet and she had absolutely no idea that her life would now soon be in danger!

Chapter **62**

E VA WALKED INTO THE LAB, THIS TIME WITHOUT the usual Monday morning coffees or the playful banter with her colleagues. She hung her coat on the stand, switched her phone to silent and sat it down on her desk.

John Greer stood at the entrance of her half opened door; he tapped gently to let her know he was waiting.

"Oh hi, John. Do you have the test samples ready?" asked Eva.

"All ready to go," he replied.

"Let's go then, we have a pile of work to do and I want some answers."

They both left her office and headed for the lab.

John had all the test subjects laid out in order on the bench. He had labelled and dated each one with the substances he had used to test them. He had deliberately separated one of the samples from the rest. He rechecked what he already knew but needed to make sure there had been total annihilation of the subject before presenting it to Eva. It was now dried out, a grey powder at the bottom of the test tube. It would be impossible for any kind of cellular reconstruction to take place.

Eva donned her white lab coat and approached the workbench. There was a massive array of equipment at their disposal ranging from expensive diagnostic hardware to the usual assortment of test tubes, microscopes and computer monitors. The lab was used for initial specimen diagnostics. If the results they produced today justified it, more extensive tests would be carried out in Portaferry.

She could sense Greer's anticipation; he walked closely behind her at a slightly uncomfortable distance. She chose to ignore it for the time being and carried on with her work.

"Have you seen or checked any of the samples since we carried out the tests on Friday?" she asked

"Umm, I popped back in on Friday night to have a sneaky look."

"Really? Why was that?" she asked.

"I love my work," he said sarcastically, trying to mask his genuine excitement and fascination.

"Was there any noticeable change?"

"Nothing unexpected. The neutral test in distilled water showed no visible differences as expected. However the test subjects in both the acid vinegar and pure alcohol were presenting with partial tissue break down and limited cellular separation."

"How were they this morning?"

"Again, as expected. The neutral test showed little change. However the other two samples had experienced substantial cellular damage and in the case of the acid vinegar, bleaching and more ad-vanced stages of cellular destruction."

"Let's have a look. It's been almost thirty hours."

As they both sat down at the workstation Greer started to laugh, he was almost hysterical with excitement! All three of the samples where now restored to perfect health. Eva had to tell him to shut up as she raised the sample in the vinegar solution to smell it. There was no doubt in his or her minds. These samples should be dead or dying.

However the cold fact was, they were now better than healthy and happily blooming.

"John, are you absolutely sure you haven't tampered with any of these just to play one of your stupid childish bloody pranks?"

"Listen, boss. No way! You know it as well as I do, but if we are in any doubt I have one more sample to test."

"Let's get it in then."

Eva was trying to hold herself together.

"Just stay focused, girl. Let the science supply you with the answers."

She picked up the sample with the vinegar solution and put it to her nose and there was no doubting the familiar smell of the acid.

Greer returned with the last algae sample and held it out for Eva to inspect. Nothing had changed. She almost cried with relief as the dead algae were still grey powder at the bottom of the tube.

"See? I knew it was some kind of unexplained phenomenon. There has to be something we're missing. I don't know what it is yet, but I will. Hey, it could be any combination of things. Even the perfume I'm wearing. God only knows?"

She knew he wouldn't buy it. Why would he? Even she herself didn't buy it and she was the one who had said it.

John stood gnawing at the inside of his cheek. If he was right, then there would be no doubt of a direct connection between Eva and the algae. He reached over the bench, handing the final sample to Eva.

"Here, hold this. I want to try something."

He lifted some distilled water from the plastic container on the bench and poured a little into the tube Eva was holding. As the water level rose the algae came back to life like a green blancmange, bubbling up over the edge of the tube. She ran to the bench at the window and placed the test tube in its holder, trying to set it down to avoid any of the substance touching her skin.

John flopped into the seat speechless.

"I've never ever seen anything like that before."

Chapter **63**

GREER WALKED OVER TO THE TEST SAMPLE, cleaned the excess algae from the outer surface and lifted it out of its holder to inspect it. He took some litmus paper from one of the drawers and dipped it into the test tube. The result was almost as staggering as the event itself. Neutral colour, non-acidic, nothing. If anything, it was slightly alkaline. It would appear that the plant itself had neutralised the corrosive acid.

Greer took a swab from the rim of the test tube and put it under the microscope. As he looked down the lens he could see that there had been complete cellular reconstruction; the chlorophyll was photosynthesising before his eyes. By some miracle, the sample had come back to life! He raised his head from the scope and turned to Eva.

"You need to have a look at this Eva. It's impossible."

Greer stood and gave Eva his seat at the microscope. He was correct. The cell regeneration was like something out of a sci-fi movie. She had never seen anything like it before.

"I'm starting to get scared here, Johnny, and I'm clean out of ideas. What are your thoughts, if any?"

"My thoughts are, as unlikely and bizarre as it seems, there is no further doubt in my mind that there is a direct connection between you and this species of plant. I submersed that test sample in hydrochloric acid and watched it reduce to ashes. I even watched the smoke rise from the tube. I took photographs and put them on the computer desktop for future research. Nothing organic or cell-based could have in any way survived that, nothing, not from this world anyway. I'm an academic like you, Eva. I simply have no explanation yet as to what's going on.

"However, I think you and I should order in some food and prepare for a long night. I'm not leaving this building until I get some answers. My God, what if we've stumbled onto an indestructible regenerative new species. Think of the connotations! Bollocks, think of the money. An indestructible plant that can sustain itself under any conditions. If we could synthesise its DNA we could end global famine.

"Just think of the applications. This thing could be the biggest scientific find since they discovered the earth was round. Bigger actually! If we can get rid of some of the solid vegetable matter in the algae and purify the remaining liquid, then we can test it on a subject. If we use the samples we have and employ a neutral carrier. We can concentrate the samples in the centrifuge. At least it will tell us if this is just a freak occurrence or an entirely new species."

Eva was still attempting to absorb some of the information that Greer was suggesting. If she was in some way connected to this material like Estelle had said, how would or could that be used and just as importantly: why her?

His research was indicating that the test subject did not regenerate without being directly in her presence. She took a while to compute that thought. John was already purifying some of the first test batches. Her head was spinning faster than the centrifuge.

As Eva busied herself with the preparations and made case study notes to distract her from the reality of what was happening, Greer was thinking of his Nobel prize speech and wondering where he would buy the first of his many mansions.

"Okay, we have a sample ready boss."

Eva thought about what to do then replied, "It's your show Johnny; you've done all the donkey work."

The truth was she was afraid of what may happen. This was now becoming not just life changing but possibly world changing work and right now, that was just too big and too scary for her to contemplate.

John set up the remote camera to record the experiment then drew some of the liquid up into a syringe, forcing the plunger to get rid of any air bubbles. He then looked around for something to use it on. He spotted the dead spider plant that no one had bothered to feed or water, sitting on the window ledge.

"This is as good a first test as any boss. Are you ready?"

Eva nodded, indicating that he carry on, secretly not wanting any reaction from the injection of the liquid.

He plunged the needle into the base of the dead plant and waited for the miracle to happen. He stood back as if he'd lit the fuse on a firework. The anticipation on his face would have been comical if it hadn't been so serious.

He checked his watch then checked the plant. Nothing.

Greer rechecked his watch. One minute had passed and still no reaction. He looked at Eva hoping for an answer she didn't have.

"What do you think, boss?"

"I think you're an idiot and stop calling me boss! This is, as I suspected, a fluke, a red herring, for God's sake. What did you really think was going to happen?"

She felt guilty. Unlike Greer, she had inwardly been hoping for no reaction. But his disappointment was clear; he looked like a scolded child. The Noble prize and the house on Lake Como were vanishing before his eyes.

"I don't know. You saw what happened when we added the water to the acid sample. Wait, what are we thinking of, we haven't added the water."

He threw the plastic syringe down into the metal basin and ran the water faucet, filled a beaker with water, almost spilling it as he hurried back.

This time he didn't wait for any instructions from Eva, but poured the water into the dry earth filled pot containing the dead plant.

The result was instant. The colour immediately began to return to the plant. Its leaves straightened and opened and it even began to produce a flower. It appeared like he was watching a time capture photograph happening right here in real time in front of his eyes. They both heard the glass smash as the beaker slipped from his hand and hit the floor!

They stared down at the broken glass then back to the plant. He turned again to Eva.

"I can't believe what I'm seeing. Can you believe what we're seeing? What have we got here, Eva?"

"Listen, John. We have to stay calm and measured until we do further tests. Just take a second and think of the consequences to both of us if this pans out. If you're right and this thing doesn't work without me what will happen then? We have to keep it between you, me and these four walls. It cannot, I repeat, cannot get out. It could not only destroy us professionally, but possibly put us in danger!" said Eva, her face, panic stricken. "Just think about it please! This is very early days, with heaps and heaps of work to do. Now let's calm down and get a research plan of action figured out. Okay? John. Okay?"

"Okay, plan right. What's first?"

Greer was still trying to absorb what they were dealing with but he was finding it difficult to concentrate. He lacked Eva's patience and was almost dancing with excitement. Eva decided to inject some sobriety into the situation.

"John if you think you will have trouble dealing with this, I can talk to the head of staff and have you reassigned."

"What? No! You can't! Not on this one, Eva. No way!"

"Well, okay then. Let's focus on the task in hand and get on with it, shall we?"

The thought of being shut out of the discovery of the millennium snapped him back to his senses. He sat down at the computer and opened a new project file. He then refreshed all the research on the algae thus far and entered the new data including photographs, film footage and images of the experiments with the acid and the injecting of the spider plant. He saved what he had and downloaded it onto a memory stick. *God knows*, he thought, *Can't be too careful.* The stick was put in his drawer and locked. He had the only key and he would keep it that way.

Chapter 64

A GREAT DEAL OF CARE WOULD BE NEEDED with her next delicate task. Kay walked carefully over to the basin in the private room she had so rudely commandeered. She raised her hands up to the lamp and inspected them. The outer skin that she had sprayed on after the contact with Valentine was still intact.

It was difficult to see the transparent membranes; the first layer on her right hand was covered in the formula she had received with the instructions. The second was applied over the first to seal the chemical after it had done its work on Valentine, by what was disguised as a container of sanitising foam that she pretended to sterilise her hands with before washing out Valentine's eyes in the back of the car. She had hoped the protective drying foam membrane had a neutralising effect on the formula as well as offering protection.

The instructions that had arrived with the package had been direct and simple.

There were three containers; the first an aerosol based solution that she surmised to be a protective Lycra coating. The second and third contained the protagonist and the neutraliser both housed in grey unremarkable tubes.

The directions were specific:

1-Apply the protective spray covering all areas of the hands.

2-Apply the protagonist immediately after applying the

protective spray.

3-Perform the required task by making direct skin to skin contact with Valentine Sere.

4-Apply the foam sealant to stop the protagonist then remove all layers using running water.

If she had been in doubt, the all too familiar symbol that was placed across the sealed folds of the package had left her assured of the sender.

The anonymous benefactor that had guided her to her current lofty position in BION had never asked her to do anything that would put her in danger up to this point and the requests had always been of direct benefit to her. Coating Valentine's hand with what she assumed was a chemical of some kind wouldn't lead the police or law enforcement agencies to her in the unlikely event that he should come to any harm.

Whatever her role was, it was not a simple assassination that could be performed by any hired thug. No. Whatever purpose and reason for her career going beyond this point, it wouldn't end with the death of Valentine Sere.

Both membranes were applied using an almost odourless pump spray. No sound and only the faintest of aromas could be detected during their application. She now reapplied what she hoped was neutralising foam as double protection. *Here comes the tricky part,* she thought. *If one molecule of that filth hits my skin I could be it serious trouble.* She had no idea of what it was composed of and had no intention of finding out!

She looked around the shelves and trolleys in the treatment room and found a plastic tongue depressor. She moved her hand back under the lamp and very gently eased the tip under the membrane nearest the skin at the front of her wrist and below the heel of her right hand. She then used the depressor as a lever to hold the covering away from her bare skin without tearing it, as she gingerly manoeuvred both hands over to the lever to run the water faucet.

She cursed herself for her own stupidity of not turning the water on previously, now making the removal of the coatings a trickier task and even more dangerous.

Using the index finger of her right hand she managed to turn on the cold tap to a trickle and held the opening under it. The material began to slowly expand as the water seeped down to the ends of the latex creating finger sized water balloons. It created just enough room for her to remove the hand covering with the depressor and drop both into the basin. A bead of sweat had rolled down her nose and followed the transparent skin down into the sink. It lay like a see-through snakeskin.

As she increased the water pressure, the membrane dissolved completely and disappeared down the waste pipe, leaving the plastic tongue depressor circling in the swirling water. She did the same on her left hand. She moved across the room and sat up on the bed swinging her legs like a child, at the same time lighting a cigarette and dialling a number on her phone.

Finally the call was answered. The male voice on the other end spoke almost in a whisper.

"Is it done?"

"It's done."

There was silence on the other end of the line until she posed the idiotic question, "May I assume that you attended Rachel Cohen's funeral service today? I trust you were not harmed during the event?"

There was a long pause.

"Harmed?"

"Harmed, yes?"

The continuing silence from the other end of the line caused her heart to race with panic. This was the most dangerous of people, someone who could end her world at the snap of a finger. She became increasingly nervous and mentally chastised herself for asking such a stupid question. After what seemed a lifetime the silence broke.

"No child, I was not harmed."

"I'm pleased about that."

Her reply was equally as pointless and idiotic as her question. These people didn't do small talk.

This person had no concept of joy or pleasure, only pain and ambition. They had never met in person and she had no desire to ever do so. They had been charting her career since she left college.

Kay came from a humble background. Her parents, juggling two jobs, had saved their money to buy their only daughter the best education that they could afford. The first contact she had with her benefactors was when she wrote a thesis as part of her degree on the positive results, if unpleasant and dreadful, of the medical advances gained through experimentation on inmates of the concentration camps during World War Two by the Nazis. One week after submitting the paper, her and her parent's debts were paid off and an arrangement was made for a retainer for her services to be paid annually. She had tried to find the source of the money but came up blank each time she investigated.

Her parents were grateful for the help. They assumed, as no contract or binding documents had preceded the monthly donations, that they may have been sent by a long lost friend or relative who preferred to remain anonymous.

Over the years the odd request would come for her to provide contacts or bits of, in her view, pointless and/or harmless information that neither troubled her morally nor physically. There was however an eventuality. Back when she was ascending the corporate ladder by means of her own merits and abilities, a male colleague had mistaken her then charming ways as an invitation to behave inappropriately.

When at an office Christmas party he drunkenly forced himself on her in one of the unoccupied offices, she fought him off, biting hard on his lip until it bled. He slapped her hard enough across the face to leave her bruised and swollen and having to make excuses to her parents that she had been mugged on the train and her purse stolen. No one had been witness to the assault but her.

Two days later they found his naked body hanging from a lamppost on the freeway. It was later confirmed as suicide, as a note in his handwriting had been extracted from his rectum during the post-mortem. It explained why he had become a serial rapist and this was the only way he felt that he could atone for his past sins after finding salvation through religion. Kay received a telephone call from her benefactor apologising for her assault and hoping that

215

she had been satisfied with the retribution. It was then that she had the opportunity to end the relationship but she declined. She liked the idea that she had a guardian Angel to protect her from harm with the benefits of having little or no personal cost to her.

Over the years, many more brutal executions were carried out against anyone who got in her way in her rise to corporate favour. She was a clever girl. She understood that the people who were protecting and guiding her would have no hesitation in carrying out similar atrocities on her or people that she cared about if she was ever foolish enough to cross them.

The line went dead and she exhaled noisily; relieved that the brief conversation had ended. Kay chastised herself out loud, "What the hell were you thinking of trying to engage in small talk with them? Do not, under any circumstances, ever do that again!"

She continued scolding herself until her heart rate slowed down to nearly normal. It was true when they say that saying a little is better than saying a lot. The worst parts of the conversation for her had been the pauses between sentences. She could imagine the caller on the other end looking down at his fingernails deciding whether to call for a manicurist or an executioner. Sweat still gathered on her brow and she took another deep drag on her cigarette. She wiped the sweat away with her finger, flicking the moisture across the room, then ground her cigarette out on the floor, not bothering with the ashtray. She was desperate for some fresh air. She left the room and made her way to a bench outside, took a seat and lit another cigarette. It had been a long, trying but fruitful day. *Better check on the patient and see how he's doing, bless him.*

Chapter **65**

T HE NATURE OF THE INJURIES THE PATIENT HAD sustained was explained to Ted Duval by Harmony as they walked down the corridor on the way to Valentines treatment room. Ted read the notes regarding the initial diagnosis, flipping the pages over the top of the clipboard.

"This isn't looking good Harmony. Has he retained any of his vision?"

"I wouldn't want to influence your prognosis Ted. I think it's best you just take a look yourself."

"That's not the Harmony I know. You generally get ninety-nine percent of things right."

"This patient was in the terrorist attack on the BION board members at the funeral of Rachel Cohen this morning. He's the son of the bigwig and I need the best in the business to treat him, Ted. You're the best in the profession, so please help. I'm way out of my league."

Ted Duval got the message and went straight to business.

"Okay let's go take a look at him."

Harmony turned to address her senior nurse.

"Jaclyn. Would you bring Doctor Duval to the treatment room to see Mr. Sere, please?"

It was a hollow request; she never wanted to look into those eyes again as long as she lived.

Jaclyn was of the same mind, but Harmony paid her wages. She knocked on the door of Valentine's room and entered.

"Mr. Sere. This is Doctor Duval. He would like to examine your eyes. Is that okay?"

Valentine nodded. Ted introduced himself then approached the basin to wash his hands. It was his usual procedure. He removed his glasses from his breast pocket, put them on, and stood over Valentine drying his hands on a paper towel.

"Now, Mr. Sere, let's see what we can do for you."

He matter-of-factly removed the gauze nearest him and momentarily lost himself in the mirror finish on the surface of the patient's eye.

His brain and years of practice wouldn't allow him to register what his own trained eyes were telling him. The next bit happened so quickly that he doubted his own sanity.

Valentines eye returned to normal. The metal appeared to change from its greenish mercury state and was absorbed into the back of his eye.

He did the same to the other eye, but it too was normal when he removed the gauze. Ted Duval stood over his patient and directed the beam of his penlight into each eye, stalling for time until he gathered himself enough to appear unfazed at what he had witnessed. The light from the penlight shook as his hand trembled. After the examination, Ted Duval pretended to re-scan his notes, to give himself enough time to come up with an answer to what he knew the patient was certain to ask. Valentine tentatively asked Ted for his opinion, not sure if he was prepared for what could be bad news.

"What do you think, Doctor?"

Ted almost jumped in fright. His mind was still processing what he had witnessed. He desperately tried to be professional.

"What do I think? So far I don't see any permanent damage but let's get you up and have a better look."

Ted Duval had no idea. If this was some kind of practical joke they must have used some of the best *FX* guys in Hollywood on it because it was the most convincing special effects he had ever seen.

Ted guided Valentine up from the gurney and led him across to the chair where he could pretend to examine him further.

It was a mixture of dread and professional fascination. He performed a series of routine tests, but apart from the initial observation, he could see no indication of trauma or damage to the eyes themselves. There were surrounding superficial abrasions that should heal within a week to ten days. He knew he also wanted to get the hell out of this room as fast as he could!

"Okay that seems fine, Mr. Sere. I see no indication of any permanent damage. I think some rest for the next week or so should sort you out. I'm going to have some dressings put over your eyes to let them recover fully. Harmony will supply you with eye-drops and antiseptic ointment for the scalds around your eyes and give you the instructions on how to use them. I don't see any need for me to see you again. However, if you have any complications or concerns I'd be happy for you to call me. You can get my number from Harmony," he lied.

Truth was he would rather go blind himself than see this guy or look into those eyes again. He felt that he had been violated in some strange way for a moment or two.

He left the treatment room and made his way to the exit. He was in shock and wanted to put as much distance between himself and the clinic, as quickly as he possibly could. Harmony saw him attempt to leave and caught up with him as he exited the building.

"Ted! Ted, wait! Were you going to just leave without a word?"

"Look Harmony. Your patient is fine. There was no damage done to either his short or long term sight."

"Did you notice anything unusual?"

Ted knew that Harmony must have witnessed the same thing as him. He really didn't care. Denial was as good a course as any at this juncture and he wasn't prepared to discuss it in a public car park.

"*Unusual*, in what way?"

What he did know was what he saw could not be explained and if he tried to, he may well lose his license to practice medicine, in this State anyway.

"Unusual, bizarre, out of the ordinary. Come on, Ted, I'm utterly baffled and frankly scared. That woman Kane who brought him in is an evil bitch and if I don't have some answers for her, God knows what she'll do."

Ted Duval was in conflict between telling the truth and fleeing.

He could see his car parked twenty feet away and seriously gave thought to making a run for it.

Ted and Harmony had a very brief romance when they were in medical school. They had parted friends and stayed in touch over the years. If he could talk to anyone it would probably be her.

"Okay Harmony. What was your initial evaluation of the patient?"

"Cuts and minor lacerations around ocular sockets. Localised scorching. Nothing life threatening."

"Is that all?"

He was fishing, and he wasn't going to commit to the event until she did. By the looks of things she was doing the same.

Harmony was stalling for time, trying to come up with a sane explanation. She couldn't. She was also desperate to have someone who wasn't in the clinic when the casualty arrived to give a second opinion that may make sense of things. She decided that telling the truth was her only option. This man may think she was insane but she had little choice. She described the whole examination and the opinion of her most experienced senior nursing sister.

Ted listened carefully to her recount of the morning's events without saying a word. He looked her straight in the eye and said only two words.

"I concur."

"You concur?"

"I concur," Ted repeated.

"You concur with what exactly, Ted? Do you concur with the fact that a casualty was brought in here with catastrophic ocular trauma, or the fact that his eyes turned into liquid metal? I saw every sin I ever committed flash across those eyes, from lifting my skirt in first grade to show Tommy Scott my panties to lying to my mom about sleeping with my first boyfriend. So what the actual fuck do you concur with Ted?"

Harmony needed to hear affirmation from someone she trusted but Ted was deliberately being evasive. Who knows what he had seen in there. Her temper was officially being lost.

Ted Duval rarely got himself in hard to get out of situations. He always had a metaphorical back door to open, but not this time.

"Okay Harmony. I saw what you and your nurse saw. However your patient is no longer presenting with any signs of trauma. I just hope that you're able to get him the hell out of your clinic as fast as your professional courtesy will allow. If I were you, and I'm glad I'm not by the way, I would go inside and tell the charming Miss Kane that the dressings over the patients eyes are under no circumstances to be removed for at least four days. Give her some eye drops, ointment and a box of placebos.

"I would then put as much distance between you, Mr. Sere and his evil sidekick as I could. I for one never want to see him again. If these folk are tinkering with some new product they're developing, then heaven help them. This goes against everything that we were taught in medical school.

"To be honest, if what I saw looking into those eyes of his ever came to fruition, I wouldn't want to meet either her or him ever again. If I were you, I would call the realtor, withdraw whatever money you have instant access to, then phone in sick tomorrow and book a vacation somewhere in India, or even better Afghanistan. At least you could wear a *Burka!* Goodbye Harmony and please don't try to call!"

Harmony watched him leave long dark lines on the road surface as he screeched the tyres of his Porsche leaving the car park.

Afghanistan?

Good idea. I really haven't travelled enough!

Chapter 66

FOR THE FIRST TIME IN OVER TWO MONTHS there was a welcome chill in the air. The temperature had dropped to 20 degrees, positively chilly by recent standards.

Hugh Doggett stood outside Saint Malachy's church looking up at its gothic architecture; the newly refurbished stained glass windows and decorative brickwork confirmed its permanence to the next generation of worshippers. The wrought iron gates were open as usual, but they seemed uninviting and foreboding to the excommunicated.

As far as the *Holy See* was concerned, he was damned to hell for eternity. Strange he thought, given the recent bad press regarding real sex offending priests and Vatican cover-ups that his eternal soul was to be forever banished from God's grace.

He, an innocent man accused by a bratty teenager. Vindicated by the law and the state, he remained and always would be an outcast from the church. He contemplated going in out of defiance. He missed the comfort of its surroundings and wanted to see what changes had been made since the last time he had prayed there. He turned to walk towards the centre of the city and home to his council house when he heard his name called.

"Doggy...Hugh."

He turned to see Father Desmond 'Dessie' Flynn, a young priest that he trained with in Maynooth College while studying for the priesthood. Maynooth had been established in the late seventeen hundreds and by the mid-eighteen hundreds it was the largest seminary in the world. Hugh and Dessie had spent time in each other's company and often sneaked off into Dublin for a night on the town with some of their fellow students. They were both ordained on the same day. Dessie was younger than Hugh, but they got on well enough given the age difference. They were never to be best friends, but friends they became and remained.

"Ach Dessie how's tricks? When did you get drafted down to the lovely St Malachy's?"

"Hugh Doggett, the most dangerous clergyman on the planet, apart from his Holiness the Pope, of course, and maybe Bishop O'Connor on confirmation day if you fluffed your lines. The vile man had always hated children, God rest him!"

They both laughed and Dessie grabbed Hugh's hand in the fondest of friendly greetings. Hugh felt his shoulders slump a little as he relaxed. He had worries and concerns about meeting some of his former brothers considering the recent allegations that had been made against him.

"I read about some of your troubles Hugh. I hope you don't mind me saying."

Hugh returned to his normal guarded self.

Here we go, he thought.

"I was delighted that they came to the right verdict. Anyone with eyes in their head would have seen that wee bollocks had been kept on the tit for too long! Anyway, have you seen the church since she's had her makeover?"

Hugh started to make an excuse that he had an appointment but Dessie Flynn was having none of it.

"Come on in, for God's sake. I've the very best of altar wine round the back of the vestry. Failing that, Father Toner has a bottle of Black Bush whiskey stashed. His liver is shot to bits so he just stares at it to torture himself. I think it's only merciful that we should ease his suffering by relieving him of temptation."

They both walked through the heavily studded wooden doors of the church. Hugh stalled as the familiar smell of waxed pews, incense, lilies and the hope for salvation wafted into his nostrils. Nothing and nowhere else in the world smelt quite like it. Dessie was still talking, then realised that Hugh had stopped to look at the statue of the Virgin mother on her altar as she smiled down forgivingly.

"Follow me in when you're ready Hugh. I'll be around the back of the altar if you need me."

Dessie Flynn took being in church for granted. It was both work and vocation. He loved the faith, but similarly now too many young priests felt powerless and disillusioned but understood that priests were getting thin on the ground and people still appeared to need them regardless of some of the terrible things that had happened to the innocent at their hands. He left Hugh to his thoughts and headed for the refreshments.

Hugh fully pushed open the second set of fifteen feet high wooden doors and was faced with ornate altars and frescos. He looked towards the newly restored stucco ceiling and admired the craftsmanship of the artists who lovingly restored it to its original beauty.

He had often before had thoughts of all the prayers that had been sent through the roofs of churches and wondered if any had been trapped and absorbed into the wood and plaster on their way towards God's ears. He had a friend in the army who thought the same about golf courses in a polar opposite way.

Candles were, as always lit on the various altars of the many preferred saints. Every member of the congregation had their favourites; a different saint and a different prayer for a problem that needed solving or a question that needed answering.

He was stirred from his thoughts by Dessie, coming towards him holding two glasses and the bottle of whiskey. He had them up at head level while singing *Party Rockers*, but quickly attempted to be as reverent as he could manage when he realised that Hugh was frowning.

No one else was in the church so he took a seat on a pew and gestured to Hugh to join him. The first glass was poured when Dessie had them stop.

"Hold on, Hugh, we need water. I filled the baptism font this morning and as we both know, you don't get a hangover when you use holy water as a mixer."

He came back with two glasses half filled with water and

224

poured some of the bottle of whiskey between the two crystal tumblers.

"Bloody hell, Dessie. They will say I led you on the path to damnation if they see those measures!"

"You know what, Hugh? I'm past caring anymore."

Dessie's mood darkened and he became more sombre.

"I'm thinking of leaving the priesthood anyway. I've taken to removing my dog collar when I go out in public these days. Folk look at you in a different way now. Some of them pull their children to the other side when they pass by. I wouldn't even dream of speaking to a child now even if their parents or guardians are with them. The nearest I ever get is visits to schools for catechism class or hearing confessions and I'm not that happy about them doing that without an adult present. Oh they still would say good morning Father and how are you Father? Lovely sermon you gave last Sunday Father, but you know in your heart that the trust has been broken. I don't blame them one bit. I would think the same myself in their position. However, they still seem to need us for the time being anyhow. So until I make up my mind for sure or things change for the worst, I'll stick at it. Anyway, there had better be a whisky distillery in heaven Hugh or I'm not for playing anymore."

They talked about old times and had a laugh remembering the antics in college while they were training for the priesthood. They were halfway through their drinks when Dessie asked, "I know you've been through the mill Hugh but you look like a man with other troubles on your mind. Is there anything I can do?"

Hugh sat for a moment without answering or saying anything and Dessie gave him time to consider if he wanted to confide in him.

"Dessie. I know it's against the rules, but would you hear my confession? A lot has happened and I'm short on sympathetic ears."

"Of course, Hugh. The church may not have changed, but that doesn't mean its shepherds haven't. Sorry, we do not believe that the innocent should be persecuted as a publicity stunt for the church to take the attention from the real monsters that lurk within it. There have been enough innocent lambs brought to the slaughter.

I know a little of your past in the armed services, Hugh, and I know you have been witness to some awful things in your time. There are none of us without sin, so you are welcome here for confession and communion anytime night or day. Maybe not night, I like my bed too much."

He smiled and stood as he placed his now empty glass on the pew.

"I'll take my seat in the confessional. You come in when you're ready."

Dessie out of respect closed the mesh screen completely between them. Hugh spoke more of his past in the next twenty-five minutes than he had in the last twenty years.

When he was finished and made his act of contrition, there were no 'ten hail Marys and Our Fathers.' No punishment at all. Just a simple, 'God loves and forgives you as one of his children. Go now in God's good grace and sin no more.'

Hugh 'Doggy' Doggett waited for his friend outside the confessional. He then did something he hadn't done in a very, very long time. As Dessie opened the door of the confessional box, Hugh was waiting for him. No words were passed. Hugh simply put his arms around Dessie and thanked him.

Dessie felt the surge of energy pass between them. His head swam and his stomach churned. He felt the whisky return to his mouth then forced it back down again wincing.

"Jeepers. Thanks mate. I think Paddy Toner must have spiked the whiskey, my heads spinning like a top!"

"Man up, Dessie. You'll be grand! Thanks for the heart to heart. If you don't mind, I'd like to stay in contact. Some strange things have been happening and I'd appreciate if I could run the odd thing past you."

"Unusual in the *gender confusion* unusual, or unusual, as in the *X Files* unusual?"

"Now I know why I had so much trouble deciding whether I should kill you quietly or set you up as a suicide in Maynooth."

Dessie had a genuine look of fear on his face.

"It's okay, Dessie, relax, it's a joke. Now you know why most people do their best to avoid me."

Hugh Doggett had once been a man of violence. Not random, opportunistic or, momentary impulsive violence, but the kind the armed forces see and exploit to their fullest. You became a tool, or an asset and a weapon. They couldn't care less about the programming you received in training when you left or were killed or maimed. They didn't have an exit strategy, or re-domestication course made bespoke or tailor made for ex-servicemen. You got dumped back into society to make your own way of life with the guilt of conflict and the night terrors that followed. That look never leaves you. Was it any surprise that so many ex-special forces became dysfunctional, reclusive or alcoholic drug addicted homeless cases!

When Hugh Doggett spoke to you, you made sure that you listened. He tried his best to recompense his past sins, but the fact was undeniable. When you'd killed and were applauded for it, adorned with campaign medals and commendations from your commanding officers, something at a cellular level changes in your being. You couldn't alter the way you moved or the fact that death was as much part of you as the clothes you wore on your back.

The thing was, you just had to accept the fact that it didn't matter how many good deeds you did or how many old ladies you helped cross the road. If you had the heart of a killer then a killer you remained.

Hugh reckoned that Dessie had had enough of reunions for one day. He said his farewells and promised to stay in touch. Dessie agreed. *That would be a good thing*, he thought to himself.

That didn't make him any more comfortable with the feeling he just experienced, if Hugh became a regular part of his life. The man had freaked him out in college and, to some extent, still did.

However something had changed. Something, for whatever reason had drawn Hugh Doggett to him. He had no idea what that could be. Maybe it was Divine intervention, but he doubted it; he knew that God was too busy to take a personal interest in him. It was as if your best friend had just told your girlfriend a really dirty joke and she was laughing a little too much at it; that feeling of uncertainty in how to feel or react.

"Still, I can at least put some of it down to the whisky," he said out loud. "Now what will I do? I have a free day. No one has died and I don't have mass until six?"

Out of habit he massaged his ankle. It tingled a little now for the first time in ages. He had a bone chipped in his foot while playing a soccer game at school and it had never healed properly. There had been talk at one stage of a professional career, but that ended after the tackle that had put the dream of someday playing in the big leagues down the drain.

For no particular reason, Dessie made his way up to his room in the Priest's house. He poked through the drawer of his dresser and found the tracksuit bottoms he was looking for. He pulled them on, and slipped on the old knackered pair of trainers he kept for lounging around the house.

For the first time in ten or so years, Dessie felt like going for a run despite the alcohol. His ankle wasn't bothering him now and the whisky was wearing off.

Father Desmond Flynn began the first of many runs that he would now enjoy. There was no further pain in his ankle. He wouldn't give it a second thought until he, like many like him, would begin to question their strange healing.

Chapter **67**

THE WORKING DAY FOR ESTELLE WOULD, AS usual, be full of lies and misdirection. She would of course render the prosecution groundless. This particular case she was defending was concrete or 'new handbag money' as she liked to refer to it.

Being lied to was part of her daily routine. She took most of her cases *Pro Bono*. She didn't need the money but she did however need some reward. Her cases were usually chosen on merit and not out of easy, no-brainer pay cheques. When the accused was obviously out for revenge or financial gain; she was the girl to sort it out. She despised liars and cheats; if she got paid money to expose them, all the better for it.

The days were beginning to shorten now and the heatwave seemed to be finally over. It was now no longer as easy for her to get up at five thirty and be in the pool at seven as it had been a week or two previously; so she arranged her first meetings for 10.00am and would go to the pool at 08.00am instead of her usual 07.00am.

She made her breakfast the night before as usual. It was the same basic formula; fruit salad doused with seeds then covered in yogurt, strong coffee, a puff on her asthma inhaler, followed by a cigarette. Her past asthma attacks could come on at a moment's notice. The swimming expanded her lungs and for the most part kept the attacks at bay. She had tried her hardest to put the bizarre events of the vision and swim at the Lough to the back of her logical brain.

There had been no contact with Eva or Hugh for the two days since the event but that still didn't make it go away. It was here in her mind and it was there to stay, clawing away at her sanity and desperate to force its way to the forefront of her thoughts at any opportunity. She was smoking again and drinking too much. Sleep was evading her prevented by the images of writhing tortured children drowning in the black water. She was avoiding bed, watching rubbish on late night TV. The event at the Lough should have been earth shattering for all of them but it seemed that not one of the three appeared willing to talk about or discuss it.

She hated the thought of guidance counselling but eventually she knew she would have to talk to someone; someone who was impartial and whom she trusted. It slowly dawned on her that she had no such person; no one she could really talk to or confide in. When had that happened?

She used to be such a social creature with a wide circle of friends, dinner parties and days at the races to go to. She sat in her apartment looking out over the river and cried into her hands. She had never felt so alone. How sad and lonely was she? All the resources you could wish for and no one to share them with.

She picked up her smartphone and scrawled through her list of contacts. All were business names – no-one personal at all. How had she become so isolated? She had never thought to even try social networking on her phone or laptop. A user name and a password was all it took. She searched for old school and college friends. People she hadn't thought of or been in touch with for so long.

Elle sat on her settee and began to lose herself in the past. The view from her apartment bathed her in the new light of coming day. The clock read 04.50am.

I think I'll throw a 'sickie' today. I'm fed up working and I'm still too drunk to drive. Maybe I'm coming down with something? she lied to herself. *I'll call Pauline and have her cancel and reschedule my appointments for later in the week.*

She left the message on her secretary's answer service and relaxed back into her settee. She hadn't taken much notice lately of how beautiful the first rays of sunlight were that crept their way along her floor and slowly up the wall.

It appeared that golden rays were rising out of the river as she came out onto the balcony to fully appreciate the new dawn. It gave her hope that the beauty coming across the black water may provide the cure for the deceased images that had hurt her soul.

The sound of car horns and traffic faded away as she lost herself in the beauty. Estelle Ballantine was at peace with herself for the first day in a very long time.

She was ready to sleep. Sleep unfettered. She could retire in the morning if she desired it so. There would always be crusades she could go on, noble causes and quests to seek.

Not today though.

No lies. No swimming and no wine. Possibly an Indian carry out later, though.

Oh bugger. Who am I kidding?

Indian, wine, eBay and a fag. I definitely, without any reasonable doubt, need a new Mulberry handbag! Hello internet shopping.

Chapter **68**

PATIENT AFTER PATIENT PASSED THROUGH HIS hands on average every fifteen minutes. From postnatal mothers to hypochondriacs – the steady stream of health issues seemed unending.

Tom Derrick sat in his leather swivel chair angry at the world. Thirty-five years practising medicine; billions pumped into cancer research and development worldwide and the best they could come up with was to feed you something so toxic that it made your hair fall out, or simply set about the patient with a knife and start loping bits off. It was medicine from the middle ages and he fucking despised it!

He was already mourning for the loss of his friend; giving the prognosis to Lyndon that his time on this earth was to be cut painfully short was the hardest thing he had ever had to do. Dordi and Lyn were the best of people. It just wasn't fair, when there seemed to be so many evil people in the world that had never so much as caught a cold.

He sat scowling at the anatomical poster on his wall when his cell phone rang. Dordi's number came up and sudden panic arose in him and gripped at his heart! He grabbed the phone and almost cut her off in an attempt to answer.

"Dordi. What's the matter?"

Dordi sensed the fear and concern in his voice.

"It's okay, Tom. Don't blow a vessel. I got someone here who wants to talk to you."

There was some talking in the background as Dordi handed the cellphone to Lyndon.

"Well, you old quack. It looks like you boys got my notes mixed up."

"Sorry, Lyn, I'm not following you. What notes?"

"My test results. My cancer diagnosis. They're wrong. They got it wrong! I've had myself checked here and there's no sign of cancer. I'm as fit as a flea!"

Tom sat at his desk staring at the patient that he was currently treating. He put his hand over the speaker on the phone and addressed his patient.

"Miss Loretta, would you please excuse me for two minutes? I have a personal matter to attend to on the telephone. Magnolia will fetch you some iced tea and I'll call you back in just as soon as I'm done with this call."

Miss Loretta was ninety-one years of age and still had the hearing of a bat and a nose for gossip like a bloodhound. She reluctantly made her exit, still trying to listen to the phone call for details to share with her sewing circle of friends.

"Hello, Tom. Are you still there?"

Tom waited as Loretta slowly closed the door behind her, then rejoined the conversation as if he'd never left it.

"Yeah, I'm still here. Listen, that's not possible, Lyn. I took those blood samples myself and I saw the results from pathology. I had them Fed-Ex'd here specially. There was no misdiagnosis."

"You sound a little disappointed,Tom."

Lyn's tone hardened. He wanted his friend to be happy so that they may get to fish together again. He didn't take into account that Tom was being presented with a medical miracle from three thousand miles away. How tough it must have been for him. He hadn't even thought of it because he was thinking about himself and Dordi so much.

"I'm sorry buddy. That was uncalled for. Something has happened over here. A prayer has been answered."

"What are you telling me Lyn? You know what? Put Dordi back on. I need someone sane on the line!"

Lyn passed the phone back to Dordi. He had an apologetic

look on his face. Dordi took the telephone and silently scolded Lyn for being such an idiot.

"Hi' Tom. What Lyn said is true. We had an episode here. We took a break from the coach trip and went for a walk in the countryside. Lyn stumbled and fell into a ditch filled with water. The folks around here think there's some kind of cure in the water that was in there. I can't say I disagree now that I've spoken to the doctor here."

Lyn was pacing around his office, wanting to talk to his friend again and make things right between them. Dordi put her hand over the mouthpiece of the phone and scolded him again for his lack of patience, then carried on her explanation to Tom.

"All the symptoms that Lyn had been presenting are gone. There are no cancer cells or indications of cancer anywhere in his system. It sounds crazy, I know Tom but I'm not looking a gift horse in the mouth. This doctor who's treating Lyn doesn't know his past medical history, just what we've told him. He just checked him over and did a few standard tests. Everything came back normal. Better than normal. I feel like going back up there and getting waste deep in that well myself!"

Tom Derrick sat on the other end of the line wondering what to say down the phone next. If Dordi and Lyn needed to hang on to some kind of false hope to get them through, then who the hell was he to stop them. Lyn's cancer was at an advanced stage. It had spread to his rib cage and as a result the bone marrow. There was, quite simply, no treatment known that could stop it.

"Okay, Dordi, do me a favour. Have the doctor there email me his exam notes and I'll take a look at them."

"Will do, Tom. He's right here if you want a word with him?"

"Sure, Dordi, why not, put him on."

A strong and professional well-educated English accent introduced itself to Tom down the phone.

"Doctor Derrick? Hugo Tomlin here. How may I be of assistance to you?"

Tom did his best to control the tone of his questions. If this country quack had given his friends an over charged half-assed check-up, without knowing any of the facts, he would sue his ass off! Tom explained the situation regarding Lyn, his prognosis and the past and ongoing treatment of his terminal illness, trying his best to hide his anger at the English doctor's obvious mistake.

Hugo's tone never wavered as he answered professionally and unemotionally, but there was an unmistakable air of 'hear this pal, you're wrong and I'm right' in his answer.

"Doctor Derrick. I have given your patient a thorough medical examination. I have also taken the liberty of carrying out a full screen blood analysis. Your patient is not presenting with any yellowing or discolouration of the skin, abdominal pain, or indeed any of the other symptoms associated with pancreatic cancer, or any cancer for that matter. There are no indications at this moment of your patient having cancer at any time in his recent past."

Hugo decided to reinforce his observations of Lyn and resented the tone of Tom's voice.

"Let me just say, Doctor Derrick, at initial testing, your patient is in good health. I, with your permission and his, would like to carry out some further more intense screenings. I will forward on immediately any results that are found to your good self and whomever else you deem necessary. If, as I am certain, your patient is in complete remission from his disorder, then let us all thank the good Lord for it. Here, unlike in your own great nation, it will be carried out completely free of charge and at our Majesty's pleasure.

"I look forward to reviewing your patient's results and as I am rather busy here in a country practice, I am prepared, as time allows, to discuss the matter at more length either by telephone or any electronic medium that you may desire."

Tom changed his mind. He now on second thoughts liked the tone of this guy. It sounded like he had that speech already printed out on faded tea stained paper and hung framed on his wall and that he'd most likely recited it a thousand times to anyone who had ever been stupid or foolish enough to second guess him!

"I'll look forward to reading your notes, Doctor Tomlin."

Hugo Tomlin declined to bid farewell, instead handing the telephone back to Dordi. She thanked the doctor and again restarted the conversation with Tom.

"Well, Tom, that's just about it. Lyn and I are making a quick trip to Oslo then cutting the vacation short and coming home. I'd like to see the old country and Lyn insists that we go. We'll be back in a week or so in time for the start of Bass season. We'll call to see you first thing. Okay?"

"Sure, Dordi. You kids enjoy yourselves. Let me know if anything changes or you need me."

She hung up the phone and hoped this English doctor had got it right. She knew they'd have to dance through the same medical hoops when they got home, with more tests and forms to fill in. Dordi could accept the fact that her husband was all better now and his illness had been a misdiagnosis, but niggling in the back of her mind was the thought that if Lyn hadn't fallen over into that English well, he'd have been a goner by Christmas.

For now and the next week, she would enjoy having her husband and their life together back. Even if it was, as she thought Tom reckoned, 'fleeting.' She turned to Lyn.

"So, miracle man, are you ready to get us out of here?"

"Ready when you are, my little Scandinavian troll," came Lyn's reply.

Dordi took Lyn's hand in hers and they left the surgery. Whatever would be would be. They had more time together than she would have dared dream to be possible. They bade England goodbye as they climbed the steps of the plane. As she reached the top, she turned around and mouthed the words 'thank you' into the British air, then left for her ancestral home.

Part Two

Chapter **69**

Belfast

THE MORNING ALARM WENT OFF TO THE SOUND of the Angelus. Father Dessie Flynn met the bright new day with a heavy heart. He was to perform a baptism at 11.30am, then a funeral mass at 2.00pm.

There was no doubt which one he was dreading more. Mrs. McKinstry, the housekeeper, had his breakfast laid out for himself and Father Toner as usual.

Standard breakfast fare spread out with bone china crockery and silver cutlery. Dessie enquired for the hundredth time if he could have his tea served in a mug rather than a cup?

"No mugs at breakfast, Fathers. If I don't count you two that is."

She laughed at her own joke as she expertly slipped the runny fried eggs and perfectly cooked sausage and bacon from the hot tray she was balancing over and around their heads as she served them. Mrs. McKinstry was *old school* and a stickler for order and routine. Dessie had once tried to force her to serve him his coffee in a mug instead of tea in a china cup and cereal instead of a cooked breakfast. That had turned out to be a huge mistake.

She knew Father Toner would eat anything she served him but also knew that Dessie was a fussy eater. As a punishment she informed them that her daughter had bought her a cookery course in the local college on vegetarian cuisine and as a consequence there would be no meat for supper or fried breakfasts and that included the flesh of any poor dead or defenceless land living creature. Meat would not be served in the house ever again! Instead it would be good healthy bran for breakfast and if they were lucky, the odd bit of steamed fish for dinner.

Father Toner took to the new diet well for the first day or two but then gradually appeared to make more home visits than usual to his parishioners at any given opportunity, usually around meal times by odd coincidence.

He often returned home with the smell of what was unmistakably fried meat of one kind or other on his clothing.

Dessie tried as he might to stick to the new diet. He knew what she was doing and considered it a battle of wills. That particular campaign had lasted for just short of two miserable meat free weeks. From then on there was never any doubt, tea in bone china cups was served at the first meal of everyday, never ever 'your fancy American coffee.'

Today's funeral would, as always, be an emotional affair. The eulogy he'd written was sympathetic and he had chosen an appropriate psalm to give comfort to the friends and bereaved. The funeral however was not his primary concern.

Jim and Patricia Napier were having their only baby christened this morning. They were both the best of folk and in Dessie's opinion hadn't deserved the awful cards that life had repeatedly dealt them.

They had been trying for children for the last fifteen years with no positive results. Patricia had gotten pregnant four times over the course of their marriage only to miscarry three and have their fourth child stillborn at full term. They had tried every avenue available to them to have a child, spending thousands of pounds on corrective gynaecological procedures on Patricia and tests on Jim to check his sperm count. Despite their efforts, success had evaded them and they had borrowed, and spent, thousands on fertility treatments in the hope of Patricia becoming pregnant.

Dessie had spoken to Jim in the past regarding Patricia's growing obsession for a child. He had expressed fears for both their marriage and her health. They both desperately wanted children but in Jim's words, "not at the cost of losing my wife's sanity or life.'

Dessie gave the best advice he could. He told them that if it

238

was God's will for them to be blessed with their own family, then eventually it would happen and that they should try not to force things too much.

He knew it was poor advice that bordered on the patronising but what else could he do? Then one day out of the blue and without any warning or medical intervention Patricia got pregnant for the fifth time. They were ecstatic with excitement but Jim feared the worst.

He knew historically how poor their chances of a healthy birth were and what depths of depression his wife would yet again sink to if the pregnancy failed to produce a child.

The nursery was made ready. Prams, toys even names were chosen for their new arrival.

Surprisingly as the birth approached, all the signs appeared good. They even debated what birthstone they should buy if the child was born under Leo or Cancer. They never factored for her to be born a Gemini and delivered five weeks premature.

As a result of the early birth, their new baby girl was born with a complex congenital heart defect and associated bowel disease. Their beautiful baby, Elyse, would not be expected to survive.

It was the last hope for children as the birth of Elyse had resulted in complications and Patricia was forced to have an emergency hysterectomy. It was the last chapter for a family and most likely their marriage and Patricia's sanity.

Dessie greeted the couple in the entrance hall of the Church.

Jim held Elyse loosely in his arms as Patricia was aided and supported by her mother and two sisters. The baby wore the most beautiful flowing christening gown that Dessie had ever seen; pure white lace dotted with countless pearls sewn on every available space of the gown which covered her tiny body from her neck, flowing down and cascading over her tiny shoeless bare feet.

She lay in Jim's arms peacefully sleeping and seeming to all what appeared to be a resting angel, which Dessie supposed that she soon would be. Dessie said a silent prayer, pleading that God would save them all from the inevitable heartache that was to come.

Dear Lord, I beg you. Please intervene and help these poor people get through this and help me get through it with them. Because the next time I see them all gathered here, they will carry baby Elyse in a white coffin on her father's shoulders instead of in his arms.

He greeted the friends and family as well as he could have hoped and quietly ushered them into the church.

Patricia was looking into the baptismal font, staring blankly down into the shallow depths of the holy water that would christen their dying infant; while her sisters stood at her side supporting her and expecting her to faint away at any moment.

Dessie had spoken to Jim the night before and asked him did he want him to use a cup or his hand to pour water on the baby's head? Jim couldn't, understandably, care less, so Dessie thought using his hands would be more personal and caring.

He took Elyse from Jim's arms and held her over the water. He began the sacrament of baptism by asking the family.

"By what do you name this child?"

"Elyse, Veronica Napier," Patricia's sister Catherine, the godmother replied.

Dessie gently held the child, being careful not to disturb her. The baby gave no indication of movement. She lay limply in his grasp barely breathing. He held her over the baptismal font and took a small handful of water into his cupped hand.

As the water fell on the child's head Dessie performed the sacrament of baptism.

"I, by the Grace of God, so name this child Elyse Veronica…."

Dessie could feel Elyse squirm slightly. It was the first sign of consciousness or any indication of movement from the baby that he had felt up to this point. Her tiny face began to redden and her eyes became crinkled as she started to cry.

He took a second handful of water to complete the ritual and again poured it over the child's brow. The next thing he heard was the most deafening shriek from the infant that he was now struggling to hold in his arms. She opened her eyes and bawled directly into Dessie's face in protest. Such was his shock that he

240

almost dropped her in the holy water.

He stood perplexed as the friends and family gathered round to see what had happened.

He nearly said, "It wasn't me," as he handed Elyse quickly back to her father Jim.

Jim stared into his daughters blue eyes, which were now, for the first time since entering this world, fully opened and alert. She squirmed and continued to scream at the top of her voice. Her face went deep purple with the effort! For the first time that day Dessie saw Patricia animated enough to take interest in the proceedings.

She shoved and elbowed her way towards her screaming baby, ignoring all else in the effort to reach her daughter. She then snatched her from her husband's arms and held her tight against her breast. As she looked down into her daughter's eyes, she could see life blooming in all its glory.

Patricia kept tight hold on Elyse and watched as the baby settled and breathed deeply into its lungs for the first time since her birth.

Patricia's sister was the first to say it: *Miracle.*

It wasn't the last time that word was used by the family that day, or any day after, when they gathered, or told anyone who would care to listen.

Elyse Veronica Napier was taken to the ante-natal clinic of the Royal Victoria Hospital within twenty minutes of her first scream. The family had bundled into whichever car whose driver could reach their car keys first. Dessie stood at the wrought iron gates of the church, looking down at his hands as the convoy of cars screeched off into the distance. He didn't remember climbing the steps that led back up to the wooden doors or sitting on the empty pew staring up at the stucco ceiling for the best part of thirty minutes. However, he did remember where the second secret stash of Father Toner's whiskey was kept and decided that he needed to again aid the ageing priest in his fight with his addiction to the bottle.

Two days later, Elyse Napier was discharged with a full clean bill of health. The hospital had decided to put her heart condition down to an unidentified mystery virus. It appeared that it was the best excuse that they could come with.

Over the same two days, Dessie Flynn was still drinking Father Toner's secret supply of the finest twelve year old Irish whiskey plus the extra bottles he had purchased under his name at the supermarket. He poured his first measure of the day at breakfast, only slightly diluted by a mug full of his fancy American coffee.

Chapter *70*

DOCTOR JAMES E. PAYNE WOULD SEE MORE than thirty patients on the same day that he had treated Audrey Walsh. His concentration wavered as he did his best to treat the mundane everyday skin rashes and bouts of haemorrhoids. His thoughts continually returned to the Walsh woman with the sight issues. Who the hell was that woman?

He checked and rechecked her notes, pulling and twirling at his eyebrow until he extracted a wiry hair. He inspected the silvery dermal bulb on the end of the hair's shaft, then repeatedly nipped it between his teeth until it flattened. He swallowed it then placed the base of the hair in his mouth and stripped the cells from the shaft.

How could it possibly be that a patient presenting the indications of advanced diabetes could suddenly appear to be free of all the symptoms? He would have to wait until pathology sent him the results of the blood tests. In the meantime, he decided to email a colleague he trained with at medical school who specialised in *endocrinology* at Leeds University.

From: Dr James E Payne jep@btru.co.uk
Subject: Patient
Date: 22 August 2014 16:14:29 BST
To: Dr Simon Darcy: dar1@leduni.net

Dear Simon

I have treated a patient this morning presenting with a history of advanced case of adult onset diabetes. All the usual symptoms are present in the patient's historical notes.

I am in the peculiar position, that on seeing the patient for the first time today, I can report that she appears to now be free of all related symptoms. Your thoughts and advice would be greatly appreciated.

Regards
Doctor J.E. Payne

Simon Darcy drank like a fish and partied hard. He was the middle son of three, all involved in medicine in one capacity or another. The last person in the world he ever expected to hear from was James whatever Payne!

Do I really want to be in contact with this fool? was his initial thought.

'Doctor James E. Payne' was how he had always introduced himself, regardless if it was a lecture or on one of the rare occasions that he attended a social gathering. He was not a popular man either at school or university, purely by his own choice. Not being popular wasn't the issue. Being aloof with a detached superiority complex and a tinge of narcissism, did not endear him to becoming part of any university social scene. It was usual that everyone fitted in somewhere at university. Not James. He would move from lecture to lecture studying his notes and keeping his head down into his papers; thus avoiding any kind of social intercourse with his fellow students.

He ate alone and rarely spoke to his fellow classmates other than to criticise the poor or sagging standards of medical teaching that had obviously seeped into the curriculum.

Simon Darcy knew him from the lectures that they jointly attended and had seldom spoken to James except in passing. Simon was a talented athlete as well as a gifted student, with a large circle of friends. He had skied with his family since early childhood and became the youngest scrum half in the history of school rugby and regularly played for Ulster and Ireland.

His upbringing had taught him to be tolerant and understanding of people and their diversities. His father had been lost to leukaemia at thirty-four years of age, leaving his mother to raise three boys under ten on her own until she met his stepfather. When she married; the boys took on his name after he legally adopted them. His own wife had died in a drowning accident, leaving him with two young daughters. Simon and his brothers had two new sisters and a new family.

His paternal father had had little time for recreation or sports, however Malcolm Darcy, his new stepfather, was a former hockey international and encouraged all the children now under his and Simon's mother's joint care, to embrace as many sporting activities as they desired. He was a kind and honourable man. He was also the clinical director of the biggest hospital in the North of Ireland which provided him with the means and finances to have all the children properly educated and travelled.

He, with the assistance of Simon's mother Isabel, had taught their children well. Simon along with the rest of his family, were impartial, from either creed or religion.

If you watched sport or liked to embrace life, he was your man and generally ready for fun and games.

Doctor James E. Payne was interested in none of the above. He was raised an only child and taught by his parents, that God himself had broken the mould when he finished making him. No one was quite good enough to share his company and that was especially true of girlfriends.

As a teenager he chose solitary activities like cycling or playing Nintendo games in his room; spending hour after hour alone, bullied into studying by his overbearing and underachieving father.

Simon had historically tried inviting him in passing to various events and opportunities to widen his social life, but all offers were rebuffed.

Simon had been willing to embrace anyone in friendship but James continually made little or no effort with him, or as far as he could see any of his fellow students. They were the exact opposite as far as personality was concerned. It would be unfair to say that he didn't like him. He had not been in his company enough to form any strong opinions.

His gut feeling, however, contradicted his sense of fairness. There was just something fundamentally unpleasant about the poor man.

From: Dr Simon Darcy: dar1@leduni.net
Subject: Patient
Date: 22 August 2014 16:14:29 BST
To: Dr James E Payne: jep@btru.co.uk

Hi James
Good to hear from you. Unusual set of circumstances.
Please send me the patient's blood test results and history of medication. Could there be a clerical error?

Kind regards
Simon

James' reply had all of his usual charm and warmth.

From: Dr James E Payne: jep@btru.co.uk
Subject: Patient
Date: 22 August 2014 17.12
To: Dr Simon Darcy: dar1@leduni.net

No. History on its way.

Regards
Doctor James E. Payne

Simon chuckled to himself.

God I miss that guy, all the personality of a wet day on holiday. The one constant in an ever changing universe, he dislikes everyone.

Simon received the email from endocrinology on his smartphone while on lunch and he briefly scanned the results, not paying any particular attention to the report. The charming Doctor Payne had obviously made a clinical error and needed verification that he may not after all be infallible.

He was off to play golf at 6.30 tonight with three of his friends. It should stay light until at least 10.30 so 18 holes looked possible if he hurried.

He later found the email that he had received from James Payne that had been sent directly to his work computer. They were the results of his patient' further blood screening, which he speed-read as he changed out of his shirt and tie and into his polo top for golf:

Medical record:
Audrey Louise Walsh, 14 New Bridge Street, Belfast, BT18 E3P
Tel no: 028 90 104 111
DOB: 18/02/1951
First diagnosed: 02/04/1989
Condition: Diabetes Mellitus

Fasting Glucose level	-	Normal
Haemoglobin A1c	-	Normal
Bun/creatine levels	-	Normal
HbA1c	-	Normal
Iris neovascularization	-	Not present

End of report.

He held the half eaten apple in his mouth while draping his work shirt over his arm. A quick reply should finish the email conversation with the charming Dr James E. Payne.

He typed the message quickly as he was leaving the office, with the hope that this may be the last time they would have any further communication.

From:	Dr Simon Darcy: dar1@leduni.net
Subject:	Patient
Date:	22 August 2014 17:34
To:	Dr James E Payne: jep@btru.co.uk

Your patient is not and has never been diabetic.

Kind regards
Simon Darcy.
End of message.

The email hit James like a hammer blow. He already knew that the test results he had received had shown no indications of the patient presenting symptoms of diabetes.

He just needed it confirmed by a specialist and Simon Darcy was regrettably in his opinion as good as they come.

His own personal dislike for the arrogant fool had no bearing on his decision to contact him.

In the meantime, what was he going to do with dear Mrs. Walsh? There was no question now that the complete reversal of her condition had somehow occurred.

If this person by some miracle has acquired the ability to either find a cure or indeed cure herself then she was one very valuable old lady.

There would be plenty of companies that would be interested in getting their hands on her. Her bone marrow would be priceless. Her DNA could be used as a template for an infinite array of healing applications. Even he could only begin to imagine its uses. Of course he had to obtain more tissue and blood samples and that would take some creative thinking on his part.

Doctor James E. Payne congratulated himself for being what he always knew to be 'a genius'. He sent his receptionist an internal email to have Audrey Walsh recalled as a matter of urgency.

This would all have to be done with the utmost speed and stealth. Her regular doctor would return within the week and he should not be allowed contact with the 'test subject' as he now referred to her.

He went into the surgery's main computer and removed Audrey's medical records from the database. All traces of her ever having existed were deleted except for the medical notes and contact information that he now only briefly kept until he transferred her details onto his laptop.

The email was received by the receptionist the following morning and before she left the office for her lunch break, she sent the letter to Audrey, requesting her attendance at the surgery.

James E. Payne would shortly no longer prefix 'Dr' at the beginning of his name. He would of course be struck off the medical register if anyone ever discovered his involvement in tampering with a patient's medical notes, but he was more than prepared for that eventuality.

However he considered that interfering with medical notes would be the lesser of his crimes. He held humanity in such low esteem that the thought of kidnapping someone and performing medical procedures on them would cause him no remorse whatsoever. If discovered, it would land him in prison for years without any hope of parole.

On the up side he would be very wealthy. He detested the sight of the wingeing bastards anyway and had, in the past, often considered prescribing medication that would have rendered at least one patient in particular being left in a vegetative state for the rest of their worthless life.

Why didn't I focus on pathology? At least then I could have diced them up and not had to listen to them droning on about their petty, fucking ailments?

The email pertaining to Audrey Walsh was the last one sent that day from the receptionist's computer. It was only a matter of deleting it then going home.

The cleaning staff arrived as he was leaving and as normal he ignored them. The last thing he wanted now, or at any other time, was to be engaged in mindless small talk.

James E. Payne left the surgery for what he hoped would be one of the last remaining days he would ever have to spend there. The soon to be ex-Doctor Payne pulled up at the nearest wine shop. He wasn't a drinker and knew little of fine wines but tonight required celebration.

Anything over twenty pounds should be good, he thought to himself.

When he arrived home he realised that he didn't possess a corkscrew. The thought had never occurred to him to buy one as he

249

had never had any occasion to use one in the past.

His townhouse interior, like him, was bereft of either warmth or hospitality. The small television that sat in the corner of the room was his only connection with the outside world.

He sat the wine bottle on the kitchen work top and removed the wax covered wrapper, then forced one of the legs of his stethoscope down on the cork which eventually submerged with a *plunk* into the contents of the bottle. This subsequently caused a fountain of red wine to splash over the table almost destroying the computer laptop with Audrey's valuable details on it.

His heart almost jumped out of his chest as he pulled the computer to safety, wiping the excess wine still seeping into the device against his trousers legs.

Phew! Almost lost you there, Mrs. Walsh.

He brought up Audrey's records on the laptop and scanned her medical history again to ensure that they were safe. Thankfully, the details were unharmed.

He took the single glass tumbler from the cupboard and poured his wine as he sat down at the table and turned on the internet search engine.

Now let's you and I have a drink together and see who your new friends will be, shall we?

The coming hours would provide him with most of the contact information he would need to market his priceless new product.

Chapter *71*

THE SECURE HAND DELIVERED PACKAGES WERE delivered to Kay Kane and Senator Gregory Hamill at approximately the same time. There were other recipients globally, as yet unknown to any of them.

Valentine would not require or need the contents of the package but had received it anyway. It was a gift for him to decide later whether or not to use or donate.

Kay tore at the heavy white plastic bag. Inside was a platinum casket, similar in shape to a computer mouse. She held it at eye level to find a way to open the object as there appeared to be no hinge or seam along its length. Neither was there an aperture for a key to be inserted. *Nice gift*, she thought, *whatever it is*.

She rechecked the plastic bag containing the casket for a return address or clues that would reveal either its origin or sender. The only marking was a bar code and some distorted writing where she had pulled at the white plastic. She returned her attention to the object.

This was certainly to be something of importance. The security service that delivered it was of the highest standard. One individual put the package into her hand and performed a retinal scan with a hand held device, while one other stood behind and guarded the elevator and hallway. They were well trained and very expensive by their appearance.

The object certainly was not a toy or a trinket to sit on her non-existent mantelpiece. Kay squeezed and twisted it with little effect other than frustration, tossing it away; it clattered along the counter. She then looked back to the plastic wrapping.

Bar codes. What am I supposed to do, bring it down to the supermarket?

Then the idea slapped her in the face. She picked up her smart phone and downloaded the bar code reader from its application selection. She stood over the object on the counter, shifting her attention from the downloading bar code reader then back again to the platinum mouse. She desperately needed to go to the bathroom, which only heightened her frustration. *Come on, come on; I'm bursting!*

The App only took seconds to fully download and open. She first ran it the length of the plastic container, then hovered it over the object itself. The platinum casket's vacuum seal split with an almost inaudible hiss and a minute release of vapour as the bar code App completed its purpose. Inside was a single gel encased pill resting on a purple cushion with a label attached.

'The Jester's coming, you should eat me!' was the singular instruction. She wasn't sure if she liked the reference to *Alice in Wonderland.* That hadn't ended very well for the poor Queen of Hearts.

Kay looked at the vessel containing the pill. She held it up to the light to see it contained an amber liquid and appeared to be innocent enough.

I'm not swallowing something I got delivered in the mail. Who do these people think they're dealing with for fuck's sake?

She also knew that the liquid and the pill that contained it must be important. The container alone could fetch two thousand dollars in any jewellery store.

Kay had seen what the liquid on the membrane she was instructed to wear at Rachel Cohen's funeral had done to that idiot Valentine even if he wasn't aware of it yet and she wasn't prepared at this or any future time to end up the same way.

Let's put this on ice for the time being and see what events unfold in the Far East.

If the secure information she was still receiving regarding the rising death toll from an unidentified virus were correct, she may have no choice but to take the instruction and swallow the pill. She wondered if anyone else had received a similar package.

She carefully placed the small shiny casket containing what she suspected could be an antivirus in the hidden compartment inside her freezer.

The white pain that was now screaming from her bladder sent her almost crashing through the bathroom door. Her pants were only half pulled down when the heavy flow of urine splashed against the still water of the toilet. The sensation was more than bliss. Relief relaxed the muscles in her face and shoulders as she slumped back against the cistern. Her legs splayed out in an 'X' pattern as the water continued to flow heavily from her bladder. She raised her head to stare at the white ceiling.

God, why is it they go on so much about sex, when something as simple as a pee gives you infinitely more satisfaction than all that sweaty grunting and post coital cuddling?

Business done, she resentfully pulled up her pants, not bothering to wipe herself. They were going in the laundry anyway and she wasn't the one who would be washing them so what was the point.

Last night's wine was as cold as winter as it frosted the glass she half filled. Her conundrum now was what to do with the package and why was it sent to her?

The remote motion sensor switched on her TV as she passed.

Chapter 72

THE NEWS CHANNELS REPORTED THE THIRTY-first death in Japan was being put down to a newly identified strain of a mystery virus. A press interview had been arranged, explaining what little information had thus far been gathered on the new strain of disease.

The spread was unprecedented. No virus or hostile bacteria had ever been recorded as reaching contagion saturation so rapidly. It would be more commonly referred to as *The Jester* although in truth, there would be little amusing about the symptoms, as nothing like it had ever been recorded before and the science community was at loggerheads on how to treat it. The virus was equally both fascinating and terrifying. *JSTR* was a cocktail of diseases that appeared to be deliberately genetically manufactured.

Researchers at the Institute for Viral Research in Okinawa suspected that this outbreak was the result of a terrorist attack but the resources needed to develop this kind of strain could only be produced by the latest viral research and development facilities and that pointed more towards an act of war by a hostile regime rather than a single terrorist group.

The ferocity of the strain was so highly infectious that the symptoms increased at an unprecedented rate and trying to find an antidote in the timescale available seemed impossible. The reports of cases coming in were staggering.

The gestation period from first symptoms detected at initial infection to fatality were anywhere between fifteen to twenty-nine days. So far the outbreak had produced only thirty-one fatalities but hundreds were now infected. Soon it would be thousands. From then on, no one could tell.

The new disease was a much more virulent strain of the four conditions it was associated with.

So far all the most acute cases and fatalities were children aged between newborns and preteens. The young appeared particularly vulnerable to one specific strain of the virus, cranial mutation. The rest of the symptoms consisted of:

'J'...Jackson-Weiss Syndrome: *Premature fusion of the bones, preventing further growth of the skull and shape of the head and deformities of the feet. In this strain the abnormal growth is greatly accelerated causing excruciating intense localised pain.*

'S'...Swine flu: *This new strain was resistant to any of the vaccines already in use.*

'T'...T cell lymphoma: *Associated with an aggressive strain of leukaemia virus-1.*

'R'...Rectal Hemorrhaging: *Leading to catastrophic internal bleeding resulting terminal blood loss and subsequent death. This was the final stage of the illness.*

The early symptoms were similar to that of the common cold or flu. No one paid much attention at first. In Japan the infected wore face masks while out in public, but at that stage it was already too late as the virus had continued to spread. The new disease was transmitted through touch as well as now becoming airborne. Cases were being reported in Tokyo and Kyoto as well as some of the more remote towns and villages where communication was limited.

People were scared and they were right to be. Panic buying of bottled water and canned food had begun to leave shops and supermarket shelves empty.

Train stations and motorways were becoming increasingly deserted except for the brave few who dared to travel or emergency services.

Panic so far had been confined to densely populated areas of towns and cities.

Around the world, media stories of the outbreak were just

beginning to air as minor items of news. After Swine flu and Bird flu, most people, as well as the press, had had enough of pandemic scares to take much notice of another one that again, regardless of how much it was hyped by the press, in all likelihood wouldn't kill them.

The Japanese premier was being advised to play down the seriousness of the outbreak. This had been the most trying of premierships. First the earthquake, then the tsunami, followed by the nuclear disaster at Fukushima, and now this! If he told the public the truth, there would be widespread panic.

Rumours were already being leaked to nervous domestic market investors and unease on the financial markets was just the beginning. The internet was buzzing with stories of the rising death count. There would be no cure for this virus in the time scale given. All he could do was pray for his people and hope for a miracle.

It was old news to Kay. BION was doing its own research into the outbreak and like the rest of the world's laboratories had so far failed to find any breakthrough in finding a cure.

Chapter 73

AGATHE BESSETTE TOSSED THE LONG STRAND of damp hair away from her left eye, then spat her used gum out on the pavement. Most of her clothes were bought in vintage or charity shops and deodorant was considered unnecessary as her lack of personal hygiene had never been a concern.

The laces of her boots were permanently undone and cut short to avoid snagging in the wheels of the skateboard that she carried like a handbag under her arm. She coloured her own hair, changing it from week to week depending on her mood. Her current look was shaved at the back and one side with the other backcombed out into a faded green bird's nest of tangles and knots.

The little details that most people missed about her were that her frayed black denim jacket had the remains of the *Yves Saint Laurent* label she had cut off. Or, if asked, she said that the *Bell & Ross* black ceramic faced wrist watch was a cheap copy she had bought from a stall on the Rue de Paris.

Agathe, as usual, had paid cash for the watch in one of the many designer jewellery stores on the Rue de la Paix. As was the norm, the assistant called for her manager to check that the money she was using wasn't counterfeit, meanwhile looking the teenager up and down; doubting that a street kid with body odour issues could afford such an expensive item of fine jewellery.

She was accustomed to the suspicious treatment and understood, up to a point, their hesitation in handing over such an expensive timepiece. Her long isometric hairstyle partially covered her face making it near impossible to identify her on their security cameras.

It wasn't every day an eighteen year old girl walked into their shop, tried on a watch then casually pulled a crumpled bundle of bank notes amassing to €5,000 from her breast pocket, counted out half and pushed the wrinkled notes across the counter top.

She put on her headphones and waited until the manager was satisfied that he was neither the victim of a counterfeit scam, nor was he losing a valuable piece of merchandise.

Satisfied with the deal he approached Agathe with her new watch. He apologised for the delay and began fumbling to adjust the strap to perfectly fit her pale thin wrist.

Coffee and iced water were now speedily placed in front of her in the private booth that had just been made available.

Nothing now was too much trouble for the first assistant that had been initially attending her. This part she found the most irritating. Everything about the appearance of the girl annoyed her. Her clothes were neat and tidy, her nails were manicured and her shoulder length highlighted hair was loosely pinned back. Agathe earned more money from one phone call than this robot earned in a year. The receipt was written and the watch was left on her wrist as requested. The assistant asked her if she would like to take out insurance.

As she explained the importance of insuring such a valuable item, Agathe ignored her and replaced her headphones as the assistant continued determinedly with her rehearsed sale of the benefits of having such a precious object insured. She didn't reply but simply stood, adjusted the volume to *loud* on her music player, picked up the empty box that had contained the watch, mumbled 'Merci' then left.

She tore up the receipt and tossed it and the empty box in the nearest waste bin. The staff inside the jewellers remained a little uneasy, still wondering if this girl had fooled them in some clever way.

The wheels of her skateboard clattered along the pavement as she weaved her way through the pedestrians walking down the

Place de la Concorde. She felt the vibration of her smart phone as an incoming message purred against her thigh.

The phone was programmed to detect any communications that were detailed unusual or worth checking by her Head of Section. She brought the skateboard to a stop, unlocked the keyboard and then scanned the readout. The email had been detected by the spy software she had modified from the computer she had been supplied with by her anonymous employer. It was faster and more accurate than the programme they had installed.

The first of two names appeared on the screen, followed by the details of the sent email to one of three drug manufacturing companies.

Subject: Patient.
Sender: Doctor James E. Payne <jep@btu.co.uk>

It has come to my attention that a patient presenting with stage-1 diabetes with related retinal dysfunction has recently appeared to have a complete reversal of all symptoms.
There furthermore appears to be complete regeneration of any damage to her pancreas and vision.
Please advise if interested to the above email address or mobile number 5556670039.

Agathe stared at the screen in a mixture of shock and amazement. Her English was perfect and she no problem reading the formal email. This guy had to be the stupidest person on the planet or the most naive one she'd ever come across. Sending an unsecured email like that through the net. What were they doing giving medical degrees to such idiots?

She had to act fast. This could be picked up by anyone! In her bid to red flag and forward the information, it occurred to her to scroll down to the end of the message.

She hacked into James E. Payne's laptop and within seconds, she was into his email program and a full history of the patients he'd treated over his brief time in the surgery.

A child running by crashed into her almost knocking the phone from her hands. She screamed at the boy for his stupidity. The parents pulled the infant into their arms threatening to call the police and have her arrested. She had let herself be distracted and quickly apologised, not wanting the police involved. The last thing she needed was the police confiscating her phone and discovering her history of hacked access to private calls and messages.

The child and its parents walked away, frequently turning to scowl at her as they departed, discussing how the streets of Paris had become so dangerous. Their scathing looks were wasted on her; her eyes were focused on the screen of her phone. A report from the endocrinology department in Leeds University was the last entry on the computer sent by a research consultant. The information she was searching for would be there. She then hacked straight into the main database in the endocrinology department and searched for anything relating to Doctor James E. Payne, including conversations via the net.

The search result was almost instant.

Email sent to Doctor Simon Darcy from Doctor James E. Payne:
Subject: Test for advanced indications of Stage 1 Diabetes.

So that was confirmed. The test and emails were legitimate. Her next move was to find out who the last patient this Doctor Payne had been treating with Stage 1 diabetes. She placed the phone between her teeth and hauled herself up on to the wall of the *Pont de la Concorde*, one of the many bridges that spanned the River Seine. His laptop had been synced with the surgery's WiFi and it must have been there that he had been treating the subject. No names of anyone with those symptoms appeared on his laptops hard drive. She looked out onto the waters of the Seine, waiting for the answer to materialise. Then it struck her.

Of course. He has deleted the name. That was the only smart thing he thinks he's done so far. That makes things easier for me now.

She searched through the historical record section of the deleted items on the surgery's file. Two names appeared: Melvin

Philip Campbell - deceased 06/09/2013; Audrey Anne Walsh - currently undergoing treatment.

Voilá!

She cut and pasted the information she had gathered and forwarded it to her main server. The ping that it had been sent came through her headphones. She jumped down off the wall and stretched her arms above her head admiring her new watch then checking the time before letting her arms fall down by her sides.

Maman would have supper ready at seven: *Tartiflette* tonight and that was her absolute favourite. This had turned out to be a very good day.

She flicked the skateboard from its resting place against the wall using her foot, having it expertly land right side up on its nylon wheels. She pushed along the footpath of the bridge and jumped aboard, smiling in satisfaction as she made her way towards the nearest Paris Metro station.

Chapter **74**

JOHN GREER GROGGILY WOKE AT 05.30, TWO HOURS earlier than usual. It was already light outside and the thin gaps in his blackout curtains let swords of daylight stream into his bedroom.

His tongue was stuck to the roof of his mouth. It felt rough and cracked, so he closed his mouth again, forcing saliva to accumulate at the back of his palette. He then pushed the saliva forward enough to eventually moisten his arid tongue. He lay with his eyes closed, refusing to open them and hoping for a reprieve from what he prayed wouldn't be the end of his precious night's sleep. It would have been simpler to just get up and get some water, but that meant that he was definitely up for the day and at this unfriendly hour that would be a bad, bad thing.

He started, eventually, to fumble his way towards the bathroom. He knew that he would, as usual, hate the taste of the water from the faucet.

The tap ran on full in an attempt to let the liquid get as cold and fresh as possible. He knew it would still taste foul no matter how long he let it run (only the Irish believed that water had a taste to it).

He was still too lazy to walk the extra fifteen feet to the kitchen in the remote idea that if he did he would never get back to the beloved sleep that he cherished so much. As usual, the sound of the water running triggered his 'pee response.' Still trying to keep his eyes closed and supporting himself with one hand against the wall, his own water began to flow with the comforting safe sound of his good targeting.

Business done, he put his face down sideways under the running water from the faucet, allowing the fluid to return some of the lost feeling to his tongue.

When he bought the apartment one of the older construction workers still working on finishing the building had told him not to drink the water from the bathroom taps. John didn't know if he should believe him or not.

"Listen pal, don't be drinking the water from the toilet," he had said.

It would have been the furthest thing from his mind and he wondered how desperate you would have to be to put your head into the toilet bowl? The builder could see the man was an idiot and had misunderstood what he had said.

"I don't mean the toilel, pal. I mean the toilet. You know, the toilet? The bathroom? The taps in the bathroom!"

John had stood, staring at him in polite fascination.

"I was working on an extension one time and we once found a dead bird and a rat in the water storage tank. They were all bloated and rotten; they'd probably been there for months, just festering away in the tank. People had been drinking from the taps in the bathroom for ages. Odd thing - none of them complained and nobody got sick. Weird, right?"

Greer had tried his best to continue to appear even remotely interested in what the man was saying. The thought of dead and decaying vermin in water storage tanks would nestle in the back of his mind forever but still wouldn't deter him from drinking it. This happened most mornings as he slurped the water, thinking of what could be decaying in the communal water tank.

It would not, however, be a strong enough phobia to cure his general laziness and his need for hydration of a sandpapered primary tasting organ. The same thought occurred to him each night while in bed: *I should fill a glass of water and take it with me to bed.* But by the time he remembered he was always tucked up and couldn't be bothered going back into the kitchen.

His tongue was regaining some return of sensation and the

263

memory stick he had removed from the lab was burning a metaphorical hole in his pocket. Realising that he was now up and almost fully awake, Greer began to make his way towards the living area of his apartment. He sat himself down on the settee and searched between the cushions for his now missing packet of cigarettes and lighter.

As luck would have it, he found a crumpled £10 note which momentarily distracted him from the bottom of the 'parrot's cage' that was his mouth. *No more wine midweek for you, big lad. It's not worth feeling like this in the morning.* He made the same promise most mornings and by 20.30pm on the same night he only had half a bottle left.

The living room was still in semi darkness and the zebra print appeared to take on a more sinister, almost predatory persona.

One of these days I'm going to shoot that fucking zebra. Maybe I should get a print of a lion and put it directly behind it, or even better some of those African hunting dogs. They'd disembowel the bastard nice and slowly!

The thought of that made him feel ill so he changed his mind to a lesser scenario.

At least I could move the poster of them closer every day and stalk the bugger.

Kettle boiled and coffee poured, he inserted the memory stick and settled at the computer screen uploading the contents of the experiments and results onto the hard drive.

He had a friend who specialised in marine microbiology at the National University of Ireland in Galway. He knew Eva would never approve of him using an outside source to help in the research they were doing, but he needed someone else's opinion on what was going on.

She seemed too overly secretive and in denial of the obviously peculiar relationship between her and the test subjects. It was then that the complete and outrageous demands that she had made on him registered in his head. No matter how strange and bizarre it seemed to be, this girl had what appeared to be, an almost supernatural power that was capable of controlling a limitless and abundant life source. He had seen with his own eyes, a completely decimated form of plant life restored to more than full health simply by her presence in the same room.

He had injected a dead spider plant in her presence, which had not only recovered, but had bloomed in front of his eyes. What he omitted to tell her was that he had performed the same experiment later in her absence on a different subject and the plant stayed as dead as it had been before the procedure. Greer had wisely curtailed his excitement in lieu of common sense.

Growing up in Northern Ireland in the midst of the civil unrest, made you think twice about the information you passed over mobile phones or more recently the internet. Too many people could know your business and limited paranoia could be a lifesaver.

He inserted a new memory stick into his computer and downloaded the data on the first device. He marked it by scratching it with the sharp unfolded end of a paper clip and put it in his desk drawer. He would email Andrew and arrange a call to Galway using his landline and seek his advice.

I mean, what's the worst that could happen? It's only a phone call to get advice from a friend.

Chapter **75**

EVERY POSSIBLE DIAGNOSTIC CHECK SHE COULD think of on countless new test subjects were checked then rechecked. Eva slumped back into her office chair confounded, hard as it was to accept.

There was no further doubt in her mind that there was not only a definite connection with this plant, but a symbiotic relationship between her and this new species. The algae responded to her and despite her own concerns she felt slightly safer when she was in there with the subjects.

I'm supposed to be some sort a real life Poison Ivy character from the comic books? From what I've seen so far I'm not sure I can see any real practical use, if its only me the algae reacts to, then what are the wider applications? I can't be everywhere at the same time!

She was frightened. She had neither asked nor wanted to be special in any way. Why of all the people on the planet had this happened to her?

Stop wallowing in your own self-pity. Do your job and get on with it. Who knows, you may not be the only one with this connection. There could be hundreds for all you know.

The tests that she had performed on both living and dead plants had all reacted positively. The next stage was to perform limited tests on non-floral test subjects.

She had been generally ignoring the text messages she was receiving from Estelle, but she knew her sister would run out of patience soon. It was the lawyer in her and she needed answers. She hadn't spoken to Hugh since the swim at the Lough but was in no doubt that Estelle must have by now. She could understand how worried they must be and she did wonder had either of them experienced any further odd episodes?

One final test, then she would arrange a meeting, initially with Elle, then Hugh.

Decision made, she decided that the best way to settle any doubt was to perform an experiment on herself. It was to be both painful and extreme but necessary. She went across to the storage cupboard and withdrew a bottle containing a glass jar of sulphuric acid. She carefully removed the glass stopper and decanted thirty millilitres into a flask. She rolled up her sleeve and sterilised a small area of her forearm; the sensitive skin in the crease of her elbow would be perfect for the test.

She then took one of the test tubes containing the algae samples and placed it within easy reach. This was going to hurt! Her heart quickened as she immersed a glass rod in the liquid acid then withdrew it. She left it balanced on the rim of a beaker, replaced the glass stopper back in the bottle and returned it to the cupboard. She was stalling for time. The metal tongs were still holding the cotton pad. She dribbled the acid on to the pad and watched it smoulder as the acid burnt the fibres of the cotton.

Oh Lord. Do I really want to do this?

The perspiration gathered on her forehead and she could feel the trickles of sweat run down her back and gather at her waistband. She withdrew the acid soaked pad and allowed the excess liquid to run off into the ceramic basin. If she was going to do it then she had better get on with it. Without further thought she pressed the pad against the tender underside of her forearm. For a moment nothing happened. No pain or even itching. Then the burning began. The pain was reaching unbearable. The perspiration now ran freely down the arch of her back, down between her buttocks. She squeezed at her arm in an attempt to dull the pain but it was useless against the acid.

She couldn't take any more of the burning and ran to the water faucet to plunge her damaged skin under the cold running water. The relief was bliss but she knew that when she removed her arm from the water the pain would come screaming back. Eva could already see the damaged flesh peeling away. She needed to get an alkali to neutralise the remaining acid but that would have made the experiment pointless. The last thing she wanted to do was take her arm away from that water. Her legs were weak with the pain and effort of intentionally burning her own skin. She leant on the basin using her elbows and cried into the water. The algae sample was less than four feet away.

She could reach it at a stretch. She almost made it, partially withdrawing her burning arm from the water. The waves of pain instantly returned as her arm left the sanctuary of water washing over her. She steadied herself and got ready.

You have to do it Eva. You knew what you were letting yourself in for.

She found the rubber stopper for the porcelain sink and continued holding her arm under the tap for as long as she could. The sink was now half filled with cold water. The wound on her arm was now starting to burn even though she kept it submerged.

OK, OK, here we go!

She lunged at the algae sample, breaking the tube in her efforts to get it. The delicate glass broke on the stone surface of the basin surround, leaving a mixture of tiny broken shards of glass mixed in with the algae.

Oh crap! You bloody idiot!

There was no other choice. She scraped up the mixture of broken glass and algae and placed it onto her damaged wet arm. The pain of the powdered glass on her acid burn was almost enough to have her lose consciousness.

Chapter *76*

WITHIN SECONDS OF HER APPLYING THE mixture the burning abruptly stopped. There appeared to be no direct contact between her and the plant. It just slid off her arm after she applied it and disappeared into the water. The itching began after the cessation of the pain. Her wound slowly was reduced in redness and the remains of any damage disappeared in front of her eyes! There was no drama. It simply appeared like nothing had ever happened. She stood staring down at her now completely healed arm.

Oh my Lord, oh my lord, what is happening to me?

Eva flopped back down into her seat and continued to stare at the flawless arm. There was no doubt remaining. This thing, whatever it was, worked, on her anyway.

Let's get on. Pull yourself together.

She stood up took a paper towel from the dispenser and dried her arm off. Determined now to find answers, she left the lab and made her way down to the *Caves*, as the basement was known generally by the staff.

It was a short walk down one of the many corridors that led to the basement of the building. This was where the freezers and stocks were kept that contained an assortment of small dead animals, delivered weekly along with laboratory supplies, clerical documents and old paper records. She greeted one of the three porters that maintained the department with less than her usual cheeriness.

Eva mostly overlooked the fact that she was young and attractive and ignored the comments that she could sometimes overhear or the remarks they made when she, on the odd occasion, came down to the *Caves* to personally collect supplies.

Two of the three were pleasant enough guys but one of them in particular freaked her out a little. *Dark Eddie* or *The Gimp* to his friends would always stare at her for just a little too long and as she walked away she always knew that he was continuing to ogle her from behind.

Frankie, the oldest of the three, a man in his late fifties greeted her with his usual informality.

"Afternoon, athlete. What brings you down to this subterranean hell?"

"Hi, Frankie. I need a couple of dead chicks if you have any handy?"

"Should be able to arrange that for you," he replied. "Fresh or frozen?"

"You have non-frozen?" asked Eva.

"Yep its delivery day, they're still warm. Should have been headed for the zoo but the delivery driver hit a bollard on Botanic Avenue and the engine overheated so we were his nearest call. He said they'd go off in this heat before getting to the zoo so we got the python's share."

"Excellent! Can I go and grab a couple?"

"Help yourself. Take as many as you want before *Smack* here puts a couple in his sandwich and eats them for his tea."

The third of the trio, *Smack* as he was nicknamed, forced a sarcastic smile and just shrugged his shoulders at the regular teasing. Eva smiled at Frankie and thanked him, then entered the storage room.

Two cardboard trays containing the dead chicks lay side by side on the bench. The scene was marginally grotesque and reminded her of the long gone poultry shop that used to trade in the high street in her hometown. She would pass it on her way back from school and was horrified at the sight of dead chickens and turkeys hanging by the feet from hooks in the window. Sawdust sprinkled under them to catch the blood as it dripped from the wounds on their throats. She would never forget the empty stare from their dead, opaque, eyes.

Back then they still had their heads and feathers attached and she had wondered since, what their marketing strategy could possibly have been?

One thing guaranteed to turn you vegetarian was the sight and smell of the butcher gutting the dead foul and assembling the neck for stock offal for the customer if they chose it. She held two of the tiny dead birds in her hands, gently stoking their soft down feathers then almost jumped, dropping them back in the box at the sound of Frankie shouting to her if she was OK?

"Yeah I'm fine Frankie. Just got lost in memories there for a minute."

"Right you are. That's grand. Do you not want me to turn the lights on?"

"Sorry Frankie?"

"I don't know how you're finding your way about in there in the dark, Eva!"

Dark! What was the man talking about? She could see perfectly well. Frankie flicked the light switch on and Eva's eyes instantly adjusted to the new level of illumination.

Frankie was less than ten feet from her when he stopped dead in his tracks.

Chapter **77**

A T FIRST THE SHOCK AT WHAT HE THOUGHT HE had just seen left him lost for words or able to take a conscious breath. He stared at her in disbelief with his mouth gaping ajar.

"What's wrong, Frankie? You look like you've just seen a ghost!"

It took him some time for the words to form in his mouth. He blessed himself and mouthed, "Holy Mother of God and all the Saints protect us. Your eyes, Doctor Ballantine!"

"What do you mean? What's wrong with my eyes?"

"I know you're not going to believe this, but until a second ago you had no whites to your eyes. They were totally black. You were standing there stroking two of the dead chicks when I came in and switched the lights on. When you looked at me they returned to normal. I've never seen anything like it!"

Eva's iris had automatically adjusted to the lack of illumination in the room. It wasn't a conscious decision on her part and she was unaware of the change. Any ambient light source had been magnified to enable her to see as clearly in the dark as in daylight. It hadn't been the same perception as the night sight goggles used by the military and bat watchers. It was quite simply, perfect.

Eva could feel herself tremble and shake a little; this was too much to take after burning her arm with the acid back in the lab. She needed to get out of there, and quickly put up a line of defence.

"Have you been drinking the formaldehyde, Frankie?"

It was the best she could think of under the circumstances. His face was bereft of colour and she reckoned he was probably thinking the same thing. This time when he spoke his tone was hard and direct. He would rather slam his fingers in a door than spend another unnecessary moment in the same room as this woman.

"Take whatever you need, Doctor, and leave please."

Eva understood what he meant was take what you need and get out! He turned and left, leaving the door to the storage room open behind him in a gesture for her to leave and not in the same space as him.

Eva made her way to the canteen rest room to splash cold water on her face. The remark that Estelle had made to her the day they met in the coffee shop regarding her wearing contact lenses came streaming back into her mind.

She'd put it down to Estelle being unusually dramatic or simple confusion. However one more thing was apparent. This relationship with the algae had in some way changed her and she needed to do one more experiment to see if the others had had similar effects or experiences.

She left the rest room and made her way back to the lab.

The experiments on the chicks could wait until tomorrow. She made an entry in her journal to remind her to prepare the last of the algae test samples for possible regeneration. It was when searching in her coat pocket for a pen that she discovered the vial containing one of the algae samples that she had taken from the storage cupboard before the acid burn. She shook the vial then held it up to inspect if anything had changed or happened to the sample? Nothing. Nothing unusual. It just sat in the tube appearing as uninteresting as ever.

Her next thought sobered her from the monotony of the experimental procedures.

I seem to be taking all of this a bit too easily, Frankie just told me that my iris's had expanded to utterly engulf the whole of my eyes, turning them black. How is it at all possible that I could see as well in the dark as in the daylight? The man had just seen something extraordinary and I tried to make light of his shock and worm my way out of it. This is becoming too normal too quickly. The only people I can talk to about this are only a call away.

"It's time to get Elle and Hugh round to my place. Failing that, I have to get to them," she said out loud.

Frankie on the other hand tried to pour himself a glass of water but his hands were shaking too violently! Smack watched him stare blankly at the table then pour water all over most of the delivery invoices.

"Are you all right, big man, you're spilling your water?"

Frankie could hear the question. He just couldn't purge the image of Eva from his mind long enough to construct a reply. He eventually forced himself out of his stupor long enough to string a few words together.

"Clock out for me will you son. I'm not feeling well," he lied without conscience.

He quickly left without saying another word to Smack or Dark Eddie. He forgot he'd left his car in the staff car park and made his way to Belfast City Hospital on foot where he knew he would find the nearest ecumenical chapel inside the hospital building. The incident had shaken him to his core and he needed to touch and feel objects that he knew for sure were real and made sense all of his life.

What he had witnessed just was not possible. He eventually calmed as his brain tried to reboot his memory and supply his mind with a rational diagnostic of the event that just occurred. He was a fairly simple creature so it hadn't taken much effort to come up with several sensible explanations for his mind to rationalise the episode.

Eva's eyes weren't black, you moron. You must have had a reaction to something you ate. I bet those two bastards slipped something into my tea for a laugh. That creepy bastard Eddie has been trying to get one back at me since I put that stuff they give to bulls for breeding in his coffee. The poor sod couldn't go out for two days with the erection he had. I mean, a cat couldn't have scratched it!

He remembered Eddie wrestling to retain some dignity as he attempted to leave work with the stiffest erection he had ever known. His bus journey home must have been priceless!

Simple explanation sorted, he left the chapel and made his way to the pub.

I mean what were you thinking? The girl was just standing in the dark lost in her thoughts for feck's sake! I'll have to make it up to her.

He thought he should apologise the next time he saw her but knew he wouldn't. Frankie was old school. So saying sorry was a rarity especially to a woman. He would never mention it again and let it be forgotten.

Smack returned to the storeroom to collect the dead chicks for freezing. He began to stack one box on top of the other to save himself a second journey, as he did he noticed two of the chicks were attempting to climb out of the box and away from their dead brothers and sisters!

"Never seen that before," he mumbled to himself, "and I've seen thousands of gassed chicks. I think I'll hold on to these two for our Christine; she keeps chickens."

He placed a chick in each pocket of his brown store coat, and checked through the rest of the batch to see if any more had survived. None had so he carried on with his original task of freezing them. He transferred the live chicks from his coat to side pockets of his cargo shorts, clocked off for the day and left. He could hear them chirping merrily all the way to the front door of his house.

Chapter *78*

T HE SOUNDS FROM THE GARDEN FILTERED INTO the room while Valentine sat quietly waiting and listening to the birds outside squabble for morsels from the feeding table. The nurse was to finally remove the dressings that covered his damaged eyes.

The French doors were fully open, letting the sounds of the splashing fountain into his summerhouse room in the grounds of his mansion. He heard the knock on the door and hoped it would be Charlotte his nurse and that he didn't have to provide any more ridiculous answers to unimportant questions that Kay now seemed to need his every opinion on, no matter how trivial. He hadn't decided if it was some sort of latent 'Mothering' instinct or just insecurity.

Ever since the explosion she refused to leave his side for more than an hour and he was beginning to find it increasingly more irritating. *I mean what the hell is wrong with the woman? It's not as if she caused the explosion!*

Time in the darkness had given him plenty of time to think and ask questions of himself and the events leading up to the incident.

Valentine was now fully up to speed on the name and history of the bomber. His security staff had squeezed the right people in a way the police never could. They had called in favours and greased plenty of palms. The suicide bomber's name was Steven Dearie. There hadn't been much left of him after the

276

explosion to do a complete post mortem on. What was discovered, however, was the unusual cocktail of drugs gathered from a blood sample taken from the remains of his severed calf muscle. How he had managed to set detonators and a dead man's switch found in the debris was a mystery? He shouldn't have been capable of biting his own finger, considering the amount of narcotics in his system.

All the components found and fragments retrieved from the scene could have been bought over the counter from any hardware store. That wasn't the puzzle. What was confusing was, among other things, the accuracy of the blast. According to his experts, he would have to have had specialist military training to be that precise when directing the bombs force. It radiated at exactly ninety-seven degrees in each forward direction. How did he know that positioning himself against the clay wall of the grave would send the blast exactly where he intended?

There were only so many details you could pick up on the internet and that wasn't one of them. The other curious thing was why had he bothered to attach a steel back plate? Why would he need to be so specific unless he only wanted a particular section of the mourners directly in the path of the blast? How could he as an amateur know that there would be only slight residual damage to the rear of the blast and why?

Surely if you wanted to take your own life and the lives of the people you thought responsible for animal cruelty, you would attempt to kill everyone.

It didn't add up. Not unless you had a specific target or targets with no regard for any innocent bystanders.

There had to be to be more to this than a crazy with a grudge, added to the fact that this guy had no past military training or that he had ever been convicted of an act of extreme violence. Dearie had been a nobody. So why all of a sudden did he choose the funeral of Rachel Cohen to make such a public display?

Valentine also began thinking about his parents. Where were they and why had they still not been to see him – they knew he'd been injured.

Valentine's mother had phoned to ask after his welfare but she appeared generally disinterested regarding it. His father had his assistant send a cactus in the shape of a penis with two testicles and a 'get-well' note.

They should have been killed with the rest of them or at least had major injuries even if the front row had absorbed most of the blast! Had their injuries been worse than he had first been led to believe?

His chief of security had made one more very troubling observation. Why were the fragments and residue from the vest that the bomber had worn contaminated with rat's faeces and urine and why had they found no traces of this on what remained of the pieces of Steve Dearies body tissues other than in the fragments themselves? There had been no traces found on what remained of his clothing. Even if he did wear gloves it would have left the slightest trace somewhere on him. There should have been some residue somewhere, but they could find none. If this act was premeditated he wouldn't have cared if his fingerprints and DNA were splattered over everything. Why should he? He was going to die anyway? No suicide note or video was sent to the media explaining his actions or who he represented. Too many unanswered questions.

Valentine's nurse Charlotte entered the room. He heard the trolley she was pushing rattle across the marble floor.

"Good morning Mr. Sere. Are you ready for the unveiling this beautiful morning?"

"Good morning to you Charlotte. I trust you're well and have finally washed those hands of yours?"

Charlotte laughed and made her way to the open French doors closing them and pulling the shades across.

"I'm just pulling the drapes, Mr. Sere. You have been in the dark for a while and we need to let those eyes of yours adjust a little."

Valentine nodded that he understood. Thoughts of the event kept bullying their way into his mind. This should have been a tense moment but he was distracted by questions that he couldn't answer. At least, not yet.

"Now let's get these bandages off shall we?"

Again he nodded that he understood. She would put it down

to tension and nerves. His mind was starting to tumble with memories of the blast before he lost his sight. Why also had Kay been so business-like? He knew she was tough but she had been as close to the blast as he was. He hadn't sensed any distress in her voice, just irritation at some receptionist while on the phone in the car. Pennies were beginning to drop.

"Hold on a minute Charlotte. I have a call to make. Could you wait outside or get yourself a coffee?"

Again Charlotte put it down to nerves.

"You take as long as you like, Mr. Sere. I'll be just outside when you need me."

He heard her leave the room and shut the doors behind her. He felt for the buttons on the hand set of the phone and depressed the number six button twice. The call was answered instantly.

"Mr. Sere. What can I do for you?"

"I need a word in private, Paul," Valentine replied.

"I can be there in ten minutes if that suits you, sir?" said his Head of Security.

"That's fine. Do you know where to find me?"

"Of course, sir. You're in the garden room of the villa."

"That's why you're my Head of Security."

"Thank you, sir."

They both hung up at the same time. Then Valentine rang his hand bell again for Charlotte.

"Ready when you are, nurse."

Charlotte entered again without knocking this time and made her way to his side.

"Shall I call Miss Kane, sir? She asked to be present when you had your dressings removed."

"No Charlotte. That won't be necessary. Let's continue without observers, shall we?"

"She won't be pleased, sir. She was very insistent that I should call her when I was removing your dressings."

Valentine's patience had reached its end with Kay Kane's now constant meddling. He was in a hurry and didn't need his hand held by a person who, on second thoughts, he may have promoted too quickly.

"Charlotte. Please don't have me ask again."

"Of course, Mr. Sere. My apologies."

Valentine felt the cold metal of the scissors against the side of his cheek as Charlotte slipped the blade under the dressing. In his heart he knew his sight was fine but there was always a risk. He was able to see tiny slivers of light through some of the mesh bandages when he awakened in the morning. He hadn't thought of Harmony Rodgers since she had treated him at the clinic and now wondered why there had been no follow up call from her or any member of her staff to check on his recovery?

"Charlotte. How's that boss of yours doing these days?"

Charlotte withdrew the scissors before she had finished removing the dressing.

"Oh, Mr. Sere. Of course, you wouldn't have heard. Dr Rodgers and that lovely Mr. Duval had a terrible accident. It appears they had been having an affair for years and decided to make a new start of things together somewhere in the Middle East. Saudi Arabia, if I recall correctly. It was awful for their families. Mr. Duval had three young children under twelve years old but sadly it mustn't have been a happy marriage. I'm sure they must have been planning it for ages. They both decided to take a desert safari I think, yes that's right, it was a safari in one of those SUV's and it's reported that it rolled over down one of those huge sand dunes and landed on its roof. From what the newspaper articles and police are saying, they had appeared to have drowned in sand. When they performed the autopsy both of their lungs were filled to bursting with yellow dust! I have never heard of such a thing; those poor people. What a terrible way to die, especially when they were both so young and talented."

Charlotte returned to her task of removing the dressings. Valentine's 'danger radar' started beeping faster in his mind. Too many people were dying suddenly to be a coincidence for his liking.

"Now, Mr. Sere, if you would slowly like to open your eyes while I put some drops in."

Valentine's thoughts returned to his sight and he did as instructed. The light, even though dim, stung and he closed his eyelids to ease the pain. What Charlotte had briefly seen was the most beautiful shade of amber going onto gold in the pupils of his eyes. She was fascinated and urged him to try to open them again for her.

She had fallen instantly in love. The rational part of her brain that resisted the magic, was telling her to pull herself together and act at least some of her fifty-six years. However the rest of her reason was dreaming of open car rides and holding hands with the most alluring creature she had ever seen.

Chapter **79**

IT WAS LIKE FIRST LOVE ALL OVER AGAIN. SHE HAD not experienced the rush of pure emotion for such a long, long time. Her face flushed pink. Charlotte could feel the beginnings of a nervous rash spreading up her neck and throat. Whatever this man asked of her, she would do without question. It took most of her reserve to avoid behaving like a love struck teenager. She managed to regain some composure before speaking again.

"OK, everything looks fine, Mr. Sere. If you would just try one more time to open your eyes, nice and slowly for me now."

He tried as requested and eventually succeeded in fully opening his left eye, then his right. Charlotte, as discretely as possible, sought just one more glance into the amber-gold pools of his eyes. The colours swirled and swayed in circles around the golden pupils. She moved her gaze from one to the other, pretending to look for any remaining damage. Her breathing became heavy as she leaned ever closer towards those golden eyes.

Valentine snapped her out of her trance!

"What are doing, Charlotte? Do my eyes look OK?"

"Oh yes, sir, they're beautiful. I have never seen such a beautiful thing."

She almost drooled as she said the sentence.

"Beautiful! What do you mean *beautiful?*"

"Oh Mr. Sere, sir, it's like liquid light - all amber and gold, swirling and twirling."

He pushed her to the side as he rose to his feet, spilling the

282

remaining contents of the tray onto the floor. Charlotte was still in a stupor following his frantic efforts to locate a mirror.

This was his own house and he couldn't find a stupid looking glass to check his own reflection! He thrust open the doors of the sun room leading him into the hallway where Paul Sloan, his Head of Security, was sitting patiently on the chair waiting for him.

Paul immediately leapt to his feet to aid his employer.

"Are you all right, sir?"

Valentine hadn't noticed him until he spoke.

"Help me find a mirror please, Paul!"

"This way, sir," replied his Head of Security.

Paul led Valentine to the nearest of the several bathrooms and opened the door for him to enter.

"Wait here please, Paul."

Valentine shut the door behind him and walked to the mirror. His reflection was the same as he remembered it before the bomb blast. The only remarkable thing was the lack of scabbing or evidence of any damage to his skin. His eyes were their normal grey blue. He gave an audible sigh and began to relax a little. *That nurse is acting like a frigging love struck teenager! My eyes are the same as they always were.* He opened the door to find Paul and Charlotte waiting for him outside the bathroom. Charlotte's spell appeared to have broken and, thankfully, she seemed to be back to her normal self.

"Mr. Sere. Are you all right? One minute I was removing your dressings and the next thing I knew you were gone. I don't even remember you leaving the room. You were just gone."

"Charlotte. What colour are my eyes to you?"

"Why they're blue with a fleck of grey, Mr. Sere."

"Do you agree with her, Paul?"

Paul, regardless that the request was strange, inspected them from a distance, like eyeing up a target.

"She's right, sir. Blue and some grey."

"Thank you both. Charlotte, that will be all."

Charlotte picked up her bag and made her way toward the exit. Paul opened the door for her as she left. Valentine ushered Paul back into the sunroom.

"Take a chair please while I let the light in."

The drapes swished open and as the light flooded into the room, Valentine saw the living space as if it was his first time being there. It was as if he was wearing the wrong prescription glasses all of his life and by some miracle no longer needed them. He saw the paintings and rare objects that adorned the room. All bought for their rarity value, not for their beauty.

It's only when you may lose something do you truly value it, he thought to himself.

He returned his attention to Paul.

"Let's get down to business. Paul, first things first; the nurse who was treating me, Charlotte Aiken, is that correct?"

"Yes, sir. She is one of the senior nurses on the register and a former employee of the late Doctor Rodgers?"

"Get rid of her. She's deranged. Oh and I don't mean get rid of her in the living breathing way. Just make her go away. Somewhere else, some other position. You know what I mean?"

"Of course, I understand. No problem, sir. Oh one more thing Mr. Sere. I think you should know that your Vice Chairwoman, Miss Kane, has requested that any information destined for you should be redirected to her during your illness. I'm sure that this may go against your wishes."

This was the first time Paul had seen his boss rattled and not fully in control of any situation.

Valentine seethed with rage at the actions of Kay without informing him. It was beyond over stepping the mark. He would take enough time for his temper to settle then come to a decision on her future as his second in command.

Chapter *80*

THE LIGHT SHEET WAS KICKED AWAY AS NURSE Jaclyn Gates dream intensified. Perspiration ran down her neck and settled into the wells between her chest and collarbones. She'd seen it all in her time. Gunshot wounds, industrial accidents, the list was endless.

Years of nursing had left her numb to the sight of broken bodies and human tragedy. She hadn't seen her daughter or ex-husband in almost ten years. None of her birthdays were celebrated and holidays were spent alone. She'd had relationships over the passing years but they'd never lasted more than a year at best. A person couldn't love someone if they hated themselves as much as she did.

The same recurring dream that was an irregular constant; how many tragic mistakes could one individual be allowed to make in their lives before even they couldn't forgive themselves?

She woke in the usual way, throwing off the now damp sheet and staring out at the glare of the afternoons setting sun.

The fan above her bed chopped at the humid air, doing little but shifting warm air from one part of the room to another. The packet of cigarettes was almost empty. She took one from the packet and lit it. The heavy smoke dried her mouth and made her head spin.

She curled her knees up and rested her head against the synthetic headboard as she stared out of the window at the passing traffic. She could see Lake Michigan in the very far distance or at least she told herself she could.

Her tee-shirt was wet around her waist so she rolled it up revealing the brand on her stomach; a simple circle with an inverted cross, burnt into the tissue. Healed long ago but the scar was as fresh today as the day she had received it, a permanent reminder of a sin that could never be forgiven.

That was the day she had sold her new born son!

Chapter *81*

VALENTINE OFFERED PAUL A DRINK AND WAS about to explain why he had asked him to be there, when the *for your eyes only* function on his phone vibrated and the signal automatically switched all the electrical devices in the room to standby mode.

It was protocol if his *Techies* had intercepted any important information that they thought would warrant his immediate attention.

The screen flashed red with the words CONTACT, CONTACT, CONTACT embossed across the black surface in bold white capital letters. He excused himself and requested that Paul momentarily leave the room.

"Sorry, Paul, I need to take this. Could you give me a moment?"

"Of course, sir. I'll be waiting outside."

Valentine pressed the contact number at the bottom of the screen and the call was swiftly answered.

"Dial your horoscope. How can we help you?"

Valentine answered in one word so bypassing the system. "RAPTURE."

The dial tone changed and he was put directly through to one of the controllers. He had installed the system with trapdoors and logarithms that only this particular system would understand. The connection was encrypted as was the conversation between him and the senior controller.

He hadn't wanted some spotty teenager or a nosey government agent to accidentally discover his covert information-gathering network.

All of it was illegal. Prying into computer systems and government security would land him in jail in a list of very unsympathetic countries. All that considered, it was more than worth the risk. He had recruited patsies; men and women that were well paid and would take the blame in the unlikely eventuality that such a situation ever arose.

He or she had hacked the communication system and knew if any *red* calls had been made or received. The call was transferred directly to his answer service. That way if it ever went to court, there had been no direct conversation between him and the caller and it could be construed as a misdial. Valentine hung up and waited for the recorded message to arrive.

His phone vibrated again as the voicemail icon lit up on the screen. He connected to the service and held the phone to his ear.

"Hi, baby, it's me. Got a call today from your niece in Paris. She's pregnant and wanted to tell you herself but you must have been out of service. What great news! I'm forwarding you the email she sent of her trip to Ireland to meet the baby's grandparents. She sent some lovely pictures of the countryside along with the locations of some of the sights for you to go see if you get a chance to visit while you're there. You'll love them. Call me when you're coming home. Love you!"

The details and medical history of one, Audrey Walsh, also the particulars of one Doctor James E Payne downloaded onto his phone. This was then transferred to the seventy-inch widescreen TV on the wall that appeared from behind the oil fresco of the prancing horses.

The details of Audrey's recovery were genuinely mind blowing. This woman had complete reversal of symptoms and this Doctor Payne was, what looked like, preparing to do God only knows what with her! As a doctor it would break his Hippocratic oath and that was a worry. If he was willing to do that then, who knew what he was capable of. Valentine had seen similar scenarios before and none of them had ended well for anyone.

Valentine couldn't care less for the subject. Her fate was sealed one way or another. It was simply that if his competition got hold of her first then they would hold, not only a controlling share of the pharmaceutical market, but countless others as well.

How in the hell did this happen? How could someone just be cured of Stage 1 diabetes? It wasn't possible. If this really does turn out to be genuine, it would be the biggest medical breakthrough in history. Scratch that. *It would be the biggest discovery of any kind in history!*

No time to waste. His eyesight was perfect again and his adrenalin pumping. He summoned Paul back into the room. Valentine was on the telephone to his own private airfield as Paul entered.

"Yes, yes. One hour. Fuelled and ready. Yes, it's not domestic. Put Jonus on the line."

Valentine placed his hand over the speaker part of the telephone and spoke to Paul.

"Do you have your passport with you?"

"Of course, Mr. Sere. I keep it in the car."

"You had better go get it."

Valentines technical wizards weren't the only ones to intercept the email from France. His systems had been infiltrated with a particular program that even his unlimited funds could neither have manufactured nor detected.

Chapter *82*

THE FAMILIAR SYMBOL APPEARED ON KAY'S cellphone as it vibrated on her desk. The symbol on the screen left her again in no doubt who was making contact. The circular image faded as the first message came through. Details of the experiment that had taken place in the lab in Belfast flashed across its screen including the contact details of Doctor Eva Ballantine, John Greer and any individual involved in the same department or were listed as university staff. Audrey Walsh and her recent medical reports along with the contact details of Dr Payne were downloaded onto her handset.

Kay stared at the results in disbelief but she knew that if it came from her benefactors then it was genuine. The medical report concerning the Walsh woman was equally astonishing.

Her first thought was this was too much of a coincidence not to be somehow related. She needed to contact Valentine and tell him of her discovery. She was just about to bring his number up on the screen when the second message came through.

"You will no longer be employed by BION pharmaceutical. You will tender your resignation immediately. You will go to Ireland and get the girl Ballantine by whatever means necessary, but keep her alive. She is vital to our pending plans. Keep her away from Valentine Sere at all costs. He must not be contaminated. Do not contact him. This must be done by you and those you require to accomplish our orders. You will be protected and armed with the necessary weapons. Do not under any circumstances disappoint us as the consequences shall be dire."

The circular peace symbol reappeared to signal the end of the transmission. Kay watched it fade to black and vanish from the screen again. For the first time since her association with her benefactors, Kay gave real consideration to disobeying them. Even she had trouble imagining the global impact of such a find. This girl could hold the key to life itself! One way or another she would have her at her mercy and God help her!

The peace symbol reappeared on her phone for the second time as if they could somehow read her thoughts. The screen then again faded back to black. Kay rubbed the edge of the cell phone across her brow. The girl was as good as got, that would be easy, but what's the connection with Valentine apart from the similar obvious commercial interest that motivated her? She opened her handbag and dropped the phone into its depths.

Looks like I'm on my own again. Given a little more time I would have stripped that company to the bare bones and left Valentine and that wretched family of his penniless. Oh well, onwards and upwards; time to requisition this latest product.

The symbol on Kay's cell phone was the international sign of Peace used by the CND.

The more sinister and alternative meaning of the symbol, that Kay was oblivious to, was that it mocks the cross of Christ and appears on many senior SS and Nazi officer's headstones. It is less well known as *Cross of Nero* or *Gesture of Despair*.

Kay, like so many others, was oblivious to its less benign usage and sinister history.

Chapter *83*

JONUS LEPP HEADED UP VALENTINE'S TRAVEL research team. His adventures took him into some very unstable and inhospitable regions. He needed all the information he could get and Jonus was an expert on likely trouble spots wherever they were on the planet.

"Who's running things in Ireland these days Jonus?"

"We are, of course, sir. Do you mean the whole country or just the North?"

"Just the North. The source indicates Belfast."

"Ah the badlands," replied Jonus. "Right now, it seems stable under the circumstances. Devolved set up comprising ex-terrorists and loyalist right wing religious types. Despite the divides between them, it appears to be working. No direct threat of danger to tourists or visitors with the exception of the usual muggings etc. Enjoy your trip, sir."

Valentine hung up and turned his focus back to Paul.

"Have you ever been to the Emerald Isle?"

"Yes, sir, once in the mid-1980s during military covert operations."

"And your thoughts on the place?" asked Valentine.

"Bad roads and worse weather," Paul replied.

"Sounds delightful. Now grab your raincoat. We leave in ninety minutes. In the meantime, find out the location of one Dr James E. Payne. He sounds like a charmer and he may already have something in his possession that we need to procure with the utmost urgency. We have to find him and locate his discovery then remove and extract the subject that he plans to hold for ransom. Payne's expendable, so no need for kid gloves. I want all his research material and anything pertaining to Audrey Walsh, his 'test subject' as he refers to her. I can't ascertain yet what he's done to her or what condition she'll be in when we get to her."

"Do you need any assistance in obtaining this individual?" continued Valentine. "I'm sending you everything you need to know. Also, do we have any contacts in Ireland?"

"Of course, sir, and if I need indigenous help I will have no trouble in recruiting them, but I don't foresee any problems with this operation."

"Call them anyway, please," Valentine replied. "Tell them what we need. I don't want any hiccups on this one. This is belt and braces time. I want her ready for transport and in my hands within forty-eight hours. I want her house searched for anything that may have aided in her recovery from her past condition. Take everything medical from the house including home remedies, homeopathic medication and whatever else looks like it could give us a clue to her non-prescription medical history. Get your boys on the ground to stage whatever they need to do to get it done. I don't care if we have to take the neighbours as well. This will be standard extraction protocol. No debit cards, no credit cards and absolutely no use of cell phones while we stay in Ireland. Have Jonus get us whatever sort of currency they use there and make sure the long range walkie-talkies are available for us to communicate.

"Also, find out what you can from your contacts about this Payne guy. I want to know what buttons to push when I meet him. He sounds the greedy, heartless type. Email this doctor from one of the secure systems with a substantial offer and have him meet us somewhere public yet discrete. I want him softened up when I eventually find out what he knows. I have a feeling it won't be the most difficult deal I've ever had to broker.

"Finally, tell our contacts to have Mrs. Walsh sedated and ready for the flight. Find out from her medical records if she has any special requirements. Have them organise whatever she needs to keep her healthy until we get her back."

"Where will we be taking her, sir?"

"I'll let you and the pilot know when we're in the air. I haven't decided our final destination yet, but bring everything anyway - clothing for all of us and for any conditions.

"This should be a simple 'in and out'. You've done it a hundred times. I know I don't need to tell you any of this, Paul, but I'm just trying to run it through my own mind to get it fixed in there. I'm not expecting any dramas."

Paul hesitated for a moment, "Sir, will Miss Kane be joining us? She has asked me again to keep her fully informed of your condition."

Valentine's face turned white with anger. *How dare she make demands on my private Head of Security. I think it's time for Miss Kane to find a new interest.*

"No, Paul. I think I need our legal team to look at Miss Kane's contract. I may reassign her to our Kazakhstan facility."

He typed the message to Kay while the wheels of the jet were still spinning as they left the ground.

Hi, Kay. I'm off for a well-deserved holiday on the beach. Eyesight's fine. Keep things ticking over at the office and make sure the Cairo contract gets signed in my absence. I know the details will take some fine tuning so you have the next forty-eight hours free from interruption.

He sent the message then called Joanne his personal aide. The phone rang only twice before being answered.

"Hello Mr. Sere, sorry Val, how can I help you?"

"Jo. Contact Henry Thatch for me and have him dig out Kay Kane's contract. I want her put on garden leave for the next month."

"Of course, sir. Anything else?"

"No that will be all, Joanne."

Valentine then hung up the phone and settled into his seat for the flight.

Chapter *84*

THE EMAIL FROM VALENTINE'S FRENCH ASSET was received by Andrus at almost the same time as Valentine. Kay's contacts had intercepted it and forwarded it onto her. She sent it on to Andrus as soon as she realised its gravity.

His boarding passes were sent to his smart phone, first to Newark airport then directly to Belfast, Northern Ireland, under the name of 'Gavin Heart' as requested. He was given the same instructions and urgency to retrieve Mrs. Walsh and extract whatever information this Payne guy had on her by any means he deemed necessary. Kay's message was to the point.

"The primary target is the Ballantine girl and any or all information regarding her work and experiments. If time allows, we extract all further information by any means from anyone associated with her. All, including her friend and sister are dispensable."

His reply was short.

"It'll be expensive. Is this a race?"

The response was almost immediate.

"It's a sprint!"

Kay suddenly realised her own stupidity. Valentine was having his dressings removed that morning. Even if he wasn't, he would be using the BION jet to get to his holiday destination, maybe a nurse would be travelling with him. Putting Andrus on a commercial flight was the height of stupidity. She sent him another email.

"Make your way to O'Hare Airport. I'll have your transport organised when you arrive. I will be joining you. Further instructions will follow en route. Do you have contacts that can supply you with anything you may need over there?"

She didn't receive a reply. This guy was obviously self-sufficient and lacked conversational skills. He was efficient she couldn't deny that. He would need the fast transport to be on call as and when he needed it. He would also need to be supplied with resuscitation equipment and an array of medicines if Mrs. Walsh incurred any injuries during kidnapping or the extraction.

It was time for her second call to her favourite Irish playwright. She would have to use her own personal cell phone this time and she wasn't happy about it. She knew for damned sure he wouldn't be! The tone rang three times as usual.

"Darling, you appear to be calling from an unsecured line! Hang up at once and I'll forward you a number of a public landline. Wait for five minutes until you call. Kiss, kiss."

Kay knew Oscar was furious with her for breaking security protocol. This was probably the last time he would take any more of her calls.

The number of the payphone came through on her cell. It had a prefixed international code. Nothing she hadn't already suspected. She dialled the number and waited for it to be answered.

"Miss Kane. What can I do for you this one last time?"

The theatrics had gone from his voice, replaced with that of a middle-aged man who had obviously spent most of his life in an arid country. His voice had grown to a grumble now that there was no need to disguise. The accent was unmistakably German or Austrian.

"I need a contact in Belfast, Northern Ireland."

"A reliable contact will be on its way to you by the time this call ends. Take it as a parting gift. I'm sure you are aware of the consequences of contacting me again, Miss Kane."

"I understand fully."

The connection was severed. A moment later the name of 'Mervin Robinson' appeared on her cell's screen along with his contact details. *I'll call him from the plane*, she reasoned.

Kay would miss Oscar. He was one of the rare people that she could be honest with.

OK, who do I have on a string with a transcontinental jet at O'Hare? Of course, the Goldstein's. They keep one permanently at the ready there for the family's personal use and the odd corporate jolly.

She rang Rina Goldstein, passed on her condolences again and asked could she rent the aircraft for two days? She would return the favour as a matter of course. Rina told her not to be so silly and she would call the pilots and have them at her disposal immediately. It was the least she could to do to return the kindness she had shown since Ira's death.

"You've been very kind to us, Kay. I don't want to hear another thing about it. Take the Gulf-stream for as long as you need it. I'll have Thomas fuel it and ready it to go for you. Is there anything else that you need?"

"No, Rina. You've already been more than generous. If you could just have Thomas make security aware of a Mr. Gavin Heart, he will be travelling with me."

"Oh I see, naughty weekend, you rascal. Have a ball."

Kay didn't see the point of protesting. It was as good a reason as any. She was getting a head cold and it had gotten heavier combined with a splitting headache. It would all be worth it if this miracle woman bore fruit. She wasn't in any doubt that the people she answered to would be disappointed to say the least if she let this one slip through her fingers.

The flight details were forwarded to Gavin or whatever his real name was, with the added information that she would be joining him on the flight. She knew he wouldn't like it and she may be placing herself in danger.

From experience, Kay knew these types of people cherished their anonymity and rarely had direct contact with their employers. This fact however may be overlooked when he saw the offer she was prepared to make him. He would never, if he desired it, have to work again. BION would underwrite any amount to secure this woman, but that wasn't her agenda. If there was such a thing as a blank cheque in business, she had the power to write it for this one, then do whatever her old benefactors desired with her.

The emergency suitcase was packed with several passports under various pseudonyms, including the usual assortment of kit and clothing for any occasion, 10,000 dollars and a further 10,000 euros. A tracking device had been installed in the lining in the event of theft or kidnapping.

The clock was ticking. Valentine could be in the air already for all she knew. She called for her driver to fetch the case and have the car brought round to the front of the building. She was quite looking forward to meeting Gavin. Oscar Wilde had given him as good a resume as she had ever seen and he was a person not given to compliments.

She picked up her lipstick from the counter top and turned to leave. It was then that she remembered the platinum pillbox still sitting in the freezer where she had left it. The vapour rose from the platinum case as it made contact with the kitchen's warm air. It remained as mysterious looking as the last time she had seen it. She considered it for a moment and for some strange reason felt the urge to take it with her. It had been delivered for a purpose and this one seemed as good as any.

Kay trusted her gut feelings about most things but this felt different. She had her contacts down at the HLOB laboratory put the pill through a spectrum of toxicology tests. They all came back with the same result; water, with a small amount of *acetylsalicylic acid*. It was an aspirin for God's sake; plain and simple.

Why the hell would someone hand deliver a placebo in such an ornate box that contained a good old-fashioned headache pill? No time for this now. She dropped it into her handbag along with the lipstick and slammed the door shut behind her.

With the pain she was having in her head right now it may just serve a purpose. She despised taking medication when she was working as she believed it dulled her senses.

Her car was waiting for her with the driver holding the door. He greeted her without her returning the pleasantry as she slid into the rear seat.

"Let's go. I'm in a hurry."

"Of course, Madam."

Kay closed the window dividing her and the driver as she stared at the handbag that she had placed beside her on the seat.

Her curiosity got the better of her. She opened the bag and again stared at the platinum container lying on its side partially covered by an eyeliner pencil and lipstick smeared tissues.

If someone chooses to harm me there are countless ways to do it.

The pulse in her temple was beating so strongly now she could feel it moving her skin to the rhythm. She had to close her eyes and rest her head back against the seat as she tried to cope with the increasing pain. She had never suffered a severe migraine before and now regretted dismissing it as a mere headache to anyone who had ever mentioned having one in the past. The aches were spreading into the rest of her body and the feeling of nausea combined with the motion of the car was returning the yogurt and fruit breakfast to the back of her throat.

She had to be fit and well for this trip. If this was the beginning of a flu', it couldn't have come at a worse time. The tissues in her bag were pushed to one side as she retrieved the pill case. Decision made. She had to do something to ease these symptoms. The catch on the pill box made the same familiar hiss as she scanned it with the barcode reader on her phone. She didn't need the plastic bag that it had arrived in anymore. The box was now responding to the scanner. She didn't even notice as her head felt like it was going to explode. The lid hissed open again and a tiny amount of cold vapour escaped from the seal spilling down into the palm of her hand.

This thing must have its own cooling unit. Maybe lined in dry ice or something similar.

The pain in her head continued to intensify and she could now barely see out of her right eye as she stifled the urge to vomit on the cars navy blue carpet. These symptoms had come on so quickly they had taken her completely by surprise. Sudden horror shot her into full alert. *Am I infected with the JSTR virus?*

No time for doctors. She removed the pill and put it in her mouth rolling it over then under her tongue. No taste or indicators of poison so far. The fridge in the car was stocked with soft drinks and alcohol. She unscrewed the lid of a bottle of *Grey Goose* vodka, half-filled her mouth with the liquid and swallowed the pill in one gulp.

If my time is up, I may as well enjoy the experience.

The vodka burnt the back of her throat and the inside of her mouth on the way down. She winced and swallowed another shot to anaesthetise the effect. That was followed by a swig of water to wash the vodka down. As she lay back holding her head in her hands, she prayed for the agony to stop. The effect was immediate. The searing pain in her head ceased instantly and her hands flopped to her sides, banging her wrist off the buckle of the safety belt causing her to swear at it. She adjusted herself in the seat nursing her wrist and watched as the buildings went past. She turned her attention to the back of the drivers capped head.

Where did the headache go? What the hell was in that pill?

Whatever it was she wanted the formula. She removed the vanity mirror from her handbag and checked her reflection.

That's impossible!

It took several rechecks to confirm what her eyes were telling her. The pockmarks she had acquired on her cheeks from chicken pox as a child were gone. She scrubbed at her face to remove the heavy make-up she used in public to disguise them. This was real. There was no sign of scarring. For a second she was struck dumb in amazement.

A barely audible whisper escaped from her lips as she pushed the button on the intercom.

"Stop the car."

"I'm sorry, Madam. Did you say something?"

"Stop the car, please, driver!"

This time the command was louder. The driver pulled to the curbside while Kay continued to stare at her reflection in the mirror.

"Do you have a handkerchief?"

"Of course, Madam."

He passed her an immaculate white handkerchief from his pocket with the initials *J S* embroidered on it. She stared at the monogrammed handkerchief wondering what the initials stood for. He interrupted her thoughts by suggesting she use the wipes provided in the cold compartment.

"Thank you."

She attempted to pass the handkerchief back through the open dividing window.

"Please. Keep it, Madam."

Kay dropped the handkerchief into her handbag and retrieved the wet wipes from the side pocket of the fridge. The scent of lemon as she withdrew the moist tissue filled the inside of the car. She removed the remainder of her make-up and continued to stare in disbelief at her reflection in the small hand mirror. No lines. No broken veins. Even the scar on her chin she received through an accident at school while playing lacrosse had disappeared!

She returned her focus to the box containing the used pill. The purple material that it had rested on had changed to white with two hand written words in platinum lettering, 'Justly Deserved.'

She snapped the lid of the box shut in fear and threw it back into her bag. She then returned her gaze to the mirror to make sure this hadn't been some clever illusion. Her image remained the same. Someone, somehow through whatever means, had managed to turn her clock back fifteen years and she wasn't looking a gift horse in the mouth.

How did the lacrosse scar disappear? I was twelve when I got that.

Again out of curiosity she tentatively retrieved the pill box from her handbag for the second time and reopened it. A new transparent pill lay resting on the familiar purple nest of satin with a new note attached, 'For whom you deem worthy.'

The rest of the journey to the airport passed without her noticing it. She was lost in her thoughts. Occasionally checking, then rechecking, her reflection in the mirror.

Chapter **85**

W HO HAD MADE THAT PILL, WHAT WAS IN IT, why hadn't the lab detected anything and why hadn't she known about it?

The car stopped in the exclusive departure section reserved for private or corporate jet owners. She remained in the car as the driver removed her small overnight suitcase from the trunk. He opened the door of the limousine for her to exit. He averted his eyes as trained so as not to embarrass female passengers wearing dresses or shorter skirts.

Kay eased her legs out and touched the tarmac with both her feet; the way she had been taught at finishing school, tucking the lower half of her skirt behind her legs.

Today she couldn't care less, but old habits were hard to break. She stood for a second inhaling the air that was tinged with avionic fuel and the noise from the jet engines as they warmed up, preparing for take-off.

She became aware of the driver's aversion to making eye contact with her. His manners were impeccable. She made a mental note to mention him for a salary increase and have him retained for her own personal use.

"Thank you, driver. You were both kind and considerate during the journey."

"My pleasure, Madam."

"I would be grateful if you would collect me yourself on my return."

"Of course, Madam."

She liked his manner. There was something about his detachment that appealed to her solitary nature. He appeared to be in his mid to late sixties with a fading tan from a recent holiday. His accent was hard to define. The slight inflection at the end of some of his words would have led her to think Australian but the formation of his sentences pointed to English or a hybrid of both. She felt calm and relaxed, which was most unusual for her. She even felt good about herself as a person, which again was unlike her. She was aware of her public persona. She should have been; she'd worked on it for long enough.

She hadn't reached her lofty position on the corporate ladder by being popular. Things got tougher as you climbed, especially if you were a woman. The *Boys Club* still didn't like it.

Today, though, even considering the urgency of the trip, and the pressure of failing, she felt unburdened and at peace for the first time in recent memory. There was a tight deadline to meet. The pilot could worry about that for the time being. A minute here, pain free and feeling this good was worth the pause. She turned to leave and heard the car door close behind her.

"By the way, driver, I didn't get your name?"

"Of course, Madam. It's Sol Newsier, at your disposal, Madam."

"Thank you again, Sol."

"You're most welcome, Madam."

"By the way, Sol. Where are you originally from? Your accent seems a little of Australian or English but your name sounds almost French?"

"I'm from many different places, Madam," her driver replied. "My parents had me educated in various international cities."

"And now you drive for a living?"

"I, like so many others in these troubled times, have recently been made redundant."

Great, she thought, *another loser.*

She didn't bother to say goodbye, instead turning and entering the terminal building, her familiar coldness and detachment returning. She wondered again what her paid assassin looked like. Mental images of the usual ex-military types with cropped hair and haunted gaunt faces from dirty campaigns of either too much or not enough killing.

This guy's a tool to use like any other, she told herself. *Get on with it.*

The security was, of course minimal, as few government departments reckoned on terrorists owning their own jets. As the flight hadn't been logged as international, no one even bothered to check her passport, but it was unlikely to be the same when landing in Northern Ireland so appropriate bribes would be necessary if required.

The jet sat on the tarmac with its engines running. The door was open and two of the female cabin crew stood at the bottom of the steps, waiting to greet their passengers. Kay opened the terminal doors and was tempted to protect her ears from the deafening sound of the twin engined jet as it brought the turbines up to optimum temperature.

The short walk across to the aircraft took but seconds. The crew greeted her as she approached.

"Good morning, Miss Kane, welcome aboard. This is Tara and I'm Lucy. We'll be attending to you on your flight today."

"Has the other passenger arrived yet, girls?" Kay enquired.

"No ma'am. You are the only passenger listed for the flight."

Kay thought about it for a second. Where was this guy? *I'll email him from the plane.*

She hesitated before boarding.

"Listen, I won't be needing in-flight hospitality. You two take a few days off."

She took the platinum no-limit credit card from her purse and handed it to Lucy.

"Go buy yourselves a party somewhere and get some new dresses while you're at it. I will expect that card back with a large hole burnt in it on my return."

Both the girls stood shocked at the more than generous offer. They were well used to tips by their wealthy employers but this was by far the best yet. Tara had slept with guests for less and both sexes at that! They simultaneously thanked her with the kind of enthusiasm you would expect from two teenagers asked to the prom for the first time.

"You won't need a pin number. Just sign it with a 'K'. Out of interest, where will you go?"

They turned towards each other hugging at the same time, then back to Kay and shouted, "Vegas!"

"Enjoy," was Kay's response.

She smiled as she watched the two girls hold hands and run to the terminal building, disappearing down the corridor still chattering to each other about the plans for their impromptu weekend. Kay turned and made her way up the steps. Once on board she reclined into one of the armchairs. She took out her phone and emailed her absent co-passenger.

"Where are you? I'm on board."

"As am I. Enjoy the flight."

If I look out the window and 'action man' is walking on the wing I'll piss myself laughing.

The idea brought a smile to her face. The sound of the pilot's voice came over the intercom.

"Good afternoon, Miss Kane. We will be on our way in a few minutes. We have programmed the navigation with the destination you requested and should be on our way. Please make yourself comfortable. If you would please be kind enough to fasten your seat belt for take-off. If you need to speak to me directly, just pick up your handset."

She picked up and almost barked at the pilot. Her old form returning at the realisation of how much time she had wasted on the ground.

"What's our flight duration, Captain?"

"I estimate six hours and fifty minutes. We have a slight headwind today that will slow us down a little."

"Could you do it in five?"

The rehearsed tone of the jet's captain changed to a more casual one.

"Sure, if I burn the engines out."

"So burn them. I'll pay for any repairs."

"You're the boss," was the reply. "I'll drop altitude and catch the jet stream. It won't be the smoothest flight."

"Let's go, Maverick."

She couldn't resist the *Top Gun* reference tinged with the surplus amount of sarcasm. These guys really couldn't get over themselves. Where the hell did they get those accents? There must be a module at flight school to teach you how to speak like that because she hadn't met anyone else who did! Speaking of accents, where was that slippery little Balkan bastard?

The genuine co-pilot of the plane had received a call telling him the flight had been cancelled and to wait on standby. If he hadn't received a call to fly within the next hour he was to consider it paid leave.

Of course, the call to work never came so he loaded up his mountain bike, drove to the hills and hit the happy trails.

Chapter *86*

NEW CASES OF THE JSTR VIRUS WERE BEING reported on the news channels of the world almost hourly. Cases were now verified in small, but growing numbers in most countries that could boast an airport. Scientists were still no closer to a cure or even treating the symptoms with any degree of success.

The disease was mutating and becoming increasingly more aggressive particularly in young children. Their metabolism appeared to accelerate the bone deformities at a vastly increased rate. The strain on the blood supply to the skull was causing haemorrhaging as the blood vessels and muscle structure strained with the abnormal rapid growth. New cases were registered every minute.

China, Russia and most parts of Europe were now reporting outbreaks. The first case in the United States had been detected two days ago. Since then several more had been registered in numerous states and cities, ranging from New Jersey to Mexico City. It was spreading at jet speed and the reports of those who had been newly infected were multiplying at a startling rate. Quarantine areas had been set up to deal with new intakes of patients.

It was now becoming commonplace to see people wearing surgical masks on the streets as they went about their daily routines. Schools were being advised to close and public meeting places to be avoided. It had so far not been termed a pandemic but that was only a matter of days away.

Senator Hamill had been appointed the head of the national task force due to his history in pharmaceuticals and he loved the power.

He had a full spectrum of resources to exploit at will and he was raping the government funding to the limit. He was also syphoning off millions of dollars which had been set aside in the event of natural disasters. The money he took was whisked around the globe to hundreds of small banks where he could access it at his leisure when the opportunity would arise.

I think another trip south of the border could be warranted soon. The last one had been too long ago for my needs and requirements.

Chapter *87*

JOHN GREER SAT AT HIS HOME COMPUTER AND inserted the memory stick containing all the test results on the algae project. The data began to upload onto the desktop. Greer opened Andrew Conlon's email address from his contacts. Andrew had studied biology at Cambridge University. They met ten years past at a blues festival in Clifden, County Galway. That part of Ireland drew tourists from all over the word for its friendliness and natural beauty.

They had swapped email addresses and mobile numbers. They worked in roughly the same field of research and had many things in common. There was little contact between them over winter and spring but when the days began to get longer their thoughts returned to the week-long festival and the emails began to flow.

John clicked on the new email from the menu bar at the bottom of his screen then minimised it as the data from the memory stick revealed the historical test results on the screen. Just to be sure, he saved it back on his hard drive again. The computer made its whirring sounds as Greer typed a brief note to Andrew requesting a second opinion on the new research in which he was involved.

He arranged to call him at a convenient time then passed on his regards. He hit the send icon at the top of the screen and watched as the words 'message sending' appeared at the bottom. It was taking longer than usual; Greer put this down to a slow internet connection. Taking advantage of the pause as the message was sending, he opened, then poured himself a glass of his favourite Spanish Rioja, filling the glass as close to the top as he dared without spilling any of the contents. The thought hadn't occurred to him to simply bring the bottle with him. His next task was to wrestle to open a stubborn bag of crisps ripping the bag with his teeth and spilling half the contents on to the counter top.

Bollocks. Balls to it! I'll eat them in a minute anyway. Must be diet crisps. I can't get the bag open.

He returned to the computer and saw the message was still being sent. Cursing the slow broadband connection he slurped the wine into his mouth and reclined back into the office chair he'd bought for a pittance from Queens during a refit of the labs. The computer pinged telling him the message had been sent.

OK. I'll see what he thinks in a minute.

He then continued to scan some of the numerous unopened mostly spam emails waiting in the inbox. Offers to buy his car. Cheap home insurance deals. Dating offers from females who would be considerably way out of his league unless he paid for their company. Most of the rest of the messages were in Russian.

What the hell did I ever buy from Russia and how do these people get my email address?

The ghostly email reply slowly appeared on his screen. It hit full resolution and was a speedy reply from Andrew.

"Hi, Johnny. Got your email. It's a large file so I'll need to take some time to go over the data. Get back to you when I read it all. Look forward to September, some great bands lined up. Best regards Drew."

Large file! What the hell is he talking about? I only asked him to give me a time when I should call him.

He clicked on the 'sent email' icon and opened the email he'd forwarded.

Along with the request to arrange a phone call, all the test results and experiments on the algae had been sent by mistake. The names and locations of the points of origin and collection of the samples taken and tested on were included. Also a list of names of research staff including his and Eva's were included in the file.

310

There was nothing Greer could do and he was almost blind with panic! The only course of action was to email Andrew and beg him to delete the email as it contained private information and had been sent entirely by mistake.

"Andrew. Sorry for sending you that file pal. It was an error on my part. It contains very sensitive research information. Apologies again for the drama. Can you comply and confirm?"

The return email was short.

"Sure, Johnny, No worries. Already done. Regards Drew."

John blew out his cheeks and slumped back again into his chair.

Christ that was close. Eva would have killed me!

His hands were shaking as he raised the wineglass and downed its entire contents in one gulp.

I have to be more careful with these results. Eva was right. This doesn't belong to me.

The temptation to share the information was increasingly becoming more urgent. The idea of fame and wealth as a result of their discovery was becoming impossible to purge from his thoughts.

Steady yourself fat boy. Patience, have some patience.

His heart rate slowed down and the shaking eased. The desire to be involved in such a big discovery was clouding his judgement.

Crisis averted he returned to the kitchen and began hoovering the spilled crisps from the counter top with his mouth, almost choking and spluttering half eaten crisps back over the counter.

Second glass poured, he settled down for an evening of chat shows with the odd flick onto the adult channels to see if there was anything worth looking at on the free-view channel before retiring to bed.

Chapter *88*

THE PHONE HUMMED AS IT SHUDDERED ITS WAY across the bedside table. Agathe Bessette wiped the sleep from her eyes as she watched the cell phone's screen light up, gently illuminating the underside of her yellow chiffon lampshade. It was one of several handsets she had bought herself without company knowledge. Each one was set up with different hacking programs for specific *red flag* scenarios.

Having one handset was crazy. What if she lost it or it was stolen? The phone would be shut down instantly, of course, if the user tried to bypass or break the passcode.

That, however, wouldn't help her if she received any new information quickly enough. And even with the technology available today, one handset would never be enough to cover all the increasing online data. She had programmed several to cover more specific grid patterns detecting even more obscure messages and emails from around the world. The system she had pre-set on all her handsets fire walled any spam mail and bombarded the sender with millions of redirected spam messages, overloading, and then quickly crashing their servers.

There had been more than one company that had regretted the fact that they sent millions of unwanted unsolicited junk emails at the click of a key, as their systems permanently crashed thanks to Agathe and her clever firewall. This was the same phone handset that she had intercepted the original red flag from the British Isles. It could be a coincidence but she doubted it.

EMAIL INTERCEPT...
Sender: John Greer. Jgreer@qub.oek
Recipient: Andrew Colon.... drewcon@guni.co.ir

Hi Drew.

Just sending you this message to arrange a convenient time for a chat over the phone. Let me know when suits?

Regards John

It was a simple and boring message. What followed however was not. All the test results including camera footage of the experiments were in the message that followed.

She watched some footage of the experiments before preparing to send it on. The grey dust that lay at the bottom of the test tube was obviously benign and lifeless. That was until the clear fluid had been added to it. The commentary and excitement from who she surmised was the sender of the message during the process; would leave her in no doubt that this was filmed in real time and not some conjuring trick or edited viral for a social network broadcast.

The look on both of the faces carrying out the experiment couldn't be faked. Whatever had been in that test tube was dead beyond resurrection. That was until the water, if indeed that really was water, had been introduced to the material.

The next piece of the film showed the dead spider plant being injected with the algae solution. She continued watching, enthralled as the plant was resurrected and then flowered.

Ce n'est pas possible!

She swung her legs off the bed, raked her fingers through her tangled hair and replayed the footage of the experiment.

What was in the syringe? This was a massive find even by her high standards. She was first to intercept internal emails from one of the technology giants regarding their prototype computer tablet while it was still in its infancy. She had been just fourteen at the time and the information she'd gathered had paid for her first designer watch along with the substantial sum of money deposited in what would be the first of her off-shore bank accounts. The selling of the infant technology to a major competitor for a tidy

313

fortune subsequently led to her being recruited by her current employer as a top-level agent. This discovery was bigger, way bigger. Before she passed on this information she would negotiate a new rate for her find and her continued services.

"So dear Agathe, let's make sure no-one else finds this email," she whispered to herself.

She docked the phone handset into her home computer and brought up the email containing the test results and film footage. She then sent a virus through the system using a worm. If anyone else received the email by accident or intent, it would instantly fry their hard drive. It didn't matter who it was. She had worked tirelessly for nine months developing the program and it had been a testing pregnancy. She stopped only to eat or sleep. It was to this point her finest work and as such, she regarded it her *perfect baby*. She knew it would be used someday when necessity called.

The contact details of the scientist and technician involved in the experiment were first downloaded onto her desktop. She froze the footage to obtain still shots of the two people involved. Within minutes she had illegally searched through both British and Irish passport offices data files and had easily hacked into their medical records and banks. She had obtained both John's and Eva's social security numbers, addresses, next of kin, mobile phone numbers and security passwords for their bank and savings accounts along with everyone else in their department.

This is the second interception within days from Ireland. Something is going on over there. First this miracle-woman, now apparently dead plants brought back to life. It was too much of a coincidence not to be connected in some way. But how?

She rechecked the Audrey woman's medical files to find out if she had volunteered for any radical or experimental trials in the university. She then checked if this Eva had ever practiced at the same surgery where the doctor who had sent the initial email worked.

What was his name? Ah yes, Payne. Doctor James E. Payne.

Agathe rescanned the email history on her computer. Normally the history of any discoveries was automatically deleted by the main frame to prevent the user passing on the information to anyone other than the intended recipient. She had however easily bypassed that and stored it as future insurance if the company ever needed a *patsy* to take a fall. With the incriminating evidence she had on them, it certainly wouldn't be her. She kept a copy of not only the information she received, but hundreds from other users. So far she hadn't been discovered.

The software used was impossible to track. She had the settings of her phones and computers interlinked with military communication satellites. The same ones the company used to intercept the messages she and the other operatives gathered. She bounced all of her communications between millions of receivers in encrypted files. By the time anyone tried to discover if she was not adhering to the company's security policy, they would be approximately one thousand three hundred years old.

She compiled a new document consisting of the names of the primaries involved, the results of the experiments and some of the footage from the email. That would be more than enough to get her employers interested. The rest she would keep to herself for the time being. Taking no chances, she printed off all the information onto paper and hid it under the loose tile in her mother's kitchen. If she played this one right her days of working for someone else would be over.

Spending the rest of her life as a skateboarder and all season snowboarding in the Alps was high up on her wish list. A cosy ski chalet in Val d'Isere and an apartment in Paris would be the first of her property investments.

Message sent to control, she checked the time on her new watch. Her phoned *pinged* to confirm the email had been sent and a message received and that any change to her contract would be reviewed later. She downloaded the images onto her home computer, then cut and pasted some of the frames of film as a taster.

It would be enough to lure her employer to rethink her financial worth and have him more than willing to offer a bonus for the entire download. She then sent the edited film to the central data collection then directly to Valentine. It was intercepted by Kay who almost wept with excitement!

Good enough for me! One way or another someone is going to give me lots of Euro.

She pulled on her still permanently untied boots, picked up her board and headed for the rues of Paris.

Chapter 89

ON MONDAY MORNINGS THERE WAS ALWAYS A faint smell of stale urine in the changing room of the gym. Not even the ultra-modern chrome air fresheners could disguise the unmistakable aroma of fermenting piss. Estelle hoped it was from the children who were allowed to be accompanied by an adult member on Sundays, although these days one could never be sure. Some people had strange ideas regarding hygiene.

I mean, why would you pee on the floor of a changing room when there were ample toilet facilities? Dear Lord! They had to be chaperoned by an adult. So do their mothers just stand watching them as they do it?

She made a mental note to complain to the duty manager at the end of her swim session. £180.00 per month was an excessive amount to pay and have the unwanted privilege of walking or swimming in some over indulged brat's bodily excretions.

Despite the unpleasant odour, Monday was Elle's favourite day for an early morning session. The weekend was still wearing off the regular early bathers. This gym had one of the rare twenty-five meter pools available for private use and was her primary reason for joining. As usual she drove her car into the car park at 6.50am, sipping her coffee from a cardboard cup waiting impatiently for the doors to open at 7.00am. She was changed into her swimsuit and in the pool for 7.10am.

The water in the pool was heated to four degrees below body temperature. This allowed the swimmers to take as much

317

vigorous exercise as they preferred without them overheating as they swam.

Despite the temperature, it still made her shiver as she stood in the water, chest deep preparing to start the swim. She inserted her ear plugs attached to the waterproof MP3 player she had cable tied to her goggles. She then fitted her nose clip and inhaled to make sure her nostrils were watertight. Lastly she dipped the goggles in the water, bending her head down to avoid pulling on the earplugs and dislodging them.

This routine was performed like clockwork every time she went into the pool and it came as second nature to her. She threw her arms out in front then swung them back and forwards to loosen the tendons in her shoulders and shake off the remains of last night's sleep. Because of the early hour, Estelle had the pool to herself. *Let's go, athlete.*

Estelle reached up and turned on her music. Antonio Vivaldi began his concerto for strings. The music flooded into her ears. The sound of the concerto changed as she submerged into the water. To her ears, the music became more magical and personal with none of the usual white noise to pollute the individual notes and tone of the music. Few people would have experienced the concerto in this medium. She doubted that even the composer himself would have been able to at the time he wrote it unless he could play the cello underwater.

Two warm-up lengths, then eighty more, hopefully undisturbed. It took three to five lengths for her to lengthen her strokes and regulate her breathing. The motion through the water centred her thoughts and all of her clearest thinking was done in the pool. Only three areas of focus, the tiles that lined the bottom, the conscious intake of air as her face broke the surface and the murals on the ceiling as she rolled onto her side to inhale. To Estelle, it was as close to meditation and true peace of mind as she could ever hope to achieve.

One stroke followed another, hands nearly closed and elbows high. Vivaldi disappearing as her mind switched to automatic. Her body performed with effortless ease. It was a strange sensation to sweat in the water. It didn't seem right somehow.

318

Why would you sweat in water? What a curious contradiction! Thought after thought came and went, stroke after stroke. Hugh, Eva, the child by the water, the events at the Lough. Her mind had made the strangest paranormal events seem matter of fact.

It was now time to put her house in order. They had all been in denial. Something momentous had happened to all of them, something both magical and beautiful.

"We all at some stage in our lives pray that a greater force governs our destiny in some way," were the words that Hugh had used. "The most peculiar thing is that when it happens, you look for a logical answer to a miracle."

He was right when he said the only explanation was a miracle. The trouble was that Estelle refused to accept the existence of miracles.

I think it's time to speak to Eva. We all need to face up to what's happened to us.

It was then that she realised that she hadn't taken her face out of the water for who knows how many strokes. She panicked at the realisation and gulped water into her lungs. She struggled trying to find a foothold, ripping off her goggles and hurting her ears as the plugs were torn out. She coughed and reached for the side of the pool resting on her elbows and clearing the water from her chest. Panic over.

Ok... Ok... I'm Ok. Still no one else in the pool yet, thank God.

She knew the session was over for the day - eighty lengths done.

Why was there still no one else in the water? Was it a public holiday? She looked up at the clock on the wall. 7.30am.

That's not possible. The clock must be stopped or I've lost count. The minute hand on the clock mechanically moved to 7.31am. *Hold on*, she thought. *Eighty lengths in twenty-one minutes? I can't swim that fast. I wasn't even trying!*

She rechecked the time on the wall by her own watch. It was right. The mural of the dolphins painted on the wall reminded her of the day, that day, at the Lough and the events that followed.

I've changed. I don't know how but there's a change in me and most likely in all of us. I don't feel any different. I don't have super powers or x-ray vision but there's no mistaking it. There is most definitely a difference.

She grabbed hold of the rails and was about to climb the metal steps leading out of the water when she noticed the figure standing at the far end of the pool. There was something odd about the way they almost appeared to blend into the giant print of water lilies. It was as if she was seeing the figure of a person through a heat haze. A shiver swept through her, chilling her to her core. A feeling of fear and panic quickly followed. She decided to be brave!

"Hello? Excuse me but what are you doing down there?"

No answer. The figure remained in the shadows, now partly concealed behind the array of decorative plastic plants. There was no reply so she tried again.

"What are you doing there? Hello! I said what are you doing down there? I think you should leave or I'm calling security."

She resisted the urge to leave the water and run. The figure stood motionless watching her from behind the artificial plants.

"I won't ask again. What are you doing? This is a private club and I'm going…"

"Be quiet now and listen to me."

The voice that reached Estelle across the surface of the water was definitely that of a man. Although his voice was soft, his tone was such that Estelle dared not interrupt.

"As yet, you are in no danger, but that time is approaching. Tell your sister and your friend not to interfere with that which they don't understand. The events that are planned are none of your concern. You may choose your own course, one of safety or the other of peril. Should you interfere, we will not be held responsible for the consequences. This will be the last time we meet under such cordial circumstances."

The figure moved further back into the shadow. There had been an inevitability about the tone he had used. He spoke in whispers but the sound of his voice filled her head to bursting point. She had to steady herself as she left the water, still not certain if he would follow her or not. She quickly made her way to the changing room as the figure continued to watch her as she left.

Her hands were shaking so much she found it hard to fit the key in the locker to fetch her towel. The strength waned from her legs and she had no choice but to sit in the cold and hope for her senses to return to normal.

At that point, two teenage girls burst into the changing rooms, chattering about their gorgeous new personal trainer. The conversation stirred Estelle from her trauma. Normally that kind of inane girlie nonsense irritated her but now it came as welcome and comforting. It was no longer just her and whoever had been at the poolside. She hardly took the time to dry herself properly or check herself in the mirror. The sooner she was out of there the happier she would be.

Chapter *90*

AS SHE LEFT THE CLUB THE HEAVENS OPENED for the first time in weeks. The smell of the rain on the warm dry ground gave her some sense of normality. She unlocked her car and tossed her kit bag into the rear seat. It took several minutes for the Bluetooth connection in the car to register her mobile phone. In the meantime she rummaged around in the glove compartment while simultaneously attempting to drive out of the car park.

Thank you, God. I knew I had a pack of cigarettes in there somewhere.

She undid the wrapper with her teeth and spat it on the floor of the car. Scrolling through the menu on the screen, Eva's number came up. She pushed the button to connect; the phone rang twice before it was answered.

It took Elle by surprise when her sister answered; calls generally went to her voice mail, to be returned sometime later. The cigarette was dangling out of the side of her mouth, Elle trying to light it with her hands still shaking and answer Eva at the same time.

"Hello?"

"Eva, it's Estelle. I'm using the work phone."

Cigarette at last lit she could turn her full attention to her sister.

"Listen we need to meet. I've just had an encounter of sorts and it scared the living crap out of me! Where are you?"

"I went into work early to pick up some things I needed, but I'm at home now. I had a bit of an episode today myself. Where are you?"

"On my way to yours, I'll be with you in fifty minutes or so. I've been for a swim so I have to call home first to get changed into dry clothes. Any word from Hugh? Have you spoken to him?"

"No, I haven't seen him. I take it that means that you haven't heard from him either?"

"No, I think he may have had enough of the Ballantine sisters for a while and I can't say as I blame him. I'll give him a call when I'm on the way down to Mum and Dad's place. I take it that's where you're going?"

Estelle knew that her sister was a creature of habit. When she was insecure or worried about something she would make for the cottage. Their parents had bought the site and built the holiday home on it when she and Eva were children. Built at the far end of the beach at Tyrella, County Down, it was an hour's drive from Belfast City and easy to access by road. It was recessed into the dunes and their father had a retaining wall built, twenty foot high by three hundred foot long, most of the way around the site, so even for its generous size, it couldn't be seen from any nearby roads or lanes. Its crescent design was fenced and secured. The location of the building was close to a former army and air force base so the community was used to high levels of security. The views from any of the eight bedrooms were spectacular and the indoor swimming pool had been constructed in such a way that at high tide, the swimmer could pass through a man-made grotto that connected to the open water of the sea. It was by any architect's standard, spectacular!

The setting was stunning; the Mourne Mountains swept down into the Irish Sea and on a clear day you could see across to Scotland and the Isle of Man. The family often picnicked on the beach when the girls had been children, scaring the Grey Seals and exploring along the strands, hunting for crabs and mussels in rock pools.

Estelle hadn't been down to the cottage since her father's death. She couldn't deal with the ghosts of memories that she had

323

associated with the house. Anyway, that was all in the past. Time to move on, she thought. *I've missed so much and been so angry for such a long time. I wonder if it still looks the same.* Her brain was attempting to aid her as it dealt with the fright she had at the club. *One more cigarette then these things go out the window; it took me bloody years to quit!*

She lit her second cigarette and instinctively tossed them into the central console of the car and not out the window as planned. Scrolling again through her contacts she found Hugh's number and connected. He answered the call with a tinge of coldness in his voice.

"Estelle. What can I do for you?"

He seemed matter-of-fact, but he was slurring his words.

"I was just calling to see how you are doing. Are you OK?"

Hugh Doggett immediately went into a full blown rant!

"OK? Of course, I'm OK. Why wouldn't I be OK? I find myself involved with two people I hardly frigging know, I experience a full on miraculous event, my scars disappear; some of them I actually rather liked by the way; I have little or no contact with either of you for the last however long it is, I can't sleep without drinking the guts of a bottle of whiskey because of the dreams I'm having and you ring and ask am I OK!"

There was a moment's silence.

"Are you at home?" asked Elle quietly.

"Where else would I be?" came the reply.

The alcohol was coursing through Hugh's system. His thought process was irrational, one minute angry the next all forgiving and regretful. He was looking forward to airing the story of some of the dreams he'd had with the only two people in the world he could talk to about it.

"Grab a bag and I'll pick you up. You need some sea air."

Chapter *91*

THE EMAILED 'RED FLAG' WITH INFORMATION regarding the Irish scientist and her experiments came through to Valentine's phone. The very idea that one of his employees was withholding information, as suggested by the attachment he received along with the information incensed him by its outrageous demand.

His employees were treated and paid more than any other people with similar talents or abilities. The French girl had been a reliable asset but was now arrogant and greedy. Valentine's internal security had detected the software she was using along with the virus stack she had stocked.

It was a regrettable but necessary command. He typed 'incinerate' on his keyboard and sent the message. Within five minutes, all of Agathe's phone handsets were wiped of their memory.

A *hydra* was sent to her laptop, home computer and computer tablets. Records of all the money she had invested in off shore non-taxable accounts were deleted. Her passport, social security number and any information regarding any trace of her were removed from all systems. She was alone and she was penniless.

There would be no further contact between her and the company. She was good on the network but Valentine's engineers were better. All she had left were the paper printouts, which he of course was oblivious to.

Chapter 92

FOUR HOURS INTO THE FLIGHT, KAY WALKED UP the isle of the private jet and opened the door to the flight deck. Two figures sat at either side of the flight controls and turned to greet her as she entered.

"Hello gentlemen. I'm buying dinner for you both this evening by way of a thank you for the late notice for the flight. I hear there's a lovely little eastern European restaurant opened in the city that makes the best *Mulgikapsad* in town. The pilot to Kay's right looked at her in bewilderment.

Mulgikapasad was a traditional Estonian sauerkraut dish. She knew that if she dropped the name of the dish into light conversation, one of them would answer quizzically.

"I'm sorry miss. I don't know if I'm familiar with that dish."

"It's OK, sweetie," replied Kay. "It's an acquired taste."

The pilot to her left smiled and continued preparing for their descent. He hadn't had Mulgikapsad since his grandmother had made it for him as a boy. It was a traditional Estonian meal made with sauerkraut, porkmeat and boiled potatoes.

"How about you, slim?"

"Why not, if you're buying."

He answered her in English with no trace of his Estonian accent. The jet created a plume of surface water as it touched down in the grey drizzle. Kay gave instructions to the senior pilot, that she needed him to refuel the plane and wait for her to call. Andrus followed her down the steps of the aircraft and they both made their way to the building where they went through the brief formalities of the easily bribed passport control.

Kay was the first to break the silence.

"Do you have any issues with kidnapping an old woman?"

"No more than I would in kidnapping a child."

He answered the question with less emotion than he would if ordering from a menu. Kay had to admire his attitude. His work was treated with the utmost professionalism. As far as he was concerned, murder and abduction were just part of his job description.

They collected the car from the hire car desk in the airport. Andrus led her through blind spots in the airport security cameras and began the retrieval. Kay quickly realised the services of Oscar's Belfast contact wouldn't be needed.

Chapter **93**

JOHN GREER DIDN'T HEAR THE COGS IN THE LOCK of his front door tumble as it was expertly picked. Andrus silently entered the hallway of his apartment followed by Kay. They found him in a semi-drunken afternoon nap. He continued to sleep; snoring as Andrus stood over him and Kay searched through the desktop files on his computer.

She casually took a seat in front of the computer monitor and adeptly found what she was looking for, including the email he had accidentally sent to his colleague in Galway.

This was another lead she would follow next if she didn't get what she needed from the girl. *No loose ends Kay*, she thought to herself.

"It all has to be neat and tidy."

She would have Andrus deal with that situation when she was flying home. If Greer knew anything Andrus would get it out of him. If he didn't, well that would be too bad. Just another tragic suicide without a note!

Greer's drunken senses registered that something wasn't right in the world and he blearily began to open his eyes. He bolted upright and was about to shout, "What the fuck was going on!" when his windpipe was closed.

It wasn't a killer blow but was enough to have him clutching at his throat as he rolled off the settee and fell to the floor. He could vaguely hear a woman's voice telling him to get up as he flayed around, gasping for air.

"Mr. Greer! If you don't get up, I'll have my friend here cause you more unnecessary harm and distress."

John was both confused and in pain. He was out of condition and not used to such disorder in his life. He brought himself up slowly, his hands still bracing himself against the floor in the kneeling position.

Kay gestured to Andrus. She was in a hurry and running out of patience. Andrus reached down and took hold of a small piece of the skin that overlapped Greer's triceps muscle at the back of his arm. It only required the smallest amount of pressure to have him jerk to his feet, uselessly attempting to free himself from the man who was inflicting such pain on him.

This only made things worse as Andrus applied more pressure resulting in him standing on his tiptoes and begging to be freed from the pain. Kay gestured for him to be released.

Andrus, while still applying pressure, directed him to the settee where he flopped down holding the back of his arm to ease the screaming pain, "What do you people want? I don't have any money!"

"Mr. Greer. Do I look like I need your money? The suit I'm wearing cost more than your annual salary."

John now registered, in his pain and confusion, that both his assailants were dressed immaculately. Obviously not your usual run of the mill burglars. His throat hurt and his arm was aching and he desperately needed to drink some water. The effect of the assault and the wine had left him dehydrated and dry mouthed.

"What do you want?" he gasped.

"Just some information," replied Kay. "I need you to tell us all you know about Audrey Walsh, Doctor J. E. Payne and…"

Greer interrupted, "Who? What? I've never heard of any of those people!"

Kay gestured to Andrus again.

"No, please wait! I don't know who you're talking about. I swear to God!"

She nodded to Andrus to stop. She was fishing and was simply eliminating any other possible connections.

"My friend here enjoys his work, Mr. Greer, and needs little encouragement from me. If at any time I think you're lying to me, he will continue to hurt you. Do you understand?"

Greer nodded his head and gave a pleading look to Andrus, which was of course wasted.

"Now, tell me everything you know about Eva Ballantine and those experiments you two are doing up at the campus. Oh and Mr. Greer, leave nothing out. I want all the details."

Greer's voice was hoarse from the trauma to his throat. He told the story of the algae and the connection between it and Eva.

"It's all on the computer. Take it and leave me alone."

"I already have. Why do you think we're visiting? I just wanted to hear it from your lips. Now where are your keys of the lab and we will need your security card and passwords."

"They are all on the hall stand, just take them and go!"

"We will. You've been very helpful Mr. Greer. Thank you. My associate here will take care of that throat of yours."

Kay began to leave. She rummaged through the bowl on the hallstand. It was all where he said it would be. She gave one final nod to Andrus as she left and closed the door behind her, hearing her assistant calmly asking Greer to stand.

The blow was swift. The cartilage in his nose was sent speeding into his brain as Andrus smashed the edge of his hand up into the base of John's nose. He stared mercilessly into Greer's dying eyes and felt the familiar tingle in his groin as trickles of blood began to drip down onto the floor from the now brain dead Greer's upper lip. His dying eyes met the awaiting greedy stare of Andrus as he died helplessly in his arms.

He fell, face forward, onto the floor, the dying nerves in his body causing him to convulse and shake. His bowels released and a pool of urine left his body, spreading outwards in a circle around his waist.

Andrus lifted Greer's head and placed the heavy glass ashtray full of cigarette ends directly under his nose then emptied the remains of the Rioja on the floor. For all appearances it would look like a silly but tragic accident. He removed one of Greer's shoes and smeared the sole with some of the spilled wine. He was meticulous, even in leaving a small skid mark of wine away from the rest of the pooling alcohol that lay by the bottle on the floor alongside the now lifeless body.

He then rolled him onto his side and poured some of the wine under the front of his thighs, faking the appearance that he landed there after slipping. The finale to his masterpiece was to sprinkle the remaining cigarette ash from the ashtray onto the floor then dust some of the ash onto Greer's face and hair to simulate where he had fallen and upset the glass container that had been lying on the floor, then position his cheek resting on the heavy glass edge. The blood from John's nose had stopped flowing and was congealing in the ashtray and between the slats of the laminate beech wood floor. He then removed any evidence of him or his client ever being there.

They left the apartment, with Andrus closing the door and removed any fingerprints or DNA from the doorknob with a bleach soaked rag that he had taken from the kitchen. Kay went ahead, leaving him to the clean-up and waited for him in the rental car.

Andrus got in, withdrew the electric cigarette from his breast pocket and took a heavy drag, releasing the visible harmless smoke.

"Any problems?" she asked.

"I've had more trying days," he said casually.

"Where to next?"

"Let's go to school," came the reply.

Chapter *94*

THE J.S.T.R VIRUS WAS NOW SPREADING AT A phenomenal rate, more infectious than any other that had ever been previously documented. Thousands were infected globally and increasing every minute.

The United States and Canada were preparing to close their borders as were Russia, Great Britain and most of Europe. It would only be a matter of days, if not hours, before their armies and security forces implemented a complete shut down and the possibility of martial law would be the next logical, if futile step, to maintain public control. The media and World Wide Web had been restricted and were being policed in an attempt to retain some desperate modicum of calm and order.

It would only be a short time before wide spread panic set in and universal chaos ensued. When international air space was shut down, no one, not even the heads of government, truly knew what would happen next. There had never been a situation even remotely similar to this global crisis since World War Two.

The clock was ticking. The stats told them that at the current rate of infection, every human being on the planet (if they weren't already) could be J.S.T.R positive within eighteen days and there was still no sign of any breakthrough for a cure. Murder, rape and looting would soon be commonplace in every major city across the globe.

For the first time since the dawn of the internet and modern digital media, coverage of anything other than breaking events went blank. No one cared or had the time to waste, to upload graphic images onto the web. They were much too concerned with what their respective governments were doing to resolve the unprecedented threat to humanity.

The sum of all fears was happening and it wasn't nuclear war. There were no shelters or silos for the rich and powerful to take refuge, churches and places of worship were packed to bursting, sanctuary was offered to anyone who wished for it; regardless of religious or ethnic persuasion.

For the first time in history, money and connections would no longer be enough to protect anyone from the germ. From pauper to Prince, everyone was in the same, rapidly sinking, ship.

Chapter **95**

INITIAL CONTACT WITH JAMES E. PAYNE BY AN intermediary over the telephone and a meeting at a public location of his choosing was selected. Valentine had already tracked Payne's cell phone using the inbuilt GPS system. The telephone's number had been in the details his recently disavowed French asset had sent him.

Payne's movements were boringly predictable. He still lived at the same address and that appeared to be where he was stupidly keeping his medicated hostage, Audrey Walsh.

Payne had contacted Audrey Walsh 24 hours previously, informing her that he had rechecked her notes and needed to take a blood sample for routine screening. He assured her that the procedure shouldn't take more than five minutes and, to save her any inconvenience, he would be more than willing to conduct a home visit.

As luck would have it, Audrey was alone when he arrived. He had briefly rehearsed the scenario if her husband or visitors were present. He would appear concerned that her newly restored eyesight required a follow up check and a brighter light in a sterile environment would be preferable. So a quick visit to the surgery would allow him to perform a routine test to help him rest better tonight, now content that his patient was permanently free at last from the degenerative disorder.

Audrey, of course, agreed and drove alone to the empty surgery, entered the dimly lit hallway and took a seat on one of the empty chairs. Payne called out to her from his consulting room to enter. He told her to have a seat and that he was just turning his phone to silent as he made his way to the door, which he locked. They chatted briefly and exchanged pleasantries. Payne indicated that Audrey should sit on the gurney and roll up her sleeve.

When she was settled, he went through the motions of checking her heart rate with his finger on her pulse. He put the pressure band around her arm and took her blood pressure, then requested that he needed to take a blood sample for further analysis. She of course agreed and held out her arm for the needle to be inserted. She watched him sterilise a small patch on her arm then closed her eyes to avert seeing the sharp steel tube pierce its way into her vein. She smiled at him, nervously, fearing the imminent pain from the syringe. As he exerted pressure on the plunger he watched the pathetic specimen of a human being cower at the sight of the needle enter her vein. The saline solution mixed with half a milligram of *Rohypnol* began to take immediate effect.

He waited, the needle still in place, until he saw her eyes begin to glaze over. It was just the effect he was looking for. She could now be moved easily without the need for him to support her as he got her to her feet.

Audrey would later remember nothing of the incident.

He then casually led her out of the hallway and into the hire car with the false license plates he had ordered over the internet on forty-eight hour guaranteed delivery. Before long, they had arrived at Payne's home. Audrey's appeal as a product intensified in Payne's mind; she was definitely his kind of person in this state. Precious, compliant and, above all, quiet.

He didn't care if he was seen, she could have been his mother for all anyone knew.

He led her upstairs, lay her on the bed, which he had covered with a rubber sheet he'd stolen from the surgery stores, and inserted the saline/sedative drip. He prepared several vials for blood samples and DNA swabs to verify the authenticity of the donor. He would continue to administer the dose every six hours until he eventually got rid of her to the highest bidder.

Payne put most of the samples in the fridge, keeping a

couple back for the meeting with Valentine. These he placed securely into a sturdy sample case that he then dropped into the inside jacket pocket of his blazer for the information briefing he would quietly present to Mr. Sere at the hotel.

As Payne had been preparing the sample, he was unaware that Valentine's head of security, Paul, together with two local assets had been watching his house. Five minutes after he left, they had deftly broken in and found Audrey Walsh lying unconscious on the bare mattress upstairs. Paul withdrew the saline drip from her arm and allowed a little blood to trickle onto the blood toxin analysis device he had brought with him; a small black case that had a circular plastic receptacle at the top and a digital analysis readout that ran the rest of its length.

He applied a cotton swab to the wound but didn't cover it, instead allowing the wound to seep.

The device indicated *benzodiazepines.* He found the necessary antidote in the satchel that he had also brought with him. He filled his syringe and injected just enough of the drug into the same wound to make Audrey more easily manageable and lucid for transportation.

After a few minutes she was strong enough to lead out to the car.

Chapter **96**

JAMES E. PAYNE WAITED IN THE LOBBY OF THE Europa Hotel in Belfast for his one-thirty rendezvous with the wealthy Mr. Valentine Sere, the new head of one of the biggest pharmaceutical companies in the world. He should have been bursting with excitement. The truth was, his hands were sweating and he was running a slight fever.

Valentine arrived suitably late, dressed in his usual blue jeans and white shirt and introduced himself. James stood to greet Valentine with a handshake. Valentine ignored Payne's outstretched hand, as he thought it best to get to the point fast without raising suspicion.

"Please, take a seat."

They both sat on the opulent armchairs across the glass coffee table.

"Mr. Payne. Do you mind if I don't refer to you as doctor?"

He didn't wait for the reply but continued on, trying unsuccessfully to disguise his loathing for the man.

"If it's not too much, may I ask how you managed to procure the information and the samples you are peddling?"

"Mr. Sere, I'm afraid that information will only be disclosed on the finality of any deal that I agree to, be that with your good self or your many competitors, whom I'm meeting with over the coming days."

The atmosphere was becoming icy so Valentine decided to alter the course of the conversation.

"Mr. Payne. I feel that I really must congratulate you on your discovery. If what you have to offer is completely genuine then I can assure you that you won't feel the necessity to meet with anyone other than myself. Now on a lighter note, let's indulge ourselves in one of your country's famous pints of Guinness."

Valentine attracted the nearest waitress and placed his order. He engaged in small talk until the black beer eventually arrived. He picked up the glass and put it to his lips; only to be stopped by James before he drank.

"You need to wait Mr. Sere. You can't drink it until it settles; then goes completely black with a creamy head. It's part of the enjoyment."

Valentine thanked him. He knew how to drink the beer but he was stalling for time until he got confirmation from Paul that the Walsh woman was safely in their hands. Valentine excused himself as a message came through on his phone. He quickly looked at the simple message on the screen... ACQUIRED; it was all he needed to know.

"So Mr. Payne, let's get down to business as I'm quite sure you're a very busy man. May I be allowed to test the samples you brought?"

Payne clumsily withdrew the case from his pocket containing the blood samples and DNA report. Valentine used an identical device that he supplied Paul his head of security with to test Audrey's blood for toxins. The device completed the task in less than a minute and confirmed they were genuine. Five illuminated bars on the screen quickly went from amber to green. So far it had all been a complete success. He had everything he needed so etiquette was no longer required. He switched off the small device and put it back in his pocket. Payne was almost on the edge of his seat in anticipation. Time to state the terms.

"Mr. Payne, I will make you one offer and one offer only. If you attempt to haggle with me in anyway, then the offer will be rescinded. I trust you will find it to your liking."

The amount of money was so large that Valentine knew it wouldn't be refused as the offer was by Payne's standards, colossal! Valentine had made a similar if less generous offer in the past to greedier, more ruthless individuals, so this was child's play to him.

Valentine confirmed that the deposit of three million dollars, a small down payment of the ninety-seven that would soon follow, would be deposited into Payne's bank account. Payne gave him the details from a card in his wallet. Valentine smirked at the small-minded slug of a man sitting in front of him.

The account had been set up the day before in the Cayman Islands. Payne had transferred his entire life's savings plus the equity from the sale of his parent's family home to have a deposit large enough to open the account, which demanded a minimum of $1,000,000.

This, of course, Valentine already knew. The deposit was confirmed as the new figure of $4,000,000 less the handling and set up fee subtracted by the bank and the deal was done.

"It's been good doing business with you, Mr. Payne. One of my employees will contact you to have the goods shipped. Enjoy your new found wealth."

Payne attempted to stand but Valentine stopped him.

"I hope you don't consider that I have been too forward, but I took the liberty of ordering a bottle of the hotel's finest champagne for you to savour as means of celebration. Also as an added bonus I've reserved the presidential suite along with the finest female company that Belfast has to offer. Please enjoy yourself with my compliments."

He stood and was just about to leave when he remarked. "That looks like the beginning of a nasty cold. Maybe you should take a pill."

By the time James E. Payne received the key of his room, Audrey Walsh was up above the clouds, safely tucked up on Valentine's private jet, bound for Kiruna, Sweden.

Chapter *97*

The Beginning

C NN WERE THE FIRST MAJOR NETWORK TO broadcast the emergency news statement. "The United States of America along with its NATO allies has announced that a total shutdown of all their collective airspace will come into force in the next twelve hours. All flights still airborne after that deadline will be redirected to their points of origin. Citizens are advised to stay at their current locations pending further information. End of message."

This was repeated every ten minutes with no explanation why so many countries had simultaneously closed their airspace. What the report hadn't stated was that all land borders and seaports were also closed. Cargo ships, ferries and trucks would similarly be turned back to their points of origin, or instructed to wait in international waters for emergency refuelling and replacement food and water supplies. Cargos would spoil and tempers would fray as millions of dollars in freight rotted in the holds and containers of stranded vessels. Queues in airports and seaports were growing with frightened passengers hoping to reunite with friends and family. Water and food supplies were running low and it was the just the beginning.

Valentine watched the newsflash from his suite in the Belfast hotel. He had instructed his aide in Chicago to delete all bank accounts relating to Doctor James E. Payne. He had tried calling Kay but for whatever reason, his calls went straight to her answer service. With all the unwanted attention she had directed towards him of late, he was surprised by her now apparent lack of communication and wondered if she had been informed of her new phase on garden leave.

He was finding it increasingly frustrating that even with his extensive list of contacts, for the time being anyway, he was stranded in Ireland.

The only logical step was to contact this Doctor Ballantine and see what, if anything, she had discovered? There would be no need for aggressive acquisition. If the news gatherers were right about the speed this virus was spreading, he would need more than the revival of a spider plant to coax him to mingle with the general populous. He still wasn't entirely convinced that there was a connection with the girl and the Walsh woman who he hoped would soon be landed safely in Sweden.

All the networks were down due to unprecedented amounts of international calls from friends and loved ones concerned for their stranded families still abroad or in transit. At least the internet was still working, so he typed Eva's name into the location search on his tablet and finally found her in some tiny village, thirty miles south east by the sea. It should take forty-five minutes to get there by car give or take.

Valentine decided to break with his normal protocol and call Eva personally. The automated voice on the cell phone delivered the standard: 'It has not been possible to connect your call. Please try again later,' message.

He rescanned through the information on his tablet and found a telephone number for the address. The main landline number appeared to be withheld so the second number listed must have been for maintenance or an Internet line. He took his chances and dialled the number. Eva could hear the phone ringing from the kitchen area of the cottage. It rang several times before she finally found the handset, buried beneath a pile of newspapers on the kitchen worktop.

"Hello?"

"Dr Ballantine?"

"Yes. Who is this?"

"Please don't hang up, Doctor. This isn't a sales call. My

name is Valentine Sere. I'm very interested in your work, specifically with the experiments you have been carrying out regarding the regenerative qualities of the new species of sea water algae that you may have discovered."

"Sorry. Who are you again and how did you get this number?"

Eva was instantly on her guard.

"My name is Valentine Sere, Dr Ballantine. I'm the CEO of a large pharmaceutical company and I just happen to be in Belfast for a meeting. I'm stranded like everyone else and thought I could maybe take advantage of the situation by asking if we could meet up to discuss your findings?"

"Look I don't know you Mr. Sere and I...."

Valentine politely interrupted her.

"Do you have internet access Doctor?"

"Of course I have internet. What's that got to do with anything?"

"If you would be so kind and Google 'BION Pharmaceuticals' and punch my name into the search engine, it may become a little clearer. Would you like me to call back?"

Valentine was on his way down to the lobby of the hotel to collect his car. It was 14.35pm and he needed to get to her and find the source of her discovery as quickly as he could. This girl and her team were for all intentions fairly unremarkable. He'd done his own research into her work. Up to this point it had been uneventful and fruitless, but if she had stumbled across something worthwhile? Well, who knows?

Eva's voice came back on the phone.

"Hold on Mr. Sere, I have you. Now explain to me again what it is that you want?"

"Just a quick moment of your time please. As I said, I'm in town and I hoped we could discuss some of your recent findings?"

"I'm very busy, Mr. Sere, and I'm expecting guests."

"I promise you, Doctor, it won't take long as I'm on a tight schedule myself. Who knows, you may be interested in what I have to say. If not, I'll thank you and be on my way."

Eva hesitated. There was something both intriguing and

daunting about this guy. The information she had hastily retrieved from the internet about him seemed genuine enough. The stories appeared to indicate that he had usurped his father recently in a hostile takeover of BION Pharmaceutical.

From what she could tell, his father had to be the stereotypical tycoon. Bullying the drugs market, buying shares in smaller companies, then tearing them down to sell them on once he had retrieved all the profits from the sale of the assets. He, by all accounts, fitted the Hollywood image of a ruthless, self-indulgent, greedy 'Fat Cat' who appeared to have little regard for anything, including his family, opting only for deals that made him richer, or maybe, even more powerful than he already was. If his son was anything like him, then it wouldn't be too difficult for her to dislike him.

The dilemma still remained that she was out of her depth and needed someone who could help her solve at least some of the questions that she didn't have answers to. With his resources and testing facilities, Valentine Sere could most probably make that happen a lot sooner than her and John alone and she was certain that the university wouldn't fast track her discovery but maybe he could. She had got her sister and her friend involved in all of this and she had no idea how to get them out of it.

His photograph was on the pages of every search on the internet while she carried on the telephone conversation with him. She had to be sure that he was who he said he was.

"Mr. Sere. Do you have a 'face to face' capability application on your hand held?"

"Of course," replied Valentine. "Would you like to see who you are talking to Dr Ballantine? It may be a little difficult as most of the networks appear overloaded. I'll try to connect. Failing that would a Skype conversation suffice?"

Valentine stopped and waited by one of the windows of the hotel and looked out at the handful of people who had ignored the broadcasted warnings and were still prepared to leave the safety of their homes, though most were now wearing surgical masks. He would have to use the hotel's Wifi to make a face to face call so for now he was stuck there.

"Either would be acceptable, Mr. Sere."

"That's perfect, Doctor, let me call you back."

Eva hung up the phone and within thirty-seconds Valentines face came up on her computer tablet. The networks had cleared, at least for the time being.

"Hello again, Eva. May I call you Eva?"

Eva didn't answer but she was satisfied that he was who he said he was.

"Carry on, Mr. Sere. Again, tell me how can I be of help to you?"

"I think you may have something my company could be interested in. I would prefer to talk to you in person if you would spare me ten minutes of your time. I have a car and I am more than willing to meet you wherever suits?"

Eva's internal radar was going crazy; she argued with herself about talking to a stranger about the results and events that had subsequently followed? It made little sense but against all her better judgment she agreed.

"OK Mr. Sere. You need to get yourself a map. I'll see you here around 4pm."

Eva forwarded the address of the cottage, with directions on how to get there. Valentine texted a thank you for the directions, though unknown to Eva, he already had the address. Jonus Lepp had intercepted the call; used satellite tracking to locate the GPS on Eva's mobile handset that he had downloaded earlier from the French assets report; then sent location coordinates to Valentine's phone.

He ended the call and nosed his car out from the hotel's car park onto what should be a busy road. It was 14.50pm on a Saturday afternoon and the city should have been thronging. Instead it was virtually empty and he drove the car out of the hotel without delay. The city's taxis and buses were still running but their seats were mostly empty. The ones that were occupied were used by worried passengers desperate to get home.

The motorways should have been crammed with people fleeing the danger, but there was nowhere to run or hide from the virus. Previously empty pews in churches were now filled with the homeless or the newly converted hoping for sanctuary or a miracle that could save them. Hospital wards were crammed with the infected. Makeshift mortuaries were being filled with the dead and the numbers of infected were still rapidly rising.

Chapter **98**

T HE SEARCH OF THE LAB BY ANDRUS AND KAY at Queens University went on uninterrupted. The corridors were unusually quiet, even for the weekend. They entered the lab and took the samples from the refrigerator or anything they didn't find on the late John Greer's home computer.

Kay's symptoms were worsening. She had gained what she now realised was temporary relief from the splitting headache she had experienced earlier. The *magic* pill had certainly worked for her, but it was now time to take another dose. She opened the pillbox to take some more of the medication. The velvet cushion retained a small indentation where the precious pill had previously sat. It had mysteriously disappeared. Her heart sank as she stared down into the empty box.

Panic ensued until she brought herself under control. She began to feel a hardening of the muscles in her forearms. This was more than just a headache. Her calve muscles cramped and flexed of their own will. She needed to get out of the building and walk.

She forgot formalities.

"Meet me at the car. I need to get some air." She almost barked the order at Andrus. "Clean up when you're done here."

She left without saying another word.

The summer heat wave had made a return and the hot air hit her as she left the shadows of the archway that led to the grass at the front of the university. Kay was a woman who took little time to appreciate the birds singing or the idle chatter of passers-by. She was thankfully beginning to feel a little better even without the pills to aid her recovery. The difference in temperature from the air-conditioned lab to the humid heat outdoors made the perspiration worse.

This chase had taken its toll on her. Her symptoms again began to worsen. The guy Greer this morning could have ended his days better but so what! People die all the time. She reached into her handbag, searching for one of the hand wipes that she had taken from the company limo. She found the cotton monogrammed handkerchief that Sol had given her and paused to wipe her forehead. The faint scent of his aftershave that lingered on the white linen momentarily brought her back home to Chicago.

She didn't often miss her home but today was different somehow. She felt lonely, almost homesick. She had never in recent memory felt that way about any place. Maybe she was getting older and needed to settle down. For the first time since she had been in her early twenties she now missed finding a love and having a family. Her career had always been prioritised over any personal relationships. She paused momentarily lost in her thoughts, then slipped the handkerchief back into her bag and flexed the tightening muscles that ran along the top of her shoulders to her neck. She ignored the growing tension in her back and made her way towards the car at the gates of the university.

She walked along the grass barefoot dangling her shoes from each of her hands. Her feet hurt and her jaw was stiff so she moved it from side to side and back and forth clicking the joints. She paused to let her head droop down to her chest then rotated it toward one shoulder, then the next. Tendons and ligaments that hadn't been stretched in years groaned and creaked but responded well. Better than well. Suddenly she felt all of her strength returning.

Thank whoever, this thing seems to be passing again. Those pills must have just suppressed it from running its full course.

The reports of the JSTR virus hadn't been lost on her. She clenched her fists and the veins along the backs of her hands popped up like thick blue twine. Even at her fittest, playing lacrosse for the State, she had never been a vascular person. However, she could now see the pulse beating as the blood flowed through the capillaries on her forearms. She felt the need to do something, hit something or run fast. What she didn't see or feel was the calcification above her eyes and around her mouth. She ran her tongue along the inside of her upper lip and the gap felt unnatural.

Andrus had gone straight to the car without diversion and pulled up in front of the main gates of the university. Kay spotted him and slipped back into her shoes. The heels dug deeply into the grass, slowing her progress. She first twisted to the right then the left, snapping both heels and leaving them where they'd dug their own tiny graves. She made her way to the driver's side shooing Andrus over into the passenger seat.

"I haven't driven stick shift for a while. Move over."

Andrus slid across without protest. Ten minutes later they had left the city and were on their way to find Eva Ballantine.

Adrenalin was crashing through Kay's system at an unnaturally accelerated speed. This was the mother of all steroid rages without her ever taking the drug. They were thirty minutes into their journey when she veered off their route, taking a gravel lane up towards a communication mast. She was driving like a professional on roads and at speeds that would have tested any rally driver.

She spoke to Andrus in perfect Estonian without making eye contact.

"Palju ma sulle palka maksan?" (How much am I paying you?)

Andrus had never been asked this question before as his terms were stated in the contract between him, Oscar and the client. He hesitated perplexed and a little confused. How did she know for sure that he was Estonian and when or where had she learned to speak it so perfectly? It took him a second to compute the information. He rolled his head back slightly against the headrest, wondering how to best answer.

Kay hadn't been good at languages at school and had dropped them from her curriculum at the first opportunity. Now however, it appeared she had found yet another new talent.

The blow came fast and so powerfully that it sent the bones

and tendons in his throat almost half way through to his upper spine. He was dead before he could bring his hands up to protect himself. Kay slid the car sideways to an almost stop, put it in reverse gear while taking the electric cigarette from his lapel jacket pocket. Still in motion, she slipped the gear box into first, slammed the plastic coated metal cigarette through his forehead like a nail through an empty egg shell, reached over, opened the door of the car, pushed him out and watched his now lifeless body roll into a water filled ditch.

She pulled a hard right turn, closing the door and carried on her way, rapidly closing the distance between her and her quarry.

Chapter 99

ESTELLE AND HUGH ARRIVED AT HER PARENT'S cottage. They pulled up alongside the metal box holding the wireless keypad in front of the decorative wrought iron gates. Elle tapped in the year of her mother's birth and the gates swung slowly open. They closed automatically behind them as they drove the fifty yards up the gravel driveway to pull up at the front of the cottage.

"Dear heavens, Estelle. This is some kind of weekend retreat."

The cottage was built from local stone and blended perfectly into the surrounding scenery. To Hugh, it appeared to be around the size of a small five star hotel. The front door opened and Eva stood ready to greet them.

"Hi you two, it's so good to see you?"

She hugged her sister then shook Hugh's hand putting her left hand on top of the handshake to make it a more personal greeting, considering everything she had put him through.

"How are you, Hugh? Apologies for not calling you, but a lot has happened since we spoke last."

"No problem, Eva. We've all been busy with one thing or another."

She then spoke to both of them.

"Have you two seen the news? It seems as though every country in the whole world is closing their borders and airports!"

"Yes, we heard," replied Hugh. "It's frightening and very

alarming. People are in hiding and afraid to venture out much. This Jester epidemic, as the news stations are calling it, is scaring people out of their wits and rightly so. It's spreading like wildfire. We tried to buy bottled water on the way down here. Every garage and shop is sold out of anything to drink."

"There's plenty inside, we have our own borehole here. Come in."

The cottage was exactly as Elle remembered it with a few new additions. The old photographs of her parents still sat on the teak side table along with snaps of all the family together.

"I take it William and Mrs. Poots are still taking care of the place for us?"

"Of course. You don't imagine I could keep it looking like this do you?"

Estelle just raised her eyebrows a little but didn't answer. She knew how habitually untidy her sister was.

Eva spoke again stating that niceties were over and it was time for business.

"We all have some talking to do," she said.

They sat down around the unlit fireplace, none of them wanting to be the first to speak.

It was Estelle who broke the silence.

"I had an unsettling encounter at the health club. A man threatened me, on giving further thought to what he said I think he threatened all of us."

Hugh's protective instincts took over and both girls could hear the tension in his voice.

"What did he say, Elle?"

It was one of the rare times that he'd called by her pet name.

"I can't remember exactly, but I know that he was dangerous and meant business. He said the next time we spoke that it wouldn't be so cordial and if we minded our own business we wouldn't be in any danger. He spoke so softly that I shouldn't have been able to hear him. He was at least thirty feet away but he sounded like he was whispering in my ear. The voice filled my head completely. I got out of there as fast as I could."

The three of them sat staring into the empty fireplace for a few moments; each lost in their own thoughts.

"And you, Hugh?"

This time it was Eva's turn to break the silence.

"Has anything odd happened to you, apart from your miraculous healing?"

"No, not really," replied Hugh. "Just a recurring night terror. Oh and I can't get drunk any more no matter how much alcohol I take. Believe me, I've tried!"

"What are the dreams about?" asked Eva.

"Children mostly," he replied. "Drowning, horribly disfigured, in dreadful pain. I can't sleep, hence the practice with the alcohol."

Elle interrupted him.

"But, Hugh, that's what I saw in the river at home remember? Was Eva in your dream?"

This time it was Eva's turn to butt in.

"Why would I be in it?" she asked.

"It doesn't matter," Estelle lied. "It was just a stupid dream."

Hugh spoke again and directed his question at Eva.

"Something tells me that you have the most to say Eva; without you none of us would be sitting here."

Eva became defensive but corrected herself. Hugh was right. Obviously she was the catalyst for all that was happening to them. She positioned herself on the edge of her chair and told them everything she knew, including the phone call from Valentine Sere.

"Who is he?" asked Elle.

"I googled him," replied Eva. "He's an American big wig in pharmaceuticals and he's meeting me here at 4."

The others looked at Eva in surprise at this latest piece of news.

"Look," she continued, "as far as I'm concerned I haven't told a living soul about any of this. Maybe he could help if we told him what was going on. I mean, this is the biggest thing that's happened to any of us and to be perfectly honest, I don't think we have the first clue how to handle it."

Both Hugh and Elle hesitantly nodded in agreement. It was all the affirmation Eva needed.

"Let's see what he has to say. We could adjourn to another room and decide if we want to confide in him a little? If not, we send him on his merry way. Everybody agreed?"

Again, Estelle and Hugh both nodded their heads in assent. Estelle employed her cold logic and reasoning.

"There must be some sense to these bizarre happenings, regardless of the facts. I suggest we all get on and deal with it. If there is a connection between Eva, or all of us, including the algae's healing properties, as her assistant believes, then we better find out for sure. Get your swimming gear on. We're getting back in the water!"

Chapter *100*

Six Hours until the Proposal

A T 14.50PM EVA, ESTELLE AND HUGH ENTERED the Irish Sea at Tyrella Beach. They waded in until they were chest deep, then joined hands waiting for something to happen. For the second time the familiar glow of the algae surrounded them.

There was no pain or fear this time. The water gleamed with the fluorescent plant life as far as their eyes could see. Then with no warning, the algae closest to them began to shimmer and vibrate. They could feel the water temperature rising.

Suddenly the vibrations ceased and the water became deathly still. Even the motion of the waves stopped, leaving the seas surface resembling a village millpond. It was eerily silent. No gulls shrieked or airplanes crossed the sky. They looked at one another wondering what was going to happen.

Then, with no apparent warning, the algae accelerated away from them in every direction at supersonic speed! It moved so fast that it left a ring of vapour rising above their heads, surrounding them in falling mist. Suddenly the scene returned again to utter silence.

The three of them just stood in the water staring at one another in disbelief. The first sounds of people in distress shook them and they turned in the direction of the noise. Then time after time they were aware of similar screams of pain then cries of joy. It was akin to multiple rebirths as all of their past injuries no matter how serious or trivial were cleansed and washed away.

Anyone who had contact with the water from the time the three had entered until leaving had any trace of illness or disease removed instantly. Maybe some of them had decided to have one last walk along the surf, as the plague had now spread everywhere and sooner rather than later it would reach them and their loved ones. Families walked and children paddled along the shore holding hands and nursing their babies in their arms, hoping for a miracle that they thought would never happen. As some ran to the aid of the casualties in distress, they too fell in pain as the water worked its magic. The chain reaction continued as more and more people entered the water to help the ones still in distress and so it continued.

Within thirty-seconds of the algae wave travelling, cures were experienced from southern Spain to the tip of Norway. All across the British Isles hundreds of people had reported similar cases. Anyone hearing the news began rushing to the coast hoping for the same miracle.

The three left the water utterly stunned. They were reeling by the reaction their bodies in the water had had on the algae and were not oblivious to the effect on the people at the beach. A strange, eerie light was beginning to flicker in their minds. Numb and silent they returned to the cottage. It was then they saw the news flash. People were flocking to the sea as reports of miracle healing had taken place all over coastal Europe and southern Scandinavia in the space of a few minutes. There could be no doubting it now. They had, without any further reservations left in their minds, caused this event to happen. The question was what do they do now? It was around twenty-two minutes since they left the water and arrived back in the cottage.

Hugh had tuned the radio onto a local station to find out if there was any further news of the event on the beach, or an update on the virus. Eva switched the TV to the regional news channel and waited for a bulletin.

Estelle opened the BBC news APP on her mobile phone and mouthed the words, "OH MY GOD IT'S TRUE," before saying them again out loud!

The red bar at the top was flashing the latest breaking

headlines like electronic ticker-tape. Cases were being reported all across coastal Europe of a miracle in the water. People in their thousands were making their way towards the sea. Commuters abandoned their journeys home instead making for the coast. Motorways were quickly gridlocked with people struggling to reach water. It was utter chaos all across Europe.

"Eva. Turn it on to BBC news!"

The full scale of the exodus was sprawled across the fifty-inch screen; countless thousands of desperate hysterical people knocking each other over and abandoning cars in their efforts to reach the sea.

Elle spoke first.

"Listen you two. If this is down to us, and I think we all, no matter how impossibly difficult it is to accept, agree that it is, we're going to have to be careful. Folk are going to be hurt in this kind of panic, so will we if they find out we caused it. This has happened so fast my head is spinning. How the hell did the news get a hold of this so quickly?"

They were about to try to formulate some sort of plan when the intercom sounded for the gate.

"It must be that American guy. What time is it?" asked Eva.

Estelle checked her watch. "4.35."

"He's late. I just can't send him away."

"Bring him in," replied her sister. "Lord alone knows what's happening out there."

Eva pressed the enter button on the intercom and the gates swung open. The three of them came out to meet Valentine as he got out of the car.

"Mr. Sere," said Eva. "This is my sister Estelle and our friend, Hugh. I'm afraid you've arrived at rather an inconvenient time."

"I'm sorry but with what's going on out there I didn't think I would get here at all. People are just abandoning their cars and running towards the sea in their hundreds for some reason."

Eva stepped forward, ignoring his observations.

"Come inside, Mr. Sere, I think we need to talk."

Chapter *101*

KAY HAD BEEN TRACKING EVA'S MOBILE USING a military satellite. The target appeared to be stationary at the same location. The thought had occurred to her that Eva Ballantine may have lost her cell phone and that she was chasing shadows.

She felt a trickle of blood drip down from her nose. Another followed until a steady stream of fresh blood coursed down over Kay's lips and fell onto her skirt. She tried pinching her nose as she drove but it was proving impossible. She was left with no choice but to stop.

She pulled into a gateway that led into an empty hayfield. Still pinching her nose she rummaged through her handbag to find a tissue. Then again she saw the handkerchief that Sol had given her at the airport. She held it to her nose and got out of the car attempting to hold her head back, to stem the flow of blood.

The headaches were getting worse again so she massaged her temple with her other hand. The nosebleed finally seemed to be stopping. She couldn't remember the last time she'd had one as bad as this. Probably school she reckoned. She sniffed a few times to make sure it had stopped and noticed a peculiar smell coming from the handkerchief.

That's odd, she thought! *I hadn't noticed that before. I haven't heard of any aftershave that gets stronger with time.*

She held the blood stained handkerchief out to get a better look and noticed that the monogrammed initials stitched into the corner were now seeping tiny amounts of amber fluid. She had to look again to make sure her eyes weren't playing tricks on her. She momentarily put the fluid from her mind and turned her attention back to the lettering on the cloth. She studied the JS embossed lettering, spreading the handkerchief on the hood of the car while still pinching her nose with her free hand.

The only person I know with those initials is Valentine's mother Julia Sere. Why would Sol be carrying one of Julia Sere's handkerchiefs?

She waited for a moment then returned to the car and retrieved some paper from the dash and the complimentary pen from the side pocket of the door.

What was Sol's surname?

Again she returned to her bag and took Sol's card from her purse. It was a simple business card with a cell phone number and Sol's full name.

Sol Nieswer, telephone 0000551000.

She studied the name and wrote the letters down in capitals on the paper: SOL NIESWER.

Suddenly, it hit her. Sol Nieswer was an anagram of Wilson Sere. That's why he seemed familiar, but it couldn't have been him. It didn't look like Wilson. He had the same build and height but that's where the similarity ended! She had only briefly met the man once several years back at a charity fundraiser but she was sure it couldn't be the same person.

The fluid encased in the letters continued to steadily seep out of the stitched lettering. Kay picked at the threads to find a thin, what she took to be, plastic membrane. Tiny beads of fluid filled bubbles had begun to melt away releasing their contents.

She looked at the handkerchief again in fascination as the aroma emanating from it became stronger. She began to feel faint and nauseous. Her head was spinning again as she stared down at in disbelief. The blood from her nosebleed was vanishing, making the scent from the substance it had been treated with intensify. The blood was being absorbed into the material itself and within a few seconds it was gone completely.

This was some kind of trick!

As she studied the handkerchief, she became aware of the change in her fingernails. They appeared harder and thicker than they were three days ago when she had had her last manicure. She doubted if the manicurist would have nail clippers strong enough to cut through them now. As an experiment, she raked them down the paintwork on the side of the hire car. Thin ribbons of blue paint rolled away as she did, leaving curled spirals of lacquered paint falling to the ground as she passed her nails along its length.

What the..?

She looked down at her hand to see the remains of the car's paint under her nails. The aroma returned; stronger now. She finally recalled where she had smelt it before. It was the same substance that she had infected Valentine with. Only much, much stronger!

Kay staggered back towards the front of the car and managed to get into the driver's seat before passing out.

She woke later to hear someone tapping the passenger side window.

"Are you OK in there, Miss?"

Kay turned her head to see what was happening and who was rapping at the window. The walker took a step back when he saw her. This poor lady had been cruelly disfigured or attacked. Blood covered the front of her clothing. He could only assume she had been left there by an assailant. Kay pushed the button to wind down the electric window and spoke to the man. His dog was barking at her, which only made the pain in her head worse.

"What do you want?" Her voice had changed. She now struggled to mouth the words properly.

"I beg your pardon, Ma'am. I was walking my dog and I saw you lying in there. You have blood all down your top. I would have called the police but I left my phone at home. Do you need any help? I can call an ambulance!"

The dog was barking even harder which was sending her into a rage. She had to twist the leather cover of the steering wheel to control herself from hurting him and killing the dog.

"I'm fine, thank you. I don't need any help." Her words were muffled and laboured. "Sir, could you please stop your dog from barking. It's really hurting my head?"

The man tugged at the dog's leash to make it stop the noise.

"Shut up, Gary. Your barking's annoying the lady."

The dog ignored him and continued with its warnings.

"Are you sure you're OK, Miss? I only live a mile away and can phone for assistance."

What remained of Kay's patience broke.

"Listen here, my friend, if you don't fuck off, I'll wring that dog's neck."

She made the threat without emotion and the man understood that she wasn't kidding. He was scared and even the dog stopped its endless barking. The walker retreated so quickly he almost fell over his now silent dog, leaving the woman to her fate and grateful that he no longer had to look at her dreadful face. Kay could see the look of horror in the poor man's reaction to her. She looked down at her clothes to see that he had been correct. She was covered in her own blood.

"What the hell is happening to me?"

She drew her hands up to feel her face and realised that something was very wrong. She adjusted the rear view mirror to get a better look. Her skull had enlarged grotesquely forcing her eyes forward until her eyelids could no longer entirely cover them as she attempted to close them; her jaw and facial bones had extended and calcified giving her the appearance of someone who had received the most appalling and grotesque cosmetic surgery. She was in agony! It was torture to blink, even though her eyes were dry from the lack of moisture and she was struggling to breathe without producing a rasping sound. She had to find this girl Eva before she stopped breathing altogether!

Despite her physical state, her mind and coordination were working at super speed. She checked the tracking device that showed Eva's location. Still there, no more than fifteen minutes from here. She turned the key, started the car and headed to find her own salvation and ownership of the girl and the cure that she was now convinced the girl held.

Chapter *102*

THE AMERICAN PRESIDENT, THE RUSSIAN AND Chinese premiers, made joint statements, broadcast on every national television and radio channel that the threat from the Jester virus was now under control and that the related deaths had ceased.

They all advised that citizens should remain calm and stay alert to information updates as to any further developments.

At 13.00 eastern daylight time the President of the United States made a plea to the American people to thank Almighty God for the end of the global epidemic. The Russian, Chinese and European premiers did the same. They were all lying of course. None of them knew for sure that this event was finally over. They simply hoped for the best and were keeping their fingers crossed like everyone else.

The US President called for Senator Gregory Hamill to meet with him and his advisors in one of the secure rooms at the White House to update him of any progress in finding a vaccine or how he intended to deal with the countless dead if this thing restarted.

The President, his Chief Medical Advisor, his Head of Homeland Security and Military Chiefs of Staff sat at one side of the thirty-foot long table with holographic computer monitors built into the table-top. It was the latest in touch screen holographic technology.

Senator Hamill was out of his depth and he knew it. He

hoped that the others didn't. He could answer their questions with some degree of credibility. He walked to the end of the room and ran what seemed like an ordinary computer memory stick along the outside edge of the table, then saw the integrated screen illuminate along its length. An image appeared and hovered at head height above the table. It appeared to be a magnified rendition of a cell or virus, although nothing like anyone had ever seen before. It constantly changed shape morphing from one form to the next. It hovered in the air rotating in front of them.

The President spoke first.

"What is this thing?"

The Senator did his best to answer.

"As far as we can tell, no-one has ever seen anything like it before. It self-replicates and changes form each time we try a new vaccine on it. We've even tried hitting it with radiation. It shrinks a little then regenerates. If we try the same thing again it doesn't even respond! What we do know with certainty is that it is not man-made. If someone out there had been developing this thing they could never have kept it quiet and we would have known about it."

The President's Head of Security asked the next question. "Senator. Are you suggesting that this germ is indestructible? If so, can you tell us who has the technology to make something like this and why?"

The Senator hesitated before trying to provide his answer.

"General Shanks. If we had a lifetime using our current technology, we still couldn't destroy this organism. If it starts killing people again we are at this moment defenceless."

"Could it be of alien origin?"

"Anything is possible General, stuff falls to earth on meteors every day. We just simply don't know."

President James Owen ran his hands over his face in a mixture of fatigue and frustration. He gathered himself and asked the assembled group for suggestions.

"Does anyone have any ideas?"

The people in the room sat silent until Senator Hamill spoke again.

"I have put in place a plan if the germ mutates and spreads

further. We start screening now for individuals presenting with symptoms of the virus and quarantine them we..."

The President held his hand up to silence the Senator. He knew what he was going to suggest.

"Senator, there are absolutely no circumstances under which we will allow American citizens to be mass quarantined at this advanced stage of the current crisis. I won't have my term in office remembered for the collective culling of US citizens. I have spoken to my Eastern and European counterparts and they are of the same mind.

"Find a solution Senator and find it soon or I will have you replaced. You have two days. Is that clear?"

"Clear, Mr. President."

The President stood up and the others in the secure room also stood as a mark of respect as the President left. The only one still sitting was Senator Gregory Hamill. If he didn't come up with an answer fast, he knew his career was over.

Who was he kidding? He needed a fall guy to take the pressure off him; easy as squeezing lemons. He had a mental list of 'Patsies.'

Chapter *103*

Five Hours until the Proposal

ON THE OTHER SIDE OF THE ATLANTIC IN Ireland it was 16.50pm and Valentine was asking all the right questions.

"Now that you all have told me what you think I need to know, I'll fill you in on some of the details that you don't know as a sign of my good faith."

He told of the kidnapping and rescue of Audrey Walsh and the Doctor who was now, by his reckoning, living on borrowed time. He also told of another case involving an American doctor communicating with a doctor in a rural part of southern England, detected again by intercepted emails. It was the case of a man being cured of advanced pancreatic cancer. He knew that he and his wife had boarded a plane from Britain bound for Oslo, Norway. But since neither this gentleman nor his wife used cellular phones or credit cards, he had no way of knowing their current location; other that they hadn't crossed any borders where passports were deemed necessary.

Unusually for him, Valentine found himself being honest. He needed this girl and time was running out. This wasn't just about power or money any longer, although that would still be a primary motivation. He could see from the news how desperate the situation was becoming worldwide. The girl, Eva, intrigued him. He could see she had an innocence about her. Her sister on the other hand was a closed book. At the other extreme, their friend Hugh had a blackness surrounding him.

That man has had a troublesome past.

He saw it all as if it were colours. He could tell when they were being guarded and when they opened up by the light that glimmered around them. The auras surrounding each of them wavered and changed as their mood swung from open to defensive. It was subtle but there was no doubting it. He realised that this ability was a new one. He could instantly tell if someone was lying or being honest by the changing of their aura. *That could be handy at the next board meeting*, was his first thought.

He, like the others, just seemed to accept these new skills and changes that were happening to them; events that, a year ago, they would have likely sought psychiatric intervention for. He halted his train of thought and readdressed Eva.

"Eva, from what you've told me these events originated with you receiving a laceration to your foot while getting out of the water, where was it again?"

"Strangford," answered Eva.

"Strangford?" repeated Valentine. "Is that far from here?"

"No it's a thirty five to forty minute drive from here at the most."

"Could we go see it?" he asked.

"What, now?"

"Why not?" he replied. "I have nowhere else to go and I'd like to see the point of origin and maybe take some water and dirt samples. If the airspace was open I would have a team inbound as we speak."

"Would you excuse us for a moment, Mr. Sere?" asked Eva. She guided the others into the next room, out of earshot of Valentine. "Are you two up for this?"

Both Hugh and Estelle looked at each other and agreed to go. Elle wasn't leaving her sister and Hugh wasn't leaving any of them. He didn't trust this guy but he may be of help to provide some of the answers that they all desperately needed. Estelle went into the utility room and opened the key box mounted on the wall. She removed a set of keys and held them up to show Hugh.

"Hugh. There's a Range Rover 4x4 parked as you enter the garage to your right. The roads could be blocked with people and we may need to go cross country if we should run into any trouble." She tossed the keys to Hugh and he caught them in mid-air as he moved towards the door.

Eva and Estelle gathered their belongings and prepared to leave along with their guest. Eva excused herself and made for the bathroom. While she was gone, Estelle used the opportunity to speak to Valentine.

"Mr. Sere. If you haven't gathered already, my sister is very precious to me so I must tell you that when she first mentioned your call and your interest, I made a few enquiries of my own. I know who you are and indeed what you are. If I feel at any time that you have an agenda that in any way, shape or form would put my sister or myself in peril, I have a friend here present who will be quite prepared to get rid of you and bury you in one of the numerous Gypsy sites that are known only to him and his Gypsy brethren. Even God Almighty himself couldn't find you where he will put you. Saying that, if you are of use to us, then no harm will come to you. Don't think for a moment that trying to tempt us with money will make any difference; as you can see, my family is wanting for nothing. Do we understand each other?"

"I understand, Miss Ballantine. I mean you no harm."

"Excellent," said Elle. "Let's hope for your sake that that continues to be the case. Oh, one other thing, leave your cell phone with me. I'll give it back to you when you leave."

Valentine was about to protest as Hugh pulled up with the car. He dug into his pocket and reluctantly handed the phone to Estelle who put it inside her shoulder bag.

Hugh was looking at Valentine in the same way a cat watches a rat before he tires of it.

"You get in here beside me, Mr. Sere; we'll let the two girls sit in the back."

Eva closed the door of the cottage and both she and her sister got into the car. Estelle placed her handbag on her knee, took out a packet of cigarettes and threw the bag over her left shoulder into the rear of the jeep.

She put the cigarette in her mouth lit it, then opened window.

"Let's go. And Hugh, I don't want to hear any crap about passive smoking. I think we can agree that we have that one covered!"

The tyres spun noisily on the gravel and they were on their way, leaving the gates to automatically swing shut behind them.

Chapter *104*

T HE CELL PHONE BEEPED THEN VIBRATED ON Kay's handset to indicate that the Ballantine girl was on the move; as luck would have it she was less than four miles ahead. The alarming thing was that someone else she had been tracking was travelling with her. Somehow Valentine had got to Eva Ballantine first and that was about as bad as it could get.

The instructions she had received had been clear. Keep him away from the girl. Her options were narrowing by the minute. She fully understood the consequences of not carrying out her benefactor's wishes. A decision would have to be made and it was looking increasingly like she would take the girl for herself.

She hoped he was driving close behind her or, in the worst case scenario, in the car with her. It was a surprise but not unmanageable. His new gift could have him charming the birds down out of the trees. There would be no negotiation. She needed the girl and no one was going to stop her now. Her mind was concretely fixed and her decision speedily made. Neither Valentine Sere, nor his father Wilson or whatever name he was going by these days would stop her. Her benefactors would need to find a new *Gopher*.

She pressed the accelerator pedal down harder and watched the tracking image on her handheld as the distance between her and her prize decreased.

The four sat in silence as they made their way towards the Lough and the site of Eva's initial experience. Valentine understood how much danger he was in even travelling with these three. There were bound to be people out there much more ruthless in their quest to obtain this girl and her companions. He adjusted himself slightly on his seat so he could address everyone in the car.

"Are you three and now recently me, the only people who are aware of your connection to this phenomenon?"

Estelle was the first to answer.

"Well, I haven't told anyone!"

Hugh didn't answer. If he'd told anybody he would have said so.

Valentine directed his question at Eva.

"How about you, Doctor Ballantine?"

"No, of course not!"

In the back of her mind Estelle always told her sister that she could never keep a secret. She waited for Valentine to turn away then mouthed the words, "Are you sure," to her sister. Eva gave several short nods of her head to reassure her. Valentine turned fully back around in his seat to face front.

"Then you've all done well to remain anonymous."

Hugh now spoke for the first time since leaving the safety of the beach house.

"We haven't done that well, Mr. Sere. You managed to find us!"

Valentine didn't have an answer for that one, so turned his attention back to the road ahead in silence. Eva stared out the window at the passing scenery. Then she remembered Johnny Greer.

"Wait a minute, there is someone else."

Val spun around again now remaking eye contact with her.

"Who else knows, Eva?"

"My lab assistant, John. He helped with all my experiments. It was he who suggested the tests on the spider plant."

Valentine silently scolded himself. How could he forget her assistant? It was all in the email from his former French asset.

"Have you spoken to him lately?"

"No, why?"

"Because there may be many very unpleasant and ruthless

people out there, all hell bent on trying to find out about this and you in a big, big hurry!"

Hugh used the opportunity to remind Valentine that he still didn't trust him.

"Does that include you, Mr. Sere?"

Valentine again did his best to ignore the question.

"Have you tried calling him, Eva?"

"No, of course not. I hadn't even thought of him until you mentioned it."

"Why don't you give him a call and find out if anyone has tried to contact him."

Suddenly Eva felt concern for her friend and brought his number up on her phone. The networks had now cleared and the full five bars showed for perfect reception.

"He won't answer. He rarely does out of work hours."

The phone rang and after several rings a female's voice answered, "hello?"

"Who's that?" asked Eva; she wasn't expecting to hear a woman's voice. "Who is that please and why are you answering John Greer's phone?"

"My name is Sergeant White of the Police Service of Northern Ireland."

The colour drained from Eva's face.

"What's happened to John? Where is he?"

The rest of the passengers in the car were listening intently to the conversation. Estelle urged her quietly to put the call on speaker-phone. The sound of the police sergeant's voice filled the inside of the car.

"Can you give me your full name and relationship to Mr. Greer?"

"Of course, I can, it's Ballantine. Doctor Eva Ballantine. John is my lab assistant! What's happened to him?"

"Doctor Ballantine. Mr. Greer has been in a fatal accident, which we are currently treating as suspicious. I'm sorry to be the bearer of such bad news."

Eva sat stunned, barely holding the phone in her hand.

"Doctor? Doctor Ballantine. Are you still there?"

"Yes, I'm still here, Sergeant."

Estelle had put her hand on her sister's shoulder in sympathy.

"Doctor, we may need to ask you some questions. We would like you to come into Dublin Road police station in Belfast as soon as possible so we can eliminate you from our enquiries. Is that possible?"

"Yes, yes, of course, Sergeant White."

"I'm sorry again for your loss, Doctor."

"Thank you, Sergeant."

Eva ended the phone call and told them what they already knew. Estelle put her arm around her sister and tried her best to comfort her.

"What happened to him Sis?"

"You heard her, she didn't say. They're treating his death as suspicious. My God, poor Johnny."

Hugh and Valentine exchanged glances and knew that his death probably wasn't an accident if they were treating it as suspicious. If there had been signs of a struggle or a break-in, the police would have said.

"Any thoughts, Hugh?"

"Yeah. We're in trouble!"

Hugh answered without addressing anyone in particular. He knew when they reached the town of Strangford and were isolated out on the Lough they would be exposed and vulnerable. The best thing now was to head for home. It would take longer to turn around and head for the cottage again than to get the ferry across to Portaferry on the other side of the Lough, then down the peninsula to Belfast.

He made the decision for all of them.

"Girls, if you don't mind. I think we'll scrap the fact finding mission for today and make for home. It's been a long day and I'm sure we could all do with some time to digest today's events. I'm sorry about John, I know you were fond of him, Eva. I'd leave the visit to the police station tonight. We can all stay at my house, toast John and talk about the happy times you had together. That invitation includes you, too, Mr. Sere."

It was a command rather than an invitation and Valentine knew it!

"Of course, Hugh. Thank you for inviting me."

Hugh didn't bother to look or acknowledge him, instead he continued driving towards the ferry.

Estelle was about to suggest that it would be quicker to turn the car around and return to the beach house when they suddenly became aware of the sound of a cell phone ringing from somewhere in back of the car. Estelle released Eva from the embrace and looked around the car to hear where the ringing was coming from.

"Is that someone's phone ringing?" she asked, not at all phased by asking the obvious. It was Valentine who replied.

"It's mine. Do you mind if I answer it?"

Valentine knew only a handful of people had his number and they all understood not to call him unless it was important. Estelle leant over the back of her seat, found the phone in her handbag and handed it up to him. She saw the name on the screen and waited to hear if he called the caller by her name. She put her hand on Eva's knee to make her focus on the conversation Valentine would be having.

"Kay. What can I do for you?"

Kay was now struggling to form coherent sentences.

"You can stop the car and give me the Ballantine girl you're holding."

She now understood that he was no longer following them but was in her company, the sneaky little bastard, he had beaten her to her quarry. No one could maintain a ten foot distance for long at fifty miles per hour behind another car without them noticing.

"I'm not holding anyone. Are you out of your mind! Are you threatening me? Where are you and what's wrong with your voice?"

"I'm much closer than you realise, now stop the car!"

"I can't stop the car. I'm a passenger. Now, where the hell are you?"

This was a huge oversight on his part. He should have had her tracked once he had made the decision to replace her.

"Do yourself and whoever else is with you in that vehicle a

favour, pull over now and give me the girl."

Her temper was close to exploding. It took every bit of her resolve to stay calm. Her brain felt like it was going to burst out through her eye sockets and she was bleeding again heavily from her nose.

"Who the fuck do you think you're talking to! You work for me remember?" shouted Valentine.

"Listen to me you 'silver spoon sucking ingrate', stop that car now. If you don't I can guarantee that I'll tear your fucking throat out and everyone else in there with you, except the Ballantine girl, of course. I have so many plans for her future."

Kay spoke as well and calmly as she could, given that her lips and tongue were struggling with the words. Her actions on the other hand were the opposite. The leather covering of the steering wheel was now hanging off as she had twisted it so hard the leather bindings had failed. She ripped it off and threw it in the well of the passenger seat.

Valentine was genuinely shaken. She must have lost control of her senses, or taken God only knows what sort of drugs.

He knew by the way she spoke to him she meant business and he had no idea who she had in the car with her. He tried bravado, but she could hear the tremor in his voice.

"I see, Miss Kane. I've never heard anyone hand in their resignation like that before. You may, of course, consider yourself to be fired."

"Fired? What a fucking blow and if you're speaking to that bastard of a father of yours tell him I'll be knocking on his door when I'm done with you. Now stop that fucking car!"

Valentine hung up, threw his cell phone out of the window into a passing ditch and quietly addressed Estelle.

"Estelle does your cell phone have email capacity?"

"Of course, why?"

"The individual who just called me is a very determined and ruthless being and she may want to harm all of us if we don't do as she asks. As you have witnessed I have thrown my cell phone away. Eva I would advise you to do the same. I need to contact one of my colleagues and have her monitored to see where she is and where she's going. Please trust me on this as I may be in as much danger as I ever want to be and I'd like to keep us all safe."

Estelle spoke to Hugh.

"What do you think Hugh?"

"Give him your phone, Elle. It's OK, I'll be watching."

Estelle passed her phone across to Valentine who typed in the address and then two short messages.

"Valentine Sere. Password, 'Rapture.' First, give me immediate GPS tracking on Kay Kane's cell phone and redirect it to this number. Use the air force satellite control network. I want to know where she is to within five feet of me at all times."

The central control sent the signal to the satellite and it immediately aborted its pre-programmed orbit. Lights were flashing and bells were ringing in Schriever Air Force Base in Colorado, as their computer was hacked, sending the spacecraft into its new orbit.

Valentine knew what was happening and could only imagine the panic in the Airforce base.

"Secondly, give the rescued woman in Sweden whatever she wants. End of message."

He passed the phone back to Estelle.

"You can check the message if you want, Estelle. Eva, your phone!"

Eva reluctantly put the window down and dropped her phone out, then watched it break into pieces as it hit the road surface behind the car. Val straightened up and looked forward again. He spoke to Hugh without turning his head.

"I'd get a move on if I were you. We need to put some distance between us and our pursuer. She's a very dangerous woman. What's more, she's behind us and who knows what resources she has at her disposal? Get us to the ferry, Hugh. I'm not for turning back and driving towards her."

Hugh took it onboard and put his foot down hard on the gas pedal.

Chapter *105*

AUDREY WALSH PACED THE POLISHED WOODEN floor of her room. The view looking out over the Swedish Lakes and the reflection of the red-orange sunset would have been spectacular if it hadn't been for the fact that she had no idea where she was and why she was here. Her arm hurt where the needle had been inserted for the drip and she wanted her own clothes back. She was frightened. She had no idea how long she had been away from Cyril and she knew he would be distraught with worry.

Erik Alfsson knocked on the door before entering Audrey's room. She didn't answer so he edged open the door and spoke.

"Hello, Missus. I am Erik, are you there?"

Audrey stood beside the window refusing to answer.

Erik was half *Sami* or *Laps*, one of the indigenous people of the North. His mother had married outside of the tribe, unheard of in those days. He was seventy-three years old, his hair and beard were both pure white and his face was a mass of weather beaten lines as a result of a lifetime spent in brutal -50 degree winters. Valentine retained his services because of his knowledge of the land and his gentle manner. You just couldn't but like the man.

He spoke to Audrey in a thick Swedish accent. He introduced himself again and poured her some warm *Lingonberry* juice, then handed it to her.

"Where am I and what do you want with me? Where's my Cyril?"

"Missus, you are in Kiruna, Northern Sweden inside the Arctic Circle and you are safe now. A man, a doctor I'm told, drugged you and was intending to harm you. We rescued you and now for the time being you are here."

"I want to speak to my husband and daughter!"

"Of course," replied Erik. "I will have a telephone brought to you at once."

"I want to go home, please."

"That is a little more difficult. While you were under this man's sedation, the epidemic that has been spreading has resulted in the closure of all the airspace and borders. No one is going anywhere until they open them again. In the meantime you can treat this home as your own.

"Let me know if you would like to go walking or fishing. The mosquitoes are not so bad this summer. I will try to accommodate whatever you may wish. I will go with you and be your guide. You may find it beautiful here and we should maybe have a good display of the aurora lights this evening.

"I will have new clothes brought for you. If you need me just call. Press the intercom on the wall; press 00 and I will come. This is your home until such times as we can get you back to your Cyril and your daughter. You will need to put the prefixed code I have written down for you before the number you wish to dial. The telephone is active and entirely at your disposal."

Chapter *106*

Four Hours until the Proposal

A N E-MAIL ALERT SUDDENLY FLASHED ACROSS the screen on Estelle's phone. She opened it and a live feed using the latest mapping and tracking technology filled the screen of her handset. Two images, one green, the other blue appeared on the screen moving in the same direction approximately three miles apart. She passed the phone over to Valentine.

"I think she's close."

Valentine studied the phone not answering her, and then showed it to Hugh.

"She's gaining." he said.

"I know. Is this as fast as this thing will go?"

The car surged forward as Hugh depressed the accelerator and the turbo kicked in. Within minutes it was clear that their pursuer was now falling behind. Kay could see the same on her tracking device. She tore the headlining from the ceiling of the car in anger, swearing and spitting saliva over the already shredded dashboard. She floored the pedal willing the car to go as fast as she could round the winding roads. Cars coming in the other direction swerved into whatever space they could find on the narrow bends in their bid to avoid the oncoming car that was travelling on the wrong side of the road.

Side-mirrors littered the road as she tore through the traffic tearing metal out of the sides of the cars that got in her way. Valentine could see on the screen that she was gaining again and quickly.

"She's catching us, Hugh. Better start taking some chances!"

Hugh again responded. He had been trained in tough evasive driving manoeuvres in the army and now was the time to put those skills into practice. He swerved in and out through the slower traffic making its way to Strangford for the last ferry of the evening.

Valentine turned to speak to the two girls in the back.

"You two are from around here right?"

"Not far, why?"

Although they were both scared by Hugh's driving, they were more frightened by the crazy woman that was chasing them.

"What time's the last boat over to the other side?" asked Valentine.

Eva quickly confirmed with Estelle the last time the ferry sailed from this side of the Lough. They both knew the timetables backwards but needed the reassurance from each other that they were right, given the circumstances. They spoke in unison.

"It's 6pm; 9pm at weekends."

Valentine looked down at the phone. Kay was still gaining somehow. His watch told him it was 17.50pm.

"How far, Hugh?"

"We're here!" Hugh replied.

They rounded the last bend that took them into Strangford village and drove the short distance down to the ferry terminal. They were the last but two cars to board and the wait was agonising as they collectively willed the steel ramp of the ferry to rise!

Valentine studied the phone with the other three who now gathered around him to watch, seeing how the green dot was getting steadily closer and closer. He didn't bother to look up from the screen as he posed the question, "Does this thing always leave on time?"

"Always," Estelle answered without taking her eyes from the display.

The sound of the ferry's engines increased as it prepared to leave on its last crossing of the day. The water boiled around its sides and the shrill sound of the alarm went off to announce their departure. As the barrier came down and the ramp began to rise, they could feel the ferry begin to move from side to side as it left the stability of the concrete slipway on which it partially rested between trips across the Lough.

Eva and Estelle momentarily raised their eyes from the screen and breathed in relief that they had all made it safely. Hugh and Valentine watched the approach road for any sign of Kay. The ferry was now ten feet out of its mooring with the boarding ramp half way up when they heard the screams of protest coming from the tyres on Kay's rental car and watched as pedestrians pulled their children to safety and away from the speeding vehicle as it mounted the kerb stones, smashing the wheel rims on the granite road edgings. Kay's car now came into view as it screeched around the corner sideways with the passenger side wheels leaving the ground.

There was no indication that she had any intentions of stopping. The four watched the car come speeding towards the ferry until Hugh grabbed Estelle and Eva and pulled them back and around shouting for them to run! Valentine saw what Hugh was doing and fled away from the oncoming car. Only a few of the other passengers on the ferry saw the rapid approach of the vehicle. Those that had not, talked amongst themselves, oblivious to the approaching danger as they admired the views from the boat.

The car's engine screamed as it left the ground! With the sudden absence of road surface the revs shot through the dial. There was a momentary silence as the car defied gravity and became a 60 miles per hour two tonne airborne missile. Observers watched in horror as the dried, caked mud and dust flew down and out from under the tyre wells, free of their earthly confines. The wheels extended downwards, allowing the shock absorbers to extend to an unnaturally obscene length without the weight of the car to compress them.

The front section hit the painted steel edge of the still rising ramp, crumpling the front hood and bumper and shattering the windscreen. The glass from the headlights and plastic from the grill turned into shrapnel, shooting shards of glass and metal across the steel deck. The impact sent the car spilling over, first landing on its side, before settling on its roof shattering further what still remained of the windscreen and side windows. It rocked back and forth with the engine still screaming until it found its balancing point.

The siren wailed from the ferry's alarm breaking the silence brought on by the shock of the eye-witnesses. Screams of fear and protest followed from the crew and passengers on board the boat.

A mixture of anger and concern for the driver or passengers in the car filled the quiet few moments until Kay eventually released herself from the wreckage. The seat belt had jammed and the car's airbag had inflated, doing its job well by wedging her firmly inside.

Hugh got Eva and Estelle to relative safety and watched Kay rip her fingers through the reinforced rubber and canvas of the airbag, bursting it with ease. She was screaming in frustration at the snagged seatbelt. She was attempting to bite her way through the fabric of the restraint.

The dust was still rising and the wheels of the wreck were still turning as the curious and confused passengers approached the upturned car in a mixture of fascination and genuine concern.

The crew of the ferry started directing the passengers away from the upturned car in an attempt to restore calm and order. The likelihood of the vehicle catching fire was a real possibility. Some of the passengers, still in their vehicles when the incident happened were now clambering from the wreckage of their own cars and pickups.

One of the crew ran towards what was left of Kay's car with a fire extinguisher as the smell of gasoline was obvious even in the breeze coming from the Lough that swept across the deck. He was accompanied by a young deckhand, who pleaded with the passengers to 'please stand back and away from the danger!'

The ferry was midway across the fifteen minute sailing to its destination when the door of the upturned car was forced open with enough violence to crack the hinges.

Chapter *107*

KAY KICKED HER WAY OUT OF THE UPTURNED vehicle. An electrical fire had begun inside the cabin of the car and was spreading fast. The flames grew in intensity as it found the combustible accelerant and ignited the fibres of Kay's gasoline soaked clothing. She tore at her burning suit, leaving herself almost naked. She had sustained injuries to her chest and face that would have hospitalised any normal person for months. She teetered slightly then oriented herself as to her location on board the ferry.

She could see no sign of either Valentine or the Ballantine girl. Gasoline was continuing to flood out from the ruptured tank of her car and a pool of the inflammable liquid surrounded her feet.
The ferry's captain decided to make for shore as fast as the vessel would allow.

The increased roar from the diesel engines could be heard over the screams of panicking passengers as the ferry sped on towards shore. The service between the two towns located on either side of the Lough had been operating for the best part of four hundred years. No one had made the crossing in such a fast time, or likely ever would again.

As some of the passengers began to recover from the shock of the crash, their initial concerns now turned to anger, as they made protests followed by threats ranging from calling the police and having her arrested, to actual physical harm. All sympathy for the 'mad woman' had long since been lost; their anger was now directed towards the half-naked, seemingly oblivious, partially burnt casualty who ignored them as she jostled her way toward the crowded passengers at the stern of the boat.

For Valentine, Hugh, Eva and Estelle, the small ferry could provide no hiding place apart from the passenger waiting area or the engine room, which was now locked down as a result of the crash. Hugh knew that if he could stall for time, they were only minutes from berthing on the other side of the Lough and away from harm.

He guided the sisters to the last car parked at the rear of the boat, making it the first to leave, as the boat had ramps at both ends so avoiding the need to turn when docking. He knew it would likely end in conflict as he told the driver of the car that he would need it to ensure the girls safety. The driver, as Hugh predicted, objected, making threats and stupidly putting his hand on Hugh's chest to push him away in anger at his request.

"Who the fuck do you think you are telling me you're taking my car, short arse."

Hugh understood that the man was angry. He just didn't have the time or luxury for tact or diplomacy.

"Look, I'm sorry man, truly I am, but I have to commandeer your vehicle."

He watched some of passengers be pushed aside as Kay made her steady progress towards the stern of the ferry that ultimately led to Eva and Estelle.

"Listen, asshole. You're not taking my fucking car and if you even so much as lean on it I'll break your face!" was the reply.

The man was in his mid-twenties with far too much muscle and an attitude that came with chemical enhancement associated with bodybuilding. He weighed upward of two hundred and forty pounds and was used to getting his own way. He moved a step too close to Hugh so he was almost nose to nose. He jabbed his finger into Hugh's chest again to reinforce his point.

That was his second and final mistake. Hugh snatched his right finger in his left hand pulling it down sharply towards the ground, twisting it counter clockwise, putting catastrophic pressure on the knuckle joint until it snapped in his grasp.

Using the crumpling effect of the pain and the unfortunate

opponents own weight, he sent him tumbling uncontrollably forward and down towards Hugh's waiting knee. Hugh changed his mind. He instead threw his opponent further off balance using a quick rotation of his hips, then simultaneously drove the heel of his right hand up and under his chin using his opponent's downward momentum and body weight to reinforce the blow. The man's head snapped backwards and upwards leaving him exposed. Hugh slammed a fist into his floating rib and the conflict was over in less than thirty-seconds.

Hugh felt sorry for the guy, but he had to get the girls to safer ground. Both Eva and Estelle stood in a mixture of fear and amazement at the casual manner and speed that Hugh had easily used to overwhelm his opponent. It took a second or two of staring down at the giant sprawled on the deck of the ship for them to remember the peril they were in.

Hugh looked at the figure of the badly injured woman who was making her way towards them. She had seen at a distance the struggle that Hugh had with the owner of the car and it helped her to zero in on Eva. Kay recognised her instantly from the film footage she'd seen on the late John Greer's computer.

She speedily squeezed through the tightly parked cars on the deck, ripping her fingers through side mirrors and the fabric top of a convertible to test her new weapons as she made for her target. She was less than fifteen feet away when Valentine stepped out in front of her, halting her progress. She tilted her head to one side, confused as Valentine had the surprising will to even contemplate stopping her after the threats she'd made.

The still panicked passengers and crew could feel the ferry making contact on the mooring ramp and could hear the keel of the boat scrape heavily against the concrete slipway as it bullied its way up to expose almost an eighth of its entire length to allow the cars and foot passengers to leave the vessel as quickly as they possibly could. The captain was trying his best to follow berthing protocol even in such extreme circumstances. Some of the foot passengers were jumping over the sides of the still moving ferry to avoid the growing danger on board. The upturned car was now engulfed in raging flames, igniting two other cars parked close by. Escaping passengers awaited the inevitable explosion as the fire quickly spread. The water around the boat bubbled and foamed as the vessel eased its over-revved engines and steadied itself for an emergency disembarkation. Eva and Estelle had reluctantly taken their seats in the little two-seater roadster and they now craned their heads around to see what would happen between Valentine and his estranged vice president.

Hugh was watching as well. He had to admit that the man had balls. He'd seen what she had done to the airbag of the car and several of the passengers who got in her way, sweeping them aside like protesting bugs.

Hugh spoke to the sisters without taking his eyes off Valentine or Kay.

"Start the car, girls."

"What?"

"Start the car now," he repeated.

Estelle turned the ignition key. The car shuddered then stalled. She swore out loud and frantically turned the key over and over in her panic to get the car moving while Eva focussed on the melee behind.

Valentine was shouting at the oncoming woman, "Kay, please, this is crazy. You've hurt people here and you are badly injured yourself. I beg you, please stop, nothing's worth this!"

Kay didn't answer just simply lifted him and threw him over the wavering side of the boat. His head hit the hard concrete as he landed on the rippled stone slipway. The water helped cushion his fall leaving him dazed and bleeding in the water.

The engines were still running creating a vacuum effect now trapping him under the boat and snagging his legs. Eva and Estelle jumped out of the car and leapt from the still moving ferry, running down the ramp to see where Valentine had gone.

"Jesus Christ, Eva, he's trapped under the keel. He's going to drown!"

Elle screamed. Eva didn't respond but instead ploughed into the water, grabbing at Valentine under his arms trying to get his head above the boiling water while avoiding the still erratically moving steel hull of the stricken ferry.

The boat violently swayed from side to side making it ever more difficult and dangerous for both of them. She could feel and hear the panicking drivers race off the ferry, crunching the undersides of their cars as they smashed nose first onto the slipway in their efforts to get away from the danger as fast as they could.

Chapter *108*

HE WAS DROWNING. VALENTINE'S BODY WAS convulsing due to the lack of oxygen. Eva took a deep breath, held his nose and breathed air into his lungs. Both their heads were underwater as Eva tried to pre-empt the erratic movement of the boat in a bid to protect Valentine and herself from being drowned or crushed under its massive bulk.

Valentine's eyes had been closed as he drew closer to suffocation. The contact with Eva as she gave him the kiss of life, jerked him back into consciousness. She tried her best to administer more oxygen but he was thrashing and protesting against her from making any further contact. The more he protested the more water he took into his lungs.

Eva finally gained control of him and was about to administer a second breath when his eyes flashed open under the water making her pause. She stared down through the cloudy sea at him as he finally gave up his struggles and allowed Eva to now inflate some air into his partially flooded chest. Her eyes now made direct contact with his. The ferry moved down and to the left as the last of the cars screeched off the deck making the boat lighter. It was enough for Valentine to eventually kick his way free with Eva dragging him to land. The brief contact continued as Eva still held him.

The colour of his eyes changed from grey through deep amber to emerald green. Tiny metal flakes of black swirled across his corneas like ebony snowflakes inside a toy snow globe, then quickly vanished leaving him with a now piercing turquoise cornea and blue within ice blue iris and pin point black pupil. He was free and with Eva's help, hauled himself further up the slipway and onto land. His eyes slowly changed back to their normal blue grey as he staggered to the relative safety of the small port.

For some unknown reason and for the first time that he could remember, and even under such extreme and dangerous circumstances, Valentine felt cared for. He felt part of something more important than he had ever felt before. Blood was trickling down his face from the cut he received to the side of his head in the fall from the ferry. He put his hand up to feel for its source but could find no indication of a wound.

"Where are Kay and Hugh?"

Eva turned to look up at the deck of the ferry. Some of the passengers were still unwilling to pass the half-naked and badly injured crazy woman and the man who blocked her path. Estelle was standing behind Hugh as would-be reinforcement. Eva steadied Valentine and spoke directly into his eyes.

"Mr. Sere, no matter what happens, get my sister to safety. Do you understand? It's me that woman wants."

Valentine took his eyes away from the scene on the ferry deck to address Eva.

"Eva, please don't go up there. God only knows what that woman has in store for you."

"That's my sister up there and she's in trouble because I stupidly put her there. I have to help her and Hugh. I have to go."

Hugh still blocked Kay's progress as she watched Eva come back up the steel ramp to her sister's aid.

"Look, Father. She's coming to me of her own free will."

Hugh baulked at the mention of his former vocation and could sense that Eva was coming, but refused to take his eyes from his enemy. Estelle turned around to see Eva walking up the ramp towards them.

"Stay back, Eva. Hugh and I will deal with this."

"Oh, will you indeed?" sneered Kay. "Is she right, Father? If you don't get out of my way I'll let you watch me kill your friends first, then gut you."

Hugh knew that she meant it. How the hell did this woman know he was once a priest? He shouted to Eva over his shoulder, "Stop where you are, Eva!"

"Father, I won't ask you again!" snarled Kay.

She dropped her head to one side again and prepared herself. Hugh adjusted his body weight and Kay saw it. He centred his weight, moving his right foot slightly behind his left, a shoulders width apart. He held his hands up, palms facing Kay as if to feign appeasement. In truth, it was a tested technique used in martial arts to allow speedy movement to parry an attack. Kay moved forward to grab at Eva, ignoring Hugh's attempts to placate her. He responded by dipping low as she made her move, crashing his fist into the inner part of her thigh, causing severe trauma to the thinner inner leg muscles and blood vessels. It compressed nerves and tissue against her thigh bone. It was an attack that would have normally caused the recipient to buckle and fold in agony.

Kay took it as a minor irritation and didn't so much as break her stride. She grabbed at Hugh using her left hand on his shoulder then snatched the waistband of his jeans. She flung him with ease against the heavy wooden handrail that ran along the top of the ferry's siding. It splintered and cracked as did Hugh's ribcage as he made impact with the rail, sending shards of wood and part of the metal bracket that held the rail up into his side. He was hurt and he knew it. Just as importantly, Kay knew it.

He lay both stunned and surprised at her speed and strength. He could do nothing but watch and wait as his breath returned and the stars stopped spinning in front of his eyes.

As he tried to regain his senses he became aware of Estelle's efforts to protect her sister. Kay now refocused her attention back to Eva, ignoring the injured Hugh as he lay on the deck holding his damaged side, struggling to breathe. She no longer saw him as an immediate threat.

The next thing Eva saw out of the corner of her eye was Valentine pulling the safety pin from a distress flare. He aimed it directly at the fuel soaked Kay and fired it as hard as he could. The flare hissed loudly as it passed by the side of Eva's head, a trail of acrid smoke filling the air as it flew towards its target.

Chapter *109*

K AY WAS SUDDENLY ENGULFED IN FLAMES and red smoke as the flare struck her in the chest, instantly turning her flesh to molten wax. The flames flashed upwards encasing her head and torso in the fireball. The screams of indignation and fury were inhaled into her lungs along with the flames and smoke, driving her to her knees. Hugh hauled himself to his feet as Kay rolled back and forth in a bid to extinguish the flames. He shouted to Valentine through the smoke, "Go. Get out of here!"

Eva ran to help Hugh. She put his arm over her shoulder as she guided him to the safety of the commandeered roadster. Kay's hand reached out through the smoke as they passed, grabbing Hugh's thigh and digging her fingers deep into the muscle tissue and tearing through his flesh. She found the only target available to her coming up short of his groin. The tear ripped into his femoral artery spraying blood as she withdrew her fingers. Hugh mustered his strength and flung himself away from his burning assailant. He was haemorrhaging badly. His hand covered the wound trying to apply pressure to stem the blood loss as Eva dragged him towards the abandoned car.

Kay raised herself to her feet, looked at her fleeing prize, then threw herself over the side of the boat, hitting the now calmer water with a hiss. Eva could see Valentine and Estelle standing on the slipway. The keys were still in the ignition and she levered Hugh into the passenger seat, while attempting to help him apply pressure to the wound on his thigh. She tore at the zipper of her hooded sweatshirt, pulling it off and applying a makeshift tourniquet to stem the blood loss. Hugh squirmed as she tightened the shirt around his leg.

"Put pressure on it, Hugh!"

Hugh pressed into his thigh absorbing the pain, trying to remain conscious. Eva ran round to the driver side of the car and jumped in. She fumbled with the keys, trying once again to start the car. After the second attempt the roadster roared into life as she jerked the gear stick, released the clutch sending them forward towards the off ramp. Her head was violently yanked back, almost lifting her out of her seat as the smell of burnt flesh filled her nostrils.

Kay had re-boarded the ferry and came up on the car from behind. She grabbed a fist full of Eva's hair attempting to pull her backwards out and over the back of the car. To Kay this was no longer about the fiscal rewards that the girl could bring. She urgently needed her to save her own life! Eva threw her hands up to stop the pain of the attack, but Kay had her gripped firmly. She swivelled her head around to see her attacker and try to find some way of escape.

Hugh pushed his right foot down on top of Eva's left, depressing the clutch. He then crunched the gears into reverse. Eva realised what he was doing and revved the engine harder. Kay was still gripping her tightly leaning over the back of the roadster with her legs partially lifted from the deck of the ferry. The car accelerated backwards, smashing into one of the abandoned cars still remaining on deck of the now deserted ferry. The momentum shot Kay backwards landing her on the bonnet of a stationary car, taking a fist full of Eva's hair with her!

Eva jammed the gearbox into first again and sped off the ferry leaving her assailant in her wake. Valentine and Estelle saw them go and followed in pursuit, leaving Kay Kane lying injured on the deck. Less than a minute into their escape and Kay was back on the chase. Valentine felt the phone vibrate in his pocket and saw the green icon on the screen gaining on them. Estelle saw him check the phone.

"What's wrong?" she cried.

"She's coming," Valentine replied. "She must have taken the tracker from her car and found another vehicle!"

It only took a second's lapse in concentration. The car in front containing Hugh and Eva had vanished.

"Where are they? They've disappeared!"

Estelle's voice now strained with fear.

"Call them!" shouted Valentine.

"I can't! Hugh doesn't carry a phone and you made Eva throw hers out the window. Remember?"

It was getting darker, and the sun was beginning to set lower in the sky. Estelle slowed the car in the hope of seeing a turn off that Eva and Hugh may have taken. Valentine rechecked the phone. The moving icon indicating Kay on the screen had taken a right turn up ahead and was still moving fast.

"Turn Estelle, Kay's moving in another direction. She must have done something or thrown something into Eva's car too. Shit! Of course, her watch! All the senior board members had one at BION, it was compulsory to wear it in case of kidnapping. She must have activated it and tossed it in the car when she grabbed Eva on the boat. Turn, turn the car!"

Eva was driving through the country lanes as fast as she could. The wind blasted through her hair as the cooling night air began to chill her. If she could just get Hugh to the water she could maybe help him. She hadn't given any thought to her welfare in her bid to extricate her friend, but now it was very apparent. Her adrenalin was slowing allowing her to calm a little given the still dire circumstances. Why was she still so wet? Her T-shirt was saturated and she was exhausted and cold.

The wound that Kay had inflicted on her was barely a scratch on the surface of her skin, but it was enough to make a thin but lethal slice through and into her jugular vein without her realising! She was bleeding badly and now struggling to stay conscious and remain focused, driving with one hand on the wound on her throat and the other on the steering wheel. Hugh had passed out on the passenger seat. She saw the sign for Tara Bay. Water! She managed to stay conscious long enough to see the white

391

washed hand painted stone placed at the side of the road with Saint Cooey's Wells written on it. She veered the car right and drove down the lane, then into the car park situated above the wells that looked out onto the darkening silhouette of the sea.

Chapter *110*

HUGH SENSED THEY HAD COME TO A STOP AND awoke startled! "What happened? Where are we? I must have passed out some way back."

"I'm hurt, Hugh! There are wells down there somewhere and I can smell the sea."

She limply dropped her hand away from her neck, too weak now to concentrate on maintaining pressure on the wound on her throat. She was spiralling down into unconsciousness and knew that she would soon be done for.

Her only chance and it was a slim one at that, would be to get to the sea and hope there would be enough algae in the water to heal the wound the way it had worked on the burn on her arm during the experiment in the lab back at Queens.

What if she was wrong? There had been a concentration of the algae in that test tube she had used back then. What if there wasn't enough here? It was too late to get to a hospital and the Kane woman was still chasing them.

"Oh God we're both going to die here and there's nothing I can do!"

Hugh came as fully to his senses as his own injuries would allow and now saw the extent of Eva's blood loss.

"Jesus Holy Christ, Eva, you're bleeding, you're bleeding so badly, how, how did this happen?"

"No time, Hugh...No..."

Eva's lips had turned purple caused by the lack of oxygen

getting through her system. Hugh did his best to ignore the white pain coming from his side as he yanked his shirt off over his head and jammed it against the wound on Eva's neck. He knew from experience that the wound was a mortal one and the lack of colour in Eva's face was equally alarming! Her hands were freezing and her shivering had stopped, all the wrong signals for a recovery. He flung open the door of the car and stumbled out, then hopped round to the driver's side.

The makeshift bandage had slipped from its position allowing what still remained of Eva's blood to flow again down her neck and onto her already saturated shirt. There was so little pressure in her system now to pump what remained of her life force through her veins. It seeped out and down in diminishing narrow ribbons of liquid red. Her car seat was sopping wet with her blood and pools had formed in any crevice or well in the leather upholstery.

He reapplied the now soaking shirt to her neck hoping it would hold there and stem the bleeding. He knelt down on the gravel and almost screamed as a sharp stone found a tender spot on an already damaged knee. He hesitated, briefly resting his head on the car door and waited for the pain to ease.

He desperately ransacked his way through the glove box looking for any means of securing Eva's dressing until he got her down to the sea. He hoped she was right; it was the only chance of saving her now. She'd be dead in minutes so there was no possibility of getting her medical attention. The short time that he had lost consciousness in the car had stiffened him up. He could barely weight bear on his own damaged leg and his breathing was laboured from the impact of the throw he'd taken on the ferry.

"Come on! Come on, there has to be something!"

He could just about see through his pain the dim light illuminating the litter packed glove box. It was now almost totally dark as he franticly threw the contents aside until he found something that would work to secure the dressing on her neck.

"Yes, Yes!"

He yanked out an LED headlight torch from the back of the glovebox and pulled the elasticated securing strap over Eva's head then down and around her neck. He adjusted the strap tightly enough to secure the dressing but not so tight as to impede her already shallow breathing. Job done as best he could manage, he put one arm around her waist and the other under her legs and lopsidedly lifted her.

The crescendo of pain swept through him like a bolt of electricity almost taking his breath away. Eva was now unconscious as he managed to take her up in his arms. He looked around and saw the steps trailing down to where he supposed the wells were located and hopefully a path down to the sea. No time to waste, he hobbled over, tortured by Eva's added weight, to the metal hand rail that led down to the vague hope of salvation.

Hugh was beyond desperate and if he could even get her to one of the wells or the sea, then the girl in his arms could be saved.

He could hardly bear the weight of Eva in his arms as he struggled to negotiate the first of the many steep steps of the path down, with no knowledge of how long the journey to the sea would take.

The muscles in his shoulders and forearms screamed with the effort. His lungs were burning, refusing to accept any more air. For the first time in his life the thought occurred that he could well be beaten. Blood was haemorrhaging through his own makeshift bandage, stemming from the arterial wound on his thigh. The dead weight of the almost lifeless girl in his arms was pulling him down. He could smell the sea.

So close now, Hugh. Get her to water and she can maybe heal herself!

Chapter *111*

HUGH LOOKED DOWN AT THE DULL METAL edge of the step as if it were the most daunting task he would every have to muster up the courage to take. The fading sunlight reflected off the scratched edging. It looked slippery and steep. He readjusted Eva's weight and gathered what was left of his depleting strength.

This is gonna hurt, but there's no other choice, he told himself.

The pain was almost sublime as it rose in waves when he stepped down. His head swam with the agony. *Take another step Hugh, that's as bad as it can get,* he lied to himself. He had never been that good a liar. The second step down was worse than the first. He contemplated vomiting as the pain tried to force him to empty the contents of his stomach less he choked on his own sick when he passed out.

He stood firm through the nausea, holding tightly on to his ward. The next ten steps down took minutes but it seemed like hours. He battled his conflicted mind telling him to set the girl down and leave them both to their fates. The mental anguish was as bad if not worse than the physical one. The girl was dying and probably, so was he. He'd never given up in his life but this was it. He couldn't go on. He was coughing up blood now as a result of his punctured lung and his breathing was becoming increasingly laboured. Ten more steps to a turning and a viewpoint. He could pause there if he got her down those ten steps.

No one would reach them in time to save them; it was up to him and him alone. He took the ten steps into Hell, then lay Eva down on the rough wooden floor of the viewpoint and gulped in welcome lungfulls of air. He raised his head up to the sky in an attempt to make his airways clearer. The twin beams of the headlights above raked across the darkening sky and he knew their pursuer was on them. Adrenalin pumped through him at the thought of falling into their assailant's hands.

This was important, too important. I have to get to the water. He silently pleaded with his maker, *If there was a greater plan for this girl then Lord, for your sake, please help me!*

He struggled to picked Eva back up, then stumbled and fell forward down several more of the unforgiving steps.

He tried his best to protect her but landed forwards and sidewards down hard onto his shoulder, smashing against the sharp steel edge of the wooden foot guard that ran the length of the descent. The pain numbed, then seared as the muscles compacted against the shoulder joint. He was doing his best to ignore the agony and still trying to keep grip of her to cushion and protect her head against his chest. At last, a new surge of fresh adrenalin was helping.

He got up but stumbled again losing his footing as his head crunched into the steel handrail. The impact tore a deep gash over his left eye. Blood streamed down and now left him almost blind and on his knees.

He adjusted her weight as he knelt. Balancing her as best he could, all the while knowing that their pursuer was gaining with every second he hesitated. His personal battle waged on and he was losing to blood loss and fatigue. He would have to set her down. There wasn't much time for first aid.

Chapter *112*

WHY HAD THIS GIRL BECOME SO PRECIOUS to him he barely even knew her? He stood holding her in his arms, again trying his best to gasp enough air. The pain in his chest from the sustained punishment he'd taken had driven the broken rib deeper into his lung. He could hear the rattle in his chest when he inhaled and knew that he was drowning in his own blood as he wiped the bubbles of red foam from his mouth. His legs buckled and his knee smashed into the edge of the step and with the added weight of Eva in his arms, it almost tore his kneecap from its joint.

He held her tight, refusing to let her go. He wiped the pain, blood and tears of frustration away on her shoulder. The agony raped its way into his brain.

Don't get up, you're destroyed! Rest, set her down. Leave this stranger be. You've done your best. You're too old now, Hugh. Let her be!

The fact was, she was more important than him or his smashed limbs or damaged chest. Hugh Doggett had always understood that he was dispensable. The military and his adopted father had taught him that. He was a small cog in a big machine and the machine was more important, but now, looking at Eva lying in his arms and the thought of what this woman or whatever it was chasing them would do to her, he realised that for whatever reason he loved her. Not in any romantic sense. He just couldn't imagine life without her being in his world.

The thought of losing her here and now was too much to bear. He gathered strength from the pit of his soul and teetered to his feet scraping up a handful of mud and caking it into the open wound above his eye to stem the bleeding. He could hear the banshee wails from above and the pounding against the wooden steps as their enemy closed in on them.

No time now, Hugh. Get up you idle bastard!

The wound in his thigh was now freely haemorrhaging. No time left to adjust his bandage.

Chapter *113*

W E'RE THERE EVA. YOU HOLD ON NOW. HOLD on for me." He was trying to convince himself rather than her that he could make it. Kay Kane was almost on them as she leapt down the steps three at a time. Hugh could hear her gaining but didn't dare turn round. *Keep going, man. This girl is not hers for the taking.*

Hugh Doggett finally stumbled to his knees still holding Eva. He didn't make it to the elusive sea. The best he could manage was to get her to the first of three shallow sacred wells that lay on the path to the old ruins of Saint Cooey's church in the near distance. The sea was less than fifty yards away, but it may as well have been fifty miles. His life was draining away. The wound on his leg was bleeding freely as the makeshift dressing had long gone.

His breathing was reduced to a series of desperate gasps as his punctured lung finally filled to total saturation with his blood. He could barely feel the sharpness of the long nails as they tore through his flesh as the vice like grip of their pursuer took hold on the meat of his calve. The second of the two talons found its way into the open wound on his already injured leg. The nails dug deep into his flesh as her grip was secured.

The gravel from the path rode up under his shirt as she pulled him backwards to his destruction. He had little defence left against her. Kay's speed and strength had grown unlike his, which had waned between the effort of saving the girl and the mortal blood loss. Even at his fittest and keenest, he doubted his chances against her. In his current state he was lost and she and he both knew it! He heard the gasps of excitement from her rancid breath; as she anticipated the torture she had waiting for him.

It didn't matter. He was resolute. *It's been a long time coming Doggy and thank God for it,* he thought to himself.

Hugh looked down at the passing trail of gravel that he left in his wake as his body slowly came to rest. Whatever he had been destined for must have now been accomplished. His body slumped and his fingers ceased trying to find purchase on the loose ground as she dragged him away from his mission. *This is OK. It's better than I'd hoped for; I'm going home.*

Images from his past streamed into his mind. The greedy rips and slashes rained down on him from above by his executioner. He could sense her hands flailing down from above but any sensation of pain was gone. He knew now how close death was.

People that he had both saved and killed in the past now washed before his eyes like fleeting photographs that fluttered in a silent breeze across his dying brain.

Hugh Doggett was at peace and more than ready to die. What remained of his almost spent supply of adrenalin activated any part of him that was still functioning.

Fuck you! I'm not going without taking you with me!

He reached up through his agony in a last effort to snatch Kay's wrist and attempted to force her into a roll to pin her to the ground. She saw the move and easily countered. She took his hand in hers and quickly twisted his wrist then pushed her knee against the back of his hand using the ground as a stop to hold his arm up vertically between her and the earth below. He felt the pressure on the joint, then heard the crack as the bones gave in to the onslaught. That was it. He was finished. He lay face down, exhaled for the last time and let her do her worst. She let his broken arm drop, stood over him, and for some unknown reason suddenly ceased the attacks.

The barrage of blows stopped and she dragged him slowly up by his collar, wondering why he was still breathing. The stones and dirt that had gathered up the front of his shirt fell back down onto his lap. He was caked in mud and his own blood. He could see that he was being raised up for execution and he could feel her firmly gripping him, holding him fast in her fist. He could sense his own weightlessness as his body hovered inches from the damp earth, legs still sprawled out in front. His arms dangled down by his sides, uselessly. For whatever her reason she hadn't killed him yet.

She stood silent, stroking the side of his neck with her rakish razor sharp finger, to emphasise how easily she could slip it across his jugular vein, ignoring his helplessness. He lowered his head preparing for the final blow.

He looked down at his broken body, wondering again why the blows from above had ended. The grip that she held him in was released. Why had she let him go?

Hugh raised his head up and looked round to see Eva standing over him, her hands held up opened palmed in a command for Kay to stop. Hugh looked up at her in disbelief.

"You're alive, Eva! How? How can you be alive?"

He mumbled the words into his chest, as the strain of lifting his head any further was too much of an effort. Eva spoke in whispers, "We are not alone here, Hugh. Come with me."

"I can't, Eva I'm broken."

"You can." Eva stared at Kay and gently stooped to touch the dew covered grass. She barely brushed Hugh's hand. "Now get to your feet, Hugh, we have work to do here."

Hugh's head swam as he slowly teetered to his feet. He looked round to see the Kane woman casually checking her finger nails for damage and passing him an uninterested glance through raised eyebrows as she looked in his direction, her head still lowered, indicating that he no longer warranted her full attention as any threat he may have once posed had now vanished.

Eva led, and Hugh managed to raise himself onto his feet and stagger behind. Eva brought him to the same shallow well that he had laid her down beside before the attack. Too exhausted to speak again, he slumped against the rough stone wall and allowed himself to slide his body down and take a seated position, resting his head against the cold stones with his legs spread out in front of him. He used the strength in his relatively undamaged arm and exhaustedly managed to bring his grotesquely broken wrist up to rest between his legs. His blood seeped into the stones from the injuries Kay had inflicted on him. He left crimson trails running down the grey granite stones and disappeared behind his shattered body.

Eva stared across at their assailant. Kay was still maintaining a safe distance, like a boxer sent to a neutral corner of the ring, waiting patiently to be permitted to finish her opponent off. Eva turned her attention back to the dying Hugh. She ran her left hand over the wound on his head then down onto the deep slash on his thigh. She placed the other in the gently running water that trickled into the wishing well. His pain abated and the blood stopped flowing from his wounds. This time there was no pain as the bones in his broken wrist and chest appeared to magically reset.

He pushed himself up using the wall as a brace and stood hunched, still weak, but mended, beside her. For the first time he now became fully aware of his surroundings. Not far away, a small structure stood. Its four sturdy stone pillars supported a slated roof and a small wooden topped altar sat below. Hugh surmised it would be for holding outdoor mass or baptisms. A summer breeze was picking up and the gentle gust forced its way through the heavily laden branches of the ancient hazel tree to the left of the structure overhanging its roof. Eva was content that the water had mended Hugh's injuries. It would take time for him to return to full strength. She somehow knew now that something had drawn them to this place; she had no doubt. The wind was intensifying in strength, heaving at the heavy branches of the trees and chasing its way through hedges and gorse. She brushed her hair away from her eyes and she could sense that a new presence had now joined them.

A male's voice spoke directly into her head and appeared to be coming from somewhere behind and to the right of the Kane woman.

"His life isn't yours to save, girl!"

Eva turned her attention away from Hugh to where she supposed the voice originated and made her simple reply, "We shall see about that."

There was no anger in her retort, just resolution. She surprised herself at her new found courage. Apparently her relationship with the algae appeared to affect her resolve as well as her body. Hugh stood in silence, shaken and bewildered, trying to follow the direction of Eva's statement and assuming it was towards the Kane woman who had suddenly lost her previous disinterest in them both and was growing ever more agitated. She sensed that one of her benefactors had somehow joined them; nothing would surprise her at the reach of those people. Some degree of her rationale still remained.

She hadn't been permitted to finish her work for reasons still unknown to her. It was just that something deep in her brain had told her to stop and so she now understood that she had to cease in her attempts to kill the girl, Eva. The others, however, were still fair game and her need to destroy had become overwhelming!

The message reached in through her frustration; a new target was approaching. If she could use the opportunity to get the priest again or the girl's sister, maybe she still had some leverage to redeem her failure before her benefactors and comply with their desires, whatever they may be. She bolted off and up through the thicket to intercept her new prey.

Eva spoke to Hugh.

"Where's my sister, Hugh?"

"I don't know, Eva, I lost her getting you here. She was running with Valentine towards a car when we fled the ferry. I thought they would be close behind us."

Eva closed her eyes and placed her hand back into the water in the well. She screamed loud enough to shatter eardrums!

"Estelle. Where are you? I need you here beside me."

Chapter *114*

ESTELLE HEARD HER SISTER'S SCREAM AND slammed her foot down hard on the brake pedal. The tyres shrieked, leaving long dark curved lines on the road and plumes of acrid smoke in the air as friction melted the rubber, bringing the car to a sideways stop.

She smashed the gear stick into reverse, not bothering to fully depress the clutch. The gears crunched and ground in protest as she bullied the cogs to comply, using both hands to enforce her will on the vehicle and have it stubbornly shift into reverse, ignoring the grinding protests. She could be only minutes from her sister's side.

Valentine forced his hands down hard onto the dashboard as the breaking car attempted to throw him through the windscreen.

"What the hell are you doing? Where are we going?"

"Didn't you hear that? That was Eva screaming!"

"Yes, of course I heard it. I thought my head was going to explode!"

Estelle had no time or desire to explain her actions. She had a singular task and no time for elaboration. She was too busy concentrating both on driving and looking down towards where she hoped would be the shoreline and her waiting sister.

The road took them back towards Tieveshilly. The panic and despair filled her to the point of screaming. If this Kane woman had got to Eva, she was as good as done for.

She supplemented her fear with harsh motivation. *You're*

running short on time, Elle. Get your ass into gear or that bitch will slay your sister!

Valentine paled as Estelle ignored the road junction ahead almost crashing head on into an oncoming car. Its driver slammed down hard on the brake pedal, almost rolling the car onto its side and only just avoiding them. The irate driver had come to a stop with two of his wheels wedged firmly in the side guttering of a drainage ditch. Valentine screamed for her to stop. She ignored him, checking her rear view mirror to see the offended driver standing by the side of the road, swearing and shaking his fist at them as they drove away into the distance.

"Estelle, you could have killed that guy!"

Elle rechecked the rear view mirror again, not bothering to reply to Valentine's protests, content that the driver was unharmed then refocused on reaching her sister.

Two miles later she caught site of the shoreline and the roof of the old church. She instinctively knew her sister was down there somewhere and took the most direct route. She pointed the moving car towards the church which sent them crashing off the road and down through the dense thicket towards the wells and shore.

The headlights did their best against the heavy foliage and steep gradient until they blinked out under the onslaught of rocks and fallen branches. The windscreen shattered inwards, showering them with razor sharp splinters of glass as the car laboured on through the decent, continuing to bounce hard over ruts and boulders sending cascades of loose earth and stones into the interior.

Elle wrestled with the steering wheel to keep the car straight and moving forward. She could just see out of the corner of her vision what appeared to be an old shelter or shrine of some sort through the lines of trees. Valentine had both feet up on the dashboard, using it as a brace, holding his arms up over his face to protect his eyes.

The car came to a crashing stop against the stump of a fallen pine. She tried several times to restart the engine, cursing it for its lack of cooperation.

"Come on! Come on, for fuck's sake start!" The vehicle

was finished and going nowhere. She yanked at the handle to open her door, but it was blocked by brambles and scrub. She screamed at Valentine, "Get out! Go. GET OUT OF THE CAR!"

Valentine released his door catch and leapt from the car. He watched as Estelle shimmied across the seats and fell out through the passenger side door landing on her hands and knees. He was about to help her up but she pushed him aside and began running as best she could over the rough terrain.

Valentine tried his best to keep up but became diverted. Movement somewhere to his right caused him to change course, then purely by chance he stumbled upon an easier path down. An old partially overgrown sheep trail was just visible through the tall grass that made his progress easier. He lost sight of Estelle as he sped his way down towards the shore. He was panting hard as he negotiated the tricky path. He finally caught sight of the wells shelter and the sea off in the distance. He attempted to close the final distance but stumbled and fell over the heavy thicket landing hard against a small pile of rocks.

His vision was blurred. He'd fallen heavily, hitting his head against the rock pile. He rose up to rest on his elbows, praying hard that his senses wouldn't fail him. The surge of whatever was left in his stomach had risen and was burning his throat as it made its way to freedom only to be thwarted by his swallowing the acid remains of food back down into his gut. A steady trickle of blood flowed down from the gash on his forehead, leaving a line of red that led down his nose and into his mouth.

He put his hand up to check the damage and could taste the metallic blood in his mouth. His head swam again and his legs weakened; his strength and consciousness was again fading. He focused on the pebbles and stones that lay beneath him to try to stay conscious but he slowly began to fade again as he slipped away into the darkness.

A peculiar heavy aroma stirred him. It floated in the air all around. It filled his mind, numbing his senses and making him easily compliant. He barely felt the arm being placed under his that led him away.

Chapter *115*

U NKNOWN TO ELLE, SHE WAS LESS THAN TWO hundred yards from Eva. Hugh was gone, dead maybe for all she knew, he'd been so badly injured, but that wasn't her primary concern now. She had to find her sister.

She crashed into branches and nettles, cutting her face and hands, and fell through brambles that ripped at her clothes and hair. The cuts and bruises on her knees were showing even in the fading light.

I have to get to my sister! she told herself through the gasps and pants. She was breathing hard but making speedy progress.

The movement to her right stopped her dead in her tracks. She could sense someone close. She brought her hand up and put it over her mouth to silence her breathing. Her panting still made too much noise as it whistled through her fingers. The effort to stifle the noise almost made her pass out with the lack of oxygen.

She couldn't move fast, not through this much rough ground, without drawing attention to herself. She wasn't even sure how many people she was hiding from but the urgency to get to her sister was overwhelming.

Her heart thumped against her chest and it seemed as though her eardrums were going to pop with the pressure! Her mind was racing, all the while trying to stay hidden and bring her breathing under control to avoid giving away her position. Her mouth was parchment dry so she ran her tongue over the front of her teeth sucking moisture from her saliva glands.

What's it to be Elle?

Her thoughts ran riot through the panic. She was terrified of the woman that was chasing them. The carnage she had caused on the ferry was frightening. She'd seen with her own eyes the damage she'd caused but given all of her fear, she still had to protect her sister and protect her with her own life if necessary! Something truly terrible was happening and she had no solution to get them out of trouble!

Hide or fight? Hide or fight?

She kept repeating the words over and over to stall for what little time she had before that awful woman found her. She had dispensed with Hugh without breaking her stride on the ferry; so God only knew what she was capable of doing to her! She was becoming desperate. Suddenly she saw what she hoped was her sister's outline beside what looked like an old shelter. She quickly worked out the most direct route down through the tangles of tall weeds and brambles.

Attempting it at speed would cut her to pieces and would most certainly allow whoever was chasing her to close the distance. She heard more noises moving behind, closer this time. She didn't dare move or even chance a look! She could see that Eva was less than thirty yards away waiting for her to come, Hugh stood to her left some five yards behind. Eva was talking to someone, but as yet she wasn't able to see who it was as the trees obscured her vision. The only thing she could think of was that Eva had somehow managed to use whatever power she possessed to reason with this Kane woman and bring her to her senses.

If it wasn't Kay Kane, then who the hell was chasing her and where was Sere?

She refocused on the task at hand. *OK, come on Elle, you're out of time. You don't know how many of them are after us so you're going to have to move...Fuck it!*

Estelle took the shortest line she could see to where her sister would still be waiting for her. She ran faster than she thought she was capable of, shredding the skin of her hands and legs as the brambles did their best to halt her progress. Ignoring the pain, she leapt over fallen branches and thicket, once almost losing balance and twisting her ankle in an abandoned rabbit warren. Eva could see and hear her smashing her way towards her and the wells.

"Come on, Elle I can see you, you're almost with me!"

Tears rolled down her checks in desperation at the thought at what this woman would do to her sister. She screamed for Estelle to hurry!

Hugh had worked his way around towards the direction he thought she may be coming and was hoping to outflank Kay if she reappeared. Eva could now clearly see her sister charging and bullying her way through the undergrowth.

"Come on sis! COME ON! You're nearly here!"

Eva held her arms to welcome her into a safe embrace. Then she smelt it, the scent of distilled corruption.

"Noooo!"

Chapter *116*

EVA SAW KAY RACE FORWARDS TO INTERCEPT, then watched as she leapt on Estelle, causing them both to somersault through the last of the thicket and land heavily fifteen feet in front of her and there was absolutely nothing she could do about it. The conversation she had been having with the figure, who still hid in the shadows, had made that abundantly clear. She was at least for the time being, helpless.

Hugh was suddenly yanked off his feet from behind, by someone or something unknown. He lay dazed, fighting for breath and attempting to release himself from a bind around his throat. He clawed at a restraint that had him bound but could find none. He had no option but to lay still. The more he struggled to free himself the tighter the hold became.

Kay got to her feet first and smashed into her side on, knocking her to the ground.

Estelle felt the impact as Kay smashed into her, lifting her off the ground by the sheer ferocity of the attack. The air was knocked from her lungs. She had no breath to scream or fight. She somehow managed to roll onto her back and her arms instinctively went up to protect her face and throat.

That area, however, wasn't the primary target. Kay tore at Estelle's stomach shredding the waistband of her leather belt and jeans in an attempt to eviscerate her.

Kay's face was now horribly deformed and contorted. Anger, greed, murder; a whole litany of past sins all now manifested themselves as tumours and ulcerations, oozing and weeping rancid fluid and pus, misshaping and destroying what was once a very pretty girl. Pain and disease raked across her features.

Whatever this person had done in life, she was atoning for it now.

She was semi-naked apart from what used to be expensive designer knickers and the remains of a skirt and ankle boots. Her determination to reach Eva had stripped away what had been left of her wardrobe and melted skin. Eva could see what used to be breasts. One still enlarged like an obscene blister on her bony chest. The other silicone implant had been torn away; the remaining gel still leaking a mixture of blood and silicone fluid down her torso. She was focused on her single objective.

Elle could hear the bones in Kay's fingers break as she franticly clawed to get to her stomach. She was getting weaker. The stench filled Elle's mouth and nostrils as the discharge from the ulcerations dripped down onto her face and into her mouth. She desperately tried to wriggle free.

She rolled over, made a dash for it and got a few feet away until Kay caught her and set about her again, pinning her to the ground face down. She grabbed her hair and yanked up her head almost breaking her neck, like a trophy waiting to be taken to please the crowd. Kay's fingernails were all now broken so she scrabbled around and found a thick piece of flint and held it to the left side of Elle's throat waiting for approval.

Eva stood helpless. She was about to witness her sister's execution at the hands of a she-devil and there was nothing she could do.

Kay made eye contact with her, savouring her moment. Eva could see the look in her eyes. She was enjoying the anguish she was giving her sister. Then Eva noticed what appeared to be a pendant half embedded and half protruding from the melted flesh of Kay's chest; a turquoise stone in the shape of a 'K' barely legible through the burnt opaque skin. The pain from her injuries must have been unbearable. She had become unrecognisable as the diseases and fire had destroyed any resemblance to her ever being anything but the monster she had now become.

Whatever had happened to this person, Eva appealed to what still remained of her humanity and sanity.

"Stop! You have no right to harm her. She's done nothing to you!"

Kay smiled at Eva through blistered lips, then teased the flint blade across Elle's throat.

Eva decided she'd had enough of playing by someone else's rules. If she couldn't help directly, maybe the water could. She ran to the well, saw an old abandoned wooden pail and filled it full of the water. She quickly turned, almost falling and threw the water towards Estelle and Kay, splashing them both, leaving a wet trail running back towards her. She threw herself on the ground, slapping her hand onto the soaked earth. What happened next was as if time itself had slowed to an almost complete stop. She watched as the droplets of water rose from the impact of her hand on the wet grass.

Countless beads of moisture rose from the earth then hung only inches above the damp ground. They glistened like a crystal curtain defying gravity then froze, hovering in mid-air. Suddenly they shot forward towards Kay and Estelle like glass pellets fired from an invisible gun. They spread across both of their bodies, coating them briefly in a sheen of pale green luminescence. For the briefest of moments the entire scene went still. Eva could hear the screams of protest from the shelter.

Two voices behind hissed at her and bayed for vengeance. Eva could barely hear the threats as she watched the tiny droplets of water that had gathered amass over the faces of assailant and victim. The droplets hung from Kay's eyelashes and a trickle of moisture slowly dripped down from the end of her nose. Kay's hand slackened its grip on Estelle's hair and the flint blade grew heavy in her hand, dropping a fraction from her sister's throat. Eva seized the opportunity and watched as time returned to its normal pace.

"Miss Kane. Please don't kill my sister. We are all each other have."

The water had worked its own magic. Neither Estelle's nor Kay's wounds were healing but something was happening now for certain. Kay shook her head back and forward repeatedly, desperately trying to ignore the alien feeling of pity, which began to take hold and instead fought to stay focused on the task of slaughtering her secondary target. An old spell began to break and Kay was losing her fight.

A look of complete and utter confusion took over her melted features. Somewhere in all that pain and suffering a piece of what once had been Kay Kane remained. The Kay that had her first kiss or the Kay that remembered a time before, when she hadn't been solely driven by power and greed. The hand holding the flint knife now slackened and dropped away from Estelle's throat. The drug or whatever had been used to change her, had found its antidote in the water and Eva's desperate plea for mercy for her sister.

A past life triggered a nerve synapse buried deep in her memory. She now understood that she had been expertly groomed as just another means to an end for whoever or whatever had been pulling the strings. Being in control of her own destiny seemed a far-away fantasy now. She was destroyed from her soul to her smile.

She stood over Estelle with the beginnings of a tear appearing in the corner of her eye that trickled down onto her calloused scorched cheek. It had only been a matter of days since the beginning of the change but it had felt like years.

Eva continued to speak to her, now seeing the faintest sign that Kay had heard her plea and had stopped her assault.

"Kay. I know it's still you."

Kay Kane dropped the flint blade and released her grip on Estelle. She looked down at herself then her victim with confusion and shame for this act and the countless crimes she had orchestrated in her past. She stood still, silent and unseeing as Estelle crawled away.

A second tear joined the first and slipped down what had been Kay's once pretty cheek. Her head slumped forward. For the first and last time in her adult life, Kay Kane was truly sorry and ashamed. Not of her nakedness in front of strangers, but for the countless bad and selfish decisions she had made in her life. The lives and the promising careers she'd ended without the slightest

414

regard for all those who may have been affected. The underhand way she had obtained information causing deaths and destruction all over the world. All for money and position.

Now she stood here on a patch of Irish earth both naked and deformed, with every sin manifested on her diseased body for all to see. This was no more than she deserved. She accepted it and let the feelings of remorse and sadness sweep over her like a wave. She was sorry for so many things. She looked down at Estelle trying to crawl away and did her best to smile through a deformed blistered mouth.

Her voice, now ravaged by disease, was able to produce little more than a half whisper, "I'm sorry, you can go."

Kay stood up straight and moved away from Estelle. She was turning to leave when she saw Hugh, now free from his bindings, coming at her with the long curved blade of a scythe in his hand. He had found it resting against a wheelbarrow and had broken the rotten shaft off leaving him a dull rusty blade. It was all he could find to use as a weapon and it would have to do.

Kay lunged forward grabbing his arm at the elbow, turning the weapon and jamming the point against his chest. Hugh stood trapped and transfixed, staring at the tears rolling down her face. Why was she crying?

Kay had his arm in an unbreakable lock. She was suddenly stronger and faster than ever. He could struggle, but knew it was useless. The shadowy figures had positioned themselves around the altar of the well. She spoke directly to them.

"You gave me the potion in the pill. You let me believe that you would always protect me. I delivered the girl and as a bonus, her sister and her friend, then you ruined me with the handkerchief! Why?"

Chapter *117*

A FEMALE VOICE ANSWERED FROM THE DARK-ness, still hiding. She spoke to Kay callously and uncaringly, her voice patronising. "Oh my dear. You're right. I did promise those things and over the many years of our relationship I delivered on them. I just didn't say how long I would continue to protect you and besides, you did not fulfil your end of the agreement. You didn't deliver the girl to us, as you see. She stands here before you with the rest of these people, here by her own will and not by your hands as instructed."

The veil of control she was displaying was beginning to fray.

"Dear girl, when we needed finesse we supplied you with the finest education and means to carry out our instructions. Now however, in these circumstances we needed a blunter tool, so needs must and your transformation was a necessity."

Hugh was both fascinated and appalled by the dialogue between the two females. He didn't have the strength to break free and still remained at Kay's mercy. Her grip was as solid as ever. He knew she wasn't even trying, as it was little effort for her to control him, so all he could do was listen and watch.

Kay stood utterly transfixed as for the first time she was face to face with her benefactor, defeated with the horrifying truth that their plan for her was ending with her destruction. Kay looked up as a second female emerged from the shadows.

"I'm sorry, truly I am."

"I know you are", said the voice. "I can take care of you now if you let me. They have no desire to have further hold on you. If you wish I can have you sent home?"

"I'm tired and would wish for nothing more," replied Kay.

Her head slumped further down this time as she waited for the inevitability of the instruction.

"Then finish what you have to do and let's get you on your way."

Kay turned away from the figure and looked deeply into Hugh's eyes. She caressed his cheek with the back of her free hand, then adeptly placed her foot behind his left heel. It happened so quickly that he didn't see the move and could do little to parry it even if he had. He had no time and was still too short on strength to avoid the take down. They both fell over as Kay easily swept him to the ground. He landed on top of her with his full weight as she turned the weapon on herself. His weight sent the scythe deep into her chest piercing through her heart almost cutting it in two. Hugh tried to roll off her but she held him fast until she was sure that the rusty blade had done its work. Now at last she let him go. She reached out again, gently this time and took hold of his hand. The blood and saliva was beginning to foam around the corners of her mouth.

"Please, Father."

Hugh couldn't believe that she again had let him live. The request from Kay was lost on him as he stared down at the blade protruding from her chest.

"Father, please, the rite of passage."

Hugh now understood what she wanted. It was his duty as a priest, even a lapsed one. He let go of her hand and fumbled in his jacket pocket then looked down at her now as a simple sinner rather than the monster she had become.

Some habits were impossible for him to break. He still carried a small suede pouch containing a crucifix and a tiny vial of oil. He retrieved it from his pocket and emptied the contents into the ground. He picked up the little silver topped glass vial containing the *Chrism* oil for performing the last rites and rested it in his palm.

Kay still gently held his hand so he released the cork with

417

his teeth and spat it on the ground beside him. He spilled some Oil of Chrism on his finger, knelt further over her and made the sign of the cross on Kay's forehead anointing her with the oil as he administered the last rites. She closed her eyes as the fear and terror of dying gently began to leave her.

Hugh's hands were shaking as he recited the sacrament.

"Purify me with Hyssop Lord and I shall be clean of sin. Wash me and I shall be whiter than snow. Have mercy on me God in your great kindness. Glory be to the Father, the Son and the Holy Spirit."

Free now from the hold her benefactors had on her, Kay Kane lolled down onto her back and exhaled for the last time; the strain and burden of the sins that she had carried for so long now, at last released. Hugh continued to kneel over her while saying a silent prayer. He then slowly returned the oil and crucifix to his pocket knowing now why she had let him live.

Her head had slumped to one side and, as the last vestige of life left her body, Hugh noticed the inverted cross surrounded by a circle that long ago had been branded into the skin behind her left ear. The raised scar tissue where the hot iron had made its mark, now faded and disappeared, leaving no trace of it ever having been there.

He blessed himself and stood away from the lifeless body of Kay Kane. He made his way towards Estelle who was also staring down at the deformed, now lifeless body that had tried so hard to take her life.

"Why did she let us go, Hugh?"

"I don't know, Elle", replied Hugh. "I'm just grateful that she did."

Chapter *118*

THEY MADE THEIR WAY TO EVA'S SIDE, WHERE she held out her arms waiting for their embrace. From the shadows to the right of the shelter a child appeared. Estelle recognised him instantly as the boy who had presented her with the vision.

"Hugh. That's the child I saw, the one by the water outside my apartment. He lured me down to show me the vision of all those poor children struggling to be free of their pain and Eva was with them drowning by their sides. Remember?"

"I remember, Elle. Now let's see what they want with us."

A second figure now joined the child; she held the boys hand in hers as she moved forward to greet them. She looked directly at Elle and Hugh but addressed Eva first.

"Do you remember me Eva?"

Eva's tone was firm and steady. For whatever reason she wasn't afraid anymore although she thought she probably should be for all of them.

"I remember you. You were on the shore of the Lough the day I hurt my foot. You smiled at me as you moved your hand around in the water. I thought you had mistaken me for someone you knew."

The female smiled.

"It is not just our friends here that can make some little changes in you."

Eva was puzzled.

"So it was you who made the underwater turbine malfunction, that means that by your actions on that day, you gave me the ability to cure myself and others?"

The female refused to be drawn any further on the subject, but instead introduced herself and the child. Eva noticed that she wore the same simple dress and sandals as the day she had seen her at the Lough side but the colour of her eyes had changed to the most beautiful shade of turquoise blue, with a whiter than white iris and an almost pin prick black pupil.

Eva felt intoxicated just looking into them. The child's were the same but with flecks of deeper blue scattered throughout the iris. A gentle breeze flowed through the boy's honey coloured hair as he moved closer to what Estelle took to be his mother. Even in the dim moonlight her beauty radiated and mesmerised, as did that of the child by her side. Her voice drifted like mist into their ears.

"We are envoys of the *Daoine Maithe, The Good People*. You will all be party to a meeting here tonight but only Eva will remember this. Should she decide to tell you of the events that will unfold at a later time, then that should be her choice and hers alone. Are we agreed?"

There wasn't any option but to comply so all accepted the proposal.

The figure that had been standing back in the shadows now moved a little closer. As it did so, Estelle, Hugh and Eva moved as if to retreat. They held each other's hands as the figure's face became clear.

There was nothing to indicate anything that seemed remarkable about the person other than they inexplicably knew they were in the presence of pure and undiluted evil. The figure refused to acknowledge their presence and indicated to the Daoine to proceed with the ancient rite of introduction on her behalf. She appeared to be in her early sixties and was immaculately dressed in the finest of designer clothes.

The only exception was that she stood barefoot which betrayed her usual height in high heels. Her jet black hair was combed up into a perfect bun and her white satin blouse was unbuttoned to reveal just a little too much tanned, wrinkled cleavage. The diamonds on her necklace glittered in the new moonlight exposing JS initials on a pendant. She was in her own way equally as fascinating as the Daoine, though infinitely more terrifying. She stood aside, ready to be formally introduced. The Daoine stepped forward again.

"This is *The Slaugh, The Host*. They are *The Unseelle Court, The Unblessed*. She will speak to you now if you will listen."

The figure stepped forward again, closer this time and did her utmost to bow slightly to whom she considered an unworthy audience. The beautiful diamond pendant came into full view. The sparkling letters danced in the air below her throat, as she directed her attention towards Eva.

"I see that you have met and saved our son Valentine from the waters of the Lough. He is not our actual son, of course, we acquired him at a very young age. Such a disappointment he is to us now. We had hoped, anticipated and engineered such great things for him. That little trick in the water you performed by the ferry put paid to those years of work. Well done you! Where is he, by the way? Ah yes, of course, my husband has him."

Eva could almost taste the extent to which this woman, if indeed she was a woman despised her and would happily send her and her sister to an eternity of pain and degradation if she got the opportunity.

"My husband, who will join us in a moment, was almost beside himself with grief."

Her voice could only partially disguise the hatred and malice she had for all of them. She never once looked toward the Daoine Maithe for either approval or objection. Eva sensed a long history of distrust and conflict between them. Whatever plans these two had for their son now appeared to be a thing of memory and they were very, very upset.

"Ah, here comes the golden boy now."

Wilson Sere came forward, leading Valentine towards Eva and the others. Valentine was bewildered, whether it was from the knock he had taken to his head when he fell or the fact that both of his parents were standing around a well in this remote part of

Northern Ireland. His head began to clear.

He addressed his father first who ignored him. He then focused his questions at his mother.

"Mother, would you please enlighten me as to what you and my father are doing here and who are these people?"

His mother answered in her customary manner.

"Valentine, my dear, I'm sorry to say that you left us no option but to make the best of your ridiculous failure."

"Failure! What failure? What are you talking about?"

His mother raised her eyebrow slightly at his tone of questioning and the graze he'd received when falling against the stone started to bleed heavily. He felt the rush of blood stream down his face and into his eye. The green metal flecks gathered across his iris as protection and it was then he saw his parents for what they truly were. They were both almost serene with utter contempt for him, but more specifically he saw their anger at Eva. He could now see the plans they had for him written across their minds and souls, if they even had souls which he doubted. The blood dripped down from his chin onto the mossy ground. He held his hand to the wound on his head to stem the bleeding and used the other hand to wipe away the blood that was seeping into the corner of his mouth. He answered their question; it was simple and final.

"Never!"

He turned from his parents and walked over to the well to wash away the blood from his face. Eva went to help him. She cupped some water from the well into her hand and placed it on his forehead. In an instant, the bleeding stopped and the wound perfectly closed, leaving him with drying blood on his shirt as the only reminder of his injury. He thanked Eva and made to leave, but she pleaded for him to stay.

"Please, Valentine. They've told me that Estelle and Hugh will remember none of what will happen here tonight. These are your parents. Why did you say 'Never' to them? What were they asking of you?"

"I can't say, Eva. I don't even want to think about the plans they had in store for me. I cannot believe that those two monsters are my parents!"

Eva's options were limited and time was running out, but the least she could do was to tell him the only truth she'd learnt tonight.

"I'm sorry, Valentine, they're not your natural parents, in your mother's own words, 'they acquired you.' I don't know how that's going to make you feel but at least now you know the truth. Who knows, if you stay we may find out the identity of your birth mother and see what these, whatever they are want from us?"

Valentine was staggered by this information, but somehow it made perfect sense. She was right, there were unanswered questions here and it may be his only chance to find out who his natural family was.

"OK, Eva. If I was meant to be part of this, regardless of the role I was intended to play, then so be it."

They both walked back and joined the others around the old shelter of the well.

The Slaugh, Julia Sere, spoke again.

"Ladies and gentlemen, shall we at last get down to business?"

There was a tinge of defeat and unwillingness in her voice. The child turned to Estelle and Hugh.

"Please join us."

Estelle came forward still holding Hugh's hand. The four joined them at the end of the covering as Eva spoke.

"What do you want from us?"

The Daoine addressed them. "You, Eva, have been armed by us, the Daoine, to restore a lost balance."

"What do you mean a *balance?* A balance where?"

The Daoine looked around to see that she had the approval of all the gathered to answer her question. Again no objections were voiced so he continued.

"Nowhere and everywhere, Eva. You will bring order to what may still be chaos. This is why I chose you."

"Why me? What are we to you?" she asked.

"We have always been with you, or should I say, you have always been with us. Our friends here of The Unseelle Court despise you and your fellows and always have. They believed that

423

to change you was a potential mistake but the Daoine were more powerful then so The Unseelle Court reluctantly agreed to the alteration.

"However the tables have turned and they now have the upper hand. The more you suffer the mightier they become. They have found a way to feed in perpetuity on your pain and sorrow. However we, the Daoine, are not without resources. The one thing that we both agree is that science extends your life and your numbers continue to grow: it makes you too valuable a resource. Your emotions not only make us stronger but are addictive to us. It is by mutual agreement that we all stand here tonight."

Estelle put her hand on Eva's shoulder to move her gently aside.

"Please forgive my stupidity, I still don't understand. Could you explain further?"

"The Unseelle Court would have you suffer. Your pain makes them greedy. If they have universal control they will turn on us, makes slaves of you and eventually devour themselves. So the balance is lost yet again. It's why I gave your sister the power over the algae and the water. She can cure the world under one agreed condition."

"Condition? What condition?" asked Eva.

"That will be answered soon enough," came the reply.

"Why do you need us? You seem powerful enough?"

"As I have said, we take nourishment from your emotions; The Daoine Maithe from the softer, kinder and loving side of your being and The Unseelle Court from your darker side. It's why we arranged to set the seed of your change from the apes you once were to what you have become today. It was they who introduced the recent virus and they can, if no agreement is reached, continue to make you suffer for an eternity should they will it. Your science may strive to find a cure but will never attain one. We of the Daoine do not condone their actions, but we understand them."

Eva, Valentine, Hugh and Estelle stood in silence trying their best to absorb what was being said. They looked at each other confused and speechless until Estelle, almost childishly, raised her hand.

"If I may, please, beg another question: who or what are you?"

The Daoine smiled at her and answered, "We are the First."

"The *First*?"

"Yes."

The statement was spoken with no emotion in her words.

Chapter *119*

ESTELLE LOOKED TO THE OTHERS, SEEKING assurance that she should continue with her questions. Hugh nodded his head for her to keep going; it was her job after all. She took it as unanimous and restarted.

"Would you care to explain what you mean by the 'first'?"

The Daoine came forward and stood before Estelle.

"Have you ever asked how old are your kind? Permit me to answer that for you. In your current stage of development the human race is less than three million years old. Let us then suppose that in that brief time you have climbed down from the branches, stood erect and become one of the most dominant species on the planet. Yet you have creatures existing alongside you in the same form for hundreds of millions of years. Haven't you ever wondered why? Why you and not others? Why was your species the only one to develop so quickly, to learn language, make tools, or to change your environment to suit your needs? No other creature can do it! Do you really suppose this was by chance or accident?"

"Why have we never encountered you before?" asked Estelle.

"You have, many times over millennia."

"Are you like us?"

"Similar. We've been with you from the beginning. We watched as you created hopes for the new day and fears of the darkness of night. In your history one set of emotions grows as the other wanes and that is why all through your past a balance is lost

426

and must be restored or one side will, for a short time prevail, as is the case now."

"You told my sister she must restore this new status quo. What does it mean to us and why should we care about your balance?"

"Because that loss of the status quo directly affects you; you have grown so quickly and attained so much power that it threatens us. You use only one-third of your brain. In another three million years you will use all of it – that's if you haven't destroyed yourselves before then. Through no choice of our own we are all connected and have been for eons. It was an unforeseen mistake. We had no wish to be entangled in your lives and could not have predicted the events that have unfolded since your development. We believed we could sip at your emotions as the bird sips nectar from the flower. We couldn't know that the flower would eventually grow thorns. We have become as intertwined in your wars and conflicts as you are yourselves. The feelings and emotions you have are now an erasable part of us. We have somehow changed to feel as you do. It is not the first time this has happened."

Again Estelle questioned the Daoine.

"So, let me get this straight in my mind. You and your kin are prepared to make us suffer for your own greedy mistakes?"

The Daoine, for the first time, grew darker with rage. They had tinkered and made the subtle change to the ape, but now the ape had justifiable reason to question their actions. The colour of the Daoine returned to normal, the anger abated and answered Estelle.

"You are, of course, correct. However, we must deal with the consequences of our poor decision and regrettably not for the first time in our joined history."

Estelle continued, "How often have you interjected in our lives?"

"The Daoine Maithe have made changes or passed gifts to some of your people in the past to oppose The Unseelle Court's desire for more power. Many of those you have martyred in the most gruesome ways imaginable. By the influence of The Slaugh, who have changed and raised your tyrants to achieve mass obliteration of your own kind in their continued thirst for domain.

427

They had almost completed their latest plan to elevate Valentine Sere to reign over you, and so, to yet again send the world into chaos. We discovered the plan and made the decision to oppose them. It was left to me, with our peoples' instruction, to give your sister the ability to reverse the effects of the virus they've cursed you with. However, what we couldn't predict was how well she adapted to the change. Not only can she cure the virus and pass the gift on, when she does, there is no limit to the life span of the recipient of the gift, be they healthy or infected by the Jester. To simplify they could live forever and this, of course, is catastrophic, both for you and us. Do you understand?"

Eva came forward; she had some questions of her own which she was determined to get answers to.

"Please excuse my tone. If you are to be believed and I neither know nor care that you are what you claim to be, and have made the changes in humanity that you say you have, surely the tables have turned now. You meddled with something that you shouldn't have. How dare you, all of you gathered here, tinker with our fate. We are not puppets to have our strings pulled by you or anyone else. You have opened Pandora's box and have been trying ever since unsuccessfully to close the lid back down. You've chosen to burden me with this *gift*, a gift, by the way, that I didn't know of or want, and you had me, without my knowledge, pass that ability on to my sister, her friend and Lord knows how many others.

"You, The Daoine and The Unseelle Court have toyed with us for the last time. We know of your existence now and what you are. We know what balance is and you are the very creatures that have upset it, and so it is up to us now, as you say, to again restore it, to correct the mistakes that you have made. The question is why is that? Why can't you just wave a wand and make everything better, reset this balance yourselves? The truth is, I don't believe that you can, and that's why you continue to need us. It may take time but eventually we will find a chink in your defences, after all, we know your weakness now!"

Both the Daoine and Unseelle were furious.

"How dare you threaten us, we could destroy you at will!"

"I'm sure you could, but you won't," said Eva. There was

no fear remaining in her now. She knew she was right and just as importantly so did they. "You have stood by and allowed the most appalling of events to take place to satisfy your greedy desires. Shame on all of you. You have led us to believe that over time you, The Daoinne, have been benevolent and kind. Over centuries you have represented yourselves as Fairy folk or Angels? And you The Unseelle Court, you, I suppose, are to be Imps or Devils, am I correct?"

Neither answered, but she knew she was correct.

"It entertains you to watch greedy tycoons who squander their time and wealth on selfish unimportant trivialities. You ignore the desperate hungry faces of children in the most terrible, dangerous and appalling circumstances with impunity and disinterest because they live on a different level of reality. You take pleasure from feasting on their misery or enjoying the taste of their joy when hope returns. These are peoples' lives; their hopes and dreams, failure and misery, all emotions that you greedily relish the taste of. You are the true tyrants here and it takes tyranny to begin a revolution. That will be your legacy and that is how we will regard you."

The Daoine let Eva finish.

"We understand your anger. We have made many errors in the past, but you, too, must take at least some responsibility for your actions as a race. We've sent or changed countless people to readdress our past mistakes, but you shunned, ridiculed or murdered them! John the Baptist, you beheaded. Joan of Arc, you burnt at the stake. And Jesus Christ, he was the one you both tortured and crucified for telling all of you to love one another. In the last 3,000 years the human race has been entirely at peace for less than 300 of those years and that fact is for the best part attributed to the Slaugh. This is what makes us again take a stand against her and the Court.

"They're greedy, they always have been and they always will be. They had the upper hand until now and to a lesser extent they still do. So now we gathered here before you have reached a compromise with our counterparts and will now put that proposal to you. Their protege who you see standing there silently beside you was their greatest hope and he may well still be, if he reverses the decision that he made earlier. He could rule over creatures much more powerful than what remained of the woman you saw perish here tonight. She and her like have been written about in your past and turned into mythical creatures by every race on the planet.

"From the Trolls of Scandinavia to your Irish Banshees all historically turned from greedy selfish humans and transformed by their cruel desires into what the true nature of their souls would physically appear. Changed and used to accommodate the appetites and goals of our opposites here gathered with us and it will happen again. Their adopted son who now stands beside you was to be their instrument of chaos, but you, all of you without any prior knowledge or planning have given him the gift and for that I'll make no more apologies. Their plans are destroyed and so at least for this time our purpose is served. When their Queen hears of their failure their punishment will be severe. That is, as I've stated, if their protege still chooses not to stand at their side."

Estelle stepped forward, "Their Queen! Is the Slaugh not their ruler?"

"She is the ruler of the Unseelle Court. Not the ruler of all the unblessed. Their Queen is an ancient creature from the time of the creation of Adam."

"Are you talking of the original Adam. The Adam of the Old Testament?"

"I am," came the reply.

"Then you are saying Eve is their Queen?"

"Not Eve. She was not his first wife."

"Not his first wife?

"No. In the beginning two were made from dust by The Sovereign of the Universe. One male, one female, both made equal. However, she would not be subservient to Adam and fled, refusing to return to his side. She was changed into the Queen of the Demons and punished forever by having one hundred of her children die every day. The Kane creature who died here had become one of them. The Queen is the true ruler of the Unseelle Court. That was eons ago and her name cannot by uttered by the Daoine. That tale is for another time."

"Regardless of the outcome there is still a price you will

have to pay. Your fate no longer rests in our hands. You, Eva Ballantine, shunned your responsibilities when your sister needed you in the wake of your parents' deaths. It is due time that debt was paid and so we have placed this burden on you. You, and only you, can orchestrate the fate of your people. If Valentine Sere joins you then finally the plague that torments your people may be over. This is all I have to say and will give no further explanations."

The Daoine withdrew, allowing The Unseelle to speak to their son.

"Valentine!"

Valentine turned to face his father.

"It is true that you have disappointed both your Mother and myself, but it is still not too late for you to redeem yourself and reconsider your decision. We can, if requested, reverse the effects of the girl's touch. We still have such high expectations for you and trust that you will reverse your decision. It has taken us two thousand years of planning to reach this point. All of our efforts depend on the reversal of choice that you will and must make. We have blazed you a path in preparation for your coming. This world is yours for the taking. We have the means to keep these *things* suffering and in pain for centuries in their infected state. Feeding us, feeding you, destroying the cursed Daoine and making us stronger. You need only say that it is your desire and it will happen."

Valentine took little time to answer his father.

"What will happen to me, Father? Who will I share this power with?"

"Why, the girl Eva, of course, or anyone you may choose! You can use her as a tool, a toy or whatever you desire. Their time of happiness has passed my son. You are the new Word."

"And the alternative?" asked Valentine.

His father darkened with rage and lunged towards him, but was confined by the agreed boundary that still contained him and prevented him from crossing. Wilson Sere was spitting through his words.

"For you there is no alternative! This is what you are boy. We have worked tirelessly for the opportunity to grant you this privilege. It is not a negotiation. It's your birth rite. Now take it!"

This time Valentine addressed the other two figures of the Daoine.

"I ask the same question of you. Is there an alternative?"

The child came forward to speak.

"Yes."

"What are my options?"

"We have put forward a proposal and your parents have reluctantly agreed. The recent disease that is currently destroying your people was, as you now know, created by them. You have had plagues in the past that cemented, united and focused you; again many of them were their doing. This isn't the first and won't be the last. You have suffered catastrophic losses before, yet you survive, stronger and, briefly, more united. Because of a shift in power your parents may now dictate the terms of the proposal. They can keep everyone infected, in pain and torment for as long as they desire. Children and new generations will be born with this disease or any other should they wish it. However, as stated, we are not entirely defenceless, and so we will lay out the terms of the solution."

"What are these terms and do we have free choice with no influence or intervention?"

"The choice will be yours and yours alone."

Eva, Hugh and Estelle gathered closer to Valentine to hear what the child would offer.

Chapter *120*

ANYONE WHO CHOOSES THE CURE WILL STEP into the water at a designated time; whether it be the sea, a lake or a stagnant pool, as long as there is contact with the water. If they choose not to enter they will live out the natural span of their life in their current condition.

"We understand that through your advances in medicine and understanding of the human DNA genome that the time is coming when you will be capable of extending your life expectancy. However, this environment will be incapable of sustaining you and, as a result, us. That, all of us gathered here agree, cannot be allowed. So we have constructed a compromise. From the beginning of this conversation there has and will continue to be, a total cessation of the virus spreading. The deaths relating to the germ have, as you will soon become aware, now ceased. It is however dormant pending the choices you must make."

"And your terms?"

"Each person, from newborn to elderly, will be free of the diseases that would have hitherto shortened their lives, except for new non-terrestrial or mutating viruses. The Court has agreed that there will be no interference from them and that they ensure future impartiality. You will be free of any known disorder from diabetes to cancer until your eighty-eighth year.

"That will be your final year. At some time during those last twelve months you will die. Accidents that cripple or maim, or acts of war, or violent death will not be subject to the agreement.

Each or any person who enters the water will be subject to these terms. We repeat, EVERYONE WHO ENTERS!"

Eva, Hugh and Estelle looked to Valentine hoping that the choice he would make would be the right one. All of their futures hung on very thin ice that could crack at any moment. However, Valentine had more questions of his own. He looked directly at the Daoine and Unseelle,

"Who are my natural parents and where are they?"

It was the Slaugh, his mother, who answered.

"Your father is dead, but your mother still lives."

"Where?"

"Chicago, Illinois."

"I would like to meet her."

"You already have."

"When?"

"Recently, she bathed and dressed your eyes at the Clinic you were brought to."

"Jesus Christ. Is there no end to your evil?"

Valentine was momentarily speechless. How could any creature be so cruel? He gathered himself and continued.

"Is she like you?"

"No, she's of your kind."

He was clever and his brain was in overdrive.

"One final question: this has happened before as you have stated. Am I correct?"

The child answered.

"We have made a similar agreement with you in the past only this time the terms are more finite."

"When and with whom did you make the last agreement?"

"That time is recorded in the Psalms."

Valentine struggled to comprehend the gravity of the conversation. His mind reeled as he wrestled with the idea of mapping out and jointly agreeing to Man's future.

"This is not our decision to make!"

"Who else, if not you? Should you all agree, you Valentine, must turn your back on your parents' wishes forever, and if both you and Eva will it, all of your people will be united in a common

434

understanding, that they are, indeed, not alone in the universe. They may refer to us in whatever context they desire, that is if you choose to tell them. You all must think hard about that decision. What may happen to them if they knew for sure that imps, angels or fairies truly existed?"

Valentine remained standing in front of them appearing to contemplate their proposal, stalling for time to gather his senses.

"Are you truly telling me that it was you who sent down the commandments with Moses from the mountain and then further agreed to a limited number of years for us to be allocated life? Where is this last agreement?"

"No, not down with Moses from the mountain. We had no part in the formation of the commandments. We interjected in one of the conditions of the written Psalms to ensure the term of your mortal life span. Your eternal soul is none of our concern. That is the business of a much greater power than us. We simply interfered with the mind of the scribe whose task it was to write the Psalm down and not that of the author. It was simpler magic then."

"You tinkered with the Psalms!"

"Not all, just one."

"Which one?"

Traumatic and fascinating as the conversation was they all wanted to know the answer to Valentine's question.

The Daoine turned her attention to Hugh.

"Father, would you care to read from that small worn out version of the King James Bible that you carry so close to your heart?"

Hugh brought his hand up to his breast and felt the reassuring holy book against his chest. He had no idea how they knew that he carried it, but removed the little bible from his inside jacket pocket and held it in both hands. Estelle, Eva and Valentine watched in stunned silence.

"Father, would you read Psalm 90:3-12 for us?"

Hugh understood that the request wasn't a matter to be thought over but instead a command to be obeyed without protest. He knew the Psalm she was referring to and he was now also beginning to understand the enormity of this event!

He thumbed through his tatty Bible and found the Psalm as instructed. The dimming light now appeared to have no issues with his once failing vision as the tiny words in his Bible became clear and bold on the worn pages. Hugh's mouth simply vocalised the written words on the thin parchment of paper as he read.

"*3: Thou turnest man to destruction; and sayest, return ye children of men*

4: For a thousand years in thy sight are but as yesterday when it is past, and as a watch in the night.

5: Thou carriest them away as with food; they are as sleep: in the morning they are like grass which groweth up.

6: In the morning it flourisheth, and groweth up; in the evening it is cut down, and withereth.

7: For we are consumed by thine anger, and by thy wrath be troubled.

8: Thou has set our iniquities before thee, our secret sins in the light of thy countenance.

9: For all our days are passed away in thy wrath: we spend our years as a tale that is told.

10: THE DAYS OF OUR YEARS ARE THREE SCORE YEARS AND TEN; and if by reason of strength they be fourscore years, yet is their strength labour and sorrow; for it is soon cut off, and we fly away.

11: Who knoweth the power of thine anger? Even according to thy fear.

12: So teach us to number our days, that we may apply our hearts unto wisdom."

Hugh closed his bible now they all fully understood. The two sisters held each other's hands as the words of the Psalm resonated in their minds.

The child addressed the stunned Valentine.

"We have amended the last offer to be more precise with this one. Four score and eight, or EIGHTY EIGHT YEARS, is our only and final offer."

The child directed his attention back to Valentine.

"If you are to choose your parents' path, all will fall before you and chaos will reign until the next rebalance. There is no more for us to say. The choice is yours."

Valentine turned his head around to face the three people who had put their lives at risk to save his. He had been indulged in every way since he was a child. The finest schools and education that money could buy, the cars, the yachts, the playboy life style and the bottomless pit of money. Yet the simplest things that he so desired were those that had been so cruelly denied him; friendship, care, companionship and the hope of love and children of his own in time to come.

His decision was an easy one. He addressed all the gathered elders.

"I agree with Eva, I don't know which of you I despise the most! You are not as you have portrayed yourselves in history and folklore as good and bad, black or white, angel or demon. You're nothing more than parasites, all of you. You desperately manipulate us for your own selfish ends. You are weak and dependent. This is blackmail on a global scale and I know now from what you have stated that it hasn't been the first time. Nor if you have your way will it be the last. We are no longer some pack of illiterate peasants who marvel at the sight of tricks performed in sideshow carnivals. With our advances in the sciences, we have our own magic now. We make our advances in gene therapy and who knows what other medical discoveries are yet to be found in our near or distant future; this deal won't last forever, so be warned. We will, even if it takes a millennia, eventually prevail. This is no idle threat, but a solemn oath!

"There is no choice for me but one. If I side with my so-called parents here, you will have us tearing ourselves apart and thriving on our misery until this new *rebalance* takes place. It could take a hundred or a thousand years and I would simply go down in some future history book as another despot or tyrant! This world has seen enough Hitlers to last a million lifetimes. My choice, therefore, is an easy one."

He spoke directly to his parents.

"I'm afraid, Mother and Father, that the very things you have tried to woo me with my entire life are as boring and dull to me as any promises of power that you offer now. What gain would it be to me to have everything I desired with only my own company to enjoy it, as I have since childhood? You gave me everything except the one thing I needed, unconditional love. Maybe on your future bids for domain you may consider this for your next protege. It would mean, of course, that you would become the very thing you oppose and despise and so that would be impossible for you. That is your paradox. You can't control a human manifestation of your desires without subjecting it to all the basic human emotions. You would have to provide those and you can't. It's a flaw in your own evolution. Did you really suppose that if you indulged a child with every whim and fancy without the human struggle to feel and be loved that this would result in your perfect son, your *Ruler of People*? It's naive and bordering on the pathetic!"

He turned his attention to the woman and child.

"You also imagine because you manifest as a beautiful female wearing a glowing white dress and simple sandals accompanied by a child that it makes you any less obscene or acceptable? You are every bit as dangerous as my supposed parents. You present yourself as benign benefactors, but your goals are one and the same. In short, you need us. We do not need you. You have fed on our hopes and fears for countless generations. Manipulating our decisions and steering us on a path that mutually benefits you all the way through our evolution. You are the more acceptable lesser of two evils.

"You have proposed an offer and you may not retract it. You, all of you, have brought us to this and as you say not for the first time. I promise you that I will spend the rest of my life and my future children and grandchildren's lives ensuring that we find a way to end it. This offer is a poisoned chalice. Life is precious and the fear of death, overwhelming. So, before I give you my decision, I have but one condition. The power to heal and give life with the algae and water remains with the girl."

The four 'Others' stood silent before agreeing to the condition.

Valentine continued.

"I reject my parents' offer outright and will join with my companions," he said and then turned to address Eva, Hugh and

438

Estelle. "If they will have me among them, that is?" The three nodded in agreement. "I agree to put your offer to anyone who will hear it and accept it. That established, what would you now have us do?"

The child stepped forward for the second time as Eva, Hugh and Estelle joined Valentine at his side. They now looked at each other through the same coloured eyes as the woman and child. As they gazed in wonderment, their eyes slowly returned to nearly normal coloration, but each was left with a narrow ring of ocean blue around the outer edge of each pupil. It would be the only thing that would mark them as being any different from anyone else.

"Eva, you will have the power to control the algae and thus the water, as will your children. If you or your descendants ever use the gift for selfish gain, the ability will be removed, never to be returned. Is that understood?"

Eva looked to her sister for affirmation. Estelle nodded her head for her to accept. Eva's reply was simple.

"I reluctantly agree and accept your offer."

The child didn't respond, instead stepping back toward the shelter. The Daoine spoke again.

"You, Valentine, have the means to have an announcement made to the world. Your colleague, Mr., or Senator Hamill, is in direct contact with powers that will provide the medium for such a proposal to all people and he has the means to distribute the supposed vaccine. It is already on its way to him so he can make the generous gift of the largest placebo in history. He will take credit for the antidote to the virus leaving you four to carry on with your lives as anonymous as you may wish. Now that the proposal is accepted, you, Eva and Valentine will return to this place in thirty days from now and again step into the sea. As stated, your sister and her friend will remember nothing of this meeting unless you wish it.

"It will make no difference if you stay in the sea for one minute or one day. There will be no requirement for either us, the Daoine or Valentine Sere's parents to be present there as you have made your choice. One stipulation: this offer excludes the good Senator Hamill. Your parents will take a personal interest in his future welfare once his glory for finding the cure for the Jester has been reached!"

The Daoine now turned and left with the others, leaving the four alone. Kay Kane was gone, with no trace of her remaining.

"What time is it, Hugh?" Eva asked.

"It's 10.27pm," he replied.

"So that's twenty-nine days after tomorrow right?"

"Right?"

Her hands were shaking uncontrollably at the realisation and gravity of the new role she would play.

"So, what do we do in the time in between and how do we even try to understand what has happened to us and what responsibilities we now carry?"

Estelle did what she always did in her usual pragmatic way, always giving the logical solution at the appropriate time.

"We get ready to ride the storm of panic, then come to terms with the fact that none of us will ever go about our normal lives after we, we.... sorry, I've lost my train of thought, what was I saying?"

The Daoine were right; Estelle was forgetting already.

Chapter *121*

E VA HUGGED AND KISSED HER SISTER AND TOLD her that she loved her. "It's OK, sis, we've been in an accident. The Kane woman crashed her car into the sea and she didn't survive. Now let's get you home. Those were lovely words you said, Hugh. I'm sure Miss Kane would have approved."

Hugh looked around at his surroundings, disoriented. He still held his Bible in his hand and wondered why he'd taken it from his pocket. His memory was fading as quickly as Estelle's.

Hugh and Estelle left the site of the wells and made their way up the steps to the car still parked where Eva had left it. Valentine took Eva's arm to halt her progress so he could speak to her in private.

"Are you ready for the burden of this, Eva?"

"Do I have a choice?"

"No, you don't. However, I will be of whatever help I can provide after the cure. All of mine and my company's resources are at your disposal for whenever you need them."

"Thank you, Valentine, I appreciate your offer. However, our immediate task is that we find a way to map out all our own destinies without interference or tinkering from our absent friends. I think there will be more needed between us than the swapping of telephone numbers. Agreed?"

"Of course, I agree. Let's both set to work, you and I."

They were both equally terrified and coping in their own separate ways.

They had made a deal with the devil and seen a woman slain in front of their eyes. Eva led the way and Valentine followed her up the steps to join her sister and their friend.

Epilogue

T HE PRESIDENT OF THE UNITED STATES, ALONG with his global counterparts, offered the terms of the proposal to the people. Most of them would accept, including the President and his family along with the Heads of State of every country on the planet.

The President and his staff had no idea how Senator Hamill and his team had found the antidote for the Jester Virus or how it could have been engineered to terminate its effective properties when the host reached their eighty-eighth year of life, but it was a window of opportunity and it gave them time to find a more permanent solution to the problem.

The Senator was presented with the highest accolades both for him and his team of scientists for finding a vaccine and the mechanisms of the delivery of the drug. Using the water as a medium was nothing short of a stroke of genius. The Senator was, of course, his modest self in acceptance.

On October, 11th, 2014 at 10.27pm BST 05.27 EST, approximately 5.5 billion people globally agreed to the terms of the proposal and made contact with the water by whatever means they could. Some couldn't or wouldn't but the choice was theirs.

Tom Derrick held his grandson's hand in his as he stood in the tepid waters of Lake Calcasieu, Louisiana. He was joined by his daughter, Ruth, her husband Mark, and the rest of their children and family.

Everywhere for as far as the eye could see, thousands of people stood in silence on the banks of the lake and waited, listening for instructions from their handheld radios. Similar scenes were reported across the globe. The seconds passed as the time for the cure counted down.

At precisely 05.29 EST, the biggest single synchronised simultaneous movement of people in history occurred, one that would most likely never be repeated. All over the planet people entered whatever water source they could find to receive their salvation and held their breaths as the seconds passed.

Eva Ballantine and Valentine Sere entered the water at the site of the holy wells of Templecowey at Tieveshilly, Ireland. They each held hands for as long as Eva and Valentine thought was an appropriate time to perform the act, spreading the cure to whoever would accept it, no bells or whistles, no fireworks or Choirs of Angels strumming their harps or blowing their horns.

The world seemed different somehow; a *good* different.

A new order arose up post event. For as long as it would last a new symbol of unity and understanding blossomed throughout the world. For the first time in documented history there was not one single war or conflict raging on any part of the planet. The news channels showed faces of every religion and creed rejoicing in their own ways in the aftermath. New holidays were announced globally to mark the event. Smoking bans were lifted and tobacco companies again sponsored sporting events. The world had no longer use for the worries of illness or disease.

Only two people knew that day that they were not alone in the universe and they agreed to keep it that way, at least for the time being. Everyone, each person who entered the water, now had the same time to enjoy their lives and prosper.

Well, not quite everyone.

As the news spread of the incidents of the individuals who were cured pre-event, they had become for the most part unwilling celebrities. Websites were established and forums set up to allow the lucky ones who had been cured before the global cleansing of the JSTR virus.

None of them realised that they were not subject to the terms of '88' as they had been cured pre-event. They were ignorant of the knowledge that they could live forever.

Lyndon Butterfield, married to Dordi Butterfield of Franklin, Louisiana, USA, Audrey Walsh married to Cyril Walsh from Belfast, Northern Ireland, UK, were two of many pre-cured who unknowingly stepped into the water. However, their choice would have been the same even if they had known. Eternity without the company of those they loved was not a salvation to those who were good.

Audrey's daughter Angela made the initial contact with Lyndon as she had with several others on the long list of pre-cured, but it was Dordi that Audrey had a real connection with. They first met in a *green room* at one of the many TV shows that they had appeared on.

Dordi's stoic sense of reason appealed to Audrey's no nonsense personality. They agreed to exchange phone numbers and over the weeks and months post event their friendship grew. They emailed often and talked regularly on the phone about the life and the experiences they had before and after the circumstances that led to the cures.

Angela taught them how to use Skype and they spoke over the internet for hour after hour. A trip to America was suggested where Dordi and Lyn would show them around the sites of Louisiana.

Audrey Walsh had a better idea!

By way of apology Mr. Valentine Sere, CEO of BION Pharmaceuticals, had contacted the Walsh family and offered Audrey and whoever she desired, fully paid and maintained ownership of the two hundred foot fully crewed yacht now to be rechristened 'The Lady Kay' to do with as she pleased.

They were flown to the United States on the BION private jet where they would see their new yacht. Audrey was also to have a substantial annual allowance of $860,000 plus $16 million in index linked shares in BION Pharmaceuticals and Bio Fuels as a further bonus. Audrey and Cyril would never need to worry about money again. Val thought it was what Rachel Cohen would have wanted. Kay Kane had seen the errors of the life she had made when the time came for her to die. No one would remember her. No children and no family that Valentine was aware of, so for the first

445

time her name would bring joy and happiness to the people who deserved it.

From that holiday on, the yacht had its permanent mooring changed to Miami Florida, where all four of them and their families and friends spent their summers sailing round the Gulf of Mexico or wherever their hearts desired.

Paris

A fire that had mysteriously begun in the apartment block on *Rue De Clichy* in the Montmarte area of Paris, made the local news. One body had been recovered from the ashes of the building and had been named as Christiane Bessette. The whereabouts of her daughter Agathe were as yet unknown.

The singed remains of documents recovered from the scene were now the matter of a police investigation into corporate sabotage and industrial espionage.

No one as yet had been arrested in connection with the fire in the apartment and the only lead the Gendarmerie had was that a package had been hand delivered to the address minutes before the fire engulfed the building, by a well-dressed middle aged woman with what an eye witness described as having an American accent and who had been driven away in a black chauffeur driven Mercedes.

The CCTV footage of the Mercedes showed that it carried Albanian diplomatic plates, but on further investigation, it transpired that no car matching that description had been registered in France by the Albanian embassy.

The investigation is still ongoing.

Postscript

One Year Post Event: Belfast

BISHOP DESMOND *DESSIE* FLYNN WAS NOW A partner in a chain of coffee shops that donated all of their profits to the people who had chosen to decline the cure. All monies generated, minus running costs, were used to find a cure for the continuing crippling effects of the Jester virus.

People who had declined the terms of 88 were still in a living hell as a continuing effect of the disease. The coffee chain was an ongoing project that was proving to be more profitable than any of its rival global brands. *Mrs. McKinstry's* coffee shop had grown fast from one tiny cafe on a corner to a national chain and was soon destined to dominate the European and eventually global coffee retail market. Dessie knew how much his former housekeeper loved her American coffee!

Chicago

Senator Gregory Arthur Hamill was in the process of cutting the tape at the opening of the wing of the North Eastern Our Lady of Mercy Hospital when the police arrived with the warrant for his arrest. He, of course, protested to the cameras and press that it all must be some kind of silly misunderstanding.

He later appeared on the steps of the Circuit Court, Cook County, Illinois to give an interview to the waiting press. It would not be his last public appearance.

He had previously presented with initial symptoms of the jester virus, but was later seen to somehow mysteriously self-cure himself of 'Satan's spell,' as he termed it. He then announced to the media that he had seen himself in a dream talking to an angel, who told him that he had been blessed by God's own hands and that he should run in the next presidential race for election and become the rightful, next president of these United States.

On the same day he announced his intentions to run for the presidency, a number of plain vanilla envelopes were delivered to every major newspaper in the United States.

Memory sticks and photographs that had been taken in an illicit Mexican bar room renowned for under age prostitution and child sex abuse had also been anonymously delivered to the British *Times Newspaper* containing verified cases of child sex abuse from some of his past victims, including the witness testimonies.

A further 32 men were also accused, including the bar's owner, who would later be jailed in his native Mexico for a minimum of fifteen years and permanently registered on the sex offenders' list. They had all testified that the Senator had personally financed a night's *entertainment* that resulted in the death of a nineteen year old girl who had died from massive internal injuries caused by trauma to her reproductive organs.

It transpired that the child had been kidnapped eight years previously from her parents' home in Arizona and had been repeatedly used as an under-age sex slave. This event had also been paid for in person by the Senator; the case, along with a string of others, is still undergoing further investigation.

Hamill's family, along with his former political allies, both disowned and distanced themselves from him. His now very public enemies pleaded with the judge to give the most severe sentence at his disposal, as Senator Hamill had continued all during his term in the senate to market himself as a 'protector of the vulnerable and guardian of the weak.'

He was paraded in front of the press that gathered outside the court after being found guilty and sentenced to life (in his particular case; everlasting) in the sexual offenders unit of Tamms Correctional Centre, Illinois, where he now regularly but unwillingly provides sexual entertainment for some of the most dangerously depraved sexual deviants on the planet!

Eva Ballantine took part in and won a triathlon for the first time. She used none of her new abilities and was cheered on by her sister Estelle, friend Hugh and her new fiancé, Valentine Sere, who applauded as she made her way up the slipway from the water at the Portaferry side of Strangford Lough.

Valentine was reunited with his birth mother, Jaclyn Gates, who now sat on the wall by his side holding firmly onto his arm as they watched the athletes finish the end of the run that led into the village.

The wind suddenly picked up and gusted across the Lough. He felt what he presumed was a speck of dust enter his eye and wiped the tear away with his hand. The tiny almost invisible green metal particle sat momentarily on his fingertip then magically absorbed into his skin like a melting snowflake.

He walked down to the salty water of the Lough and washed his hands, watched with more than a passing interest by Hugh and Estelle, who, for some unexplained reason, still distrusted him...

About the Author

Living in the historic village of Hillsborough in County Down, Northern Ireland, Albert McAuley has tried his hand at most things in life, finally discovering his undoubted talent for writing after being encouraged and inspired by his long term partner Helen whom he describes as 'a very strong and determined woman.'

He recalls receiving at the age of 14 an end of term report that stated: "Albert has potential, but must do better." Unknown to his parents, he returned the report to the school along with a note, saying, "Thank you for your comments. I think the same could be said of all of us." He left school the following year for a career in engineering.

'Has potential and must do better' has been his maxim ever since.

"With Helen's belief, influence and guidance I feel that *'potential'* may finally be close to being reached."

Albert is working on the follow up to 88.

She had been young and beautiful once. She'd had her whole life ahead of her until they took it all away in an instant. He had been born with a burning hatred in his heart and lived a cold and loveless life until he had found a reason to exist.

When both worlds collided, security agent Nick Savvas found himself in a race against time as a suicidal plot unfolded to tear the heart out of the British Establishment.

As journalist Lyndsay Mitchell discovered, a very black Friday was to descend on the House of Lords, and the closer she got to the truth the more dangerous it became for those around her.

From the poverty stricken streets of Bogota in Colombia to the halls of power at Westminster and Whitehall, THE HUNT FOR BLACK FRIDAY is the explosive follow-up to the international thriller and top Amazon download, THE ICELANDER.

In 2008, Dr Allen Baird designed and delivered the UK's first university course for Jedi. It exploded like a thought-bomb on the worlds of Education and Media. Was it an attempt to gain global notoriety, work out childhood demons, or revolutionise adult training?

Whatever Dr Baird's motives, the results were impressive, most impressive. Journalists gave him international publicity. Colleagues praised his attempt to reach out to the uninitiated. Ordinary citizens scratched their heads in wonder and smiled. The light was not to last. Local academics soon resented Dr Baird's attempts to unlock the secrets of knowledge with the key of pop culture. Others whispered censorship, and accused Dr Baird of stirring religious debate in a country too used to its incendiary effects. But the darkness was yet to fall.

Part indie novel, part autobiography, part training guide, this book tells the tale of a one-day university workshop that changed the course of a galaxy, not so far, far away.

On September 21st 2012 Vitali Nevski and Artyom Novichonok discover the comet ISON just beyond Jupiter's orbit. Heralded as the comet of the century all eyes are upon ISON as it blazes a trail through our solar system – and it's not only humans who are spellbound by its beauty.

Having entrusted the training of the newly appointed Karma to Sister Sarah Arellano, God can now focus on much more important things – such as the newly discovered comet that conceals an ancient secret. But the human race is no longer simple and neither is the newly appointed Karma.

As an ex-con with a troubled past the new Karma is more than a handful for Sister Sarah. His own troubled history as well as the complexity of his first three cases causes him to question the validity of the entire set up.

Why does God allow bad things to befall good people when he has the power to prevent it? If God wasn't so engrossed in trying to stop China and the US from laying claim to HIS comet, he might have put those issues to rest. But time and unforeseen occurrence befall us all...even God.

Printed in Germany
by Amazon Distribution
GmbH, Leipzig